UNTAPPED

The Completionist Chronicles Book Twelve

DAKOTA KROUT

MOUNTAINDALE
PRESS

ACKNOWLEDGMENTS

As always, thanks to my wonderful wife for her amazing support as she joins me on this journey.

A specific thanks to my assistant, Ella, and several of my most supportive friends and fans on Discord who act as lore masters on my behalf: NeoRyu777 and Grand Fungus.

PROLOGUE

The air in the audience chamber *crackled* with power as Grandmasters from all over Vanaheim slowly filled the room. It didn't matter if they were swordsmen, paladins, or mages; nearly all classes and professions had a representative.

As the attendees became more numerous, factions and cliques began to become apparent. Various groups glared at each other, and a dividing line slowly emerged, wide enough for two of the tower-shield-focused classes to walk along side-by-side. Yet, despite how the room was becoming literally charged with power and tension, the central, raised area remained calm and serene, with powerful figures both male and female lounging almost too casually as they chatted amongst themselves.

The roiling mana in the room went still and docile as it approached those elevated figures, turning the turbulent air into a gentle breeze. Eventually, the door closed, seemingly on its own. One of the people in the central area let out a sigh that reverberated throughout the cavernous space, silencing the murmurs and heated voices while simultaneously drawing all eyes to him.

"Well… I suppose we should get started." He gently waved his left hand, and enormous, blocky numbers appeared in the air. "As the Water Sage of the Elemental Mage's Tower and host of the one hundred thirty-four thousand, nine-hundred and twenty-seventh meeting of the tower representatives, I declare this meeting officially-"

Without waiting for the official ceremonial opening to be completed, a man bedecked in an immense amount of armor stepped forward, slammed the pommel of his war hammer on the ground, and shouted, "We've been waiting for the opportunity to have our own Sage for a *thousand years*! I demand to be recognized. The Tower of Defenders has taken the hits for all of you in the past, and if we don't get first rights for hunting the World Boss of Jotunheim now that the bifrost has reconnected to this world, the rest of you are welcome to try and do so *without* our help!"

The furious declaration rang throughout the room. Only the fact that the Grandmaster had a valid point kept the Sage of Water from drowning the man on the spot for interrupting him. Even so, it was a near thing, and the Sage's hands trembled as he worked to contain himself. Taking a deep breath, he looked down his nose at the Grandmaster and belatedly finished: "-started."

Immediately, across the room, hands were calmly raised as various groups waited for a chance to air their thoughts. To the great annoyance of all of the assembled Grandmasters, the Sage of Water instead turned around and sat down once more, content to discuss the issues of the day with his peers. With another gesture, a large swath of the previously opaque tower turned transparent, revealing a bridge of shimmering light suspended over the void in the sky. Its radiant arc served as a gateway to the newly reopened world of Jotunheim.

For a long moment, silence returned to the room as each of the people stared at the flickering expanse with conflicted emotions. Many of those on the fringes, Grandmasters all, stared with hunger in their eyes, fists clenching into white-knuckled grips at the literal path to power the Sages were there to parcel out.

Conversely, those in the center of the room looked on in various shades of disgruntlement or suspicion as they were reminded how the tenuous balance of power they had maintained for centuries was likely to be broken by the end of the meeting.

"We would be fools to allow this opportunity to slip through our fingers." The Sage of Swords spoke softly, each word carrying the sharpness of his chosen weapon. Sword intent flowed along with every syllable, easily ignored by the Sages, though some of the weaker Grandmasters needed to actively defend against the passive slashing damage he exuded. "The path is open, and Jotunheim has lain dormant with its resources untouched for a millennium. We must move quickly to allocate the expedition rights, before opportunists or the *unworthy* claim Sagehood first."

A scoff came from the opposing side of the raised central area, as a man with a frame as broad as his ambitions leaned forward, folding his arms as he glared at the whipcord-thin Sage of Swords. "Next you're going to be telling us we should take this opportunity to reconnect the rainbow bridge to Hel... or worse, *Asgard*."

"Would it be so bad to have access to a world with Mythic cores freely available... to those who can take them?" The Sage of Swords shrugged serenely, though the air around him rippled with razor-sharp lines as he moved. "Think of the number of Sages we could raise from the ranks of the Grandmasters around us-"

"-Shattering the balance of power on the Sage's Council forevermore, Eldrin!" the broad man bellowed back, though there was no heat in his voice; his normal speaking volume all but designed to be heard across a battlefield. "For a thousand years we have isolated ourselves, each of us perfecting our craft. For the same amount of time, the council has been deadlocked, unable to decide whether we should give those on higher worlds the chance to *descend* and interfere with our lives once more."

"This world has been nothing but a terrarium for us, Baccus," a man nearly entirely covered in flowering plants declared, shifting slightly and sending sparkling spores scattering through the room. Whenever they landed on someone, their tension faded, and easy smiles broke out. "Sometimes we forget we don't represent our own power... we are here to guide future generations along our path. It's difficult to cultivate and prune those who need guidance... when all access has been removed."

"Druid." Baccus inclined his head carefully at the potent caster. "All I'm trying to say is, there is more to think on here than simple expedition rights. The first Sage to be raised will either cast their vote to open the path forward or close it off for the next decade. Once either option has been chosen, the arms race will begin. Besides, what of our economy? Flooding Vanaheim with materials from the lower worlds risks undermining our own interests. An unchecked influx will-"

"Take it up with your Class Sage. I, Kaldora the Sage of Water, declare my intent to allow expeditions to begin immediately." The Elemental Sage glared at Baccus. "You may be the representative of your *tower*, but we all know that Minya, the *Class* Sage of Merchants, remains active. If you want to have your vote count as more than a proxy, convince her to step aside."

Before the Skill Sage, Baccus, could allow his thunderous expression to morph into words he might later regret, the Sage of Illusions, Rothric, smoothly interjected, "No one wants to stifle growth for control. Trust me when I say that I, more than anyone, know how much of a mirage 'control' truly is. We stand at the precipice of a new age, and I know where your heart truly lies... the fact is, our currency will not spoil. For you see, my wine-loving friend, despite what you charge for goods, our true currency is *knowledge*. The flow of goods on or off of this world means little compared to the acceleration of learning. I say let the materials flow, let the cores be used, let our ranks swell!"

Gesturing to the side, he called the attention of the group of approximately a hundred Sages to the thousands of Grandmasters surrounding them with thunderous expressions. "Or, some among these will go and do it anyway, with or without our blessing. Then, we will not gain allies... but may instead find our position as Sages suddenly vacant for one of our students to fill."

Baccus, long since used to being one of the superpowers on this planet, felt a sensation he hadn't in hundreds of years. The blood drained out of his face, and his mouth went dry. His words shifted to grumbles, and he uneasily leaned back in his seat, realizing his arguments had already failed.

Taking that moment to push his agenda, the Sage of Swords steepled his fingers and grinned wickedly. "If the expansion and distribution of knowledge is what we seek, why stop here? Since it has already been brought up, I don't mind pressing harder. The bridge to Jotunheim is open; why not unblock the bridge to the higher worlds as well?"

The resistance to his words came immediately.

"You *overreach!*"

"Scoundrel-"

"I knew you were going to do this."

The last complaint was a soft grumble from Baccus, who remained out of the argument otherwise, though he slowly shook his head as Kaldora took the floor once more. "The higher worlds were closed for a *reason*. No one of us has the authority to unseal them, and as it is not a priority of this session to discuss it, nothing we say here will convince us to unseal the way."

"Authority... or the *will* to do it?" Eldrin sneered at the expected opposition. "We possess the means. Why *shouldn't* we act? Or do the Sages on your half of the council fear what lies beyond? If we do nothing, we are trapped. Worse, to your point, Rothric, we are *stagnant*. Knowledge without the ability for action is merely wasted potential."

The arguments went back and forth, round and round, the tide of opinions shifting back and forth. Many among the Grandmasters spoke up, but their words were ignored—they were only there to witness the Sages' decisions. Finally, Eldrin lifted his hands and tried to force the decision. "Let's vote on it! Who cares if this was meant to be a discussion on something else? We are here, and *I* think the majority want the way unblocked."

The chamber rang with the sound of agreements being made, allegiances and friendships being tested, strained, and forged. The call went out, the tally was cast, and the result became clear: a tie.

As always, a tie.

Eldrin's eyes twitched as he glanced around the room, meeting the eyes of his staunchest ally, the Sage of Blood Rites. "Once more, we are at an impasse."

"No, we have found clarity," Rothric denied him, his body increasing in size and appearing in the air evenly spaced across the room. His illusions spoke to the assembled multitude. "It's time for the next generation of Sages to rise. The Grandmasters of Vanaheim wish for true influence in such matters. I say it is high time you earned it. If you wish to shape the course of our world, it's time for one of you to rise. The first to ascend to Sagehood will become the tiebreaker. Both factions on the Sages' Council shall hereby nominate one tower to begin expeditions to Jotunheim."

"I don't care if I get nominated or not, my tower *will* be marching on the bifrost by dawn!" The Grandmaster of the Tower of Defenders shouted over the hubbub, instantly needing to grit his teeth and activate a few defensive skills as the displeasure of the Sage's Council turned on him. Still, as was his path in life, he stood resolute. "Nominate me or don't. I care not *one whit!*"

"Surely you do not want to be the one to cause our world to

descend into conflict and war? Look around yourself. Do you see the world of the Sage's Ladders, where any can climb to the pinnacle of potency... or have I found myself back on Midgard, scrabbling in the dirt to gain my first profession?" The Druid Sage spoke lightly, hoping to calm some of the raging tensions. "If it matters so much to you, far be it from me to stop you. I nominate the Tower of Defenders for the stability and foundation-building faction."

"The Stormbinder Tower for the climbers!" Eldrin immediately called out, causing those on his side of the debate to nod in agreement, while his opponents winced at the nomination. "Shieldbearing defenders focused on soaking up as much damage as possible, compared to ranged damage dealers who have been weaving talismans and scrolls for a thousand years, with no one to use them on. I wonder... which of the two will be able to take down a World Boss faster?"

Each nomination was quickly confirmed, and the Sage of Swords held a triumphant smile on his face as he stood and leisurely stretched. He chipperly waved at the others on the council and turned to leave, only for the broad grin on Baccus's face to stop him cold.

"That was pretty slick for a swordslinger, but it seems there was a small detail that slipped your mind." The Sage rolled his shoulders happily as Eldrin began to fidget, not wanting to demand information and prove his lack of knowledge.

Luckily, but certainly not happily, the merchant didn't make him wait very long. "Yeah, adding another Skill Sage to the council might tip the balance in your favor a little bit. Let's call it *temporarily*. But, if the Tower of Defenders claims that core, there won't *be* another vote. All of a sudden, there will be a *Class Sage* active and making decisions again. Just as the Grandmasters had no true say today, by the time this is over... the *entire* Council could be overruled just as easily."

Eldrin went pale, but he simply huffed and turned away, storming out of the room with Baccus's laughter chasing after him.

CHAPTER ONE

Joe walked along the empty streets of Vanaheim, staring at his feet and thanking his lucky stars that his Exquisite Shell protected them from the cool surface of the smooth pavement beneath them. *Technically* he was still wearing outdoor-acceptable slippers, but they were so heavily damaged that his toes were poking out in areas.

As the small group trudged along for another hour, the eerie silence took more of his attention. Occasionally, the Ritualist would even peek over his shoulder to make sure his friends were still with him, but the uncomfortable expressions on the faces of Heartpiercer McShootypants, Socar, and even Nimue—the Nyanderthal pretending to be a regular cat familiar—did little to ease the odd tension in the air. Joe glanced up yet again at the towers reaching endlessly into the dark void of the sky above them and flinched as he was startled out of his reverie by Heartpiercer suddenly speaking.

"I guess he was right, huh?" The others looked at her, so the Archer elaborated slightly. "The vagrant we ran into a few minutes ago? He said we wouldn't be able to find our way around the planet without a local guiding us."

"Yeah, but he also wanted to be paid in cheese? Then he kept muttering 'plump'?" Socar shrugged off her concerned words. "I don't think he had all of his spoons in the drawer, if you know what I mean."

Joe spoke up, needing to clear his throat after such a prolonged silence. "That's normal here, as far as I'm aware. The cheese, at least. A while back, I was talking to Jake the Alchemist about this, and he mentioned the currency here actually *is* cheese. I don't know exactly how that works, but remember that we're on a new world. Every one of them so far has had something different going on, so I don't recommend discounting anything you're told. But… at the same time, yeah, maybe we can find someone other than a guy sleeping on a bench to confirm."

"If we even *can* find anyone," Heartpiercer murmured in frustration. "It's been hours, Joe. You said this world is one giant city, right? Isn't a city supposed to have people?"

"There's got to be some trick to it," Socar declared solemnly as he squinted and scanned the area. "I know every street and tower looks the same, but if a local can find their way around, there *must* be some way to tell where you are."

A burst of noise came from above them as an enormous gout of sparkling, magical fire blasted out a window of one of the towers. Beyond a few shouts of alarm, there was no indication that anyone saw or cared about the sudden detonation. At least, no one came running to help, and the light show ended quickly. Joe watched carefully yet couldn't even see silhouettes through the high opening before some opaque barrier closed off the space. "Well, clearly there *are* people. Just not in a place where we can get to them."

Distant laughter echoed off the hard walls, bouncing around the street and making it difficult to pinpoint the origin of the sound. Unconsciously, the group stepped closer together, hands clasping their weapons. When the high-pitched chuckles ended, Nimue let out a soft *hiss*, and Socar nodded along. "Yeah, that was pretty creepy. What kind of world did we land on? Should we... do you think we should go back?"

No one spoke, yet at the same time, they didn't turn around. After a few moments, Joe relaxed slightly and began treading forward once more, leading his friends along the endless road. After a few more hours, a bright, scintillating glow appeared in the air a few miles ahead of them, and the Ritualist stopped dead. "Did we circle the entire planet?"

"Looks like it," Heartpiercer grumbled in discontent. "I suppose that'll happen when it's a dwarf planet and we have superhuman stats. Well, if nothing else, now we have a land-mark we can use as a reference. Should we try, I don't know, taking a left turn or something?"

They took another step, and with each one, the endless path stretched onward. Soon, a soft humming of machinery distin-guished itself from the background noise, and the group looked on with interest as they closed in on a tower with extremely clear differences from the others around it. Behind the massive square wall encircling the tower's base, machines scaled the sky-scraping structure in a flurry of motion. Not only were the tire-less constructs scrubbing the exterior, they were swapping out worn down components with new, gleaming versions.

"That one looks pretty active. Should we knock?" Joe tried to keep his voice cheerful, though the oppressive silence had started to wear on him. Without waiting for an answer, he walked up to the enormous double doors set into the wall, reaching up and pounding on the metallic surface—and only just barely making a sound. Trying not to react to the stifled mirth of his friends, Joe pulled out a Ritual Orb and levitated it upward, sending it slamming against the surface to produce three sharp knocks that echoed up and down the road.

A contraption on the door itself *whirred*, revealing a complicated circuit board, complete with spinning gears, tubes filled with crackling energies, and dripping with dark oils. Joe stared at the open panel in confusion, unsure how to react, only for the protective casing to slide back over it when Joe did

DAKOTA KROUT

nothing to interact with it. "That's... what do you think *that* was all about?"

He'd tossed the comment out, not expecting a reply. So, when Heartpiercer actually had something to say, Joe's ears perked up with interest.

"If I had to guess, I'd say that was a puzzle of some sort?" Her words came out slowly, though her eyes lit up with interest. "I have no idea what we would do with that, but maybe we can find one we *can* figure out. Let's start knocking on doors."

Joe deflated slightly as he realized what she was saying. "Please tell me you don't want us to go around knocking on every individual tower on this planet until we find something that makes sense."

"If you have a better idea, I'd be more than willing to hear it." She let out a soft chuckle, examining Joe with a critical eye when he sagged in place, as though every bit of his stamina had leaked out at once. "Maybe we'll even be able to find you some proper clothes. If I had to guess, I'd say people are avoiding us because you look more like a hobo than that vagrant did. I've no idea why you haven't bothered to replace your gear, since you're wearing basic clothes that offer no bonuses, are covered in holes and burn marks-"

"I blame Stu." Joe immediately countered, only for her to roll her eyes and easily refute him.

"Joe. That was *so* long ago." Heartpiercer crossed her arms and raised an eyebrow. "You've had plenty of time to figure out some new gear. It's not like you were hurting for items to barter with. Anytime in the last... I don't even know *how* long, you could've just figured *something* out."

Joe rubbed the back of his bald head, an uncomfortable smile appearing on his lips. "It never came up? The cold didn't bother me much, since I have good protection from the elements with my magic. At least everything stays clean, and... are there really *that* many holes?"

"If you were cheese, your shirt would be Swiss, and we could have bribed that local to show us around." Socar offered

12

'helpfully'. "Even though you think it doesn't matter to you, I can tell you there have been a few people who were going to seek you out for class training, but figured you wouldn't be able to work with them because you looked so destitute. You know, not being able to take on students, or maybe your class is just so hard to learn that you constantly had to live like-"

"Got it." Joe cut off his friend's deluge of words before he was called a hobo yet again. "But... am I seriously losing opportunities because my clothes are a little-"

"Ragged?"

"Tattered?" Heartpiercer offered at the same time as Socar.

"Mew," Nimue solemnly meowed.

AutoMate took that moment to phase into being in the mug dangling from Joe's belt, reaching up with its tiny tendril of coffee and patting him gently on the shoulder. Its coffee bean eyes stared into his, as though preparing to join in the impromptu intervention. *No sad. Drink. Be happy.*

"Thanks, Mate," Joe murmured, unclipping the carabiner and lifting the mug to his lips, taking a sip as the elemental vanished, leaving behind only ten ounces of steaming beverage. "At least *one* of my friends isn't putting another hole in my pride."

"Better there than your pants," Heartpiercer remarked dryly. "Starting to look a little too much like fishnet stockings for comfort."

"I get it! New clothes, as soon as I can get 'em!" Joe threw his hands in the air and started walking toward the next tower. "You know what else? Next time, one of *you* can knock, and maybe someone will actually open the door instead of leaving us to our own devices."

"You know, the bifrost is *right there*. You could take a few hours, pop down to another world, get dressed, and come back?" Socar's innocent offer sent Heartpiercer into peals of laughter, even as Joe's ears went pink. "We'd wait for you."

The Ritualist simply shook his head instead of responding verbally, but at least they didn't have to walk through silent streets anymore, as now Heartpiercer couldn't stop herself from falling into fits of laughter every few minutes—the wind had picked up, sending Joe's clothes flapping like a flag that had barely survived a war.

Joe tossed his few remaining Ritual Orbs back and forth, leaving one to orbit his head like a tiny moon as they knocked on one gate after another. Most of the gates showed no reaction at all, though a few of them shifted and twisted with obvious puzzles like the mechanical one had done. Illusions covered the surface of one, arcane writing another: harsh, golden light that raised goosebumps on Joe's arms as it appeared—making him realize how smart it had been to use his orbs to do the knocking.

Despite the endless possibilities, none of the group could make sense of the puzzles that appeared. So, with a collective shrug, they moved on to the next, then the next.

Socar spoke out a few hours later as they twisted and turned through the roads, trying to keep the bifrost on their right, just to make sure they weren't doubling back. "Look…! This area isn't anywhere near as random as we thought it was. Here. The large road we circled the planet on is a straight line, but if you look at these smaller side roads? This one curves subtly, but every third block, the alignment is reset. Look at that… the wall around the base of this tower is a few inches shorter than the one on either side of it, which would allow the flow of ambient energy on the secondary ring of the feng shui along the northeast axis. That is, if we can assume the bifrost is landing at the magnetic north of this planet."

"I feel like you're trying to make a point but are either unwilling or unable to get there," Heartpiercer unintentionally quipped, earning herself a distracted, frustrated glance from their resident Formations expert.

Socar gestured vaguely at the tower with his right hand, making a sinuous curve with his left as he detailed a street in the distance. "I know this isn't obvious, but there should be a nexus point signifying 'spiritual growth' with a subset of earth somewhere over here. It's creating a massive funnel and should be gathering the energy… but I just don't know for what."

"Do you know where it's collecting?" Joe latched on to the concept like a man spotting an oasis in the desert. "Nothing's making sense on this planet. I'll take any lead I can get."

"Sure, it's just right there." Socar walked into the middle of the street, his eyes on the towers around them, gauging the distances between them, their relative height, the wind flow, and tapped on a specific section of the road. "This spot. For some reason, the nexus point is just hovering above ground?"

Whump.

As he pushed his index finger into a spot in the air, which didn't offer an *inkling* of being important, the perfectly smooth road collapsed slightly, slamming up and around Socar like a venus flytrap made of stone. Joe's first instinct was to attack the hard surface, but it melted away, leaving the ground just as perfectly smooth as it had been a heartbeat earlier.

There was no sign of their missing party member, but an instant before Joe gathered energy to try and resurrect his friend, who he assumed had just been slain, he heard a creaking sound off to their left.

His chin jerked toward the unexpected noise, and he glimpsed Socar's pale face just before the squealing gate slammed closed.

CHAPTER TWO

Before Joe could react, an arrow pinged off the now-closed entrance, which latched just before the projectile reached it. Forcing himself not to focus on Heartpiercer's impressive reaction speed, Joe sprinted toward the imposing gate, heart hammering as his initial panic shifted into rage.

His Ritual Orbs swirled out from where he had stored them in his ragged bandolier, swishing forward and bouncing off the metal door with a staccato beat. "Open up right now, or I'm going to *level* this entire tower! Give him back!"

Heartpiercer slid to a stop next to him, her eyes fiercely darting around as she looked for any weak point to exploit. "Joe, do you want to go over the wall? I can give you a hoist, and I'm pretty sure you can jump this."

"Do it," Joe agreed grimly, dashing into the street to get a running start then barreling forward and Omnivaulting once, landing with his feet outstretched in Heartpiercer's cupped hands and throwing himself upward in time with her heave. In an instant, he was above the wall, over it, and looking down at his friend—who looked up and met his eyes with immense surprise.

Socar was facing a few people who seemed extremely excited to see him, and to Joe's confusion, it seemed they were having an amiable conversation. He shifted his position to land safely, only for fog to swirl out of nowhere and completely block his vision for a fraction of a second. He landed, stumbling slightly, and the misty visual impairment lifted.

Heartpiercer flinched away in surprise. "I swear I saw you go *over* the wall?"

"I saw him. Some kind of magical effect threw me back out here, though." A ritual tile appeared in Joe's hands, and he began swirling his fingers as he directed his mana into the activation sequence. "It doesn't look like he's hurt, but no one abducts someone like that and has good intentions. I'm gonna raze this wall; be ready."

Heartpiercer nodded, pulling out three arrows and leaning them against her leg as she nocked one. Pulling his hand back, Joe prepared to slap the tile against the wall, only for a firm, concerned voice to cut through the air and echo off the cold wall in front of him.

"Hold on there, young man! If you directly attack the tower itself, you're going to be hunted across the entirety of Vana-heim... uh... forever."

Joe froze in mid-motion, his desire to rescue his friend warring with the hard-earned knowledge of how much it *sucked* to be hunted across entire worlds at a time or barred from them entirely. "I don't know who's talking to me, but you'd better bring Socar back out here, or I'm going to have to take my chances."

"Well, sorry to say, I don't have anything to do with that."

Joe shifted, trying to pinpoint the source of the words, only to spot a figure at the end of the block peeking around the corner and waving at him: an elderly man dressed in a strangely refined robe, with a matching shirt, pants, and boots showing below it.

Thanks to Joe's enhanced Characteristics, it was easy for him to inspect the man even from a distance, and he took in a set of gray eyes sparkling with a blend of amusement and concern, a face lined with wrinkles both from worry and laughter. The Ritualist could even see how the man was staring at the glowing ritual tile in his hands with a conflicted gaze. "Who are you, and why shouldn't I try to save my friend?"

"Oh, he's not in any danger. I'll explain in a moment, but I figured I should start with that. The name is Mak, and I'm a humble merchant." Mak motioned for them to come closer. "Come on, let me give you a little rundown of what sort of situation you got yourself into."

Heartpiercer and Joe glanced at each other, then at the wall, each of them letting out a small noise of frustration before backing away and hurrying down the road. The Archer shrugged as Joe sent her another hard look. "Worst comes to worst, he's sent to respawn. If they've thrown him in some dark room or something, we can always come back and blast the tower until it falls over."

"Fine." Joe grumbled as he tried to contain his frustration at the situation. "One thing after another here. Either it's totally empty and nothing's happening at all, or we find... what even was that? This world's version of a monster? I haven't seen any other creatures yet, so that would make sense."

They turned the corner, and the duo stopped dead, staring at the 'merchant' with a deadpan stare. Behind him was an eye-catching, brightly painted wagon which practically *oozed* festive charm. Its sturdy frame was painted with vibrant shades of yellow, white, and rich cheddar-orange colors, perfectly complimenting the wheels and wedges of cheese stacked within. Decorative awnings striped with the same cheerful colors were draped gracefully from the roof and fluttered gently with the steady breeze.

As for Mak himself, the merchant was standing centrally to the wagon, arms spread wide to the side as though to give his newest customers a hug. "Welcome to Vanaheim! Even better, welcome to my rolling cheesewagon, Mak 'n Cheese! I'm the proprietor, a true merchant Kraftsman."

For his part, Joe simply didn't have words to respond with as he took in the absolutely flamboyant display, a direct affront to his senses after the stark black, white, and silver architecture which utterly dominated the miniature planet.

Only after blinking a few times was he able to see more of the details of the wagon, such as how it was clearly designed for a single person to pull it along effortlessly. A yoke at the front was fitted with a comfortable looking harness, complete with leather straps, and polished brass fittings designed to look like wedges of cheddar cheese. Just as he finally managed to think of something to say, the smell hit him.

The air carried a mouth-watering aroma of aged cheese, but it quickly became overwhelming as competing scents—from creamy brie, to the nutty smell of aged parmesan—struck him like hammer blows directly to the nostril. Joe's lips twitched, and he leaned away to try and catch a breath of fresh air while he checked his active spells. "Abyssal Neutrality Aura deactivated itself on the bifrost, didn't it?"

"What happened to Socar?" Heartpiercer managed to stay far more on task than Joe, immediately demanding the answers they had come there for. "Why'd you stop us from going after him after he was taken like that?"

"As I said, he's in no danger!" Mak cheerfully exclaimed, shaking his head and chuckling softly at their hard expressions. "First off, he wasn't, as you say, *taken*. He was invited and accepted. Frankly, congratulations are in order. I don't think there has been a new entrant to the Tower of Formations in nearly a millennia and a half. Only the children and the children's children of the original members and their spouses have gotten in. The bright side is that this tower has almost no active feuds with any faction. If I had to guess, I'd say the only downside is the fact that they're a *supporting* tower and have little hope of ever producing even a simple Skill Sage."

"Formations?" Joe looked back down the street, allowing one of his orbs to float up and gently rest against the back of his hand. Immediately, Essence Cycle activated, overlaying his vision with the flows of power in the world. Chaotic energy shifted in a turbulent manner around the spot Socar had vanished from, seeping out and away as though a heavily compressed bubble had been burst. "He solved the puzzle for the tower, didn't he?"

"Good to see you've been able to start making some deductions." Mak put his hands on his hips and leaned to the side, flashing the duo a cheesy grin. "Vanaheim doesn't suffer fools easily! As you've mentioned, each tower has an entrance exam only Experts and above have the tools to solve. The one your friend just popped into is particularly tricky, as there's almost no way to practice formations on this world outside of that specific tower. No new buildings are allowed to be built, and nothing permanent can be placed outside of the walls surrounding each of the structures."

Here he waved at his own shop. "As you can see, even successful merchants, such as myself, need to be able to stay on the move. Everything else... well, eventually it's swallowed by the world. Ach, don't give me that look! It's not as scary as it seems, things just kinda... *vanish* if they're left in place for too long, like a good mozzarella melting onto a slice of toasted bread. *People* don't vanish, in case you were worried. It's safe to nap wherever you want to rest your head."

"Wasn't on my mind, but still good to know." Joe managed to murmur, though his mind was racing. His eyebrow quirked up, and he stared intently at the wall as he shifted his mana and activated the spell *Message*.

<Socar! Should I start blasting, or are you safe?>

Forty-five mana vanished into the air along with the casting of the spell, as his friend was out of line of sight, but it was such a tiny drop in the sea of power he had that Joe wouldn't even have noticed it missing, were he not watching to ensure that the spell activated in the first place. He let out a sigh of immense relief as a reply came almost instantly.

||Yes! Safe inside, and I still have Nimue. It was a convergence of earth and spirit, as I'd assumed! As the ground

collapsed around us, we were both converted into pure energy and pulled along a tether. Not quite a Blink or Flash spell, but something similar I had never considered before. Joe, it was a *completely novel* expression of Formations I didn't know it was even possible!||

||Right now, I'm standing with a dozen *Masters* of Formations, and each of them is arguing and competing to see who can give me the most benefit for studying under their direct tutelage! It's the opposite of every college I've ever heard of in my life. Here the masters of the craft are fighting for the chance to teach—oh! Literally fighting! It's like watching Plato in action, they just started throwing fists! I'm going to stay here for now; let me know if you need anything. Otherwise, this is a golden opportunity-||

Socar absolutely rambled for the next thirty seconds, his mental voice coming across the connection faster than he'd ever been able to speak in person. ||They're telling me right now that there are no more natural monsters on the planet, and the reason the road came up and collapsed around me was so the spiritual energy could condense and inundate my flesh, briefly converting it so I could spirit walk over to the door. Even the basic explanations they're giving me are making my head spin with possibilities-||

Joe could practically *feel* the instant his friend ran out of mana, and the spell cut itself off, as there was a small retort, and the headache he'd felt building from the absolute deluge of information vanished. Turning to Heartpiercer, Joe grinned and cocked his head to the side. "Yeah, Socar's fine. He wants to stay there and look around for a while. Apparently there are a few Masters in there competing to be the one to teach him?"

"Makes sense. Hard for a Master to reach Grandmaster status if they don't have any students, isn't it?" Mak called out. To Joe's surprise, at some point, the merchant had gone into his wagon and was now looking out of the window, surrounded by cheese on all sides as he clearly prepared himself to make a sale. "So... you two look like you're a bit low on cheddar. How about we make a deal, and I extend you a line of credit?"

"Nope." Joe firmly backed away, lifting his hands as if to ward off evil. "There's absolutely no chance of me going to a new world and finding myself in debt. That's a good way to end up picking up a new profession I have no interest in."

"Eh?" Mak stuck his pinky finger into his ear and twisted back and forth as though something were blocking the passageway. "Tell you what, why don't I give you some basic information, so you know I'm a sharp fella, and you can check things out for yourselves? No reason for me to be at odds with someone who can conquer an entire world by themselves."

Now it was Joe's turn to be confused, but before he could ask for clarification, Mak cheerfully explained, "The bifrost lit up, and suddenly your group appeared. Here's a little known fact for you: even if you got on it weeks after someone else did, since you were the first person here, you had to have been part of the group that opened it up in the first place. As the person who opened it, you'll move along the rainbow bridge faster than anyone else—the bifrost is *not* instant travel."

"That's... concerning." Heartpiercer grit her teeth and glanced at the scintillating light in the sky. "It feels very quick, at the least?"

"Oh, yes, it's fast. Just not instant. It's not a portal, right? You're having to move along that physical distance." Mak clapped his hands and beamed at Heartpiercer. "You look like the archetype of a powerful Archer; I bet you'd love to become the first Grandmaster Archer from Midgard, wouldn't you?"

"You know I'm from Midgard because..." she trailed off with a bit of heat in her voice.

"Why, where else would a human come from?" Mak paused for a moment, his left index finger in the air as he corrected himself. "Since you weren't born *here*, that is. Even then, humans are quite the small sample size of our population. As I was saying, the Tower of Bowmen would love to have a new recruit. I'm not going to pretend here, every tower is desperate for new recruits. As I'm sure you know by now, you're on the world of the Sage's Ladders. You're not going to find monsters, easily accessible materials, or anything like that here. If you're worried about it, just know that all fighting is done for *honor*, so a violent death doesn't mean down-leveling and isn't permanent for anyone."

Surprisingly, Joe felt a wave of relief wash over him at that information—he was sick and tired of constantly worrying about his Dwarven friends and how his actions might force them to turn into Elves and lose their memories and personalities. "That's... really good to know, Mak. The last couple of worlds have been constant combat and scheming. I'm really looking forward to something different."

"Then you came to the right place!" Mak held up his fingers in a 'V' for victory, "on Vanaheim—"

Joe realized at that moment that the 'V' may *not* actually signify victory, but the planet instead. Just another culture clash he needed to internally note.

"—There are only a few ways to get what you need. Everything physical is paid for in cheese. The more refined and well-aged, the more it's worth. You can purchase cheese in exchange for knowledge or by working or completing tasks for others. It's basic currency; you can trade your time for plenty of cheddar. Each tower is also given an allotment based on the Honor they've managed to accrue for themselves, though that allotment is assigned by the leader of the tower itself. If you want to learn specialized skills or gain access to knowledge not a part of your class, you must trade. In this way, the cheese flows across the planet. A very gouda system, if I do say so myself."

"There *are* some rules you must be aware of." Mak's voice turned stern, recapturing the duo's attention. "First, we have ways to tell if the cheese you are passing out has been magically altered or stored in a faulty storage device in an attempt to unnaturally age it. That's the same as passing around counterfeit currency and is actively *dishonorable*. Just remember, if you want to grow your wealth, invest in young cheeses and age them well. If you have a sharp eye, you'll eventually be able to trade it for parmesan to practice non-class skills."

"You mispronounced 'permission'," Heartpiercer told the man with a straight face, acting intentionally obtuse. Joe could practically see the gears turning in the man's mind as he debated whether or not to explain his cheesy jokes to the young Archer, but eventually he set the issue aside.

"How grate to have someone to help me out when I have shredded my words. Just in queso people get feta up with my quips," the merchant replied with a stiff smile. "Now, the tower you're looking for is... here, I'll draw you a map. But for you, my shiny-scalped young friend, I'm drawing a bit of a blank. You were using some form of embedded magic, so... I want to guess you are a scroll master?"

"Ritualist." Joe replied easily, though he went still as Mak's eyes went wide.

"Oh. Is that right?" The man winced sympathetically. "That's... I'm sorry to hear you fell into that trap."

CHAPTER THREE

Before Joe could ask for an explanation, a small head poked around the cheese wagon and caught his eye. He stared at the small-statured person, who scanned him in turn with a bored gaze before vanishing once more. "There are more people!"

"Don't worry about her." Mak shook his head and briefly rolled his eyes up to the sky as though looking for patience. "That's just Beth. She's... well, she sells fairly useless goods. She's been following me around for years, though I intentionally go out of my way not to pick up strays-"

He stopped at that moment, wincing slightly as he glanced back to see if he'd been heard. When Beth did not appear, he let out a soft sigh of relief. "Anyway, give me just a few minutes, and I'll put together some instructions for you to find your individual towers."

The merchant vanished behind his cheeses, but Joe couldn't contain his curiosity. Walking alongside the wagon, he squeezed through the narrow gap between the wooden surface and the wall built around the Formations tower, blinking in surprise as he found a dozen small, rolling cart kiosks set up behind the cheese shop. "All right, let's see what Mak considers 'worthless goods'. Hello, Beth is it…?"

His words trailed off as he stepped close, his eyes lingering on the cat ears poking through the long, orange hair of the bored-looking woman's head. All of a sudden, Mak's discomfort over calling her a 'stray' made sense: though she looked like a young human, Beth was clearly a Nyanderthal. Seeing him falter, she inclined her head slightly and gestured at her shop. "Hello. Welcome to my little shop. I have flowers, chocolate, and coffee. Feel free to browse. If you need something, I guess I'll be here."

Immediately intrigued, Joe stepped closer, looking over the far-from-worthless consumables. His nose twitched as the scent of freshly brewed coffee wafted over him, and he slowly reached forward to grasp a cup… only to recall that he had no way to pay for it. Grimacing slightly, he stepped back, only to feel a moist prodding on his wrist. The Ritualist glanced down, meeting Mate's wide 'eyes' as the elemental refilled his mug for the second time since arriving on Vanaheim.

"Oh! Thanks, Mate." He glanced up at the shopkeeper, a hint of apology in his eyes, "Sorry, I'm a little low on… cheese. Looks like I can't afford your coffee, mate."

Beth's eyes scrunched slightly, and Joe watched as she unconsciously bit the inside of her cheek for a split second. Then, as if resuming autopilot, she lifted her hands and adjusted her jacket with a fleeting motion. "Feel free to browse. If you need something-"

"You'll be here." Joe finished for her, his estimation of the Nyanderthal dropping slightly. "Got it. Maybe another time? Listen, I have a few friends among your people I'd love to introduce you to if you'd like. I've never seen one of them walking around with cat ears before; they've always either been fully cat or looking just like a human child. Can all of you do partial transformations? Queen Cleocatra was following me around for a while, and even *she's* never done that."

Beth's right ear flicked slightly, the only sign that his words had been heard at all. Joe cocked his head to the side and stepped forward to try again, when Beth looked up at him and met his eyes. "Welcome back to my little shop, customer. I have flowers, chocolate, and coffee. Feel free to browse. If you need something, I guess I'll be here."

"Uhm." Nodding slightly, he stepped away, confused over the interaction. All the way back, when he had first joined Eternium, Joe knew that the people there weren't truly non-player, scripted characters. They all acted like real people, and as far as he knew, they were. But Beth? She might've been the first true NPC he'd ever encountered. "I wonder if whoever is controlling all of this is only making people with personalities as we arrive? Perhaps I'm just interacting with people too quickly for the world to keep up?"

"Got the map, Joe!" Heartpiercer called around the cheese wagon. Taking the opportunity, he offered a polite nod to the orange-haired cat girl and quickly walked away. As he got closer, the Archer saw his tumultuous expression. "What were you doing over there?"

"Just trying to meet some locals. It was a, *humm*, confusing experience?" He reached out and took the paper written with careful, detailed instructions, impressed by Mak's meticulous work. He walked around to the front of the wagon, flashing the merchant a smile. "Thanks for the help, Mak. I'm looking forward to bringing you exotic cheeses in the near future."

"That's what I'm here for!" Mak beamed back at him, tapping the counter and waving at an oversized wheel of parmesan. "There's other cheese stores out there, but make sure not to give them your business! I'm the nicest, friendliest, most going-out-of-the-way-ing-est merchant out here. Now, I've been parked here for too long already; I need to get moving, or my wagon is going to start melting into the ground."

"Hold on." Joe firmly stated, his smile fading slightly. "I need you to explain what you meant about the Ritualist class being a trap?"

Mak's expression turned somewhat pained. "Look, my apologies, I shouldn't have said that-"

"But what did you *mean* by it?" The Ritualist pressed, not breaking eye contact until the merchant let out a sigh and showed he was ready to talk.

Even so, the merchant didn't stand idly, pulling down the awnings and compacting the wagon slightly so as to more easily navigate along the roads between towers. He seemed to be chewing on his thoughts, so Joe waited patiently as the man started hooking up his harness. Finally, he began to explain, "It's not so much that there's anything wrong with the people who *take* the class, Mr. Joe."

"Mister?" The Ritualist recoiled slightly at the honorific. "Are you about to call me 'sir' as well? You're older than me, right?"

"Respect knows no age, *sir*." Mak chuckled at the disgruntled look on Joe's face. "As I was saying, the people who take the Ritualist class are arguably among the best in their original classes. They're the go getters, the *extra* people. You know... the kind of person who wants to be able to grab cross-class skills without having to put in five times the effort to learn them. It doesn't matter if they started as mathematicians, alchemists, blacksmiths, farmers, or whatever... there's always a place for them at the Tower of Rituals."

"Sounds pretty great so far," Joe deadpanned, waiting for the other shoe to drop. "Accurate and succinct. They sound welcoming. My kind of people."

"Oh, they are! In fact, I'd even go so far as to say they have the most varied and accomplished Masters of all of the towers, which is certainly the reason they have such an... err... impressive structure." Mak tossed his shoulders as he finally got around to his point. "The problem is, it seems like the class *itself* is a trap. Of all of the towers, only that one has never produced a Sage. Not a Skill Sage and *certainly* not a Class Sage."

"That's the second time you've brought that up, but can you explain what the difference is? I've only ever heard of 'Sages', as the natural progression from Grandmaster to the next tier." Joe fell in step alongside the merchant as the cheese seller began slowly moving forward, dragging his wagon with surprising ease. "You're saying it as though there's a large distinction-"

"Ha!" Mak belted out a laugh, startling the Ritualist enough that he nearly jumped head-first into the wall behind him. "That's putting it *lightly*, Mr. Joe. Come now, there can't be *that* much of a divide between our worlds? You must know that a Skill Sage is someone who's broken through the Grandmaster ranks with *one* of their skills?"

"Right, it's the next step up after Grandmaster." Joe repeated himself with a trace of heat in his words. "That's what I just said."

"Then you should be able to *hear* yourself as you speak." Mak shot back without missing a beat, utterly unfazed by Joe's disgruntlement. "You can only ever become a Sage in *one skill* if you become a Skill Sage. It's right there in the name, isn't it? If you pick something to specialize in to the exception of all else, that's what you become. Certainly not a bad thing, but it means everything else is locked in at peak Grandmaster, or Grandmaster nine if you like, *forever*."

The merchant waved a hand expressively, "A *Class* Sage, on the other hand, is someone who has brought each of their class-related skills to the peak of Grandmaster, which brings the class *designation* skill up naturally, and bound the *Class* with a Mythic core. This allows them to bring each of their other core class skills up through the Sage ranks as well."

"That's… that's a *lot* of skills. You know, actually I do think I've heard some of this before. Who was it that—right! Cleave mentioned some of this in passing a long time ago." Joe glanced at his skill sheet, trying to estimate how many Sage-ranked skills he could have. "Mak, I gotta know why anyone would ever take just one, when you could have… what, ten, fifteen of them?"

"Of what? Sage-rank skills? What, do you think they grow on trees by the roadside, and you can just pluck them as you walk along? " Mak shot Joe a half grin, though his eyes were slightly narrowed as though the Ritualist were being intentionally obtuse. "I'm not talking about *general* skills, I'm specifically calling out the class-specific core skills. As to why someone would only choose to become a Skill Sage?"

He shook his head, plodding around a bend in the road completely unconsciously, "Think about the sheer *immensity* of investment in time and resources you need to raise even one of your skills that high. Look, it's been fun chatting with you, but if you want more information about your specific class, you should go to your tower. Then again... maybe my guess *would* be as good as theirs, since they've never managed to produce a Sage. Which, again, has the entire world convinced your class is a beautiful trap."

With plenty to think about, Joe murmured his thanks once again for the directions, though his words were muted as he pondered the concerning bit of news. He fell back, stepping onto a side street with Heartpiercer as the wagon trundled along, the rolling cart kiosks trailing after it like little lost puppies—or, in Beth's case, a lazy kitten following a dangling string.

"How much of an advantage do you think we have, since we're here before pretty much anyone else?" Heartpiercer suddenly questioned her bald companion, pulling Joe out of his contemplations. "In a real way, think about it... according to him, there're so few new recruits right now that the towers are offering enormous signing bonuses, essentially. What does that look like? I bet there are skills I've never even considered possible before, just waiting to be handed to me on a silver platter."

Perking up significantly at the idea of expanding what was possible with his class, Joe nodded eagerly and followed the Archer as she set off, following the instructions on the map Mak had given her. Since the tower she'd be entering was on the way to his own, Joe accompanied her until they arrived at yet another skyscraping building that had no distinguishing characteristics compared to the others around it. He glanced around the area, dubiously staring up at the black and silver spire. "Are we sure this is the right place?"

"This is absolutely, positively the right place." The conviction in Heartpiercer's voice drew Joe's eye, making him wonder how she was able to speak with such complete confidence. Yet, before he could ask for her reasoning, she pulled an arrow from her quiver in a single, fluid motion. The shaft twirled in her fingers before being nocked to the string with the casual grace of long-practiced mastery. Not once had she taken her eyes off something in the distance, yet even tracking her pupils, Joe was unable to find what she had locked onto. "There's highlighted critical hit points... if you have the skills to see them."

Adjusting her aim slightly, Heartpiercer loosed the projectile, which hurtled toward her unseen target almost too quickly to track. A soft sound echoed back, and a nearly invisible disk lit up, previously so well camouflaged that Joe could have stared directly at it hundreds of times and never even noticed that it was different from the rest of the tower. Thin, glowing lines sparked outward, capturing his entire attention as he wondered what the magic meant—though the Archer never hesitated. Another shaft was in the air, *thunking* against the tower, then another and another, so impressively quick that Joe's head was spinning.

The ground trembled slightly beneath their feet, yet the massive double doors set into the wall surrounding the tower slid open without so much as a whisper of resistance. Heartpiercer let a cocky half-smirk show on her face as she glanced at Joe with a look of signature superiority, "Well, that was easy."

Unable to come up with a reply, Joe simply walked along behind as the Archer strolled into the courtyard around the tower as though she owned the place. Joe couldn't help but grin as well, honestly somewhat envious at how she was able to move into every situation with effortless confidence.

Unfortunately, just as he was about to step into the courtyard as well, an arrow *thunked* into the ground just in front of his toes. Another one approached, clearly designed to release a piercing whistle as it flew. He shuffled backward, as shaft after shaft seemed to sprout from the ground in a line following him until he was fully outside of the gates—which immediately began closing.

"Guess this is where we split up." Heartpiercer tossed him a jaunty wave. "Send me a message if you want to meet up again."

"Or just to check in." Joe quickly added, to which she shrugged and offered a conciliatory nod.

"If you're really *that* nervous about this place? Sure, buddy." Then the gates closed firmly, a scraping of metal indicating they'd been barred from the inside.

"*Haah*... alone again." Joe stared at the closed entryway, swinging his foot back and forth and scuffing it against the ground while softly grumbling, "I put together a team and everything... why's it so hard to keep a group together? Maybe it's just-"

He paused as a thought struck him and turned on his heel, marching toward the Tower of Rituals somewhere in the distance. "Birds of a feather flock together. That's got to be it, right? I just haven't found the right community to be a part of yet, but there's no better place to try again than right here."

CHAPTER FOUR

Joe walked through the streets, carefully following Mak's written instructions each time he came to an intersection. He was trying to channel Heartpiercer's confidence as he walked alone through the streets of the world-spanning city, but his mind was churning with the concerns the cheese merchant had brought up.

"If the Ritualist Tower has *never* produced a Sage, that just means there's plenty of room at the top for anyone who wants to get there, right? I'm still so far away that it shouldn't matter, but... the way he said it? Like it was a foregone conclusion that no Sage ever *could* come out of there?"

He tried to shake off the gnawing concern, telling himself that eventually he'd be good enough to become a Sage, even *if* no one else had *ever* managed to in the entire history of Vanaheim. "Gah! Stop it, brain! If nothing else, he said there were more Masters in this tower than any other tower; that has to count for something, right? Plus, what if the only thing they've been waiting for is resources from the other worlds? I might not have any cheese, but there's plenty I'm going to be able to accomplish if they need stuff from elsewhere."

Taking a deep breath through his nose, he rounded the final corner, steps stuttering as he came to a stop. For the first time since arriving on the planet, he saw something other than endless rows of towers: open space. The nearly suffocating winding streets and monolithic, monochromatic towers gave way in front of him to an immense, circular clearing he could only estimate to be nearly a mile wide. At its center loomed a tower unlike any of the others, at least in size. While it still had the coloration of the others—black, white, and silver—this one was easily three times the width of its lesser counterparts.

"That's the place?" Letting out a slow exhale, Joe didn't bother trying to squash the smile slowly spreading on his lips. "Now we're *talking*."

He took a step forward into the circle, freezing in place immediately as words appeared in the air in front of him—not a system notification, but actual burning lines of energy hovering in the air.

Do you seek entrance, honor, or audience with the Tower of Rituals?

"Entrance." Joe voiced plainly, half-expecting that would be the end of it. He took another step forward, but the words didn't vanish, instead bursting into a wall of flame that raced into the distance and blocking him from proceeding forward.

Heat washed over him, and the smell of his arm hair singeing reaching his nose just as his reactivated Neutrality Aura cleared the last traces of the scent from the air. The Ritualist frowned, glancing down at his arms, which were covered with a shimmering, sparkling light. "That's odd... how did it burn me through my Exquisite Shell? I didn't take any damage, and everything should've been blocked. That must mean... an illusion?"

Ignoring the roaring flames, he slowly scanned the ground around him, finding a few chunks of rock and bits of detritus like string and such that had been left on the ground. "Oh look, litter on the surface of a planet that absorbs everything left alone on it for any length of time. That's definitely just randomly strewn-about garbage, yep."

He leaned down, poking at the sympathetic lines that had been woven with real material, grinning as he felt the silver strand of metal tied to the core of the twine. "*There* it is. Let's see. I don't have too much experience with illusion rituals; I think I only have the Ritual of the Ghostly Army to go off of here, but do I really *need* it with a Novice rank circle? Please."

Shifting one of the rocks an inch to the left, then bending the end of the wire that had been touching it until it poked into the ground, Joe redirected the flow of mana from the ritual into the ground, and in moments, the 'flames' had vanished, and his arm hair had reappeared where it was supposed to be. "There we go. I don't exactly have a lot of hair to lose, so I'd like to keep what I've got. Hey, whoever's watching, do I need to explain my work?"

He looked around, not sure why the gates to the tower in the distance hadn't sprung open as they had for the rest of his group once they'd solved a challenge. "I can do that! This is a Novice ritual illusion, which means it's fundamentally different than a spell. The spell version will rely on tricking the senses, but once someone realizes it is an illusion, it'll lose most of its power. The far superior *ritual* version keeps reapplying itself unless it's broken or someone brute forces their way through the flames. I would've felt the fire the whole way, only to come out completely unscathed on the other side. Is that good enough?"

There was no response from the tower, so Joe could only shrug and keep moving in a straight line toward the girthy spire in the distance. "No? Then let's see what else you've got."

He kept walking, and after about ten minutes, realized the tower hadn't come any closer. Squinting at the tower, then the ground around him, the Ritualist began searching for what he'd missed. "Clearly, I got caught in another illusion as soon as I broke the first, but when did it... wait. *Did* I get caught in it after I broke the first one, or *before*? This could be the same ritual that asked if I was trying to enter the tower. I bet it is."

It didn't take long for him to spot the Beginner-ranked ritual, now that he was looking for it: a simple duo of circles innocuously carved into a fire hydrant set next to the road he was trying to walk along. "Look at that. A world filled with magic, where the streets and buildings are all some kind of strange, stone-like material, and somehow I believed they'd have firefighters that needed fire hydrants. Didn't even think about it twice. Sneaky. I think I'm really going to like these guys when I get in there."

A cursory examination of the ritual circle revealed how the illusion worked. Not knowing the actual name, Joe dubbed it the 'Rotating Horizon' ritual. It was easy for him to understand that the ritual subtly curved his vision so that it appeared he was walking straight to the tower when instead he was actively circling it. Instead of attempting to cancel the effect or break the circles, he simply touched a finger to the ground next to the 'fire hydrant' and imprinted his mana signature alongside dozens of others—adding himself to the whitelist of people allowed entrance.

Standing back, he glanced to his right, where the tower had appeared to be standing only a moment earlier, only to find that he had to look over his shoulder to find it. Swiping his hands together in the universal gesture of 'job's done', he thought over the concerning fact he'd just learned. "I've never had to combat Ritualists before; would it be just as easy for them to add themselves to my rituals? There's got to be a way to obfuscate the design, somehow. I mean, with high-tier rituals, the complexity alone makes it difficult to add yourself in, but that's not the same as not allowing someone to add themselves in."

This time, before setting off, he began sweeping the area with a careful gaze. The doors of the tower had still not opened, which meant the trials hadn't yet ended. "Started with Novice, then Beginner... how high up the tiers am I going to have to climb to gain entry?"

It wasn't long before he found the next ritual circle, this time a trio of circles softly glowing with power, hidden under a layer of dirt in a poor attempt to conceal it. "What do we have here? Apprentice rank, that's clear enough. What do you do? Make it feel like I'm walking forward when I'm moving backward? Make me comfortable walking for hours on end without noticing? Or do you-"

The words died on his lips as his mouth went dry, and Joe slowly looked from the triple circle to the tower, shaking his head slightly. "Oh... it superheats a section of stone under the ground and causes an explosion of lava like a landmine when someone walks over it. That's a pretty *rapid* departure from the other rituals, wouldn't you say?"

He didn't bother with being fancy on this one, not trusting the unstable matrix to *not* detonate when he walked over one just because he was added to the white list. Coating his fingers with mana, he simply pinched two of the circles together, shaking his head as hundreds of lava bursts erupted from the ground across the entirety of the space surrounding the tower as the ritual was forcibly broken. "That would've been useful on Jotunheim, if it dealt more damage. Might even copy that one down and try to upgrade it for the next time I go there."

Now understanding that the test to get into the tower wasn't as safe as he'd initially thought, Joe moved with far more caution as he searched for the Student-ranked ritual he was certain was waiting for him. "Four circles... if I were setting this up, where would I do it? Probably closer to the tower, where it wouldn't be so difficult to maintain it if needed."

Taking measured steps, Joe approached the tower, covering nearly half the distance from the outer edge before running into a line of shimmering power. Studying it carefully, he realized he was seeing the active effect—*not* the actual source of whatever would happen if he tried to cross the line. He circled the tower for about a third of the distance before running into the ritual diagram itself, letting out a sigh of relief as he realized crossing the boundary would have only sent him outside the open area and activated copies of the other rituals he'd already finished with.

"So it would've been time consuming, but not deadly like the last one. I wonder why they're so wildly varied? Different people setting these up, maybe? They built it in alignment with their specialty?"

Just as he was about to break the ritual, Joe paused as an idea struck him. Reaching out with a strand of mana he manipulated into the circle, he inverted the direction of the transportation. Quickly stepping back, he waited to see if it would work or cause the ritual to catastrophically fail. Happily, Joe had the Ritual Circles skill at Master rank two, and a simple Student-ranked ritual was easy enough for him to take control of or redirect.

Still, there was *always* the chance of failure, and he didn't want to walk into the tower after having blown himself up. "Gotta keep that good first impression."

He crossed the boundary, and as the magic of the ritual collapsed on him, he didn't struggle against it. In an instant, he was just outside the doors of the tower, staring at a floating, rapidly rotating six-circle ritual. "Whoo. What a rush. Is this kinda what happened to Socar? Oh, nice! I got to bypass the Journeyman tier and go straight to the Expert?"

It was far different from the previous defenses, being a singular, elegant ritual with each sigil denoting its purpose precisely woven into its rapidly spinning rings. When the Ritualist had first begun in his craft, this would have appeared as nothing more than a shimmering orb of energy. But between his experience with his class skills and his massively inflated Characteristic points, he was able to easily read along the lines as they spun. After taking a few minutes to carefully study the design, he reached out with a strand of mana...

...only for it to be *slapped* away as a spark of power shot from the circles and detonated against the questing tendril of mana. Eyebrows shooting up, Joe blinked as he admired the Expert-tier ritual. "How fun. I've never seen a ritual fight back before."

Even as he spoke, the sigils drawn out along the rings of the circles began to shift, moving up and down and side to side as they rearranged themselves. If he hadn't taken the time to gather all of the information he needed before attempting to alter it, it would've been a monumental task to try and even determine its function, let alone shut it down. "Adjusting the sigils in real time to compensate for a hostile presence? Now *this* is a skill I need to learn."

Holding both hands out in front of him, Joe extended a string of mana from each fingertip, which then broke into five additional strings each. He reached forward with them, allowing his magic to flow more powerfully as the ritual tried to defend itself, allowing the threads to be as soft and powerless as the gossamer strings of a spider web when they weren't under attack, but as energized as a bolt of lightning were they under attack.

Any of the strands which managed to attach to the various runes along the outer ring were ignored by the defenses, so he pushed power along them to create additional strands from that point and shifted into the next layer, attaching the extended strands to the sigils there. After only a few minutes, he reached the innermost ring and extended the threads to the activation sequence of the ritual.

Supplying it with his own mana, Joe activated the *true* ritual contained within the defensive shell puzzle. With a precise application of intent, and a calculated pulse of power, the endlessly spinning ritual diagram came to a sudden stop. Each of the six rings folded until it was parallel with the ground, *clicking* into place one after another. Joe stepped back, expecting a dramatic effect. Some grand invitation inside, a guardian he'd have to fight, or perhaps *nothing* if the trial required going back and clearing the Journeyman ritual as well.

What he hadn't been expecting was a deep, tolling bell to ring. The sound reverberated only inward, causing a strange, almost suction-like feeling, since one of his ears was outside of the area of effect. For a long few moments, nothing changed. Then, the door swung open. Unlike the previous two towers he'd witnessed opening to invite in the new members, here there was no secrecy.

Instead, dozens of people wearing almost-matching robes were revealed running across the courtyard around the base of the tower itself.

"There's a new Ritualist in the tower!"

"His score! Ninety-eight of a hundred! Prodigy!"

"Did you see how quickly he broke through the last two layers?"

"What's your specialty?"

"Dibs! Everyone respects dibs, right?"

"Dibs doesn't work when it's been a decade since the last one entered."

"Look, if dibs isn't sacred, what is?"

"Go to the Tower of Clerics if you want to find something sacred! I only need a handful of merits-"

"You! Let me sponsor you! Looks like you can handle a hammer; I'm the best Ritualistic Forging Master in the tower!"

"Your *mother*!" Another gasped at the braggadocious shout. "I've been a peak Master in Ritualistic Forging since you *entered* the tower."

"Exactly! I've already caught up to you!"

"Those aren't muscles, look at his sleeve! Ink stains! I was a Grandmaster Mathematician before I came here, I'm definitely going to be the first Grandmaster of Magical Matrices, accept my sponsorship and-"

"-Alchemical Rituals!"

"-means nothing if you don't understand Ritual Lore, and you all *know* it!"

"I'm thirty merits away from being our first Grandmaster of Ritual Circles. I saw the way you interfaced with the final challenge; I have the best chance at refining your skills!"

"Everybody *stop*!" A single voice cut through the commotion as yet another Ritualist, this one wearing what was clearly a combat version of the same robes the others had donned. "Newcomer! Welcome to the Tower of Rituals. As you *might* have been able to pick out of that hubbub, you won't be wanting for sponsors now that you're here. To make this as fair as possible, you are, of course, welcome to pick who you would like to sponsor you in the tower, but we can make it easier if you let us know what your base class is."

Joe's smile was bright enough to illuminate the darkest night of Jotunheim. "Hello, everyone! I can't tell you how excited I am to meet all of you. Clearly, I have plenty to learn. Before we go much further with this, what does it mean to be sponsored at the tower? I only just arrived on Vanaheim, and I'm not sure of the customs."

"*Oooh.*" Came the collective sound from the gathered Ritualists, who looked at him hungrily and glared at the others with dull, red eyes as they sized up their competition.

The man clad in the battle robes spoke again before anyone else could, causing more than one of them to *tsk* in frustration at not being able to capture Joe's attention. "Sponsorship means anything from paying for your room, board, and robes to teaching you their specialties. The reason I ask about your base class is that typically people who come from similar backgrounds are going to have an easier time learning from each other. For instance, if you started as an Alchemist, you will be used to the teaching methods of your previous fellows. Depending on how you want to specialize here, you may not want that, of course. Still…"

He trailed off leadingly as Joe's thousand-watt smile dimmed slightly. The bald man glanced around at the others, "I'm a ritualist."

"Yes, we all are," the spokesman stated in a consoling tone. "But what was your *base* class?"

"*Ritualist.*" Joe stated with a touch of frustration. "I've specialized twice since then, but-"

Seeing all of the skeptical looks sent his way, Joe shrugged and fiddled with his character sheet for a moment, before displaying the details of his class and first two specializations— choosing to hide the remainder of the sheet.

Name: Joe 'Monarch of Mana'

Base Class: Ritualist Level: 30
Specialization 1: Rituarchitect Level: 13
Specialization 2: Reductionist Level: 10

Seeing all of the people around him staring at the words with incomprehension on their faces, Joe began to get a little worried. "Is that so strange?"

"Why, yes. Yes it is," the Battle-Ritualist confirmed for him. "You see, 'ritualist' is a *prestige* class. That means anyone can take it, but it becomes a new class you've gained on top of what you started with. It doesn't *replace* your base class. Frankly, I don't think anyone here qualifies to be your sponsor at the tower."

"I think the only fair thing for us to do…" The man swept his eyes around the gathered Ritualists, who, though slightly disappointed, seemed even more eager to speak with Joe as soon as they could. "…is to let the Grandmaster have the final say in all of this."

CHAPTER FIVE

"While we're waiting for the Grandmaster, why not let me take a peek at your ability with Magical Matrices?" one of the Master Ritualists excitedly interjected before anyone else had the opportunity to speak. "I'm Master Cosmo Hollows, founder of our math club!"

Joe's gaze dropped to the exuberant Wolfman's hip, but he didn't see a club anywhere. Upon self-reflection, he realized he'd taken a concerningly long time to realize that the man was speaking about a group of math enthusiasts. "A club? As in, an extracurricular activity? That's a thing here?"

"We all need to have hobbies!" Cosmo cheerfully stepped forward and clapped Joe on the shoulder, giving the bald Ritualist a close-up view of his well-manicured paw of a hand. "You have an interesting energetic field around you. In fact, I nearly mistook you for a member of the Blood Rites tower. Don't look so concerned, you'll see how this all works soon enough. Essentially, they're our direct rival right now; everyone knows they've been jealous of our tower for centuries."

"Only recently have they had the stones to step up and challenge us for Honor, though." A lady stepped close, and as he recognized her Elven features, Joe froze a moment longer than he had even when seeing a Wolfman rush at him. "Gabrielle Syme, Master of Alchemical Rituals. I'd love to see your capabilities in my field; with Ritualist as your base class, you must have had an immense amount of time to practice this craft. Maybe you could even teach *me* a thing or two, ha! Err... I don't suppose you actually *can?*"

"Unfortunately, Alchemical Rituals is the part of my magic I'm *least* competent in-" Joe tried to explain, watching as her face fell—though another person stepped forward with their hand outstretched as soon as they saw their chance.

"Ritualistic Forging!" the first human Ritualist Joe had met shouted near-desperately, "Stabilizing, Amplifying, harmonizing! You name it, I can do it. How do you feel about a sub-sponsorship from me, even if the Grandmaster-"

"Sub-sponsorships aren't a thing!" Gabrielle finally found her voice once more. "Anything other than sponsorship is just... *bribing!*"

"Are you mad that I'm doing it or that you didn't think of it first?" came the cheeky response from the man, who seemed to have slightly canine features, now that Joe was looking closer. "Levi Dren Redips, metalsmith extraordinaire! I can see by the light in your eyes that you're familiar with my craft. It's a true rarity. Believe it or not, there are more *mathematicians* joining than there are smiths. I wouldn't say this is a once-in-a-lifetime opportunity... but *you* might!"

"I'd love to learn some of the ins and outs of forging specific to Ritualists! If you'd get in trouble with helping me out like that, I have a Grandmaster Dwarf on Jotunheim who owes me forging classes, if you'd like to trade tips." The handshaking ramped up in intensity, even as others clamored for his attention. Seeing Gabrielle start to move away, Joe addressed her once more. "I also know a Sage of Alchemy there who owes me *years* of dedicated tutelage, if you'd like to make the same deal."

"There's a Sage on a lower world?" Gabrielle's startled exclamation cut through the hubbub, and the attention of the crowd was focused entirely on her next words. "It can't be... a Sage of Alchemical Rituals?"

Suddenly the weight of their collective attention turned sharper, and Joe felt like he had to force out his next words through syrup caught in his throat. "No, Alchemy as a whole. As far as I'm aware, he has nothing to do with rituals at all."

"Celestial feces, I almost had a heart attack!"

"Can you imagine how devastating that would've been to the Grandmaster?"

"Centuries of effort, down the drain."

Gabrielle now seemed far more enthusiastic at the news. "As soon as we can get clearance to descend to Jotunheim, I would absolutely love to meet them! I wonder which specialty they took the Sage position of? They've been having nearly as much trouble raising Sages as we have, though they were the last tower to raise a Sage, if I remember correctly."

"Released a World Boss somewhere, you mean," Cosmo chimed in darkly, though he tried to hide his frown as Joe's eyes turned back to him. "Ah, sorry. You may not know this, but there are a limited number of World Bosses that can spawn on any of the worlds. The Mythic core drawn from them is the only *material* required to go from peak Grandmaster to the Sage rank. Many hope to be able to make the leap the instant the option becomes available, so they hold on to a core. Wars are fought over them for this exact reason. Until the core is used, the World Boss it's taken from won't respawn-"

"Thereby artificially limiting the number of Sages that can be raised even more." Another voice finished the explanation, this one causing everyone to go silent out of respect as they turned and inclined their heads at the man walking toward them.

Joe studied the person, who must have been a Grandmaster of the tower, noting the humble air about him—the only thing that set him apart were a few circles embroidered into the sleeves of his robes. Even so, the power and authority that seemed to flow off of him was the likely reason he didn't need any garish accessories. Joe politely nodded as he was studied in turn, patiently waiting for the elderly man to speak.

"I'm glad to hear that my efforts were not in vain." There was a faint smile on the elderly man's face as he stroked his long, white beard. "It would be quite the shock to the system to put in all this work to reach the highest heights in Alchemical Rituals, only for someone else to have swooped in and snagged the position."

The group let out a collective chuckle, though there was a clear sense of unease as they looked at each other. It was then that Joe realized, no matter how friendly each of these people were with one another, each of them was in an extremely long-term competition with the others. If only five people in total could become Skill Sages, and only one could become a Class Sage, at least a dozen of the people standing in this cluster alone would never be able to ascend beyond Grandmaster.

"I hear you are bringing us exciting news." The elderly man folded his hands behind his back, rocking back and forward on his toes. "Someone with Ritualist as a base class? Two specializations on top of it and leading the way here from the lower worlds. Well, to me, it sounds to me like you have been doing our class proud. We gained a much-needed influx of Honor when the bifrost opened... now I know why."

Appreciative murmurs filled the air, and Joe felt multiple people clap their hands on his shoulders. "As Tower Master, it falls to me to reward you for the benefits you have brought us."

Something gleamed around the Grandmaster's head, causing Joe to blink several times as he focused in, trying to understand what he was seeing. A golden wheel slowly appeared in the air behind the Tower Master, becoming clearer as Joe concentrated. A thin line extended from the wheel, connecting to Joe's chest.

"Is this... Karmic Perception?" Before the elderly man could issue his rewards, something *clicked* in Joe's mind, and he blurted out, "Oh! It's *you*!"

"I hereby award you-" The Grandmaster stammered to

silence, blinking in shock as he realized he'd just been interrupted. "You… would you like to share your thoughts with the
rest of us? I was only going to give you rewards and accolades;
I'm certain those can *wait*."

Joe winced at the spicy tone, but seeing as he had already
put his foot in his mouth, he decided to explain himself. "My
apologies, Grandmaster! It's just that, when I was down on
Jotunheim, I encountered a Master-rank ritual which sealed a
vault. Back then, I swore to myself I would find the original
designer of that ritual and exchange pointers with them if they
were still around."

"A vault… you say?" the words came slowly, as though the
old man wasn't sure whether he believed Joe or not.

"If I recall correctly, it was the 'Vault of Winter's Life'."

Silence filled the area as the old man closed his eyes, taking
a long breath and slowly letting it go. "How very interesting
indeed. I was not the designer of that ritual. However, the
previous Tower Master, my sponsor and my grandfather, *was*. It
seems we have some fate together, young Ritualist. *Hmm*. I don't
mean to take opportunities from the others here, but… this may
be the best way to solve our quandary. How about this? Instead
of the rewards I was going to give you… I instead offer a full
sponsorship?"

Soft protests came from everyone in the area who'd been
hoping to be the one to sponsor him, for whatever reason. The
Grandmaster waved his hands at them, "Let me finish! I will
offer sponsorship, providing above-standard rooms, as well as
funding your first thousand hours of training with each of the
core skills under a sub-sponsor of your choosing. Yes, Gabrielle,
I understand sponsorships like this are not the norm, but *I* don't
need the merits, now do I?"

Joe glanced at the Elven woman, who had a small grin on
her face. "I should *hope* not, Grandmaster. Thank you for this
opportunity."

"As for what I'd like in return…" the Grandmaster paused,
stroking his beard as he looked around the group. "Well, let's get

you settled first, then talk business. You're going to catch your death of cold if we don't get you out of those rags. When you're wearing something more comfortable, I think *all* of us will be more comfortable."

"-Do *all* humans have five toes like that?" Joe heard someone in the crowd whispering, and he felt himself deflate slightly as he glanced down and noticed his shoes had deteriorated even further from the continuous walking around the planet since he arrived.

"Yes, I think that would be for the best," he murmured in thanks, nodding at his new sponsor. "Thank you for your consideration. As you might imagine, Jotunheim was a difficult place to be for an extended period of time."

"Excellent. Once you're properly equipped, have someone show you to my study." A token clipped to the Grandmaster's belt flashed with a green light, and for a split second, the air around the man did so as well. Then he was gone, and Joe was left *salivating* over the idea of gaining access to what was some sort of stable, local teleportation ritual. In fact, as his new hopeful sub-sponsors led him away, Joe couldn't stop asking about it.

"Does everyone get to use that teleportation function? Are there various levels of access someone can get, based on an access token? That's what that was, right?"

The others only laughed his inquiries off, not commenting on how the Grandmaster had vanished. Instead, he was led into the tower itself—though Joe did pause as they crossed the threshold, reaching out and brushing his fingers against the strange material the structure was made of. It was hard, yet still yielded slightly to his fingers, as though made from some form of fossilized organic chitin.

This set off yet another round of questioning, though this time he only got shrugs in return. "Are there truly no monsters remaining on this world? Is this what happened to all of them? A Mythic core, when pulled from a World Boss, keeps the monster from respawning, so did the leadership on this planet figure out how to extrapolate that out to the monster population in general?"

"There're monsters here, don't worry about *that*." Cosmo gestured for Joe to follow him after the newcomer had spent a long few moments studying the wall. "It's just that they're raised under controlled circumstances, either in the animal husbandry, tamer, or various farming towers. Anyone can go in and hunt, after paying the entry fee, and bring back whatever they can gather as resources for our tower. It's one of the ways we distribute resources and such. Don't worry, there are plenty of tower missions to go and bring back materials; it's what keeps the place running."

Gabrielle pulled open a door, revealing a large supply closet filled with dozens of robes. Each of them appeared exactly the same, except for small artistry embroidered along the sleeves. "You can take any of these with blank sleeves. The embroidered versions are modifiers to the standardized Ritualist garments, and you have to earn them by bringing Honor to our tower or completing tower quests."

"Right, I'm still not clear on what 'Honor' is or how it's accounted for?" Joe pulled the robe off a hanger, realizing that, though the outer portion opened as standard robes would, the inner part was buttoned up, creating a combination of a cassock and robe that ensured his modesty would be preserved. "Oh, these are nice."

"You'll be happy to know we have matching slippers that go with them." Levi chortled as he grabbed a pair and tossed them to Joe. "This first set is free, as a welcoming package for getting into the tower. After that, your sponsor is charged, or you can pay in either cheese or Honor."

"Again, about that-" Joe started, only for Cosmo to spare him a struggle with words, jumping in to fill in the blanks.

"Honor is how we determine what class is able to control which tower. You may have noticed that we not only have a tower much larger than the standard ones around us, we also control a large portion of open land. We are able to use it for practicing large-scale rituals and effects, and obviously most towers don't have such a large, open training area. They need to pay rather hefty fees to the Enchanter's Tower to have spatial enchantments maintained in their space, if they want it. As I'm sure you can imagine, when you earn major accolades that can have an impact across Vanaheim as a whole, you can earn large amounts of Honor for your tower."

"Which is why you earned us quite a windfall of Honor, according to the Tower Master," Levi chimed in happily. "Since you were one of the first arrivals to the planet, and had a hand in opening the path to lower worlds, well, that's a pretty major impact on the planet, isn't it?"

"Right," Cosmo took over once more. "You can also earn Honor for your tower by challenging someone of equal rank from another tower to a duel—or of a higher rank if you really feel confident. If you win, your tower earns Honor, and theirs loses some. If our total Honor drops far enough, a more 'honor-able class' can challenge us for control of the tower directly. As I'm sure you can understand, once you lose control, it's very difficult to wrest it back, as the other maintenance fees and such quickly pile up."

Joe nodded along as things started to fall in place. "So, Honor is literally how we maintain our position in this tower and isn't really a… let's say *spendable* currency, whereas cheese is used for personal purchases and bartering?"

"Got it in one," Gabrielle cheerfully acknowledged, handing over a pair of gloves embroidered with six perfect circles. "There you go, the gloves of an Expert Ritualist!"

Taking the offered items, Joe paused and looked at them in confusion. "But I'm… a *Master* Ritualist?"

Each of the trio who had been walking along to get him settled froze in place, their cheerful expressions dropping away into a slight desperate stare. Gabrielle swallowed hard, "You're a Master already? In… *all* your core skills?"

"No, sorry. I guess I may have misinterpreted what these represented?" Joe looked around at the others, who were now looking at him with their eyes practically shining as they waited for more information. "I'm a Master in Ritual Magic and Ritual Circles."

"Feces, don't scare me like that." Levi let out a sharp breath, "I thought we had just offered to sponsor you without being able to gain any merits in return. Not that I wouldn't help out, but being able to earn something definitely makes it easier."

"Another type of currency?" Joe inquired as politely as possible, though he was starting to get annoyed with all the variations they were bringing up.

"No, skill merits are…" Gabrielle paused, pursing her lips as though looking for the right words. "There's three requirements for breaking through the Master ranks into the Grandmaster ranks. Merits are gained by-"

Boo~oop.

Everyone paused as a loud tone rang through the tower, followed by a slightly distorted, nasally voice which drowned out all other conversation. "Joe 'Monarch of Mana', please report to the Grandmaster's office."

"Ah, you better get going. Definitely don't want to keep him waiting. You never know when he'll have time for you again." Levi snagged a different pair of gloves, pushing them into Joe's hands. These ones were embroidered with golden thread and had seven circles instead of six. "Here you go! Master of Ritual Circles gloves. I'd tell you what all of this does, but you should just put it on real quick and take a look for yourself. A little reading material as you start climbing the stairs."

"Stairs?" A flash of premonition made Joe's eyes narrow. "Where exactly is the Grandmaster's office?"

"Top floor." Cosmo snickered as Joe gave a weary shake of his head.

"*O~of* course it is."

CHAPTER SIX

After adjusting the collar of his new clothing, Joe pulled on his new gloves and slipped his feet into the well-designed slippers. Immediately, he felt a sense of *rightness* and let out a sigh of relief. A small notification popped up, grabbing his attention and causing his lips to form into a small 'o' of surprise.

Set bonus activated!

Garments of the Master of Circles.

These garments are more than mere clothing. They are a representation of Mastery. Those who are able to don the full set find themselves circling ever higher as they draw out the essence of the universe into a beginning and an end, only to begin again. 3/3 pieces equipped.

- *1 set piece equipped: Your Mana infuses the threads of your apparel, traveling out and around then back to you. You gain an intrinsic understanding of how to unravel inefficiencies, reducing the cost of creating ritual circles by 7%. 3.5% of your total mana pool is reserved in your garments and will automatically repair them.*
- *2 set pieces equipped: The cohesive fabric of intention*

amplifies your purpose, enhancing ritual effects by 7%. An additional 1.75% of your total mana is reserved.

- *3 set pieces equipped: The mental burden in complexity of creation is reduced by 7%, increasing the speed and accuracy of drawing out ritual circles by the same amount. An additional 1% of your total mana is reserved.*

Requirements: Ritualist Class. Master Rank in Ritual Circles.

For those who achieve Mastery in a broader spectrum of core disciplines, additional sets of apparel await.

"I'm glad this all fits over my codpiece. For the low price of six and a quarter percent of my mana pool, I can create ritual circles faster, more accurately and efficiently, and with additional power. Absolutely worth it," Joe murmured to himself as he looked up the enormous spiral staircase situated in the exact center of the otherwise hollow central chamber of the tower. He looked higher and higher, his neck creaking as he stepped back to absorb the sheer enormity of the stairwell. "What is *not* worth it, would be me trudging up these stairs."

Cosmo had off-handedly informed him that the highest floor was approximately thirteen hundred feet above them, and the spiral staircase wrapping around the tower's inner walls like the coiled body of an ancient serpent contained exactly two thousand, four hundred, and ninety-nine stairs. Wide balconies jetted out intermittently, serving as anything from a lecture platform to an open-air meditation station for the hundreds of total Ritualists which called the place home.

Joe had already met a couple dozen of the Masters, but each of them had other Experts they were teaching, who were in turn in charge of Journeymen, Students, Apprentices, Beginners, and Novices. Frankly, he hadn't expected this place to be nearly as populated as it truly was, especially since entering the tower from the outside required at least an Expert-ranked ability to interact with the challenges. "I guess it makes sense… a Ritualist joins, brings their family, and has kids. Those kids marry other people, have more kids. Maybe Vanaheim should be called the world of *nepotism* instead of-?"

Pausing, the Ritualist realized he was simply procrastinating because he didn't want to begin the climb. Pushing his discontent to the side, he rolled his shoulders in his extremely comfortable new robes that actually covered everything they were supposed to, crouched, and kept his eyes on his goal far above: the penthouse of the tower where the Grandmaster had called him. "This is probably some form of rite of passage, maybe a little bit of hazing? That's just fine with me."

Flexing his legs, he activated Omnivault, jumping nearly fifty-six feet straight upward in an instant. For the briefest of moments, his feet landed on one of the balconies. Then he reactivated the skill, allowing a surge of mana and stamina to flood through his muscles. With another explosive leap, he blasted upward, wind rushing around his aerodynamic Exquisite Shell. Reactivating the skill each time he landed on a solid surface, Joe quickly ascended the tower, leaving behind a shimmering streak in the air as his expended mana dissipated into the ambient energetic field.

Through his entire climb, Joe carefully studied the floors he was zipping past, his eyes easily able to distinguish the storage areas, bedrooms for low-Characteristic Ritualists who still needed sleep, practice and lecture platforms, and dozens of other unmarked rooms with intricate designs on their doors. By his fifth jump, he was beginning to breathe heavily. By his seventh, his mana was pouring out of him in massive quantities. As he pushed off for his ninth jump, his mana well sputtered in his chest, warning him that he didn't have a tenth in him.

Joe did a flip, twisting to the side and landing with his feet flat on a balcony, breathing heavily and panting. He glanced over the edge, looking at the ground far, far below him. "What was that, five hundred feet up? Almost halfway there... just need a... minute or two."

"Sir." A firm, unhappy voice came from behind him. "You are *sweating* on my ritual. Do you have any idea what kind of magical mishaps may occur if your bodily fluids interact with my enchantments?"

"I am absolutely *not* sweating on your ritual, I would never let such prime targeting material be handed out willy-nilly-" Joe rounded on the person complaining, pausing as he came face-to-face with a studious-looking human woman holding what appeared to be some form of advanced inscriber. Freezing in place, he slowly looked down, realizing that he was indeed currently standing in the middle of a six-circle ritual diagram. Before he could even begin to apologize, he was captivated by the collection of tokens placed in the circles themselves, placed where the standard runes he used would have gone.

Crouching slightly, Joe's eyes went wide as he realized each of the individual, perfectly circular tokens were, in fact, high-grade enchanted items. Peeking at her gloves, he saw a similar design to his own on the back of them, though instead of the seven circles being drawn in gold, they instead sparkled like gemstones catching the light. "Don't tell me you're making *Enchanted* Ritual Circles?"

"If you have the talent to recognize them, you certainly should have a modicum of respect for the difficulty and expense of this particular craft," the unknown Ritualist explained to Joe in a calm tone—no, not a *calm* tone... she was speaking in the same soothing voice someone would use to walk someone through which wire to cut when defusing a bomb. "Not to mention the danger that comes from disruption."

"But... you're just out here in the open?" Joe waved his arms to the sides to indicate the open air all around them. "Couldn't anyone just walk out here and accidentally scuff a line?"

She blinked at him owlishly, shaking her head and waving to indicate he should carefully walk around the edges of the circles. "No, not just anyone can or *would* randomly walk over here. This area is reserved for Masters and above, the only way to get here is to leave the stairwell over there, go through two

sets of locked doors, then come out onto this balcony. At least...
that was *thought* to be the only way, unless someone could fly."

Finally remembering his manners, Joe carefully sidled along
the platform. "So sorry! Truly, I didn't mean to interrupt here,
and I hope I didn't mess anything up. I was just so surprised to
see you that I forgot to act properly."

There was a momentary pause as the lady he had interrupted processed his words, and a faint smile appeared on her
lips. "I suppose I can understand that, at least. I'll admit I wasn't
exactly expecting to see you here either. Now, who are you, and
why are you bouncing off the walls? I understand you're excited
to be here, but...?"

"Ah! Yes, my name is Joe. I'm on my way up to see the
Grandmaster right now." Extending his hand, he held it in the
air for a long few seconds as he waited for her to shake it. To his
dismay, she simply looked at the outstretched limb, shaking her
head and glancing at the implements she was gripping.

"Well, Mr. Joe." Her words faltered briefly as she glanced at
his hands, and she started again. "*Master* Joe, my name is Hilda
Darling, Master of Enchanted Ritual Circles."

"Right, sorry, not used to introducing myself with my skills."
Joe sheepishly rubbed the back of his head with his gloved
hand. "Master of Ritual Circles. I've got to ask, how does one
become a Master of Enchanted Ritual Circles without first
mastering Ritual Circles themselves?"

"This sounds like a delightful, scholarly conversation to have
another time," Hilda stated firmly. "Suffice it to say, I came here as
a Master of Enchanting, and my skills transferred over. Now,
don't you have somewhere to be that isn't in the active effect of
the ritual I am attempting to create?"

"I do." At that moment, Joe felt his mana pool reach max
capacity, which meant he'd been standing there gawping at his
new peer for just over a minute and a half already. Before
leaping away, he paused as his eye caught on a slight irregular-
ity. "Err... not to be a pain, but you have a misaligned conduit
on the third ring. Right, uh, there. It's meant to direct the

energy flow outward, but the way it's angled will force it to curve point eight-three percent on the z-axis, creating resistance and impacting the duration of the ritual. Probably not enough to make it fail, but it'll degrade faster than it should. Shift it three degrees counterclockwise on the x-axis, and the mana should distribute evenly instead of feeding back into the matrix."

Hilda looked at the space he was indicating, but it was clear she didn't see the issue the way he did. Carefully reaching forward, and glancing at her to double check that she wouldn't stop him, Joe shifted the positioning of the enchanted token ever so slightly. "There you go, that should do it."

"You could just... see that." She looked between her diagram and the newcomer, "I know you've never seen my design before, so unless someone snuck it out to you so you could play a prank on me, that means you truly do have some skill."

"I suppose it's just what it means to be a Master of Ritual Circles?" Joe chuckled uncomfortably. "I can see what the diagram is *meant* to do and where you have things correct and incorrect. It's even easy for me to know what those tokens are supposed to do, but for some reason, the idea of creating them? The actual purpose of the tokens themselves? I have no idea."

"Hmm." Hilda bit her lip before slowly inquiring, "You must be extremely busy, especially if you are being called upon by the Grandmaster already. Still, if you find time in your schedule, I'd love to exchange pointers. Perhaps some tutelage in Ritual Circles, in exchange for teaching you what I know about Enchanted Ritual Circles?"

"I'm only at the Student-tier in that skill, so it would be extremely helpful, if you wouldn't mind." Joe flashed her a grin, then crouched down to leap away. "Until next time, Darling."

"That's *Master* Darling."

Joe flushed completely red, sputtering slightly as he nodded vigorously.

"Ahh, yeah. Bye... sorry about-" Feeling like he should go

and bury himself in a hole, Joe instead decided to shut his mouth with a *click* and leaped upward. "What's *wrong* with me today?"

A few minutes later, he was standing outside the door on the top floor, trying to compose himself before his meeting. Taking a deep breath, he stepped forward and lifted his hand to knock, only for the man on the other side to call out.

"Just get in here, newbie."

Entering the room, Joe was completely stunned to see the Grandmaster sitting in a soft chair with his feet up on his desk. The old man flashed Joe a grin and motioned for him to take a seat. Thrown off by the shift in attitude, as the representative of the tower had been stately and refined the last time he had seen him, Joe cautiously grabbed a chair, wondering if he was meeting with the Grandmaster's twin.

"I'm going to get straight to business, if you don't mind." The old man twirled a loop of his beard with a finger. "Your arrival here is extremely well-timed. Frankly, we are facing a crisis."

That made Joe perk up, and he sat forward to listen more intently as the Grandmaster casually laid out the plight of the people in the tower. "You see, Joe. Our tower has no Sage. It has *never* had a Sage. Our influence is waning, and challenges are coming more frequently. I don't often lose, certainly not within our own territory, but we still need resources. When our members go out and about, I'd say eighty-five percent of the time, they are challenged to a duel before they can return with whatever they left for. As I'm sure you understand, our class is most effective when we have had time to prepare."

"Absolutely." Joe nodded along to show he was listening.

"Then it should also make perfect sense that most of our people only carry around a few prepared rituals. Once those are exhausted by endless duels, it almost *always* means a net loss in Honor." The Grandmaster let loose a heavy sigh. "It used to be that no one wanted to antagonize us, for fear of not being accepted if they ever wanted to take Ritualist as a prestige class.

Now? Now the class itself might be at risk. I'll be brutally honest with you. We need a Sage. In other words, I *need* a Mythic core."

"Got it." Joe continued to bob his head. "Well, the path to Jotunheim is open? I'm sure you can-"

"I can't do anything, Joe." There was a soft **thump** as the Grandmaster's feet dropped to the floor, and he turned to face his guest directly. "If I were to leave the area directly around the tower, I would immediately be challenged by combat class Grandmasters from all across the planet. We were already dangerously close to losing the tower before you arrived, but even so... that merely bought us more time."

Clap!

The bright sound startled Joe, as the old man clapped his hands and beamed. "Luckily, I have a solution! Do you know how long it's been since I've been able to take a direct mentee? I'd like to not only sponsor your stay in the tower, but give you advanced training, and I am willing to give you direct guidance in your skills when you get stuck learning from your other sponsors. You're at the level cap?"

"Yes...?" Joe slowly replied, glancing at his character sheet. "At least, my Ritualist base class is capped at level thirty."

Name: Joe 'Tatum's Chosen Legend' Class: Reductionist
Profession I: Arcanologist (Max)
Profession II: Ritualistic Alchemist (7/20)
Profession III: Grandmaster's Apprentice (15/25)
Profession IV: None

Character Level: 30 Exp: 465,000 Exp to next level: 31,000
Rituarchitect Level: 13 Exp: 87,450 Exp to next level: 3,550
Reductionist Level: 10 Exp: 59,900 Exp to next level: 6,100
Hit Points: 4,171/4,171
Mana: 9,223/12,018 (2,794 reserved)
Mana regen: 115.09/sec
Stamina: 2,992.5/2,992.5

Stamina regen: 7.27/sec

Characteristic: Raw score

Strength (Bound): 278
Dexterity: 277
Constitution (Bound): 277
Light Intelligence (Bound): 283
Wisdom: 270
Dark Charisma: 229
Karmic Perception: 280
Luck: 222
Karmic Luck: 99

Doing a double take as he saw the enormous jump in his Karmic Luck, Joe refocused on what his counterpart was saying.

"The only way to become uncapped is to advance your base class." The Grandmaster patted his own chest proudly. "Even if my time is rather stretched, and my main focus is going to be my evolution into Sagehood, I can help you become a Grandmaster. That will come with a class evolution, uncapping your growth. Now, my personal attention and time does not come cheaply. As I said, I'll make you a deal. I'll sponsor you with whatever you need and make sure to give you as much time as I can spare to direct your training. In return, I need you to bring me a Mythic core."

Quest gained-

"Nope. Absolutely not." Joe shook his head, and the notification died before it even finished writing itself out. "I'm not going to trade a Mythic core for training. Not when I can do the same by going and starting a dairy farm on... celestial feces, I just realized how I'm going to pay for things here. Anyway, being able to advance slightly faster just... isn't worth it to me. I have just as many uses for a Mythic core as you do, plus I eventually want to become a Sage as well. So... get your own?"

He licked suddenly dry lips as he trailed off, the air in the room becoming oppressive and stifling as the Grandmaster glared at him. Just as he worried that he may have made a serious mistake, a peal of laughter came from behind Joe, and the tense atmosphere instantly shattered.

"Ha! I can't believe you'd even try that as a *joke*, Pete." Shifting around, Joe stared at the newcomer, jaw dropping slightly as he took in the intense, focused power that wafted off the man like heat off pavement—he had no idea how he had missed this person until now. "He's going to think you're serious if you try to suppress him like that."

"Haaa... just had to make sure he wasn't actually a plant from another tower." The Grandmaster, apparently 'Pete', offered an apologetic grin as Joe looked back at him. "Anyone willing to make that kind of trade would definitely only be here to spy on us. All right, Joe. You pass. Now, I truly *do* want you to get me a Mythic core, but here's the real offer…"

CHAPTER SEVEN

Pete, much to Joe's surprise, didn't wave his guest over to stand near him. Instead, he got up and walked around his own desk, moving until he stood just to the left of and behind the as-of-yet unnamed man. The bald Ritualist watched this interaction, recognizing the show of respect for what it was.

"This is *Sage Mirascible*." Pete paused for a moment as if that should mean something to Joe. "Nothing? Huh. You truly are new to this world. Well, while he's a rather *irascible* person, he's also considered the strongest single combatant on the entirety of Vanaheim."

"*Considered?*" the Sage jested at Pete in mock outrage. "I mean, I only have an unbroken century of wins in the arena to prove it. It has been getting a bit stale these days... maybe I should challenge the current champion?"

Pfft, Pete replied with an unflattering sound. "As if they'd let you. You break the betting pool every time you even get *close* to the place. Like I was saying, Joe. All of the parts of my previous offer stand. Resources, focused help getting through bottlenecks, and anything else I can do to help you rapidly

reach Grandmastery. On top of that, I'm willing to cash in my *only* grand favor with Mir on your behalf. Until I'm able to fulfill my end of the bargain and help you step into your power, he will act as your mentor on Vanaheim. He will teach you his combat methodology in an attempt to make you the first Ritualist worthy of fighting. Not only that, but he will hold both of us to our ends of the agreement."

Even with the promise of a Sage's wisdom, some part of Joe still resisted, since he hadn't been seeking it out. Not to mention, this was an intense *ask* that bordered on desperate. It was a bad look, and so far the leadership of this place hadn't been anything like what he had been expecting. "Look, I understand how valuable it would be to learn from any Sage, let alone Sage Mirascible-"

"Just call me Mir."

"Okay then, Mir. It's just that I don't know how that would help me with my own short term goals going forward." Joe shrugged his left shoulder, his palm lifting as he tried to articulate his thoughts correctly. "While I appreciate all of the attention, I just don't understand the real value in this offer. What I'm being offered, nor what I'd get in return. I'm... sure you think this is a good deal, but... could I get a little more context?"

Hum. To Joe's great relief, the Sage didn't seem to take offense to his words. "A little caution is always good, but you're right to ask. Still, you shouldn't let it get in the way of a good opportunity. I'll explain to you why this is worth the price of admission. First, helping your tower produce the first Sage it's ever had will solidify the tower's position on Vanaheim. If your tower births its first Sage, it cements its legacy in Vanaheim and quells every malicious voice out there. Remember that what's beneficial for the flamboyantly feathered honk machine is equally advantageous for the slightly larger progenitor."

Joe blinked, trying to process the statement—but the words wouldn't untangle themselves in his mind. With a sigh of surrender, he chose to refocus as Mir carried on. "Second, being the direct recipient of your new Sage's goodwill can only be beneficial to you in the future. Let's say you bring back the exact material he needs in order to achieve his goal. I can't imagine he would be anything but gracious and generous forevermore. The person who makes that happen won't be forgotten, and that kind of opportunity doesn't come around twice."

Something seemed to amuse the powerhouse, and he belatedly added, "Third, you get to skip the line of people trying to learn from me. In all fairness, I wasn't going to train them anyway. This way, you get a guaranteed yes, and you don't have to sit on the waiting list for a few decades just for me to tell you no at the end."

"What *Class Sage* Mir is trying to tell you is that his teachings are truly priceless," Pete pressed as his companion went silent. "There's no one better to learn how to fight from on this world or any lower ones. Perhaps in Asgard, but learning directly from a deity is an unlikely proposition."

Finally, each person in the room fell silent, all for their own reasons. Pete was carefully watching Joe, waiting for him to accept. Mir seemed to have simply run out of words for the day and appeared perfectly willing to walk away if the offer was refused. Lost in the whirl of his own mind, the bald Ritualist struggled to make sense of what was happening. Finally deciding to speak, he exhaled sharply and met the Grandmaster's gaze without flinching.

"Why?"

"What do you mean?" Pete smoothed his beard with his right hand, almost as though he were petting an emotional support puppy.

"I mean, why me? I'm the newest. You have no idea what my capabilities actually are. Wouldn't it be far more simple to get your own people to go and make this happen? Certainly, those who've been here for a long time understand the intricacies of the Honor system and what it would mean for all of us.

A grand favor must be worth *something* if you've brought it up with such gravitas. Is it that you don't trust your people? Are you uncertain of their loyalties? So… why me, and why this offer practically the first time we're meeting each other?" Joe closed his mouth before he pushed too hard, perfectly willing to patiently wait for a full answer.

"Ah." Contrary to expectations, Pete seemed relieved at the questions. "That's actually easy enough to explain. You see, my boy, anyone from this world needs to get permission from the Sage's Council for the members of their tower to go off-world, or risk their wrath. Each of the factions have already nominated a tower to go on expeditions to Jotunheim and bring back a Mythic core. Yet, after one of them succeeds, there's still an endless waiting list… and we're at the very bottom, since they don't know if we actually *can* ascend."

The Grandmaster leaned forward, searching Joe's face. "*Every* tower has Grandmasters waiting on their chance, but they will be carefully managed by the council to ensure the balance of power is kept steady. With you, we've been given a unique advantage. You can go and hunt for the cores, and no one can say it's unfair for you to do so."

Suddenly the full-court press made perfect sense. As understanding dawned on him, relief etched itself across the Tower Master's face. Bobbing his head as he considered his next actions, Joe decided to play for a bit of time so he didn't need to give a firm answer one way or another just yet. "Mir, could you explain your class and how learning from you is going to be beneficial?"

"Sure," Mir casually replied as his eyes tracked across Joe's face, looking for something but… not finding it? The man's eyes narrowed slightly before speaking again. "I'm an Elementalist, plain and simple. No prestige class, no special evolutions, just the base class in its purest possible form."

He glanced over to Pete, who was grinning as if getting ready to hear an inside joke.

Joe frowned ever so slightly. "I don't know why you think I should be shocked? I guess I just don't have the background in all this? Sure, I would have thought you'd have evolved your class at some point, especially if you're the strongest fighter on the planet. Is it because of your specializations?"

Mir let a soft snort escape his nose. "That's the thing, little Ritualist. I never felt the need to evolve my class. When I specialized, instead of chasing upgrades, I doubled down on perfecting what I already had, becoming an Elementalist 'plus', which only means I get stronger with my current class. A free lesson for you. The problem most people have is they spread themselves thin. They want *more*. Skills, abilities, and variety for days! *Pah*. What you'd learn with me is a different path. Instead of a lake of skills three miles wide and an inch deep, I went with three inches wide and a mile deep."

Lifting his hand, he curled his fingers slightly and allowed a thin bolt of lightning to crackle into existence between his fingertips, then spun it around his hands as though twirling a pencil. "The core class skills of an Elementalist are as follows: Bolt, ball, channel, cone, and impact. My first specialization is in 'bolt', the next was 'ball'. I'm sure you can guess what the next ones were. The only thing I didn't specialize in was which element I chose. I can use any of them: lightning, fire, water, earth, wind, ice, light, shadow... time. Space. Death. Life. If you can use it, I can as well, and can counter your abilities every time."

"I can see why you're so good at *combat*, I suppose." Joe exhaled slowly as he tried not to accidentally make an enemy. "But, long term, I don't think combat is *my* path."

"Then you're lying to yourself," Mir barked at him, suddenly flushing as Joe seemingly touched a nerve. "You want to make interesting things? Then you need to gather material. That means *fighting* to get what you need, whether that means hunting monsters or holding them off as you delve deep for rare components. You want to keep what you have? Then you'd better be able to keep the vultures circling instead of feasting on your corpse. How about that Mythic core? Are you just going to pull it out of thin air, or are you going to hunt a World Boss? All of that sounds like combat to me."

"I *could* try to pull that core out of Jake's Alchemy hall, but I don't think that'd go over very well," Joe murmured ever so softly to himself, glanced to the side slightly as a shiver ran down his spine. When he looked to the others, acceptance was clear in his eyes. "I understand. Look, I'm not trying to fight against this, I just need to make sure everyone has a clear understanding of what this deal is going to be. I'll get you the core, Pete. But in return, on top of everything else, if there's ever a time when I'm competing with someone else to become the Class Sage for Ritualist, you'll support me. Deal?"

The other two were stunned by his audacious statement, but it was Pete who reacted first, chuckling and shaking his head. "A Master in only one of the disciplines, and he's already got his heart set on becoming a Class Sage? Do Grandmaster skills just grow alongside the road like weeds? Sure, Joe. It's a deal. Take your time... it only matters that this *happens*. We don't need to be first; we just need to get there."

Quest gained—and accepted. For some reason, I felt the need to add that part in.

The makings of a Sage. You have agreed to Grandmaster Pete's request. He will provide sponsorship in the Tower of Rituals, training as able—no less than one hour per month—dedicated support when attempting to break through a bottleneck in your core skills until each of your core skills enter the Grandmaster ranks, support should you ever be in competition for the position of Class Sage of Ritualists, and direct mentorship under Class Sage Mirascible. Should you ever be in competition for the position of Class Sage, he will support your bid.

In return, you will provide a Mythic core to him and support him as he ascends to the Skill Sage of Alchemical Rituals.

Rewards: Maximized reputation with Pete. Failure: You will enter a blood feud with the entirety of the members of the Tower of Rituals as well as Class Sage Mirascible, unless the entire cost of your tutelage and sponsorship is repaid.

"Wow. When it's all laid out like that, it does *kinda* look like I'm getting the better end of the deal." Joe murmured thoughtfully as he read over the details. He looked over at the powerful people he was dealing with, noting the ecstatic expression on the wizened, white-bearded Ritualist. Then he glanced at Mirascible, *really* studying him for the first time.

It was clear the man was old, ancient even, but he didn't really look it. He was clean-shaven, his hair a salt and pepper coloration, and well-healed scars adorned practically every inch of his skin, some wide and vicious, others thin and shallow. His ears had a sharp point, indicating some sort of Elven heritage, though he looked nothing like the High Elves inhabiting Alfenheim.

Suddenly remembering a part of the conversation they'd glossed over, Joe quizzed the duo, "That arena you were talking about, why wouldn't they let you come back and fight again? Just too powerful?"

"Yes. Exactly that." Mir looked like he wasn't going to say more, but Pete refuted his statement with a sharp huff of air.

"As *if!*" The Grandmaster's face scrunched up as he shot some side-eye at his friend. "They'd *love* to have him back, no matter how strong he got, if it wasn't so abyssal boring to see him fight. Oh, what's he going to do next? Look. A bolt. Oh, he changed it up with a cone-"

"The fundamentals are everything!" Mir halfheartedly growled at Pete. "That's the entire point of what I teach. Who needs fifty different skills for fifty different situations, when you have five that you can adapt, shift, and use to dominate *any* scenario?"

"This is why you don't have friends." Pete playfully shoved the Sage, only to stumble backwards slightly as the man didn't budge even fractionally. "Besides me, that is."

"No, being boring in a fight isn't why I have *few* friends," Mir retorted darkly, though he didn't elaborate further. Pete looked like he was about to do so on his behalf, clearly in an exceptional mood, when the light in the tower shifted ever so slightly. Just then, the sound of a gong being struck rang through the air.

The Grandmaster's face fell, and he heaved a deep sigh. "Just like that, duty calls once more. I'll give them this, they're persistent."

"*I* could go have a talk with them, if you'd like," Mir offered as he cracked his knuckles menacingly. "You're not the only one who tires of the endless interruptions."

"No, no… if the Tower of Blood Rites wishes to continuously feed us Honor, who am I to deny them their daily tribute?" Pete half turned his hand, a green glow at his waist expanding outward and blocking Joe's vision for an instant. "Mir, keep an eye on him, would you? Make sure he follows the rules."

In a blink, he found himself standing at the gates of the square wall built around the base of the tower. Pete was in front of him, while Mir stood just to the right of the newcomer Ritualist.

Before Joe could regain his bearings, the gates swung open, and a cloying tension draped over him like a thick, wet blanket. Just beyond the wall stood a formation which exuded discipline and danger—warriors wrapped in matching battle robes, though a formal version meant to be worn *after* a victory. At their forefront was a single figure, his presence so steeped in bloodlust it pressed against the senses, utterly suffocating in its intensity.

The leader gleamed with unapologetic flair, wrapped in a black and sanguine combat robe tailored with surgical precision. Shiny crimson trim reflected the light, and each measured step closer revealed a flashy sigil stitched over his heart. But it was his hair that first demanded Joe's attention. The Ritualist felt his jaw drop in disbelief at the towering, sculpted pompadour that defied gravity, wind, and all conventional taste.

Only then did he notice that every member of the battle group wore the same style, all without any noticeable sense of irony or awareness of the bizarre appearance they had. His eyes flicked back to the leader, who was now sneering at Pete, radiating momentum and a violence that *begged* to be released—like a storm only waiting for the last drop of water it needed to create a downpour.

He remained locked in position as he stared down Grandmaster Pete, sneer fading into a knowing smirk and revealing small, twin fangs peeking down from his top lips. This was a man who seemed to already know how this battle would end and was simply waiting for everyone else to catch up.

"A vampire? Is that a real thing here?" Joe murmured in quiet surprise, clearly not quietly enough. The aggressive group's eyes snapped toward him in unison, predatory and sharp. For a long, breath-stalling moment, the opposing Grandmaster fixed his gaze on Joe, head tilting ever so slightly, as if adjusting the angle would help him figure out exactly what kind of threat he was looking at.

"How bewildering, *Stompetti*." The vampire drawled with just the slightest lisp in his silky-smooth voice from the oversized teeth. "It seems your tower has taken on a rather... *sparkling* new recruit. Youngster, that glow of yours is positively radiant. Tell me, why didn't you join my tower instead? You'd fit right in."

Only then did Joe realize he'd been ignoring a literally glaring fact—the only negative effect sunshine was having on these maybe-vampires was that they were lit up like disco balls; in fact, their skin shining with *more* than just reflected light.

"After all, that unnatural luminescence you exude is remarkable. Perhaps you've mistaken your calling? It's not too late to change your fate; the Tower of Blood Rights is always open to those who can appreciate power in its purest, most *visceral* form."

"Mir, correct me if I'm wrong here, but they're absorbing sunlight, as well as having natural bioluminescence, yes? They're basically humanoid fireflies with dental problems?" Joe's voice was pitched to carry—while he *was* actually curious, he figured that, since he'd already thrown in his lot with the Ritualists, he may as well let their enemies be his as well.

"Mind your manners, kid. Don't talk to me, answer *him*," Mir responded stoically, not a hint of mirth in his voice, no sparkle showing in his eyes. Instead, there was only a slightly pained look, as if Joe was digging his own grave.

"Ah. I see. He's as small a man as you are, Stom-*petty*. Go ahead and add him to the priority target list," the vampire casually called over his shoulder, and one of his sycophants quickly stepped forward and snapped his fingers. A perfect image of Joe formed in the air, and the Master vampire lifted a book and clapped it around the photograph before nodding at his superior and stepping back into line. "Well, I guess we're already all the way past pleasantries now, aren't we? I tried to make an opportunity for advancement available to one of your recruits before they *stagnated* like the rest of you-"

"In ten seconds, I get to shut the gates on you for a week," Pete casually called in a tired voice. "Did you bang the gong for a reason, or did you just come here to spew vitriol?"

"Fine, *fine*... I've had my say about the lack of advancement your tower has had since its inception. No Sage, no new advancements in your arts. While everyone else evolves, grows, and claims Honor, you merely survive. So, to help our world achieve *excellence*... I once more issue a formal challenge to the Tower of Rituals."

"Standard terms?" Pete tried to keep his voice casual, but his opponent was having none of it.

"No, no, no. A little birdie told me you've had a sudden, rather unexpected windfall of Honor. I'm wagering *triple* my standard, to make sure you don't have enough to keep your gates closed to us any longer. Do you dare accept? Or will you step away and sacrifice Honor without even fighting?"

"It's kind of like a big blind, if you know how wagers work with gambling," Mir whispered into Joe's ear. "Doesn't matter if you want to play that hand or not, you automatically have some buy-in just by having a spot at the table. Saying no too often just means not having enough Honor to wager when you *do* have a winning hand."

Surprisingly, at least to Joe, Pete didn't immediately accept the terms. "You seem quite confident today, Istvan."

The vampire's eyes twinkled maliciously as he exposed his sharpened teeth in a wide smile. "Ahh, but I *am*, Petti. I've finally found your weakness."

CHAPTER EIGHT

"Must you drag this out, Istvan? If you truly had an angle, you'd already be gloating about it. This sly tone you've taken is unlike you." Pete strolled out of the apparently tenuous safety of the secured courtyard, casually walking an arm's length from the group from the Tower of Blood Rights before stopping and taking his position more than a hundred yards away from the tower. "I accept the duel. Let's get this over with, so you can go and tell Violetta you've failed yet again."

Joe watched with great interest as the vampire flinched at Pete's casual mentioning of the person who must have been his superior in his tower. "Mmm. I think I'm getting the hang of this, Mir. This guy is challenging Pete because they're both Grandmasters, but he's not the Tower Master because his tower has a Sage?"

"Correct. But I'd rather not talk to you right now. I'm trying not to slap you hard enough to make a crater in the ground for acting the fool in front of Pete's rival." Mir spat to the side, giving Joe a hard look that actually strained his Exquisite Shell. "You all but announced yourself as being important to him, not to mention directly sponsored, and made it harder for Pete to refuse the fight, if he'd wanted to do so. Masters don't get to act so familiar with higher tiers unless there's a good reason for it."

"Hold on… I said nothing I wouldn't have said if I was alone. I'm not using him as a shield. Next, I've never been one to, as they say, 'know my place'." Joe stood straight and crossed his arms as he rejoined against the powerhouse. "My plan has always been to treat everyone equally until they prove they don't deserve it. I did it when I was only a Novice, and I'll keep doing it when I'm the Class Sage. Too many people blowing smoke up your rear-"

Mir placed a hand on Joe's shoulder and *squeezed*. The Ritualist's Exquisite Shell let out a high-pitched whine and shattered in an instant. "What did Istvan do to you that made you think he didn't deserve respect, then? Offer you a position in his tower? He was nothing but polite to you and frankly even has good reasons for trying to drive your class out of your tower. Just because those two don't like each other doesn't mean you needed to spit on his gesture made in good faith. The world does not always have to be black and white. You don't have to have *only* enemies or allies. I want you to stand here quietly and watch this, then reflect on your actions before we meet again."

Completely taken aback by this unexpectedly, casually violent response, Joe simply closed his mouth and looked on, though his mind was already carefully scrutinizing the events that had led him to that point. "Is this a culture thing…? Thousands of years being in a closed-off world making everyone super touchy about perceived respect?"

The Grandmasters remained a dozen paces away from each other, poised to strike. It quickly became clear what they were waiting on as the air shimmered above them, bright numbers appearing and beginning to count down. Pete slowly clenched his gloved hands, and across from him, Istvan smirked, fangs glinting as his skin flushed pink, red, then a deep vermillion.

"I don't know what your depth of knowledge is in combat yet, as I haven't had a chance to assess you, but you need to watch carefully." Mir spoke into Joe's ear, carefully modulating his voice so as not to do anything to interrupt the combatants' concentration. "Pete has been fighting for the tower for hundreds of years, and he's fantastic at it. Ritual combat isn't about speed, brute force, or enormous, flashy explosions. It's all about... control."

3...2...1...

Ding!

Even before the bright, cheery sound had reached Joe's ears, the two Grandmasters had begun moving, their hands flying through the air as they channeled their mana into intricate patterns, superimposing their will and intent on the world. Pete finished first, his right hand slicing through the air as the ritual circles on the back of his gloves flared with violet light. Joe's eyes went wide as he realized that the sigils on his robes weren't merely decorative. They must be keystones to an unknown number of rituals, which had been created and placed across the entire battlefield ahead of time.

The ground rumbled, and the air hummed as luminous blue chains erupted through the stone from seven points around the vampire, pulsing with mana and lashing out at the Grandmaster like a particularly vicious slither of snakes. Istvan dodged to the side, even managing to twist in midair, body blurring as he sought to escape from the center of the containment. Yet, the chains weren't easily denied, puppetted as they were by a Grandmaster Ritualist. Shifting dynamically, one *snapped* through the air and managed to wrap around his ankle; and from there, the rest managed to latch on.

Once each had a hold on a different part of his body, the chains went taut, each pulling in a different direction as they tried to force him to the ground. It wasn't enough, and though Istvan showed signs of strain, he was able to remain standing and moving, though his graceful movements turned slow and rigid.

Pete didn't relent on the pressure, tapping the air and activating another ritual in the distance, which launched a beam that seemed to consist of a swarm of biting insects. It impacted his slowed opponent, and the bugs vanished, leaving behind a pulsing green and black energy which slowly began to sink into Istvan's skin. The vampire let out a strangled yell, lifting his hands in front of him and channeling a catastrophic amount of power into a sphere made entirely of crimson energy. Pete glared at the orb, a hint of concern appearing on his face, but neither stopped or changed their attacks.

Another ritual pulsed with power, and though Joe didn't see exactly what it did, a moment later, Istvan coughed wetly, a dark splatter of blood escaping his lips—only for Pete to reach out with his left hand and gesture, summoning the fluid over to himself before it could hit the ground. As soon as the vital juices landed in his palm, he clenched his hand into a fist and closed his eyes.

"That was *beautiful*," Joe murmured appreciatively at the move, only to stutter to silence as the vampire finally released his spell.

"*Crimson Tribunal of Thundering Blood!*" Istvan shouted hoarsely, clapping his hands onto the bright red orb—which popped like a soap bubble and released a strange shockwave of pink-tinged power. It washed over the combat zone, then continued outward, further and further. Joe blinked as it swept past him, lips curling into a snarl as he glared at the vampire who was attacking the first person to give him a real shot at growth.

"Four worlds I've been on, and I've met exactly one person who is clear with their intentions. You want to fight him? Over my dead body!" Joe tried to launch himself forward, his mana already flowing to his fingertips, only to find his feet running in empty air as the iron grip around his shoulder held him in place.

"That's a trait of the Tower of Blood Rites," Mir calmly explained as Joe fought to rush forward. "Each of their blood-based spells creates a powerful compulsion. This must be a *particularly* powerful attack for it to create such a large-scale taunt."

Skill increase: Mental Manipulation Resistance (Journeyman 0 → Journeyman III)

Joe felt the strangest anomalous feeling, calmly reading his skill increases as they rapidly accrued, while at the same time lost in a deep bloodlust. Then the main portion of the Blood Rite began, slurping away the remnant energy that had been infesting his thoughts. Joe looked around, realizing the world had taken on a soft pink hue—only for the accruing energy to *crackle* and condense into a bolt of crimson lightning as thick as his torso.

The dense energy crashed down, and Pete dodged—or at least tried to do so. It didn't matter how perfectly he shifted to the side, flipped, or threw himself out of the way, the arc of energy simply adjusted itself midair until it slammed into his body. At the very last moment, Pete managed to block it from hitting his chest by throwing his right arm in the way, but was sent skipping across the ground as the plasma detonated against him.

The light in the area spasmed and condensed again, another bolt striking and splitting the air. Another, and another.

Pete shifted his stance and channeled mana from both hands onto his chest, revealing yet another ritual diagram woven into the fabric. With a grunt, he spread his arms wide, and a translucent bubble of mana appeared around him, lifting him slightly off the ground as it kept him in the exact center of the barrier. For his part, Istvan had moved on from the spell, allowing it to run autonomously as he began spinning his hands in the air, each forward motion creating a spike of half-fluid, crimson energy that whizzed through the air and broke against the new barrier.

"Ugh~" Joe went limp in Mir's grip, getting a conciliatory pat from the man's off hand when he realized the younger man had finally gotten control of himself. "How's he doing that? It almost looks like a ritual?"

"Blood rites are... *similar* to rituals, but they're a much more focused branch of combat-specific magic. Where blood can be used in rituals for targeting, and perhaps some alchemical purposes, blood rites specifically use the material *as* the output. It could be anything from simple spikes to creating portals and familiar contracts to, *apparently*, tribulation storms," Mir explained in a mild, vaguely interested tone. "I have to say, I don't often see innovation coming from the towers these days— nowhere near enough fresh *blood* to come up with new ideas—so this really gets me going. I wonder if I should go see what else Violetta has come up with?"

"Are you a battle junkie, or something?" Joe grinned at the powerful man next to him, his smile fading as the Sage nodded excitedly.

"But of course I am! What did you think Pete meant when the stipulation for me training you was when he said that my goal is to 'make you the first Ritualist worthy of fighting against'?" Mir shook Joe slightly, making his head lash back and forth. "When you finally become a Sage, we're going to fight for *real*."

"O-oh," Joe murmured with no small amount of concern, only for a strange motion by Pete to recapture his attention.

The Grandmaster was sweeping his arms in opposite directions, his right hand pointing up to the sky, and his left was pointed to the ground. Slowly, he began shifting until both arms were parallel, then had completely switched positions.

Istvan let out a vicious snarl. "What is that? Oh, *no* you don't!"

Joe didn't see anything happening at first, but his eyes shifted slightly out of focus all on their own, allowing him to view a golden wheel which appeared in the air in front of Pete, traced out intricately wherever his arms passed. Mirroring his opponent's movements, the vampire swiftly twisted both palms in opposite directions, unleashing a spiraling corkscrew of blood-red energy.

The vicious attack slammed into the barrier with tremendous force, splintering its surface. Slowly, methodically, the blood-drill ground its way through the magical shield, shards of energy splintering outward as the relentless storm of lightning continued to hammer down and dissipate against the protective barrier.

Pete's hands began traveling toward his midsection, finally stopping just in front of his heart. Then, he gently clapped, and an almost-imperceptible sheath of golden energy surrounded his entire body. Joe waited for some dramatic effect, but whatever the Grandmaster had done had already run its course in a terribly anti-climactic way. It wasn't until the next bolt of lightning struck that he realized that something actually had changed—since the crimson energy impacted the ground nowhere near the Grandmaster, instead sending an eruption of molten dirt flying into the air.

Whatever technique Pete had used, it had drained him heavily. His face was contorted with exhaustion, his breath coming in ragged gasps.

Joe wasn't the only one to notice this, as Istvan began mocking him. "You're getting *old*, Stompetti. Finally noticed it was your own blood targeting you, huh? Tell me what that technique was, and I'll send you a wheel of cheese as thanks."

"You're not the first person to use my blood to target me. We all have our own ways of keeping ourselves safe from being targeted at a distance—all I did was sever any ties to parts of myself not contained within my body. Where did you get it? A previous duel? That doesn't seem sporting." Pete allowed himself a ragged smile as he slowly reset his stance. "I'll take parmesan, thank you very much."

"It'll be sent to your new tower," the vampire snarled in response, surprising Joe by actually following through on his words. "*Sporting*, you say? You're one to talk, relying on your homefield advantage to the exclusion of all else. How is using what amounts to little more than pre-made traps honorable? Not that it matters, not today. You're already on your last legs."

Pulling out a bottle of what must have been Pete's blood, Istvan tossed the now-inert liquid to the side, where it splashed against the pavement. The Grandmaster Ritualist grimaced in disgust but said nothing. Instead, he lifted his hands and began rapidly tapping at the air, sending bursts of mana out and away to activate ritual after ritual. More circles flared to life, more sigils ignited, burning with a luminescent blue glow as layers of afflictions and debuffs began accumulating on the vampire.

Even as his skin burned, and his bones creaked from strain, the vampire pushed himself forward, countering the low-damage rituals with an immense amount of vitality. His regeneration almost able to keep pace with the first, second, and even fifth wave of damaging energy that latched onto him.

But as they kept coming, anger and unwillingness began to fill Istvan's expression. Shockwaves of blood left deep craters in the ground and caused the barrier around Pete to shimmer. Curses which *should* have managed to reach and effect the old man fizzled out—their ability to target him having been lost.

"Looks like you'll have to try again another time, Istvan." Pete finally allowed himself to break out in a smile as the numbers in the air above them finished their countdown. "Same time tomorrow?"

3...2...1...

"Enough!" The vampire's voice boomed across the battlefield, echoing off the towers in the distance at least twice. "You win this time, Stompetti... saved by the bell once again. It means *nothing*. We all know the truth, Ritualist. As the defender, the Honor defaults to you when there is no clear victor in the time limit. But that's all you can do. You haven't walked among us in decades, so you don't know the truth. But your time in that ivory tower is coming to an end. If you were to ever step outside of your grounds, you would become easy prey."

His sunken, crimson eyes flicked toward Joe. "That goes for *all* of you."

With a dramatic flourish, he turned on his heel and stalked away, quickly followed by the members of his tower. It didn't escape Joe's notice that they walked easily and freely, without any fear of being challenged as they left the area and walked down the streets in broad daylight. Then, his attention was caught by something odd. Off to the side of the tower, just barely able to be viewed from inside the wall, hundreds of people were starting to disperse, clearly having gathered to watch the battle.

One familiar face stood out above the others, and Mak sent him a jaunty wave as they locked eyes. A few moments later, the man came rushing over to the open gates. "What a rush! I always have a soft spot in my heart for the Tower of Rituals— truly, the most reliable place on the planet to find a battle on a regular schedule. It makes the logistics of preparing grilled treats and cold drinks so much more logistically feasible."

"You were using this *incredibly fraught battle* as a way to sell snacks?" Joe blinked and shook his head, "Abyss, man... that's brilliant. What about seating? Do you have spare seats you can set up? I bet you could charge a premium for offering a little bit of comfort."

"Ooh, I like you. Tell you what, I'll try it out and cut you in about five percent if the idea takes off. Still happy with your choice of tower? I'd love to know that I pointed you in the right direction."

"You know? I'm getting more excited by the minute."

Mak winked at him and went back to his wagon, just as Pete slowly limped through the gate, bleeding from a dozen small lacerations that Joe hadn't noticed him accumulate. He smelled of copper and ozone, and looked close to passing out on the spot.

Stepping close, Joe made sure the Grandmaster was within his Neutrality Aura, allowing the passive spell to cleanse his wounds, hydrate the man, and begin the process of healing him up. After a few moments, Joe frowned softly as he noticed the damage was barely being affected—as if it were actively resisting his attempts at healing.

"Well, what did you learn from this battle, Joe?" Pete inquired in a heavy, tired tone. "Anything new or interesting?"

"Uh... *so* much." Joe admitted freely and vehemently, causing the Grandmaster to perk up and look at him questioningly. "The way you just kept piling ritual effects up on him? I've never seen anything like that before. I lost count at ten, since I was trying to figure out what each of them did and how you did it. Let me know if I got these right... you started with that set of spectral chains that weighed him down and made it difficult for him to move, then there was one that forced him to bleed, which you then used to activate at least three others. I was pretty sure I saw you actively dehydrate him? Was that a thing, or were you doing something else to his skin? There was one that just amplified the injuries the others made, right?"

"Yes... all of that is correct. I started with Crippling Chains, hit him with a bloodletting ritual, which let me infuse him with the Ritual of the Decaying Sun. It causes his body temperature to rise, forcing dehydration and exsanguination, then heat exhaustion and collapse, if I can get through his resistances. It's especially effective on entities like that, who require fluids specifically in order to maintain their combat proficiency. But..." Pete tapped his fingers together, a troubled expression on his face. "What do you *mean* you've never seen anything like this? Many of those could be found in the first few chapters of the standardized grimoire of ritual combat."

"There's a *guide*?" Joe gasped excitedly, his eyes going wide. "Do you have a spare copy I could look over?"

"A spare...!" Pete shook his head vigorously, looking at Joe as if he'd just seen him sprout feathers and begin flapping around like a chicken. "It's the primer we give anyone who is even interested in becoming a Ritualist. I've got *hundreds* of them lying around. Come along, it's time to get you properly outfitted. Thank goodness I made the deal with Mir *before* you revealed the true extent of your combat proficiency... or lack thereof."

The gates began to swing closed, just as Mak's wagon began rumbling by. The merchant waved, and Joe nodded politely in return. Then the follow-up cart kiosks trundled in front of the gates, still determinedly following the larger conveyance. His eyes locked with the disinterested gaze of the orange-haired

Nyanderthal, and after a moment of hesitation, he lifted a hand to wave at her as well.

"Customer. I have flowers, chocolate, and coffee. Feel free to-"

"I see you're repeating yourself again." Joe half smiled at her, determined to get through to the robotic person. "I understand. I also like to have my routines and standardized practices. Keeps me happy. If you're ever looking to take a break, maybe join a tower, come chat with me. You won't find a more understanding group than the people here. After all, we're all *about* rituals."

Her ear twitched, nose scrunched, and the hand she wasn't using to grip her cart kiosk shifted to straighten out her jacket.

"Ah... there we go. I love being polite, especially since Mir might accidentally pop my head off if I mess that up again." Joe lifted Mate's cup to his lips, taking a *slurp* of the hot coffee and letting out a long satisfied sigh. "I'm figuring this place out, and I'm getting through to her. I just know it."

CHAPTER NINE

A green flash later, Joe found himself once more in the Grandmaster's office, though somehow Pete had already gathered the necessary items and piled them up.

The elderly man walked to the other side of his desk and put his hands flat on its surface as he stared up at his tower's new member with great concern. "From what I gather, your foundation is terribly unstable. For you to have come this far, it is clear progression has been efficient, but... structured it is not."

"That's fair, but it's been working for me so far." Joe opened his mouth to say more, pausing only as he stopped to think about how he was going to explain his specializations. "It's just that, on this world, I have a bit of a handicap. My specializations are mostly focused on gathering large quantities of materials for crafting, not to mention creating structures."

"Both of which are heavily regulated on Vanaheim, to the point of being entirely useless here," Pete flatly pointed out, easily processing and accepting what Joe had to say in an instant. "Anything left out is absorbed by the world, whether that be garbage or a building. If you're going to help me become the SOAR, that is, the Sage of Alchemical Rituals, flailing about and coming up with haphazard schemes in the last moments are not going to be enough. Eventually, you'll find that your creativity has been outmatched by sheer skill. So... knowing what I know now about your lack of combat ability, I've decided that your first guided session is going to be a deep dive into your current status. Let's begin with your titles."

Joe frowned at the thought of how he was being directed to begin such an invasive process and only the fact that he had a quest guarantee that Pete would help him reach Grandmastery convinced him to start sharing details. With a flick of his fingers, he summoned his title list and displayed it for the tower master. For a few moments, the Grandmaster read over the details, then glanced to Joe with something akin to horror in his eyes, and back at the list.

"What... a mess." Pete leaned away slowly, as though the various titles were going to ooze out and infect him with their chaotic nature. "Superhero lander? Seriously? How is that possibly helpful?"

"Starting at the top, I see." Joe wryly replied, pulling out a chair and flopping into it. "This is going to take a while, isn't it?"

"Not really, at least not this part." Pete reached to the side of his desk, pulling a strand of pearls out of the pile and rolling over what turned out to be a necklace. "These are called the 'Pearls of Wisdom'. It's a fairly rare necklace and earned its moniker thanks to its ability to save people from their past mistakes. What this does is allow you to set a title on one of the pearls, rendering it inactive, but keeping it as one of the possible titles you can re-equip down the line."

"So it lets me potentially double my total number of titles without having to delete them?" Joe inquired with sudden interest, reaching for the necklace and pulling it toward himself.

"Not only that, but you will gain titles quicker when you have fewer slots filled." Pete raised an eyebrow at Joe's stricken expression. "Surely you've noticed that, as your title slots filled up, you were offered fewer and fewer of them? Only for succeeding in extremely unlikely scenarios or doing something truly title-worthy?"

"That's true enough…" Joe trailed off as Pete stared at him expectantly. "My titles are very helpful-"

"Really? Would you say your 'Superhero Landing' has been truly beneficial? Especially when the damage it deals turns the kills you may otherwise accrue into terrain damage, and therefore only gives you partial credit at best? What about this one? 'Pierce the Darkest Night'. Have you found that to be exceedingly helpful when you are generating rituals to attack your enemies?"

"That's…" Joe grit his teeth before admitting that the fifty percent resistance to dark magic was mainly used when he was accidentally striking himself with his own spells or out-of-control ritual circles. "Ten percent armor piercing isn't something to scoff at-"

Pah. Pete scoffed at Joe's weak attempt to convince him. "Tell me any ritual you have access to above the Student rank which uses dark-aligned magic? Most likely you won't be able to think of one, certainly not a combat ritual—as darkness is mainly used in either illusions or weapon enhancement. Or *spells*… which, while convenient, are the absolute last resort of a Ritualist. No matter what you might think to the contrary, we are not mages, wizards, or sorcerers. Now, I will concede that your 'Tatum's Chosen Legend' has some merit, as does the 'Monarch of Mana' titles. I would keep your 'Never Satisfied' title until you complete its requirements and gain a skill, but the rest of them? Assign them to a pearl and pull them out as needed."

Hackles raising at the casual way the tower master was giving him direct orders which would impact his ability to deal and receive damage, Joe started to snap back a reply, only to grind his teeth and keep his mouth shut at the last moment. As he took a deep breath, Pete nodded slightly, a faintly disapproving glimmer in his eyes.

"As I said before… unstructured. Frankly, Joe, the quest I've given you is likely the best possible use of your time for the near future. You need to learn how to fight in an entirely new and, to you, unconventional manner. This world is too strong for you to start on that journey. More than anything, I'd recommend going all the way back to Midgard and starting over."

"*Midgard!*" Joe was on his feet in a flash. "You're telling me you want me to go back to fighting rabbits and foxes? I've used rituals to destroy thousands of monsters, build entire cities, start and end wars, and connect worlds together! How difficult do you think it's going to be for me to figure out how to use standardized rituals for combat?"

"Very." Pete kept his cool, even as he watched the muscles in Joe's jaw clench and relax. "It's not just ritual circles, Joe. It's ritual circles empowered with alchemical substances, altered by ritualistically forged tools of the craft, layered with enchantments, and calculated by matrices. Tell me, if you can, when was the last time you put together a ritual and fought a monster directly? When the ritual struck them, did it do any damage? Or, more likely, did an extremely powerful ritual you concocted basically bounce off of your enemy?"

"I've designed ritual towers that blast hundreds of monsters apart every single day." Joe's indignation began to dissipate rapidly as his mind fought against him, his subconscious repeatedly pointing at the beam of what should've been absolute death against the Jotun Brisingr. The monster was only annoyed and ended up treating the beam as a laser pointer, which caused temporary blindness and irritation.

"How about that direct fight I was mentioning? You've been able to go head-to-head with creatures or other sentients, as I did with Istvan, and come out on top… using rituals." Though the words were not spoken as a question, they were filled with doubt and coupled with a direct stare.

Joe's silence spoke volumes, and Pete bobbed his head, having fully expected this outcome.

"As I thought. Again, this is not intended to be an attack on you, Joe. You've done extremely well with no guidance, or minimal guidance from someone who's not well equipped to teach you directly. But now you're here, and you've seen a glimpse of what's at stake. Like it or not, you represent our tower simply by possessing the class. First, remove all but those three titles, and let's talk about these... skills."

Still somewhat unwilling, Joe nonetheless wrapped the necklace around his neck and concentrated on the first pearl. Taking a deep breath, he assigned his 'Superhero Landing' title to it, and the iridescent white pearl immediately shimmered with a myriad of colors before settling on a light blue. 'Pierce the Darkest Night' turned the next pearl metallic black, 'Architect of Artifacts' a deep burnt orange, 'Anti-mage' purple, 'Immovable Object' a light mint green, and 'Councilman of Novusheim' a soft pink. "That's... done. Only three are equipped me now."

"Get it down to two, and you'll find that the requirements for earning a title are eighty percent reduced." Pete's words did perk Joe up slightly, and the Grandmaster decided to throw him another bit of information as a reward for following through without further complaint.

"If you've ever run into something called a 'broken title', those are what you should truly be seeking. Titles, just like professions and certain skills, can be thrown into the mix when you are creating new things. New things being skills, titles, classes, and even items. Imagine, if you will, plucking one of those pearls off your necklace and embedding it into a building you're creating, guaranteeing it will have some form of enhancement as a *named* structure. This is what you are opening yourself up to by understanding what is possible."

"Is there a list of-" Joe's question was met with a rapid shaking of the Grandmaster's head.

"Nothing we have access to. You might be able to chat with your deity to dig up more details, but honestly? This is exactly the sort of thing your 'Never Satisfied' title was made to help with. Information about higher-tier abilities is restricted for a reason—to encourage exploration, experimentation, and genuine growth instead of obsessing over some mythical 'perfect build.' Because, trust me, what's ideal for one person might be absolute hot garbage for someone else."

Pete tapped the extensive skill list Joe was showing him, but instead of tearing into the bald man, the Grandmaster simply let out a deep sigh and shook his head. "Mir is going to have a *field* day with this. All I can recommend is that you find a way to pare this down to what you determine to be truly necessary. That, and choose only one or two combat spells to retain. The fact that you have 'Wither Plant' at the Journeyman ranks is more *confusing* to me than anything else. How about this… when you start using the Ritual Combat Manual, choose just *one* ritual to use for a few weeks, get used to stretching the bounds of what you can do by limiting yourself?"

"I'm sure that'll be fine. But, look, I've been gathering spells because I'm able to convert spells into rituals, and the other way around," Joe quickly interjected in an attempt to explain himself. "Wouldn't it be better for me to learn a *larger* variety of spells and-"

Pete lifted his hands and began to rub at his temples, then cradled his head and swept his fingers back while looking into the air. "Tell me, have you ever heard of *scrolls*? If you were to take a prepared spell at the Master rank and convert it to a ritual, what do you think would happen?"

"I'm… guessing that would create an equivalent-ranked ritual." Joe let out a heavy sigh as his stomach sank. "Why did I never think of that? I even *have* spellbinding as a skill."

"You *sure* do," Pete agreed flatly. After that, he was silent for a moment, staring at a blank space on Joe's shared information. "I see you also have a few skills you are hiding even from me… I hope they are not too terribly taboo. Though, if I'm being honest, so long as you aren't dealing with the eldritch, I don't particularly care. A few tricks up your sleeve will be necessary, just don't damage our reputation. What else, what else… professions?"

"Ritualistic Alchemist, a personal favorite... Ritualistic Metalworker, *excellent*. Grandmaster's Apprentice? Goodness. You *have* been rather busy on lower worlds, haven't you? But what is this first profession? It, too, is hidden to me, but why?" Pete waited for an answer, but Joe only shrugged in reply, unwilling to explain why he was hiding his Arcanologist profession. "Keeping that one close to the chest as well, huh? That's fine. Still, you've reached level thirty in your base class, which means you have space for six total professions. One every five levels. If you will at least take recommendations, I'd have you take upgradable professions instead of the full versions going forward."

Seeing the incomprehension on Joe's face, the Grandmaster explained more clearly. "For instance, if you would pick up something to the effect of 'Rookie Ritualistic Enchanting', which only has five possible levels, you'd be able to double the rate at which you earn Lore skills associated with the profession until you max it out and upgrade it. It will not offer production bonuses or the like, but knowledge is far more useful than saving a few materials at the low levels while you're working to rebuild your foundational class skills. I'd recommend seeking out any Master of the skill you'd like to base your profession on; they'd have information on how to attain such professions. Now, finally, a gift."

Joe's head was spinning from the sheer deluge of information, though it was clear and succinct in a way he'd never come across before. Vanaheim was a world where people came to bring their skills to the pinnacle, and it *truly* showed at that moment. Until now, he had always encountered hesitation or half-explanations from those teaching him, as if they weren't certain just how much knowledge they should reveal. But here, in this moment, it was different. The Grandmaster's promise of a clear, unobstructed path forward had not been empty words: Joe was just *starting* to experience the full weight of its sincerity.

Gulping softly, he leaned forward in a half-bow as he'd seen the other Masters do. "Grandmaster, you've already given me an incredible gift. I didn't even realize how much I didn't know."

"Hmph." Pete let a huff of air burst from only his left nostril. "Well, that's interesting. You're an arrogant man, Joe, but at least when I hold up a mirror, you aren't afraid to look at your reflection and see what needs to change. Good. A slightly *different* gift, then."

Swinging his left hand to the side, he smacked a book off the table, only for it to be instantly replaced by another that pushed its way up through the surface of the desk. Unlike the previous one, this version was ragged from much use, the pages crinkled and dog-eared, stains on the cover clearly showing it had been used as a coaster more than once. "Ritual combat, a standardized guide. I was going to give you a fresh one, but I think perhaps I'll give you my old copy. It has a few tips and tricks I've written in the margins. Don't be afraid to experiment and try new things, but this will serve you well as a baseline. Actually, take a few dozen extra standard copies. You know, in case you run into any other newbies out there."

Joe reverently received the book, his aura already causing the stains on the outside to fade as he cracked open the cover and flipped to the first page. His eyes dilated as he took in the sheer density of information packed on to every page. Just as it had seemed, the book was well-worn. Intriguingly, the thick, handwritten notes across every open space showed how this was almost equal parts formalized manual *and* the notes of a lifelong practitioner.

There was a pleasing dichotomy between the precise-printed script and the hastily scrawled handwriting. Some lines were underlined aggressively, so much so that the ink had bled through the page, while others had intricate diagrams with small looping arrows which led back to concepts in the book, then to explanations written out in the margins. A quick glance between where they led showed how the hand-drawn connections linked esoteric principles to practical applications. Even if Joe hadn't been able to realize their purpose on his own, it was easy to understand the annoyed note written next to a crossed-out section: *ignore that; do this instead.*

Looking at an actual ritual diagram, Joe saw how the standard spellcraft had been marked with symbols for alchemical injection points, though there were small notations beside them: corrections or perhaps enhancements? Either way, they deviated strongly from the standard method shown. Even at the very start of the book, it was clear to see the path Pete had been on, which had eventually led him to the peak of being a Grand-master of Alchemical Rituals. For every note he had on a different subject, he had five or six when it came to alchemy combinations.

Warnings were scattered throughout the text, ranging from simple and direct such as 'do not attempt in an enclosed space' or 'permanently dyes clothing purple', to far more alarming ones such as 'if the ritual circle starts humming, you've either done it very right or very wrong. If it's a *happy* hum, run.'

Entire sections had been viciously scratched out and rewritten, with only a single word or two as explanation, such as 'had a typo' or 'bad day' to give a clue as to what was happening. All in all, this wasn't just a combat guide, it was an absolute mutant of a document filled with trial and error, not to mention ruthless refinement. As he flipped to the back of the book, Joe could nearly hear Pete's voice coming through the now near-calli-graphically precise handwriting. He had to blink a few times as he tried to understand why such a fantastic, masterfully written note had been topped off with a crude stick figure falling apart seemingly in mid-explosion.

Under the diagram was an annotation: *Don't stand where it tells you to stand. Move three and a quarter paces to the right of the 'recom-mended' spot. Self-destruction is all but guaranteed otherwise.*

Letting out a slow exhale, Joe carefully closed the book and allowed it to vanish into his spatial codpiece. "That's… that was a lot. Thank you, Pete. This is going to be very helpful."

"You'll miss out on some of the more… *educational* bits, but as a Master of Ritual Circles already, they wouldn't have done you much good, anyway." Pete offered a rueful smile. "Last thing. If you're going to actually follow my advice and return yourself to Midgard, we have gear you can borrow for that. Not doing us much good here, so you may as well have it until we're allowed access. This is a limiter, and it's an example of what all five core skills working in combination can achieve. Here, this goes under your robes. This part connects at each joint, knees, elbows, ankles and neck. The band goes around your head, and… don't wear it in Jotunheim or above, unless you'd like it to crush you like a bug."

Joe stared at the horrifying amalgam of metal spinning with freely rotating ritual circles and what appeared to be gaseous potions contained along the length of dozens of needles turned inward along the bands. "You can't be serious. That literally looks like something you'd find in a medieval prison or a horror story."

Item gained: Tempering Body-Mind Sifting Refiner.

The Tempering Body-Mind Sifting Refiner is a specialized under-robe accessory designed for those who wish to walk upon lower worlds without violating restrictions. This is a masterpiece of ritualistic constraint, and wearing it forcibly reduces the wearer's Characteristics to a strict cap of 150 through an intricate system of active rituals, alchemical micro-needles, infused vapor channels, and enchanted mind-body feedback systems.

Effects:

1. *Forced restriction of all Characteristics to a cap of 150.*
2. *Engraved suppression rituals prevent all external or internal buffs from circumventing the restrictions.*
3. *Endless physical training by way of restriction due to constant exertion passively training all body stats. Lower stats received greater focus and accelerated growth.*
4. *Constant IV drip induces low-level agony, heightening bodily awareness and sharpening mind and reflexes through intensive self-awareness.*

"I admit, it's not something anyone would want to wear if

they didn't have to, but I can guarantee its effectiveness. It won't fail you in a critical moment." Pete spread his arms, palms up as he offered blandly, "If you'd rather go to the lower worlds and figure out how to control all of your Characteristics manually, that is *absolutely* an option. Might take a few years, but it'll be great for your willpower and patience. Just recognize that you'll most likely need to hold still in the presence of those who are far weaker than you, and that even something so simple as blinking too rapidly may cause devastation to the local area."

Joe's thoughts flicked to the king and queen of Ardania, who were forced to hold perfectly still in their own palace, so as to not accidentally suppress everyone around them to the point they couldn't breathe. Storing the gear away, he nodded at Pete, who looked on with an approving gaze.

"Despite its brutal nature, to those willing to endure its relentless nature, it offers something few accessories can: a path where every step forward brings you to perfect, balanced refinement. All it takes is walking forward covered in sweat, blood, and tears." Pete shot Joe a thumbs up, "Get down there, and make sure to take some time enjoying being one of the strongest people around."

CHAPTER TEN

"You're saying you want to join the math club?" Master Cosmo Hollows excitedly gripped Joe's hand and began pumping it up and down. "We'd love to have you! We meet every Tuesday and Thursday from-"

"I was more hoping-" Joe had to put effort into freeing his hand from the Wolfman's good-natured excitement as he slowly crushed him. "-you could get me the best profession for figuring out Magical Matrices. I have two open slots."

"That's even easier, but we could really use a few more people joining our ranks." Cosmo's voice had an edge of desperation to it. "Do you know how hard it is to keep people in the group when it's just us and our kids for the last hundred and fifty years? It's fallen out of favor, Joe!"

"I can't make any promises," the bald Ritualist firmly stated as he stepped back and away. "But maybe I can swing by when I'm in the area? The Grandmaster is sending me back to Midgard, or at least I need to go there once I realize how badly I'm throttled by my 'lack of a foundation' or whatever it is he keeps telling me."

"Hmm, yeah." Cosmo distractedly agreed with him as he

bit his lip, eyes going distant as he clearly tried to think of a way to bribe the newbie. "I suppose that's gonna have to be good enough for me. It'll work as merits, at the very least, if you get the skill high enough. Alright, really all you need to do is read this book and accept the profession at the end of it. Should take you all of... thirty seconds?"

Joe glanced down at what was essentially a pamphlet, not at all surprised a person this dedicated to math carried such an item around. Eagerly accepting the offering, he pulled it open and softly read out loud. "So, you have begun to wonder about the underlying, ever-shifting mathematics of ritual magic. Rejoice, for your ability to calculate and predict ritual flows will increase dramatically-"

He finished going through the information, slightly uncomfortable with how cult-like the information packet was reading by the end. It was bad enough that he was surprised it hadn't told him to start spending less time with friends and family in favor of exploring mathematics. Finally, he got the notification he'd been waiting for.

You have met the requirements to earn the profession: Ritualistic Numerologist Novitiate! This is an entry-level, upgradable profession, which will allow you to increase the associated Lore extremely quickly. Each Lore skill level earned will instead grant two levels and increase your profession level by one, to a maximum of level five, or Expert in the Lore skill. Reaching Expert in the lore skill will maximize the profession level. Would you like to accept this profession? Yes / No.

"This looks completely different from the other times I was offered a profession." Joe murmured to himself, mentally accepting the prompt.

Ritualistic Numerologist Novitiate (Level 0): Everything in the world, the universe, and even in various side dimensions can be explained and charted with mathematics. If it can be measured, it can be improved. A Ritualistic Numerologist Novitiate doesn't care about the doing of the math, only the knowing of it. This is a language written in numbers, lines, and sequences of power. Every angle has a purpose, but only those who don't have deep knowledge think formulas are static instead of a constantly shifting balance of power. There are no absolutes, only counterbalances and fluctuating variables.

By sacrificing the ability to make things easier for themselves, those who take this profession will be able to increase the Lore skill associated with the profession at double the standard rate. +100% skill gain when increasing the Lore skill 'Calculus and Number Theory'. -99% speed of alteration to ritual-specific matrices.

When you C.A.N.T. you can only think, you C.A.N.T. do.

"It has a detriment? It didn't tell me it was going to have a detriment!" Joe glanced up at Cosmo, who only shrugged as though it wasn't a big deal.

"You're going to need that foundation the Grandmaster was talking about either way, right? Better to get a few levels in the skill before trying something big and having a blow-up in your face."

"Yeah, about that." Joe cracked his knuckles and closed his eyes. "I'm already at Journeyman four for Calculus and Number Theory. Probably could've skipped straight to the big boy version of this profession."

"Oh? You're that close to Expert rank already?" Cosmo's eyes started shining as he leaned in. "I thought it would be years at the minimum before you managed to bring me a merit; who knows how soon it will actually be? With your help, I might be the first Ritualist Numerologist Sage! Would you like to come and meet the rest of the math club? There's quite a few around your own level."

"I... still have another profession slot to fill, and I'm not sure where I can find," Joe paused, feeling his throat close up slightly from sheer embarrassment as he finished, "*Ahem*, Master Darling."

"Her?" Cosmo's face clouded up immediately, his canines peeking through as his lips twitched in annoyance. "Don't tell me you're going to go take *that* as a profession? There's a reason there's only a handful of Ritualistic Enchanters in the tower, Joe. You think what *we* do regularly is expensive? Even forging is less than half as resource intensive. Not to mention the sheer amount of… never mind, I can already tell you don't think it matters. Okay, well, if you can afford to make toys for the next decade before making anything useful, go for it."

"Thanks. Um. Any chance you know where I can find her?"

"She usually hangs out anywhere from five hundred to eight hundred feet up the tower. If she's not out in the open areas, only the Grandmaster has the authority to bring her out." Cosmo flashed Joe a lopsided smirk that was half amusement, half challenge. "I hear she's been rather quick to bind people to the ground floor recently after someone shattered a crystalline token she'd been working on for nearly six months. Hopefully she's in a better mood these days. Look, if you change your mind, we'll be on the fourth floor, room three-one-four. *Ma~ath club!*"

His final words were whisper-screamed through cupped hands, as though to emulate a cheering crowd. With one last intense bout of eye contact, Cosmo turned and waved over his shoulder as he sped off.

Taking a deep breath and trying to put his worries to the side for the moment, Joe glanced upward, trying to determine exactly which platform he had landed on during his ascent earlier that day. Just as he picked out a likely candidate and crouched to begin Omnivaulting upward, a light cough sounded out behind him. "Master Joe, I was wondering if I could ask you a few questions."

Joe's foot slipped out from under him as he tried to cancel his jump, and he ended up falling nearly flat on his face before turning the awkward collapse into landing on the ground in a relaxed lounging position. "Master Darling! I was just asking after you, in fact. Care to join me? The floor here is surprisingly comfortable."

"You have strange customs. Is this common on other zones?" The seriousness with which she asked caused Joe to bite his lip, wanting to do nothing more than make a joke, but somehow knowing it would come back to bite him in the end.

"No, this is just a 'me' thing," he admitted with a heavy

sigh, pushing off the ground with a flick of his fingers and easily landing on his feet. "How can I help you?"

"Your honesty is appreciated," she stated in a polite, professional tone, making no further comment on his failed dexterity check. "First, how much do you know about Ritualistic Enchanting? The activation of my ritual above went off without a hitch, and I was hoping to ask your opinion on a few other prototypes I have."

Joe held up a thumb. "More than happy to help! If it's about the circles, I'm sure I can figure something out. If it's about the overall craft... I'm only at Student rank two. Lots of room to grow, and I was hoping to speak with you about getting an associated profession."

"Oh... that isn't easy, unfortunately." There was a pained look on Master Darling's face. "We don't have handy *pamphlets*."

"But you *do* recognize the rivalry with the math club. How interesting..." Joe murmured under his breath, earning a sharp look for his attempt at a joke. "What I mean is, uh, please continue."

She remained silent for a few more moments, clearly gathering her thoughts. "Master Joe, unlike other professions, with Ritualistic Enchanting, you are not able to avoid having a large base of knowledge and instead focus only on cherry picking the parts you want to use. If you want me to help you get a profession focused on enchanting, you need to start with a more general profession, then move to a specialized field from there."

"Do I need to have my Enchanting skill high enough, or...?" Joe gently pressed, not ready to rule it out just yet.

"Again, this comes back to how much you know about the actual skill." Now she had a slightly defeated tone in her voice, as though she were about to have to explain something simple for the umpteenth time.

"You see, Joe. When you create an enchanted ritual, you are delving into the most *diverse* field of ritual magic. We focus on, in general, summoning, sealing, and curse breaking. We control powerful oaths, wards, and binding formations. In essence, we are the meta magic of ritual magic, taking two separate fields of knowledge and power structures and using the best of both. Without at least a deep theoretical knowledge, Master Cosmo was correct… you'll need at least a decade of study and practice making things that are little better than toys."

"So you were listening to that, huh? Well, if I told you I was already a Journeyman in Enchanting Lore, would that change your mind a little?" Joe held back the smug smirk that wanted to crease his lips as her eyes widened in surprise, instead managing to shift it into a real smile at the last moment. "I always love catching people by surprise like that."

"How could you possibly… do you have a high level in regular Enchanting? It's almost impossible to understand the mechanics, the underlying theory, without the hands-on experience." It was clear that she was extremely interested in finding a new method of training, but it wouldn't have been terribly surprising for Joe to have other skills, having literally come from another planet.

"Nope." Not wanting to irritate her with a guessing game, Joe quickly explained himself. "I have many Lore skills that I've been working on for a long time, and my Enchanting Lore recently reached Journeyman five. Will that be enough?"

Master Darling pursed her lips, weighing a few options before slowly stating, "I *might* have something for you, but it's an ancient profession that's almost impossible to get much use out of. Unlike what you likely just took from Cosmo, this one has a *requirement* of becoming an Expert in the lore before it's able to be upgraded. It offers good rewards if you can do so, but as it is a foundational profession, it's impossible to combine or upgrade without doing so. There's almost always a better option for someone who is progressing the Enchanting skill at the same time. If that sounds at all interesting, give me a couple hours to figure out the requirements, and I'll get back to you."

"Before that, why don't you let me help you with whatever ritual circle you're working on?" Joe politely offered, not wanting to keep making requests of her without offering something in return.

"Mm." Shaking her head slightly, the powerful lady pulled a book out of her pocket and opened it—only for an illusion to spring up over the open pages and begin rotating in midair. "As you can see, I've been trying to generate a curse-breaking ritual which will be useful all the way up to cleansing Artifacts. The problem I'm having is creating the targeting sequence. Gear doesn't have blood, and shaving parts of it off to create a sympathetic bond can either weaken or destroy the item... if it's even possible to do so in the first place."

Joe looked at the spinning circles, immediately able to identify a few areas that could be better transposed, though they would work for an ephemeral construct such as a curse-break. That *should* mean it was a burst of power and didn't need constant reapplication. Still, something about how she had described the targeting ritual irked him, and it took a moment to realize what it was. "Why are you required to create a sympathetic link? Is the item you're trying to cleanse working to escape the bounds of ritual circle? Is it on the move, or something?"

"No, in fact it is almost impossible to move it, as part of the curse. It's a hammer that only lets those it deems 'worthy' lift it, and it was left in a rather inconvenient place." She let out a grunt of frustration, though it was easy for Joe to recognize she wasn't directing it at him. "Problem is, whoever created it was too literal, and now only people who have 'worthy' in their name or title can pick it up. Then, of course, they can never put it down again."

"Of course they can't." Joe shook his head at the rookie error she was describing. "What happened to the last guy who picked it up?"

"He cut his hand off to get rid of the hammer."

"Ah." Joe poked at the spinning hologram, and it rotated away from his touch. "So... I've got to ask, you do know how to activate undirected rituals, right? You don't actually need to feed chunks of your target into the ritual to make it work. If you look here, instead of supplying parts of the desired target, you could simply input the exact shape and size alongside its coordinates by using a differential equation. It takes a bit of mathing the problem, but if it can't move, there's no issue. There's an entire math club you could ask for help, if you really need it."

"Yet here I am, speaking with you. The fact is, I'm not trying to target the *hammer*, I'm trying to isolate its cursed energy pattern." Master Darling responded with a dismissive shake of her head. "Don't I need a sample of said energy to get rid of it?"

"Is this... the first time you've had to break the curse on a stationary object?" Joe didn't want to specifically call out exactly how wrong she was, as he was still working to make a good impression. "Let me tell you, making permanent *things* is what I do. I totally understand that the very concept of permanent construction is antithetical to the culture of impermanence I've found among our contemporaries. If I had to guess, I'd say it's likely due to the Ritual Combat Guide you all get right away when you are starting to learn the class. Here, let me..."

Glancing around, Joe pulled out his inscription tool and spun it about, practically *itching* to draw out a ritual for the first time in what felt like forever. Just as he was about to start scribbling on the floor, Master Darling caught his wrist and sent him a look of horrified shock. "You can't draw on the tower! What if you damaged its structure?"

"Didn't you draw out a ritual on one of those balconies?" Joe gestured in a general upward direction.

"Celestials' *sake*, man." She pulled on his wrist, starting to walk away. "Just follow me, and I'll show you where my setup is."

A short while later, Joe was a few hundred feet off the ground, staring at the 'balcony' she had set him up on. "You mean to tell me these are detachable blocks of stone? I can draw out an entire ritual on this, then just... take it with me?"

"Yes, but you don't need to do the whole thing. As you can see," Master Darling gestured at the intricately designed ritual sprawling across the ground. "The majority of the work is done, I just need to figure out the targeting portion. What do you need? I have purified silver filaments to help conduct and disperse the lingering malicious energy, but I don't know if you want to use that on its own or combine it with the salted obsidian powder to help ground the curse and prevent it from reforming while the remainder is eradicated. Or, I suppose if you're more traditional, I have some blessed chalk stashed away somewhere-"

"Just need to know what the hammer looks like and where it is," Joe responded with a hint of caginess in his tone.

"Are you certain? These *are* Artifact fragments, and I wouldn't want you to have to use your own stash for my project." Seeing Joe's face remain calm, she simply shrugged and passed him the details.

"Let's just say I'd really like to get that profession up and going." Joe's inscription tool flared with an orange light as he injected aspects into it from his newest Aspect Jar, quickly drawing out the remaining portion of the ritual and connecting it to the broader design. Master Darling let out a gasp of horror as he turned his attention to the outer rings, using the flaming substance to make minuscule adjustments to her ritual diagram. Even though she was certain weeks of effort were about to go to waste, she didn't try to interfere with the rapid, efficient motions.

Joe stepped back, double checking his work as the orange light faded away, shifting into a substance that perfectly aligned with the rest of the ritual diagram. After scanning every inch of the circles, he slowly nodded his head and gestured at his peer to take over. "That should do it for you! Anything else you'd like me to look at, or shall we call it a day? Oh, sorry, did you want to activate this right away and test it out?"

"Activate it? While I'm absolutely *flabbergasted* at whatever you just did, our methods of using rituals can't be so different that you don't understand that activating this ritual will cost over ten thousand mana for the outermost circle alone."

Even though her tone was questioning, her eyes never left the suddenly completed circles. "There's a reason every Master has scores of *Experts* working under them, who in turn have dozens of underlings of their own. "I'm estimating the activation cost of this ritual to be approximately thirty-four thousand mana, with an upkeep of at least a quarter of that per minute until the curse is fully shattered. I wouldn't touch this thing without a complement of twenty-three total Ritualists channeling."

"An upkeep cost?" Joe's ears perked up at that. "I haven't run into many rituals that have that. Not unless they're creating specific effects over and over, and even then, it's just a recharge. *Literally*, I had just been thinking curse-breaking would be a single burst of power. If that's the case, I'm guessing you need to fully remap the energy pathways, expel the foreign energy, and replace it with... for lack of a better word, clean mana? "

"There's a few more subtleties to it, but essentially yes." She finally glanced over at him, though there were many questions hidden behind her eyes. "That's part of what the enchanted tokens will do—tapping into the curse, forming the map of the pathways, holding it, flooding it, then tying it off when the cursed item's intentions have been changed."

"Ah... because even though it turned into a curse, it's still an enchantment. At such a high level, it's 'kind of' alive." Joe felt a slight chill run along his spine at the thought of running into Minya in the future and having to explain what had happened to the gear he'd been wearing. "Curses have something like intentions, then? Or more like thought patterns?"

"This is an entire lecture course, not a casual conversation," she explained while jerkily shaking her head back and forth. "Tell you what... if this profession works out for you, I'd love to exchange Mastery merits. You help me get up to Master rank in Ritual Circles, and I'll do the same for you with Enchanted Ritual Circles? Again... you will *need* to complete the requirements of the profession before I can do much more for you."

"Sounds good to me," Joe happily replied, managing to stop

himself from asking her why she hadn't just worked with one of the other Masters in the tower previously. There was no reason to question his own good fortune. "What's your skill level in Ritual Circles?"

"I'm..." She flushed and looked away, before glancing at him and offering a weak smile. "Still a Beginner. I've only been part of the Tower of Rituals for about a year and have been working on the last few circles you've seen almost the entire time. They made an exception to let me in, as they have almost zero Enchanters and certainly none at my level. These circles, well, there's a lot of crossover with Enchanting, so I was able to make it work, but... between the sheer amount of resources I've wasted and the amount of time I've invested into these, if they don't work-"

"They had a few errors, but nothing that would cause them to explode." Joe casually shrugged, not at all concerned at the thought of wasted materials. "I'm more impressed that you were able to make Master-ranked circles in the first place, as a Beginner."

"Anything is possible, if you're careful enough." She took a deep breath through her nose and stood straight. "I'm hoping that, when I fully activate them, I will gain a large number of levels in one burst. Now, I know you have other things to do, so let me go find those profession requirements."

CHAPTER ELEVEN

"I found it, but it's…" Joe looked up from where he'd settled in to wait, blinking rapidly as he pulled himself out of the depths of studying the Ritual Combat Manual. Master Darling was walking toward him with an enormous tome, a pensive expression writ large on her face. "It's even more difficult than I remembered. The first page outlines what needs to happen, and… it's considered an 'extreme' difficulty profession."

Joe immediately felt his mouth watering at the idea of getting access to the book. Swallowing hard, he licked his lips and made a small inquiry, unable to peel his eyes from the leather-bound cover. "If it's so difficult… the rewards must be pretty great on the other side?"

"Yes, in *theory*." Without further ado, she dropped the heavy book into his hands and stepped back, already able to see he wasn't about to give up on it. "Just read the synopsis, it'll explain better than my fumbling attempts. Look, I need to go gather a crew to break a curse; I'll talk to you another time?"

"Sure, sure…" Joe distractedly agreed, already pulling open the cover and letting his eyes rove across the page.

To the aspiring Enchanter, the inquisitive mind, but truly and explicitly for the worthy Scholar.

It is with the deepest reverence for the profession of Enchanting that this tome has been compiled. This work is not for the common Enchanter, those out in the world creating trivial trinkets and shaming the good name of <u>real</u> Enchanters, but for those who seek to be true Masters of the <u>art</u> of enchantment.

If you have found this profession guide in hopes of gaining a simple, foolproof method to inscribe magic on bands of metal to create the magical equivalent of mood rings, using all the elegance of a hammer on glass, I suggest you close this book immediately and walk away. This path is not one of convenience, nor should it be defiled by those who seek efficiency over understanding.

*No, the Arcane Enchanting Theorist's profession is for those who wish to question the intricate **why** behind every unit of mana, every rune, every shimmering sigil sunk into the fabric of reality. Those who throw themselves into the craft expecting results without knowledge, power without wisdom, are doomed to create nothing but baubles bound to turn on their user at the worst possible moment.*

"I bet whoever wrote this was just a joy to be around at parties," Joe murmured as he skimmed over the rest of the forward. "Let's see, strip away comforting crutches... see enchantments as they truly are…. sacred pursuit… transcend the need for mere technique? That sounds promising, at least. Ah, finally the end. 'Written by the Sage of Theoretical Enchantment, the Bane of Mediocrity'. Well, I suppose he, at least, had the credentials to act like this."

Flipping to the next page, Joe finally found both the requirements and rewards of taking and completing the profession.

The Arcane Enchanting Theorist's profession is a unique upgradable foundational profession focusing on deep, theoretical understanding of enchantments rather than their direct application. Unlike traditional enchanting, which relies on refining craft through trial and error, the Arcane Enchanting Theorist seeks to unravel the fundamental principles behind enchantment before ever touching an inscription tool. So strict is this requirement that the profession itself will not bind to anyone who has first gone out and created an enchantment without applying their knowledge to indirectly do so before accepting this profession.

Once this profession is taken, any attempts to directly enchant items will be severely hindered. Until this profession is level capped, the speed of enchanting any objects will be decreased by 99.9%. However, those who can endure the grueling process and complete the profession are rewarded with profound insights, generating a uniquely tailored enchanting skill forming at the Expert rank upon using this profession as a prerequisite to accept another profession.

Effects: This profession doubles the gain of levels for the Enchanting Lore skill. Each level of the profession will grant bonuses to identifying flaws, instabilities, and inefficiencies in enchantments.

Requirements to complete the profession: 1) Achieve the Expert rank in Enchanting Lore without directly inscribing any enchanted items. 2) Indirectly create an enchanted item using your theoretical understanding of enchanting.

Once the requirements have been completed, this profession will automatically reach the maximum level and be upgradable.

Would you like to _attempt_ to bind to this profession? Yes / No.

"Abyss, it made the system egotistic by proximity." Joe tried not to laugh as he accepted the prompt, hoping the plan he was thinking of would pay off.

Congratulations! You are now an Arcane Enchanting Theorist (Level 0).

Requirements to reach level 5 (max). Reach level Expert zero in 'Enchanting Lore', 0/1. Create an Enchanted item using theory instead of directly enchanting it. 1/1.

Hey... wait-

Joe protocol activated. Elevating issue.

Dude. Why? Fine, checking to see why this profession works for you when it should have absolutely bounced off. You think I don't see that shirt you _enchanted_ on Jotunheim? How did that not count against you? Checking... oh. I found why the profession accepted you even without having to make an exception. Well, have a good day.

"Hey!" Now it was Joe's turn to shout at the system, and

luckily, it seemed whoever was messaging him was only having fun with him.

Fine, fine. First, you're lucky it <u>did</u> work, or there would have been a nasty backlash as the profession rejected you. Secondly, it only cares about the <u>first</u> enchantment you make. Read 'without applying their knowledge to indirectly do so before accepting this profession'. Well, the first enchantment you ever made was a Mana Battery all the way back in the salt mines on Midgard, where you inscribed an enchantment in a Mana Core using a ritual and theoretical knowledge of enchanting. Wasn't even your <u>own</u> theoretical knowledge, but that wasn't part of the requirements. Happy now? The Sage of Theoretical Enchantment isn't rolling in his grave, he's actively spinning.

"Well, if *that* was enough to reanimate his dusty corpse, just wait until the next part." Joe flexed his mana, trying to lock down the ambient mana in the area around him. "Knowledge: Enchanting Lore, Calculus and Number Theory!"

Two thousand mana flooded into his mind, swirling and condensing along different parts of his brain and creating knowledge out of nothing but sheer power and skill usage.

Skill increase: Enchanting Lore (Journeyman V → Journeyman VII).

Skill increase: Calculus and Number Theory (Journeyman IV → Journeyman VI).

Skill increase: Knowledge (Journeyman V → Journeyman VI).

Profession level up! Ritualistic Numerologist Novitiate (0 → 1). Your understanding of numbers begins to override your flawed mortal perception. When viewing a ritual circle, you are able to innately understand where its mathematical structure deviates from its idealized form. Effect: 1) Minor automatic correction of mathematics to account for ambient mana fluctuations. 2) The world is no longer people and places, it is an ever-changing equation. You are no longer able to look at a poorly drawn ritual circle without feeling physical discomfort.

"Perfect." Joe all but purred, ignoring the flashing notification of some administrator somewhere reminding him 'this is how people earn curses', and focusing on the one telling him he had gained one point in Luck. "Going to get both of these professions maxed out in no time flat."

It could've been his imagination, but the bald man could have *sworn* he heard a dusty groan from somewhere in the distance. Another groan echoed the first, though this one was far more present and immediate.

Wamble. His stomach whined at him piteously, making Joe realize he hadn't eaten in... far longer than he expected, especially if there was some sort of time mishap while he was crossing on the bifrost. Having accomplished his short-term goals of filling his professions, he hopped off the balcony and bounced off the stairwells until he reached the base of the tower.

"Pardon me, where can I get breakfast?"

Joe offered a bright smile to the young man he landed in front of, getting a long, shocked stare, until he finally sputtered out a reply, "Down the hall, third door on the left. Basic breakfast is a small round of cheddar, but if you are at the fifth threshold or higher, I recommend spending a large wedge, else the meal won't supply you with enough energy."

"Right. Cheese." Joe blinked while shaking his head in continued disbelief at the world's currency. "Thanks, kid! I've got a pretty solid sponsorship going, so-"

"Sponsors don't cover basic food items." The young man's words caused Joe to freeze mid-turn, then he glanced back at the Ritualist wearing gloves with Student circles etched in them. "It covers a bunch of things, even the room you live in, but not food."

"Mine is supposed to cover meals, though?" Joe took a step closer to the cafeteria.

The look of confusion on the youth's face didn't inspire hope. "Oh. Never heard of that before; I'm sure you have a signed waiver."

"I'll... work on that. I guess I need some way to earn some cheddar?"

"Hah! Don't we all."

Frowning slightly, Joe watched the man wander off even as he started contemplating his options. Looking at his status sheet, with his two shiny new professions, he made his decision. "Not really all that much to learn until I can bump both of these skills up to the Expert rank... that's a few days at least, so I suppose I might as well go and get some practice with ritual combat."

Preparing himself for mental discomfort, Joe pulled some mana together as a packet. "*Message*, Heartpiercer McShootypants. Hi, Heartpiercer! I'm heading back to Midgard for a while to practice what they're teaching me here. Want to come with, or are you all set here for a while?"

Nearly half a minute later, the return spell delivered her answer. ←<< *I appreciate the invitation, but I'm staying put. My Tower Master is giving me direct instruction, and it's too good to pass up. Gained a quest to bring in as many Mythic cores as possible; they're doing what they can to make that happen.* >>→

Joe held shaking fingers to his ears, expecting them to come away dripping with blood as the message finally ended. "Abyss, every word felt like an arrow directly into my eardrums. She must have gotten a whole lot stronger since the last time we talked like this. From now on, she's getting messages on *paper*."

Another message, this time to Socar, gave him a similar response. After exchanging a few pleasantries, Joe began the process of channeling his 'Beam to Bifrost' spell. "A good start to this new world... made some friends, got some benefits. At this point, it just makes more sense to leave the world entirely than it does to scrub the excitement of a new recruit out of their eyes by going around begging for food."

The ten seconds of channeling completed, and Joe found himself enveloped in a thin sheen of crackling energy which perfectly matched the movement pattern of the bifrost itself. An instant later, the wall of the Tower of Rituals was in front of him—then he was through it, and zipping along the surface of the world nearly as fast as thought. The bifrost loomed large in his vision, then he hit it and shifted from moving parallel to the world to blasting up and away from it before he even recognized what was happening.

Part of his distraction was due to how he was trying to

process the enormous cadre of warriors that surrounded the bifrost, facing outward in an attempt to stop anyone from Vanaheim from getting on the rainbow bridge between worlds without permission. He took a few moments to move past the discomfort he felt at their actions then simply shrugged and relaxed into the embrace of the energetic field he was flowing through.

The world of Vanaheim rapidly shrank into the distance behind him, its cloud-piercing towers quickly becoming tiny needles poking from a deflating ball. From his current vantage point, he could see a handful of worlds spread out through the star system. Each of the realms connected to the bifrost had clear continents, weather patterns, and an energy about them which just seemed to scream *life*. Yet, each time he managed a glimpse at one of the worlds not yet linked, they simply hung in the void, covered in shadows, unreadable, their nature kept hidden even to his secret-sniffing senses.

Seconds sped past, and minutes turned into hours before his destination finally came into focus. Joe let out a soft breath as he approached the world he'd been exiled from so long ago. "Midgard... I'm finally coming back."

He hit the outer atmo-flat of the planet—as only round worlds had atmo-*spheres*—and had an exceedingly strange experience. In an instant, he moved from moving as fast as thought to having the wind blowing at him with manageable force. Halfway to the ground, he passed through another zone in the air that slowed him down, but this time, he was moving slow enough to see a spinning field of energy along the outer edge of the bifrost. As soon as he moved through it, his speed cut in half again, until he was merely falling as if he had hopped off a set of stairs.

A few dozen feet from the ground, a third slowing effect washed over him, and the remainder of the fall happened at a crawl. Joe glanced around with great interest as the bottom of his feet finally touched down. "Where'd this drop me? I would've thought it would exit in Ardania."

All around him was forest: old growth trees with boulders left behind in a manner that suggested glaciers had once carved through the area and left them there, ripped out of the ground and scattered out of place.

"Hello? Anyone around?" The words echoed back to him, accompanied by a soft breeze that ruffled his robes. "No one here, either? This is so bizarre. Why wouldn't they at least have someone here to keep an eye on new arrivals?"

Joe took a single step and immediately had his answer as he hurtled along the plane.

A shockwave erupted from where his ankle *thundered*, having split the air with a deep, guttural **boom!** Trees thrice as thick as his torso bent as if caught in a hurricane. Leaves and dirt blasted outward, followed by the enormous boulders and chunks of stone as his foot touched down and *cratered* the ground below him.

Light warped around him, a chaotic shimmer of power forcing the atmosphere around him to burst into flame from the enormous friction he'd generated, only to have a massive gout of water splash over him as a storm manifested in the air above his location. Dark clouds rolled through the sky at an unnatural speed, originating directly above him and sending lightning snapping across the sky in jagged arcs.

"Oops."

Then came the world's retaliation, as the system took notice of his position on the planet and reversed the worst of the effects as though someone had hit rewind on an old-style movie. Joe barely had time to process what had happened before he was thrown back to where he had first arrived, and an enormous pressure clamped down on him, his eyes forced open to read the system notification blazing in his field of vision.

Warning! The world of Midgard is capped at the peak of tier 4 for anyone coming from a higher world, with only one Characteristic being allowed above this benchmark for those who have never left. Limit your Characteristics to 150—at maximum—across the board, immediately. Failure to comply will mark you as a raid boss on this zone, triggering take-

down quests against you. Continued failure to comply may result in being recognized as a world-level threat, with commensurate rewards being granted for your destruction.

"Raid boss?" Joe murmured with annoyance as he reread the notification, "You've got to be kidding me."

Above him, the storm seemed to grow angry at his lack of immediate compliance. The lightning took on a red hue, tinged with gold and *crackling* at the edges with a deep darkness.

Moving as slowly as he could, Joe began reaching toward his codpiece, and spoke in a soft, soothing tone. "Just give me a second here. I need to equip my gear so I don't accidentally break things again. Look at me complying *so* hard. I love not being exiled from this planet. I certainly don't need adventurers getting emergency quests, guilds mobilizing to hunt me down, or the kingdom sending its elites after me."

A moment later, he was holding the awful accessory and trying to think of any reason *not* to put on the terrifying piece of gear, anything he could do to avoid to subjecting himself to himself to the immense suppression of *everything* that came with allowing the needles to pierce his skin and the enchanted rituals to suppress his mind and body. He glanced upward once more to take in the furious roiling in the clouds above him, accidentally moving too fast and causing a few more trees to snap in half from the motion of his chin jerking up.

"Just an accident, I'm working on it!" Joe muttered in a panic as he slipped the accessory under his robes, pressing it against his chest and firmly pressing the back down so the main portion could rest directly against his solar plexus. He heard a sharp *click*, and thin strands of metal began spreading across his torso, looping around and linking as a harness. Then the remainder of the accessory began to *click* and *whir* as it unfolded at high speed. The majority of its metal components shifted along the strands and aligned themselves with his spine.

Cold metal trailed down his sides and along his legs, as though a mouse had run into his sleeve and was trying to find an exit. Though it was an uncomfortable image, a moment later, Joe wished it could've been the truth. The metal strands circled around his knees, then his ankles, then bands began tightening around each of his joints, pulling his hips into alignment, forcing his spine straight, gripping his shoulders, elbows, wrist, and neck. There was a hair's breadth of time where Joe thought it was all over, then the micro needles slid into his skin, hundreds of them at the same time, each injecting the *tiniest* amount of fluid subcutaneously.

Taking a deep breath, Joe did his best to ignore the immense discomfort, gritting his teeth as the suppressive rituals activated, enhancing the effects of the alchemical compound and forcing his stats downward. His muscles contracted, his strength drained, and his previously lightning-fast thoughts felt suddenly sluggish. Letting out a low moan, he sank to the ground as if falling through thick syrup. The only upside to all this was how the storm above him calmed, and the crimson, threatening notification flaring in his vision flickered and changed.

You have equipped a restriction accessory. Scanning... all stats forcibly capped at 150. Adjusting world compatibility... welcome back to Midgard, Joe!

"Okay, I take it back," he grunted as he forced himself to his feet and began moving around to get used to his now greatly lowered stats. "That was way more of a welcoming party than I *ever* wanted to have."

CHAPTER TWELVE

Jogging along the primitive road fast enough that each step kicked up a small cloud of dust, Joe grit his teeth as he tried to take deep, even breaths. The midday sun was glinting off his shiny head, scintillating slightly as it refracted off his Exquisite Shell—the magical protection itself far weaker than it normally was, due to his Characteristics being so heavily degraded. Each time he swung his arms, they felt heavier than they had any right to, and the fact that he was sweating from the effort felt deeply humbling.

"At least my Neutrality Aura is working correctly to clean that away, or I'd have to figure out how to take a shower like a normal person before seeing my mother this afternoon." Joe grumbled the words aloud, mostly for the benefit of some ambient noise as he hurried along the path. "Nearly a hundred points down across the board; it's like trying to swim through icy water, with the same mental degradation."

Years ago, he'd been into cold plunges after exercise, and while 'experts' promised it was great for his health, there was always a long chunk of time after getting out when his mind felt just as sluggish as it did at this moment. "No wonder people from higher worlds don't bother coming all the way down here usually. I thought it was just because the resources weren't worth getting, but it's really because it's just so... uncomfortable."

Still, underneath everything else, the strain, the fogginess, the pinpricks of needles pulling at his skin as he walked, there was a reminder of something else: opportunity.

If the gear worked the way it was supposed to, that meant every grueling step, every slowed thought, even catching his balance in a lucky way after tripping over exposed roots was effective training he would see the benefits of after returning to a world that could handle his full power. Just for something to occupy himself with, the Ritualist pulled open the remaining notifications he hadn't yet read over.

Caution! You have access to an immense amount of power, even without your Characteristics being at their full capacity. Therefore, additional restrictions apply. Any spells or combat-focused skills at the Master rank or above have the potential to warp the ambient mana of Midgard. Please note that each usage will destabilize the region, and without taking proper precautions, you may initiate a level cap shift for this zone, if you are incautious.

If you use a single Master-ranked combat spell, skill, or ritual, the area directly around your person will become warped with turbulent mana. This effect will fade after 12 hours, so long as you do not use another similarly ranked spell. If you do, the local area mana field will become turbulent, and the time needed for it to fade will double.

From there, a third usage will impact a region, approximately the size of a Town, and large enough to affect local weather or terrain. A fourth usage will impact a domain level area, enough to shift the balance of power in a kingdom or nation. A fifth usage may make the effects permanent... but a sixth is guaranteed to do so.

Please note, using a Grandmaster or higher ranked spell a single time will bring the turbulence to the cusp of permanence, if proper protections are not put in place.

Once a world-altering amount of power has been used, the structure, rules, and fate of Midgard will shift drastically. This may include opening portals to dangerous dungeons or locations, destroying or forming continents, and includes the formation and spawning of Tyrant-class monsters.

Joe read over the information twice, once to get it down and a second time to ensure he understood it. "So, this is actually a challenge set up as a warning. I wonder what level I'll need to achieve with my skills to use all of them without concern."

Already, he was planning out an expansion of his Ritualistic Forging production, his thoughts touching on creating massive, permanent stabilizing arrays with his forged equipment. Thus far, he had mainly focused on temporary setups, but if he had a chance of accidentally breaking the place just by doing what he normally did... well, he had no interest in being hunted by all of humanity. Again. "What's a Tyrant-type monster? That sounds like a fun thing for someone else to deal with."

The flags flapping on the walls of Ardania began to peek over the treetops as Joe closed in on the city, growing steadily closer as he ran with his nearly inexhaustible Stamina. After another ten minutes, they'd only gotten a bit closer, so he let his mind wander over his status sheet as he crossed the remaining distance.

Name: Joe 'Monarch of Mana' Class: Reductionist
Profession I: Arcanologist (Max)
Profession II: Ritualistic Alchemist (7/20)
Profession III: Grandmaster's Apprentice (15/25)
Profession IV: Ritualistic Metalworker (3/20)
Profession V: Ritualistic Numerologist Novitiate (1/5)
Profession VI: Arcane Enchanting Theorist (0/5)

*Character Level: **30** Exp: 465,000 Exp to next level: 31,000 (Locked.)*
Rituarchitect Level: 13 Exp: 87,450 Exp to next level: 3,550
Reductionist Level: 10 Exp: 59,900 Exp to next level: 6,100. Talk to Occultatum for a Specialization reward!

Hit Points: 1,999/1,999
Mana: 5,610/7,310

Mana regen: 63.94/sec
Stamina: 1,590/1,590
Stamina regen: 6.5/sec

Characteristic: Capped Score

Strength (bound): 150
Dexterity: 150
Constitution (bound): 150
Light Intelligence (bound): 150
Wisdom: 150
Dark Charisma: 150
Karmic Perception: 150
Luck: 150
Karmic Luck: 99

Just as he finished reading over his status, Joe had to throw himself to the side as his attention returned to the road. Instead of slamming directly into a small adventuring party cheerfully making their way toward the gates in the distance, he instead found himself wrapped around the trunk of a tree next to the road. Bark fell to the ground around him like hail as he let out a soft groan and pushed himself back to his feet, taking a moment to appreciate the Joe-shaped indentation he'd left in the wooden surface.

Exquisite Shell: 11,869/11,919.

"Ouch, terrain damage is no joke. Fifty points for running into a tree?" He turned around, meeting the wide eyes of the small adventuring party just as their jaws dropped. "Hi there! Sorry, didn't mean to startle you."

"No. *Way.*" One of them slowly lifted a square device, holding it with shaky hands as he pointed it at Joe. It had been so long since he'd seen something similar that the Ritualist didn't react quickly enough to escape before there was a loud **click** and a flash of light. "You're *the guy*. Thought you were straight-up *tapped out*, mate."

"Did you just take my picture?" Joe was utterly dumb-founded as the small group slowly backed away from him, the person holding what appeared to be a simplistic version of a phone nodding very slowly, as though trying not to startle a wild animal. "Why? What possible reason would you have-"

"Look, being an Influencer is a perfectly legal profession." The man's open hand slowly drifted toward the small screen, making Joe's eyes bulge.

"Don't you *dare*-" Before he could finish his words, the unknown man's finger tapped on his device, and soft *pings* could be heard from the pockets of his teammates. Joe took a deep breath in through his nose, closing his eyes and clapping his hands in front of his face. "How many people did you just send that to?"

"Now *all* of Ardania knows you are here," the man whispered softly, as though trying to find the courage to stand up to Joe but having his voice fail him.

"It's fine for me to be here!" the Ritualist tried to defend himself. "I'm not exiled anymore; you don't need to worry about-"

He trailed off as a notification appeared in front of his face, glowing with golden light and having trumpets on either side appear and let out a bugling cry.

Hear ye, hear ye! Mandatory Quest received!

Joe, the Monarch of Mana, has been summoned to the Royal Court to present himself before the king and queen of Ardania!

Time limit: 2 hours.

Reward for Quest completion: unknown. Upon quest failure, the previous state of 'exile' will be reinstated.

"Seriously? Come on, guy. I was on my way to see my mom." Joe leveled a death glare at the no-longer-trembling member of the small group, who was now glancing at his phone and relaxing as a broad smile appeared on his face. "Let me guess, you just got a ridiculous amount of profession experience, didn't you?"

"*Oh* yeah." The smug grin rapidly widened further. "I even

got a multiplier, thanks to being the first influencer to gain the attention of the crown!"

"Hey, that's cool. As soon as I figure out how to do it, I'm going to find you and put a nasty little curse on you." Joe showed the man a thumbs up, then a *less* socially acceptable gesture, and he stomped away toward the gates of the city. "Hope you still think it'll be worth it."

Thanks to the… *Influencer*, his walk into the city was accompanied by the standard crowd going quiet and parting in front of him as though he were carrying a contagion, leaving plenty of space for him to march along the stone road. A subtle extension of his mana trailing out along behind him revealed a full squad of city guardsmen following him from a distance, but he didn't bother to look back—mainly because they were providing him a service by quickly intercepting anyone who started walking toward the Ritualist with a thunderous expression on their face.

"Looks like I haven't lost *all* my reputation with the guards," Joe murmured quietly as he strolled along toward the palace. "I'll have to make sure to swing by the barracks and fix up any issues they might be having."

Even with his degraded state, Joe's casual jogging speed was comparable with a trotting horse, so in no time flat, he was climbing the wide marble steps of the palace then being led through the gilded halls as the city guardsman handed off their escort duty to the Royal guardsmen, who were in turn replaced by the Throneguard—the force tasked with protecting the king and queen directly, so they wouldn't need to take action on their own. Finally, he was stopped just outside the throne room itself, where a bored-looking official waved him toward a chair, pulling out a long scroll at the same time.

"Greetings, Joe the Ritualist, Monarch of Mana, Tatum's Chosen Legend, the Architect of-"

"Please don't read all of my titles out to me." Joe interrupted as politely as possible, his eyes taking in the ticking-down timer that hadn't stopped even though he had entered the palace. "Unfortunately, I'm in a bit of a rush."

"As you wish, good sir! By sovereign will and the binding decree of the rulers of Ardania, let it be known throughout all corners of this blessed realm that Joe the Ritualist, Monarch of Mana-"

Ahem. Joe loudly coughed into his fist, and luckily the herald understood the message, skipping ahead a few lines.

"-Unifier of the Human World of Midgard, Beloved of the Bifrost, has at long last returned to Ardania!"

"I already knew that," Joe muttered as the herald continued shouting into the echoing hallway. "Actually, how do you know all those titles? They aren't equipped?"

"Spies. *Ahem!*￼ By decree of his most noble majesty, King Henry the Unyielding, and her infinite grace, Queen Marie the Forty-seventh Apocalypse, Joe the Ritualist's burden of exile, nobly borne and fulfilled, has officially been lifted. Henceforth, let no man, woman, or beast cast doubt upon his right to walk these lands as a stalwart ally of the kingdom! Let the bells toll and the banners fly! Let his deeds be spoken of with reverence and no longer in hushed fear, for he is no longer considered by the crown as a vagabond or villain, with a name only spoken of in rumors and hushed whispers, but a man whose path forward shall be in lockstep with the will of the realm as his feats continue to unfold beneath the magnanimous-"

Joe waited as politely as possible until the herald finally allowed his scroll to snap shut with a flourish, a bright smile on his now-sweaty face. "Now, Joe the Ritualist, please take a seat and relax until the monarchs are available to meet with you sometime within the next few days. A room shall be prepared-"

The man's voice trailed off as Joe shook his head, his index finger tapping on the timer only he could see. "Look, I really love the theatrics, but I got a quest to see them in the next... now only about half an hour. Do you mind if I just pop in there?"

"Do I mind? Do I *mind?*" The herald puffed up, his face

going red as he took a deep breath, only to have it catch in his throat as a deep voice rumbled from behind the door, shaking the very flagstones of the palace.

"Enough of that, just let him in." The voice, though thunderous and firm, held an amused undertone.

"As his majesty commands!" The herald practically fell over himself in an effort to get out of the way before the Thronesguardmen threw the doors open.

Joe strolled into the massive, almost entirely empty chamber. Searching the ornate area, he compared the silent, echoing space to the last time he'd been there: on trial for releasing an eldritch ritual which had sent thousands of people into a respawn cycle and likely slain many, many more who didn't have the chance to come back to life. Finally, he looked to the thrones, where two statue-like figures were sitting, and bowed slightly at them politely. "Good to see you again. I've got to say, I like this space better without the crowds of nobles howling for blood."

The twin doors shut behind him with a boom, and the Ritualist finally learned why he had been granted a private audience. To his great surprise, both the king and queen rose from their seats and stepped down, a blast of air and a wall of intense pressure setting his robes flapping while simultaneously filling him with the urge to kneel. Joe resisted, curious as to why they were moving around so casually, when before they had always done their utmost to remain perfectly still.

"Told you." Marie gently slapped the back of her hand onto King Henry's shoulder. "Look at him, he's not even buckling."

"Have you climbed higher than Jotunheim, Joe?" King Henry questioned excitedly, ignoring the love tap from his wife. "Did you go to Muspelheim or Vanaheim first? Don't tell me you managed to get into-"

"Let's not badger our guest, Henry," Queen Marie murmured. "Give him a chance to answer."

For the next short while, Joe and the monarchs spoke together, the stiff, ceremonial air that had marked the beginning of their meeting quietly melting away. At first, the conversation had been stilted, due to habit and the presumed necessity of etiquette, but as he told his tale, it shifted into something more natural. Eventually, he even found himself laughing and sympathizing with the king as the monarch lamented about having once accidentally caused a nobleman to pass out by *breathing* too hard.

"You know, a lot of people like to romanticize what it's like to be at the highest peak of power on a world." Queen Marie shook her head and let out a deep sigh, causing the windows in the room to rattle. "But I tell you what, it's quite difficult to have friends or even people we can consider peers when we aren't allowed to lower our Characteristics below two hundred and fifty. Even with as careful as we are, sometimes our passive abilities can crush someone, if we aren't remaining perfectly focused."

"System forbid we actually laugh at a *joke*." King Henry snorted, sending a blast of dust off the rafters. "Last time I did that, I needed to pay for a dozen people's healing when I ruptured their eardrums."

Eventually, the conversation petered out, and silence stretched between them, though it wasn't uncomfortable—especially now that Joe's countdown clock had ended. The king reached out and gently gripped Joe's shoulder. "Anyway, I suppose we should get to business. Ready to get your rewards?"

"Say what now?" Joe blinked at the sudden shift in the direction of their chat.

"You know, all the rewards you should have gotten way back when you got an exile instead." Queen Marie mirrored her husband but took it a step further and gave Joe's shoulder a sympathetic squeeze... breaking his collarbone and nearly liquefying his trapezius before letting go as he let out a pained gasp. "Oh no! I'm so sorry! You were just dealing with the suppression so well, I didn't think-"

Exquisite Shell: 0/11,919
Health: 1,421/1,999

"It's fine!" Joe wheezed as the last sparkles of his Exquisite Shell faded into glimmering motes of mana around him. *"Lay on hands!"*

His crushed shoulder reinflated, and his collarbone aligned with a **ping** he could feel down to his toes. To his surprise, the healing spell increased to Expert level three at the same time. "Huh. Must have been right at the edge of increasing for a long time. When's the last time I actually *used* that spell?"

"A-as I was saying," the queen stammered in relief as Joe worked his shoulder to test its range of motion. "Now that you have officially completed your exile, we can reward you as we wanted to be able to do."

"I feel like you've given me enough, even if it was a little under the table?" Joe stated carefully, intentionally not stepping away from the lady who could deal nearly twelve thousand damage with a light touch. He didn't want to break the tentative bonds of camaraderie they'd managed to form.

"That's the thing, now we can reward you *publicly*," the king smoothly interjected when he noticed the queen was still staring at the Ritualist guiltily. "On that note, I am pleased to give you three gifts. First, a tier-five advancement mandate for your guild. This is the first time we've issued one of these... ever. It's a unique opportunity and allows for a guild with a power rating similar to a small kingdom to exist within our borders. I'm certain I don't need to explain to you the potential political ramifications of misusing this chance. Normally, you'd have to be on an otherwise uninhabited world or continent, or having a power base like this would provoke an act of war against you."

Joe solemnly accepted the document, which seemed to have been made from a combination of gold, silver, and electrum. He quickly slipped the metal plate, buzzing with power, away before anyone could change their mind, and stepped back, ready to leave... only to realize they weren't done yet.

"Next is a land claim token for you to use." Queen Marie arched an eyebrow at him. "Whatever land you claim with this will be considered yours and can't be associated with your guild like the token you gave your previous assistant. I highly recommend bringing this to the edge of the kingdom at the minimum and using it to expand our borders. It will place approximately twenty miles of land under your direct control, depending on water boundaries and terrain. If we inspect and find that you have cultivated your land well, we may expand the amount of territory under your control."

"That sounds…" Joe hesitated as he stared at the shining token with concern. "That doesn't sound like something you can just casually give out."

"Not to any *commoner*," the king agreed with a sly grin. "Which brings us to your last reward. Kneel."

Marie smacked her husband's arm, the sound reminiscent of the scaffolding at a construction site falling to the ground. "He's just kidding."

"Ha! I am, and it feels good to do it. Congratulations, Joe. Upon using this land claim token, you will officially become the newest duke of Ardania." The king raised a hand before Joe could react. "Don't get too excited, as you still have us, the crown prince, grand princes and princesses, and a series of archdukes above you in the peerage. We decided that, as your third reward for defeating the Wolfman nation and securing our position, we would give you recognition and a measure of protection against retaliation for previous… *perceived* indiscretions. You will be able to call on the kingdom for aid, and we will be able to call on you."

Queen Marie lifted a hand before Joe could say anything else. "Now get out of here. If I have to hear one more petition from your mother to bring you back, I might close the bifrost just to force you to stay."

CHAPTER THIRTEEN

Joe padded along the stone streets of Ardania, the soft soles of his shoes making no noise as he pushed through the still-leery crowd. After leaving the palace, nothing was going to stop him from moving directly toward the merchant district, no matter how many sidelong glances and aghast stares he received. Thankfully, as a silver lining, he was getting used to his forcibly capped stats and beginning to compartmentalize the discomfort that came from the needles being pressed into his skin as if he had an overly eager acupuncture specialist strolling alongside him.

Actually, it *was* a little like hanging out with Jaxon, if he thought about it.

Still, despite the physical and mental discomfort—and the range of emotions he saw in the expressions around him—Joe only had a wide grin on his lips as he approached the *Odds and Ends* shop tucked away in a corner of the merchant district. He could see his mother through the window, animatedly chatting with a customer as she added item after item to the pile on the counter, much to the buyer's dismay. For a few moments, he simply stood at the window, the goofy grin on his face reflected back at him as he waited for her to notice him.

Eventually, the customer saw him there and stared, causing Brenda to cast a curious glance over her shoulder, only to do a double take as she saw him standing there. Then she was sprinting through the shop, throwing the door open with a clatter and a clang as the bell swung wildly over the frame. "*Joey!*"

An instant later, she slammed into Joe with a full-force hug that would've sent him flying the last time they'd seen each other. But now, he had to move with the momentum just to make sure she didn't take damage as though face-planting into a boulder.

"Oof! You've gotten stronger! Good to see you, Mom."

"You're taller! Um, shinier?"

"You've just shrunk, and your eyes are worse," Joe quipped right back at her. "If anything, I'm only more aerodynamic."

"I can't believe you're finally back! I've missed you so much! Do you even realize how long it's been? *Months* at a time between calls! This is why I should have had a daughter instead."

"A little over a year now, but it's not like you came to visit me, either." Joe got a smack to his chest for that joke, as both of them understood exactly how difficult moving through the higher worlds would've been for her. The Ritualist was able to punch above his weight class on a regular basis, and that had served him well as a forerunner for humanity's journey to new worlds, but Brenda had little in the way of combat potential.

"A *year?*" She leaned away to look into his face and see if he was still joking with her. "Joe... it's been well over two years since you last walked on Midgard."

"Two...?" Shaking his head in denial, Joe immediately went to refute her, only for his jaw to drop slightly as he remembered a small part of the message he'd ignored when opening the Bifrost on Jotunheim. "Time across worlds wasn't synchronized... is that what it meant? Was time running faster here, maybe to give everyone else a chance to catch up? I thought it was going slower here and faster on the world of giants? I know we talked about that before, but I thought maybe it was just the messages having to travel huge distances or something."

"No, you knew the truth, you just didn't want to accept it." Seeing that Joe was about to try arguing with her, Brenda shook her head and spoke first. "I went and talked to Boris about this, and though he wasn't too happy to see me, he did explain the problem was that you keep moving freely across worlds. Simply put, the physics of your travel have messed with time pretty seriously for you. Jotunheim is considered to be one of the largest worlds, even if it may not be the densest?"

Pausing for a moment, Brenda furrowed her brow, but she pushed on before she could be interrupted. "Imagine time flowing like river water downhill. The heavier the world is that you are on, well, it is like a stone in the middle of that river. As you get closer, the flow of water slows down to move around it, but the top of the boulder itself isn't wet—that's why you might suddenly be moving much faster. Your relative time would have snapped back to moving faster than even here. At least, according to Boris, passing through those barriers around worlds—the edge of the gravity wells—*that's* where you've been finding issues with losing months at a time."

Seeing Joe's shock, Brenda relaxed and allowed all traces of concern to vanish from her face as she gave him one last squeeze then stepped back. "Enough of that! Come in, we have a lot to talk about. I'll close the shop for the day; I'm due some time off."

Less than ten minutes later, they were sitting at an open-air cafe, being served tiny cups of coffee which both Joe and Mate looked at with disdain before he *thunked* his massive Ebonsteel mug on the table, and the elemental filled it without waiting to be asked, nodding at each other in mutual disdain.

"Still overdoing it on caffeine, I see," Brenda pointed out in passing as she got settled, then leaned forward to grin at her son with light dancing in her eyes. "So... you remember Blas?"

"Captain of the city guard," Joe agreed easily as he took a sip of his delectable fresh brew. "I'm guessing you kicked him to the curb a year ago. What happened to him that's got you so cheerful? Did he get run over by a wagon?"

"I certainly hope not, as we're engaged."

Joe had never seen a rainbow formed from light pushing through coffee, but as he spit out a mouthful of his drink, he got to witness the decidedly rare event. "You *what*? When did this happen?"

"Shortly after you were exiled, but I didn't want to make you worry about us, so I kept it to myself. Still, we didn't want to have the ceremony until you came back… and here you are!" Brenda beamed at him with such a bright smile that Joe couldn't find it in himself to plot against Blas. Much.

"Now it all makes sense." Joe settled back in his chair with a sigh, taking another sip of coffee as his mother looked on curiously. "I was just chatting with the king and queen, and they mentioned you'd been constantly petitioning them to allow me to come back or bring me back. They didn't really give me a clear explanation on that. Now I know the *real* reason was just so you could get hitched."

Brenda snorted and reached over to flick him on the forehead. "Brat! That was only to get you back here sooner because I missed you. But yes, I wasn't about to get married without my son being there."

"Well, if this is going to happen, I demand father-son time." Joe put his fingers together and cracked his knuckles. "Blas and I need to have a bonding experience that involves flying projectiles being thrown at him as I ask about his intentions with you."

"Now there's an interesting way of asking to play catch with someone," a new voice intruded on the conversation as Blas himself marched across the open cafe, his metal-shod boots *clinking* against the floor. "I've received four hundred and thirty-six reports of a wanted criminal being on the loose in the city, and after I got the description, I figured I should probably be able to handle this one myself. Welcome back, Joe."

The three of them stayed in the cafe for the next few hours, catching up, slowly eating a charcuterie board as the sun slowly dipped behind the walls of Ardania. Eventually, the conversation wound down, and Brenda pulled out a piece of parchment and quickly scribbled on it before handing it over. "It's settled, then. Six weeks from now, you're the best man at our wedding. Plenty of time to prepare, and no excuses for being late."

Joe stayed the night in his mother's spare room, though he only needed roughly an hour or two of sleep every few days to stay in top form... normally. When he laid down, it was under protest, but the next time his eyes opened, the sun was shining through his window and reflecting brightly off his head. "Ugh... lowered stats, increased sleep and food requirements. Abyss, I thought I was past this."

Active effects: Rested. After laying in a bed for six hours, no matter how poor quality, you were able to get some much-needed beauty sleep. +5% Experience gain for four hours.

"You're not beyond the bounds of humanity yet, young man." His mother's voice floated through the open door. "Now, get out here and have breakfast, then let me know your plans for the day."

Pausing at that thought, Joe frowned slightly as he wondered what he should be focusing on. His mind turned toward the future, his hand unconsciously grasping the Ritual Combat Manual he'd been studying before he fell asleep. "What's next? Training, of course. There's titles to earn, land to claim and build on. Enemies and honor duels to prepare for. But..."

He heaved himself out of bed, joining his mother as he thought about something that had been eating at him for apparently years now. When Brenda asked him what he was going to do, he responded with a firm voice.

"I need to go to the library and talk with Boris. Hopefully, I can clear the air with him, assuming he hasn't carved my name into his 'no admittance' board. I left things with him pretty bad; I never got a chance to explain what happened. He was a good friend, and I burned him. Err... he might have preferred me *actually* lighting him on fire, and as a librarian, he *hates* open flames."

After a nice brunch with his mother, Joe made his way out of the merchant district and wound through the city until he finally stood outside the library.

Taking in a deep breath through his nose, he allowed the familiar scent of leather-bound books and dusty tomes to fill his nostrils, even as his eyes roved over the stone facade and began picking out small changes. The wooden doors were the same, worn from decades—perhaps *centuries*—of use, but the old brass name plate that had been green with age had been replaced. Instead of the small plaque which had read 'Head Librarian: Boris, seven-star Scholar', there was a shiny, utilitarian sign.

Head Librarian: Lindon of the Tri-fold Path, Grandmaster-Endorsed 4 star Scholar.

"They ousted Boris? Abyss, I'm going to have even more to make up for than I thought." Pushing open the door, he stepped inside, certain that the new librarian would at least know where Boris had gotten off to. "Hello? My name is Joe, and I'm looking for the previous librarian, Boris. Can anyone help me with that?"

The quiet atmosphere remained perfectly still, though the gentle ambience he'd come to associate with libraries seemed... off. Instead of a place which felt comfortable to sit and read, whiling the day away with endless research, it now felt oddly... clinical. As if he had stepped into a laboratory wearing the guise of a library to maintain its modesty. Even so, he ventured farther inside, looking for any signs of life. "Anyone here? Boris used to sit right next to the door, so I'm not sure where I'm supposed to look for the librarian."

He felt a shift in the air, as if a buildup of lightning on the horizon were causing the hair on his arms to stand on end. His robe flapped, and a few books fell off shelves as he reached for the door to try and pull it shut. Only as he gripped the handle did Joe realize the wind was rushing *outward*. That was the Ritualist's only warning before a shape materialized in the middle of the stacks, darting toward him and slamming a golden-glowing fist into his face.

A sharp *boom* echoed in the library, following Joe outside as he went flying, hit the ground, and bounced twice before rolling to his feet and managing to bleed off the rest of the momentum. "What was that? I *knew* I shouldn't have unequipped my Immovable Object title!"

Joe felt the world tilt again as a man appeared in front of him—out of a burst of shredded papers that filled the air like confetti—and landed a glowing fist on his nose. He flew tush over teakettle, only coming to a stop as he fully crossed the road and impacted the wall of the building on the other side.

Exquisite Shell: 1,320/11,919

"Celestial feces, man! What're you doing?" Joe waved at the thick cloud of dust in front of him, clearing the air just in time to see a tall man wearing an ornate set of navy and emerald robes stalking toward him, a pair of golden gauntlets covering his raised fists as he approached. "You just attack me outta nowhere? I don't want to name drop here, but I have a pretty close relationship with the captain of the city guard."

There was no response as the bored-looking man stared at Joe through a pair of thick-framed square glasses. His close-cropped hair fluttered slightly as he dashed forward, hammering his fist into Joe's chest and watching with clinical detachment as the Ritualist folded over.

Would you like to activate Haunting Shadows? This is a courtesy request, as the skill is a combat spell in the Master ranks. Yes / No.

"No." Joe spat out as his Exquisite Shell burst into shimmering motes, giving him just enough time to slip out and away from the follow-up attack. "I've got this."

Jumping into the middle of the street, Joe lifted his hand and allowed his inscription tool to appear pinched between his index finger and thumb. Swirling the intricate implement in the air, he allowed light gray aspects to form into a simple Novice circle, flicking it with a splash of mana to activate the somatically-created ritual diagram.

The simple design hovered in midair, bursting into flame as it rapidly consumed itself from the bottom up. At the same time, the librarian's boots began to smolder, bursting into blue flames as the man rushed toward Joe.

A cheerful *ding* sounded in Joe's mind as a system notification appeared, though it remained tucked away, since he was in the middle of combat.

"Hot-footing it over here, are we?" The Ritualist slipped away from the slightly sloppy strike. "I can make Sympathetic Combustion rituals all day long, pal. Might not be a lot of damage at once, but it just keeps burning. Are you going to talk this out like adults, or am I going to start your pants on fire?"

"I am Lindon," the librarian replied with an even, if slightly accented tone. "Battle Scholar of the Tri-fold Path. Current steward of this repository of knowledge. The hammer which shall fall upon you and drive your impurities out of this world."

"Impurities? Trifold, huh? So you're a scholar, a fighter, and some kind of blacksmith, if you're using crafting terms as a threat." Quickly extrapolating from incomplete data, Joe began working out how he should best fight against this particular foe, paging through his Ritual Combat Manual as he leapt out of the way of a follow-up attack. "Not so easy to sucker punch someone if they know you're coming, huh?"

"I am going to take you with me now, Joe the Betrayer." The calmly spoken threat sent shivers down Joe's spine as he landed on the page he'd been searching for. "Once I deliver you to our smiling sponsors, we'll learn what you know then make sure you are gone *forever*."

Scowling at the incredibly creepy librarian, Joe swished his inscription tool through the air, rapidly generating another ritual made of sharp, angular lines which had multiple recursive circles within, activating it in the same motion. It flared with silvery light, and the scholar's gloves, belt buckle, and the frames of his glasses began to glow brightly as the sunlight pouring down on them focused intensely on each of the metal items he was wearing. "Ritual of the Solar flare!"

A *hiss* of pain was the only indication the Novice-rank ritual was having even the slightest effect on the Battle Scholar. In response, the warrior flicked a piece of paper into the air, where it exploded into confetti. Joe felt an immense sense of impending doom and dropped to the road as the librarian appeared next to him in a shower of paper, which mirrored the exploding talisman, barely ducking underneath the heavy strike directed at his head.

As he landed, Joe scrawled a ritual diagram on the stone road in a flash of motion, slapping the activation sequence and shoving himself backward at the same time. A heavy boot landed where his neck had been an instant beforehand, yet instead of striking the hard surface of the road, his foot sank in a few millimeters. The rock splashed upward as if it had been turned into water, coating the man's legs before re-hardening in a thin layer which slightly hindered his motion.

Very slightly.

Flexing his legs, the librarian burst through the impediment, rushing at Joe in a tackle and managing to get one arm around him. They were nearly equal in strength and sturdiness, yet with the extra momentum and use of whatever grappling skill he had, the Battle Scholar managed to bring Joe to the ground. Then he shifted around and *slapped* Joe across the side of his face, raising a stinging welt as the Ritualist gasped at the sudden, sharp pain.

Health: 1,918/1,999

"Oh, that was a very bad idea." Joe spoke softly as he turned to stare directly at the Battle Scholar, who was silently raising a fist. Even without looking down, he began quickly drawing out a circle, then another... but he ran out of time. The fist raised above him glowed faintly for a moment, then slammed into his chest, cracking at least two ribs and forcing his body to spasm.

Health: 1,010/ 1,999

Letting out a wet cough, Joe felt blood dribble from the corners of his mouth, even as he did everything he could to keep his prodigious focus on finishing the second circle. As Lindon drew back for another strike, Joe drew the last line and poured mana into the activation. Both of their attacks hit at the same time, bringing Joe down to the last dregs of his health but also sending the scholar tumbling away from him.

The Ritualist thanked his lucky stars that he'd been studying intently ever since he gained this Ritual Combat Manual, and that the Force Reflection Sheet was such a simplistic ritual design, especially for a Beginner-rank ritual. "Probably because it's single-directional and just a basic square that hangs in the air above the point of activation. Maybe I don't tell him how easy it is to counter."

Pushing himself to his feet, Joe restored some of his health with a quick activation of Lay on Hands, barely bringing himself out of critical condition before Lindon was rushing at him once more. The Scholar hit the invisible plane of force and was thrown back with double the amount of kinetic energy of his sprint, sending him a handful of feet back before he managed to catch himself. He lifted his right index finger to his glasses, pressing on the bridge of his nose and causing the lenses to flash.

"Abyss," Joe murmured just as the Battle Scholar stepped a few feet to the side and rushed him again, easily avoiding the stationary ritual effect. "Only get to use my traps once, huh? Aren't *you* a perceptive one."

Another fist flew forward, and Joe jumped out of the way, only to take a sharp inhale as he was struck anyway. The Ritualist glanced down to see a trio of sharpened pens sticking out of his left arm. "If you make a 'pen is mightier than the fist' joke right now-"

"I do not joke." Lindon made a sharp gesture, as if pulling on the air, and Joe found himself being yanked off balance. Once more, he felt a stinging pain on his face as the Battle Scholar slapped him across the side of the head.

Health: 501/1,999

A glance at his health told Joe that he needed combat to end immediately, or he was going to be heading back to respawn at the *least*. The only reason he wasn't in only double digits for health at that moment was his Neutrality Aura healing him for a hundred and twenty-one health per second. His moment of distraction nearly cost him, as the Scholar lunged forward once again, missing with his fist but managing to shift the motion into yet another ringing *slap*.

"Son of a *gun!*" Joe let out a hoarse holler as his cheek flared with purple streaks under the angry red welt. "You like slapping so much? Fine! Let's see how much you really enjoy it. *Yes.*"

The last word was directed at the system, which had once again popped up with a question asking if he wanted to activate his Haunted Shadows retaliatory spell. In an instant, a shadowy version of himself appeared next to the Battle Scholar, rearing back and swinging with a nasty backhand, striking with enough force to ring the Scholar's bell and returning a little over a hundred damage, as well as one percent of his total health.

It wasn't much, but it was enough to make a move. Joe launched himself off the ground and onto the top of a nearby building, gritting his teeth as a bubble of warp drew close to his skin. Immediately, he felt how the mana he was regenerating was pouring in slower, the ambient power trembling and thickening as the energies of Midgard grew unstable around his body. He shoved off the roof once more, reactivating Omni-vault and just barely managing to escape the Battle Scholar, who was appearing out of shredded paper.

"Coward! Get back here and face your fate!" Lindon bellowed into the open air as Joe's vision blurred further, though this time with speed, not due to watery eyes after having been *slapped*.

"I didn't come here to *fight*, you weirdo!" The Ritualist called behind him as he flipped in midair, landing on another building and once again immediately launching away.

"Yet a fight you've found!" Lindon shouted from *ahead* of him, causing Joe to curse under his breath as he seized his Ritual Orbs with his mind and blindly sent two of the meager three forward. A duo of *thumps* told him they had met their mark, staggering the librarian and giving him enough space to land and change directions.

Joe had a specific destination in mind, no matter how it must have looked to the librarian. At the speed both of them could move, the fight was moving lightning fast. But since he was focused on escaping, Joe had a far better chance of getting away than the Scholar did of dragging the battle out. Their little game of jumping mouse and teleporting, pouncing cat continued for a few long minutes, until the Ritualist dove off the building and into a courtyard, tucking and rolling to bleed off his momentum.

An instant later, he felt one of the Scholar's pens stab into the back of his thigh, dragging him backward and forcing him to tumble to the ground. Then the Scholar was next to him, lashing out with his left hand and grabbing Joe around the throat.

"It's *over*, betrayer."

"Might want to look around, random person who attacked me for no sane reason." Joe managed to rasp out, giving the Scholar pause. All around the courtyard, the soft sound of metal on leather sounded out as weapons were drawn. "Like I said, I'm in good with the city guard."

"Unhand him at once, citizen!" As the first shout crossed the distance, Lindon shot Joe a glare filled with absolute vitriol. He dropped his hand, then brought it to the other in a sharp clap... vanishing in a cloud of paper and bloodlust.

CHAPTER FOURTEEN

"Woo!" A guard recruit dressed in clearly non-regulation gear called over. "Baldy almost got *tapped*, know what I'm sayin'?"

"I literally don't. Somehow I left, and the lingo went feral." Joe tiredly rubbed at his eyes.

"Ya know… tapped." The guard looked at him askance, as though the Ritualist were only playing around. "Went to take the big nap? Body is around but no longer breathin'?"

"Enough of that chatter, get back to practicing your forms if you want your position to become permanent. As for you, citizen, would you like to tell us what that was all about?" A more senior guardsman carefully inquired as he drew closer to the Ritualist, who had flopped to the ground breathing heavily. "Abyss, is that *Joe*? That is… would you like to file a report?"

"Absolutely I would!" Joe grunted as his health quickly ticked upward. "That guy was the head librarian, and he attacked me for absolutely no reason. If I hadn't been able to get here, I probably wouldn't have survived another minute without having to make things *real* ugly."

"I see." The guard sheathed his sword and pulled out a notepad. "So you were walking down the street minding your own business, and you were attacked out of nowhere? I can see from here that you're a powerful individual; why is it you weren't able to defend yourself?"

Joe paused and clenched his jaw, knowing how his next words were going to sound. "No, I had just entered the library and was asking for assistance when he attacked me unprovoked. As to why I didn't fight back with everything I had, well..."

Here he gestured down at his body, which seemed to be covered in a thin, swirling mirage or heat shimmer. "I have combat abilities in the Master rank, and using more of them would've been... detrimental. Other than that, my class is one that thrives on preparation, and I wasn't ready for a fight."

Clicking his tongue, the guard shook his head and put his notepad away. "I'm sorry to say, there's nothing more I can do for you."

"It's because I was in the library when he first attacked, isn't it?" Joe let out a heavy sigh and stood, feeling much better already. "I get it. He probably has some kind of right to initiate combat in his area, no matter what."

"Exactly that. However, if he does hunt you outside of the walls of his territory, please come directly back here, and we will handle him. Otherwise... well, I shouldn't have to be explaining this to someone of your apparent strength, but being unprepared for combat is the standard for anyone who goes out and about, unless they're *seeking* to fight. Yet, if you're only ready on *your* terms, ninety-five percent of the time, you're going to be cut down where you stand." The guard offered him a hand, shaking it firmly as he looked at Joe with a bright grin. "Good to have you back."

"Yeah, yeah." The sour expression on the Ritualist's face faded as he smiled in return. "Mind walking me around your infirmary? Should be able to get anyone feeling a bit under the weather back on their feet pretty quick."

A quick stroll through the barracks, infirmary, and prison area generated a swarm of reputation—desperately needed after having lost two thousand reputation with the guard when being exiled so long ago.

You have gained +100 reputation with the guards of Ardania.
You have gained +100 reputation with the guards of Ardania.
You have gained...

Quest update: Living for justice (Ongoing). Every day, people are arrested. Many of them are critically injured and will perish before trial without help. Some are innocent! Most are not.

Reward: 1,300 guild and personal reputation with the city guard.

Your reputation rank with the city guard of Ardania has increased! Reluctantly Friendly → Friend.

Nine guardsmen had been injured in the line of duty, five of them severely, the others bad enough that they wouldn't have been able to get back to their patrols in the next few days. Thirteen prisoners had been in critical condition but were now healthy and hale, glowering at him with rage now that they were sure to finish out their sentence instead of being sent to respawn.

"You know, keep this up, and the next time you're having trouble with an overdue book, we might be able to ignore the circumstances a little bit and help you out," Joe's escort told him with a knowing wink. "Can't make any promises just yet, but..."

"I'm not planning to get close enough to him for there to be an issue." The Ritualist amended his words a moment later, "At least, not unless I'm completely ready for him. Thanks for the offer, but for now I'm just happy to help out."

Thinking about having fought Lindon made Joe remember that he had heard and ignored a notification in the middle of combat. As they walked through the halls of the guard outpost, he pulled up a waiting notification. His eyes went wide with interest at the immense amount of information scrawling across his vision, almost running into the wall thanks to his inattention.

Quest gained: Mastering Ritual Combat I. This is a Ritualist-tower generated chain quest consisting of five quests of increasing difficulty, which will help you determine your final specialization for combat-based rituals. You have taken your first step into the world of structured combat rituals. As you now have access to the required material to unlock this quest, the Standardized Ritual Combat Manual, the system has recognized your intent to master the battlefield through preparation and control.

This first quest is meant to help you gain an understanding of your personal combat prowess and teach you the tools required for fusing the various sub-disciplines of ritual magic for the purposes of combat. It is a philosophy few are able to master. Will you?

Quest objectives:

1. *Use 500 Novice ritual combat circles in live combat.*
2. *Use 300 two-discipline ritual combat circles in live combat. (Choose any combination of the following: Ritual Circles, Magical Matrices, Alchemical Rituals, Enchanted Rituals, or Ritualistic Forging.)*
3. *Use 200 three-discipline ritual combat circles in live combat.*

Progress toward the next quests in this quest line, such as using higher-ranked rituals, will be tracked but locked until the current quest is completed.

Reward: Upon completion, choose one of the skills used in the creation of any of the rituals you created to receive: +10 to the skill if it is currently in the Beginner rank OR +8 to the skill if it is in the Apprentice rank OR +6 to the skill if it is in the Student rank OR +4 to the skill if it is in the Journeyman rank OR +2 to the skill if it is in the Expert rank.

Additional rewards and profession opportunities may be unlocked based on your performance.

After being walked out of the building and the door firmly closed behind him, Joe started slowly walking down the street. "Well, I was just thoroughly *trounced.* I haven't been smacked around that badly since… Alfenheim? Maybe I'm just rusty. I *have* been pretty reliant on indirect combat with my ritual towers and such, building up a lot of survivability, but I'm going to have direct combat situations in the future. If any of them go like *that*… yeah. I guess Pete had the right of it; I need to get in a *lot* of practice if I want to hold my own up on Vanaheim. At least now I have a quest that'll get me motivated to make it happen."

The Ritualist had barely made it forty feet from the guard station when he was yanked from his contemplation by a low growl reaching his ears. Looking up curiously, wondering what sort of monster might be loose on the streets of the city itself, Joe felt his jaw drop as a ragged figure darted toward him out of the mouth of an alley. With a flash of intent, his trio of Ritual Orbs jumped off his bandolier and began hovering above him, fully prepared to lash out and beat down whoever wanted to test him.

He had plenty of frustration to work out.

Yet just before he attacked, he saw the man's face. Wild, greasy hair framed a gaunt, furious expression, but it was the light glinting off a pair of familiar, filthy half-moon scholarly spectacles that brought clarity crashing down like a hammer. Just before the ragged man got in grappling distance, Joe whispered, "Boris? Is that you?"

The force of the man's tackle was absolutely laughable compared to the earlier beatdown Joe had endured. The Scholar slammed into his midsection with all the force of a stuffed animal being thrown into a wall, his fists pounding on Joe's chest and shoulders with pure emotion instead of skill or killing intent.

"I trusted you! *Vouched* for you!" Boris tried to roar, though his words were hoarse and weak. Still, he punctuated his statements with an ineffectual haymaker, which lightly creased Joe's robes, any actual damage easily being repaired without Joe even noticing. "Then you were caught out and vanished just as I was dragged before the Provost himself! My life's work, taken away! Funding, gone. I don't even have a *library card* anymore, Joe!"

Not bothering to block or even raising a hand to defend himself, Joe simply stood and took the strikes. Boris vented all his rage, or at least as much as he was able, on the powerful Ritualist, but his body had clearly degraded over the last long years. Not only had he certainly been doing nothing for physical training, it was obvious he was malnourished and running on fumes. Even so, his eyes were bright and canny, burning with emotion while being ringed with exhaustion. "I've been blacklisted from any kind of scholarly pursuit. Research! Fact-finding missions! *Journalism*, for celestials' sake, and they'll take *anyone!*"

Finally, the ex-librarian slumped forward against Joe, being caught by the Ritualist before he could drop all the way to the ground. Swallowing hard, Joe bobbed his head while refusing to look away from his long-lost friend. "You're right, Boris. I couldn't find you. I never had the opportunity to come and explain myself. I only got back last night, and first thing this morning, I came looking for you. Please, give me a chance to make this right."

"Pah!" Boris tried to shove him away but only succeeded in showing how weak he had become. "You think you can make it right? We were doing amazing things, finding secrets lost to time! I thought we were building something that could be peer reviewed, and all the time you were just... just an *Occultist!*"

"I'll fix it," Joe promised the man, who simply shook his head and went limp. Lowering Boris to the ground, the Ritualist crouched until he was sitting opposite of him, watching as the last hints of fury shifted to bitter resentment. "Until then, I'll think of something to get you back on your feet."

"Haa..." Boris reached up and rubbed his face, leaving a streak of grime where his hands touched. "I suppose, if nothing else, I missed your boundless optimism. Abyss, Joe, I just wanted a proper explanation. That's all *any* scholar actually wants, though I suppose I can't officially call myself that anymore."

"Come on. Let me buy you a meal, and let's catch up?" Joe pulled Boris to his feet, noticing both how feather-light he seemed, as well as how the accumulated grime and filth that had been coating him was already melting away under the effects of his Neutrality Aura. The man merely offered a defeated nod and trudged alongside Joe, though his skin started to regain some color as his body was subtly rehydrated.

Much to Joe's consternation, at that moment, the system decided to reward him for the encounter.

Congratulations! You have managed to enter and exit combat without attempting to escape, nor attacking in return, for the 100th time! You have remained outwardly calm in these situations, no matter how you may have felt about them. Your Constitution Characteristic has been influenced by these actions and has been adjusted accordingly.

Constitution has become Stoic Constitution. This shift does not come with any immediate effects, other than the ability to absorb and integrate permanent energies which resonate with this Characteristic.

Warning! This shift has caused a cataclysmic dissonance between you and your Ritual Orb of Constitution.

"Abyss!" With a mental tug, Joe pulled out his Ritual Orb and sent it hurtling into the sky, where it promptly detonated with a massive explosion, burning away with blue and orange flames as if someone had launched a firework into the atmosphere. Luckily, no guards swarmed toward him, though several people in the vicinity began clapping and cheering for more.

The Ritualist groaned as his total Constitution was instantly halved, though a quick glance revealed it had only dropped to one thirty-eight. Bizarrely, he actually felt better than he had moments ago, as his limiting device immediately stopped restricting some of his movements. "Well... I'll need to make a new one, but there's nothing I can do about it right now."

The tavern Joe picked for the two of them to eat in wasn't the nicest in Ardania, but it *was* the closest. Boris didn't say much on the walk there, only occasionally muttering to himself or shaking his head as he found an easy counter to his own internal arguments. Still, when a bowl of thick stew and a hunk of buttered bread was pushed in front of him, Joe could see the man come alive, the glassy look in his eyes fading with each bite.

"Good stuff?"

Boris snorted and started to shake his head, then froze with his spoon hovering over his bowl. "Yes... somehow, being around you throws me right back to better days, when I wouldn't have touched this food with a ten-foot pole. Now? Now it's the best thing I've eaten in months. At least I didn't have to pull it out of a garbage can."

Giving his hopefully soon-to-be friend a few minutes to digest, Joe ordered him a second serving before finally breaking the silence. "You know, I never really understood why Scholars hate Occultists. I mean, you know, I get the general head-butting and such, but-"

Giving him a half-hearted glare, Boris leaned away from his food and slowly chewed his most recent bite, swallowing and taking a drink of water before finally responding. "Fine, Joe. You want to know why people like me are cast into the outer darkness, left to devolve into feral hobos the moment it's discovered that we've been duped by someone like... well, you? Not to put too fine a point on it."

Joe began to nod, but Boris had already started speaking again, his eyes fixed on the sad lumps of poorly cut vegetables floating in his bowl. "It's because Occultists don't care about what gets broken in their pursuit of knowledge. On the other hand, Scholars build structures, literal and metaphorical, for knowledge to grow within. What we do is tested, able to be replicated. We try to make sure the knowledge outlives us. The people on your side are like wildfire. You burn down a forest and leave behind a note that says 'fire is hot' before skipping away and leaving the devastation in your wake for someone else to clean up. Someone like *me*."

"I'll say it again, Boris. I didn't even know what was going to happen to myself, let alone you." Joe's platitudes were waved away as the Scholar angrily shoved his spoon into his bowl.

"We work with civilization to uplift it, Joe. How many Occultists' experiments are able to be replicated? Let's say you go find a passage in a book somewhere that tells you how to unleash a creature that has been pushed outside our dimension. Let's say that you go and free that creature, either on a whim or because you think you can control it. Now, even if you meticulously document every step of what you've done... the creature is free. That experiment is over. There is nothing left for others to do with that, which means the research you put together is useless. Therein lies the main difference between the two professions."

"That's not completely fair, Boris. I've handed over blueprints, documents, and lots of research that can be tested and seen by others. Abyss, I've even upgraded my profession to Arcanologist. Just because something's been one way in the past doesn't mean it always will be in the future, right? Isn't there room for both to exist?"

"Ah yes. The blueprint you handed over. You mean for that one building that was instrumental in your creation and unleashing of an eldritch spell, which ended up killing off almost all life within hundreds of miles of its origin? *That* blueprint?" Now Boris looked up at Joe, meeting his eyes with a steely stare.

"There were extenuating circumstances. I wasn't..." Joe grit his teeth before he accidentally threw his coven members under the bus, which would have made his entire exile pointless. "Let's just say I took more responsibility for that than I truly deserved. Besides, it wasn't the building that set all of that off. That would be like blaming the palace for a tyrant's decision to burn a village."

Boris returned his gaze to the stew, slowly stirring it as he thought of how to best word his thoughts. "That right there, Joe, is the other main issue. A Scholar takes responsibility for his research. An Occultist can only frantically apologize for the damage that was done."

"Then let me make it up to you, like I said I would." A flash of inspiration struck Joe. "You say you haven't been able to find anywhere to work? Join my guild. I'll guarantee you a high-level position as a researcher in anything you want to pursue, even if it has to come out of my own pocket. Then I'll-"

"Not a chance-"

"What else do you have, Boris?" Joe carefully responded,

feeling like he'd been punched in the gut as he watched his friend's face crumple.

"Then…" Boris began to nod. "You really want to take responsibility? You aren't just saying that?"

"Absolutely."

"Then accept this quest." Boris quickly tapped on the table, his eyes distant as he interacted with the system.

Quest offered: Academia and Diplomacy. You have been offered a quest to restore your friendship with Boris, so long as you manage to repair both your and his reputation with the Scholars. Failing this, so long as you are able to get Boris reinstated among the Society of Scholars, your reputation with Boris will return to 'Reluctantly Friendly'. Should you fail to complete this quest within two years, your Arcanologist profession will be stripped.

Rewards: 1) Reputational recovery with Boris. 2) A method to further advance your Arcanologist profession.

"Society of Scholars. Whoops, I've been calling that the 'Scholars Guild' in my head for a while." Seeing the determined look in Boris's eyes, Joe knew he wouldn't accept any further procrastination. Letting out a deep sigh, he shook his head and accepted the quest. "I hope this means you're taking the job."

"Under duress, but I do hope we can become friends again in the future." Boris tilted his head slightly to the side. "I guess that remains to be seen, doesn't it?"

"Sure. I assume you don't have anywhere to live, so I suppose there's nothing stopping us from heading out right away?" Joe pushed back from the table, scraped the last few coppers he had to his name out of his storage ring to pay for their meals, then stood and offered a hand to the ex-Scholar.

"Heading out? To where, if I may be so bold as to question you?"

Finally, a full smile appeared on Joe's face as he thought about seeing the people he hadn't been able to visit within the last few years. "Home, Boris. For now, at least, while we are on Midgard. Come on, I know the perfect place for you to live. You're gonna love Towny McTownface."

CHAPTER FIFTEEN

"Let's get going. If you hop on my back, I can get us there in... let's say an hour and a half?" Joe gestured for Boris to hop on, only for the Scholar to scoff disdainfully and slowly shake his head. "No? I suppose we could use the fast travel option at Tatum's shrine."

"You are *joking*, yes?" Boris crossed his arms and stayed put. "I am neither a parcel to be delivered nor a backpack to be worn. To be perfectly forthright, I'm also not comfortable using the power of your... deity. There's a reason I lived in the alleys between buildings for the last several months. I still have *some* pride, Joe. I certainly am not about to hop on your back and be carried along like a child. No, if you want this partnership to succeed, you will help me maintain whatever scraps of dignity I have left. We will walk. Perhaps the slower pace will help you put your thoughts in order? In fact, answer this, if you can. When's the last time you took it slow?"

"That's..." The Ritualist clenched his jaw and rolled his shoulders to bleed off his frustration. "Okay, *well*, in that case, I'll need to stop for some supplies. Probably for the best. I shouldn't just vanish without letting my mother know I'm leaving."

"See?" Boris spread his arms wide, as though he had solved one of his friend's many problems. "Look at that, taking your time is already paying dividends."

A short while later, they arrived at the Odds and Ends shop, and Joe found himself on the verge of seeking out some of Havok's 'compliance powder' and knocking Boris out so he could haul him to the guild's town at speed. Whether it was from long months of malnutrition, a lifetime of not building up his Endurance or Strength Characteristics, or if he were just plain trying to irk the Ritualist, Boris trudged along at a *snail's* pace. Seeing a chance to move quickly, Joe requested his companion wait outside as he purchased supplies then rushed in to begin gearing up.

Grabbing a small crate of dried rations, two bed rolls, and a lucky find of a Common-rank alchemy cauldron and dozens of empty glass vials, Joe hurried to the counter and set it all out, smiling at his mother—who had been staring at him with one eyebrow raised the entire time he was shopping. "Leaving already? I certainly hope this trip will be shorter than the *last* one?"

"It has to be." Joe shot her a knowing grin. "After all, there's a wedding to prepare for. I have a deadline now, and I've never missed one before."

"I'm going to see you *before* the few weeks we have remaining have passed though, yes? Maybe in just *one* month?" Brenda dryly questioned while ringing up the goods. "I suppose that might be too much to ask. I know how you are. Haa... all together, twelve silver and eight copper."

"Silver... right." Joe patted at his pockets, knowing they were empty, since he had scraped the final copper coins from his storage. With a sinking feeling, he realized he hadn't bothered to hold on to any of the currency from Midgard—he had filled his codpiece with far more *interesting* junk since leaving this world. "I don't suppose-"

"We don't sell on credit," Brenda firmly informed him, shaking her head at her son's sheepish expression. "I'll cover you this time, as a welcome home present, but you need to find a way to earn a living like the rest of us do. Now, since I figured this would happen, I had a friend pick up some listings. There's a bonus for bear pelts right now, what with winter coming on. Also, if you remember correctly, you can sometimes earn coin from hunting monsters directly. I think you'd be perfectly suited for that task, especially if you're planning on going out in the wilds anytime soon."

"I appreciate it." Joe accepted the papers, which immediately turned into quest notifications. He didn't bother looking at the official system messages, simply noting how hunting down any monster above level fifteen would pay a silver a head. Though Joe obviously kept his mouth shut, he only took the bear fur quest out of respect for Brenda, knowing he didn't have a good way to bring in high-quality, undamaged pelts.

Alternatively, if they were accepting singed, heavily damaged ones, *that* he could do. Pausing for a long moment, he slowly sidled over to several stacks of stone tile set in the corner of the shop, where a handmade sign reading 'flooring' was hanging. Emptying it out directly into his spatial codpiece, he sent a winning smile at his mother. "Since you're covering this one, I hope you don't mind if I-"

"The store doesn't sell on credit, but I will give you some from me personally." Brenda grimaced at him, shaking her head at his antics. "That's nearly eight gold of cut stone, Joe. Not going to just casually hand that over."

"I'll pay you back in no time flat," he promised, giving her a quick hug and running to the exit of the shop as she grumbled in acquiescence. "I'll bring you back a souvenir!"

"I think you'll regret that choice of words once you get to your guild," she ominously called after her son as he pulled the door open.

As he came out of the shop, Joe realized Boris was giving him a bemused stare and realized it appeared as though he had come out empty-handed. He slapped his pelvis, murmuring 'storage item' when the Scholar appeared shocked at the nearly-obscene gesture. "Hey Boris, I'm going to run over to the gate and start putting together a small arsenal. Meet me there?"

"I suppose I can manage to get there on my own, but I won't go any farther outside of the safety of the city without you being present," Boris replied after a moment's hesitation. That was all the confirmation Joe needed before turning on his heel and dashing away, determined to make as many rituals as possible before setting out.

Only minutes later, he was outside of the city and collecting dry wood to build a small fire. Under the concerned glances of the guards at the gate, Joe lit a fire by spinning a stick with his hands so quickly that the flames almost immediately flared up. As soon as he had a fire roaring, he pulled out his new Common-rank cauldron and put it directly on top. Flexing his power, he shaped his mana and flooded the outline of an implement with white aspects to create a simple stirring stick.

Sitting down cross-legged in front of his rudimentary setup, Joe began directing Damaged aspects into the cauldron, using his stir stick to evenly coat the inside of the cauldron as he read the recipe out of the Ritual Combat Manual with his other hand. The entire time he was working, he was mentally translating the simple component cost into its equivalent aspect version, placing droplets of glowing energy alongside the interior of the cauldron as he did so. Between his Alchemical Lore being at Journeyman five, and his Ritualistic Alchemy being at Journeyman three, he was able to brute force the Novice-rank elixir with little issue.

Unfortunately, 'little' issue didn't mean 'no' issue.

As he scooped the resulting clear, bubbling mixture out of the depths of the glorified saucepan, Joe looked on in dismay at the interior—which was now coated in a foul, brackish tar clinging to the surface. "How is there even that much in there? I barely used any ingredients, but it looks like I was just melting licorice and boiling it in bacon grease!"

After carefully pouring the single dose of elixir he had managed to make into a glass vial and replacing its stopper, Joe glanced at the oversized pot once more, hoping his Neutrality Aura had swooped in to save the day. Clicking his tongue at how only the edges had lost their burned-on substance, he reached in and began scooping out the foul mixture with his hands, trusting his Exquisite Shell to protect him both from the heat as well as any toxins caught up in the sludge.

Using his other hand to scrape away some dirt, Joe began to tilt his hand, freezing in place as a guard shouted over. "Hey! You'd better not be planning on fouling the ground. There are ways to safely get rid of alchemical residue, but dumping them in a hole is not one of them."

"Nope, I've got a plan for it!" Joe blustered with a bright, fake smile. Looking back at the hole, he frowned and reached out with his mana, forming an Ascendant Matrix as he poured the ooze into the hole. The guard let out a strangled yell and rushed to stop him. Yet by the time he arrived, Joe had reduced the gunk into Trash aspects. "See? Nothing to worry about!"

After repeating the process dozens of times, Joe had come to a simple conclusion: he was terribly spoiled by the Artifact-quality Morovian cauldron, especially its self-cleaning function. "I can't tell if it's my form or if this cauldron really is just that bad. Then again, it *could* be that I'm using a campfire with no heat regulation whatsoever. Hmm."

An hour later, and dozens of elixirs stowed away in his spatial ring for easy access, there was still no sign of Boris. Joe started to get worried, but instead of thinking about it too much, he pulled out a stack of stone tiles and switched out his stirring stick for a similarly ranked inscription tool. "Okay, I'm probably going to need a ton of these, 'cause they don't do much damage. Maybe I'll just pick a few to focus on, especially since Grandmaster Pete told me to figure out how to push the bounds on what's possible with just one? How about..."

Joe chose three variant rituals, which were actually a single ritual, technically considered a second when enhanced by a secondary discipline, then again when a third was used in conjunction with the others. "Ritual of Elemental Burst. This is how you know I'm thinking of you, Sage Mir. Now, if I use it as a simple circle, it sends out a burst of power in a cone centered on the ritual. Kinda like a flamethrower, but it gets its elemental type based on what is most prevalent in the area. Hmm. If I want actual fire, maybe I should carry a torch with me?"

"Or maybe you don't use flames near the forest?" the gate guard called out from his position not terribly far away, where he had been taking an unhealthy interest in what Joe was up to.

Cutting off his desire to make a snarky comeback, Joe reluctantly acknowledged the man in thanks for his advice. "Fair enough. Of course, now I'm going to speak quieter so I have a little *privacy* over here. Where was I? Right, the basic version is good enough, but if I enhance the basic ritual diagram with the elixir substrate and use it as an ink substitute, it'll cause an Elemental Burst based on... oh, I can set it for either 'on contact' or 'body heat'? Is this the same principle my previous proximity rituals used?"

Happily, he was able to quickly find an answer for how it worked, as the dense notes in the margin of this book explained the theory behind it, as per the standard in the book, being highly detailed for anything using alchemy. This made perfect sense, as the previous owner of the book was attempting to become the Sage of *Alchemical* Rituals.

Flipping pages, he eventually came to a section on theory. "Yeah... let's see, compounds, make ink, or substrates, yep, here it is. Alchemy creates specialized compounds similar to alloys which can change states or properties when exposed to specific triggers. If I'm reading this right, instead of remaining as static diagrams with a singular purpose, alchemy can be combined into the rituals to create potent versions which respond to ambient mana, fluctuations, or even... emotional states? How would that work?"

Joe looked up from his book, thinking about the new-to-him

concept and reluctantly agreeing with the premise. "If enchanted items eventually can be considered 'living', I suppose this makes at least as much sense. Emotions, though? How does someone bottle a response to an emotion? That'd be like figuring out how to make the *opposite* of a love potion."

Flipping back to his planned diagrams, Joe looked at the third version of the ritual. It was still labeled as 'Elemental Burst', but this time with the addition of an enchantment in the circle. When he had first read through it, the Ritualist had been greatly surprised to learn that the most basic version of the skill was incredibly simple: just add blood as a targeting material. According to Grandmaster Pete's annotations, the reason for it was simple.

-Blood carries a distinct magical signature which ties the ritual to the target, essentially functioning as a living, or perhaps a better term would be 'parasitic' enchantment. This is called biological anchoring, an ages-old substitute for creating an enchantment token for binding magic onto a target.

"Abyss, if I had still been using blood regularly in my rituals, I bet I'd be out of the Student ranks in that skill by now." Even as his inscription tool flew over tile after tile, barely needing a few seconds to design the basic Elemental Burst ritual, he compared the results of the three-skill-using ritual circle to the proximity type, which would be the result of using only the circle, and alchemy. "Adding in a drop of blood, or a splash if I'm moving fast, will cause the Elemental Burst to form on the surface of the target. If I were using fire, not that I would—just in case a nearby guard has an Expert-ranked snooping skill— that would look like... what? Instant immolation? Light the target on fire all over their body? Yeah, I can see how that would be a *lot* more effective."

"Ready to go, Joe?" Boris called from where he had parked himself just inside the city's gates. The Ritualist looked over, trying not to show exactly how relieved he was to see that the elderly Scholar had safely arrived. "Burning daylight right now, and I'd rather not get caught out in the dark without a plan."

"Absolutely! Let's get going, Boris." Joe quickly stored away all of his completed rituals and was about to stand up and get moving when he saw how slowly his traveling companion was walking toward him, leaning heavily on a long walking stick he had likely been gifted from Joe's mother.

Staring at the old man with a nonplussed expression, the Ritualist slowly settled back down into a seated position and continued drawing the simple Novice rituals, a single circle overlaid with triple triangles poking out of one side of the diagram, all facing the same direction.

Just under the triangles were symbols denoting simple concepts of the elements: a square with a circle in the center for stone, which tended to stay the same but could be weathered down over time. A swirly figure eight for wind, showing air in perpetual motion. A coiling flame which could have been found on the notebooks of eighth graders the world over, and finally a trio of raindrops next to each other to denote water.

Between his Master rank in ritual circles and current hundred and fifty points in Dexterity, such simplistic formulation required almost no thought or effort. By the time Boris had joined him next to the campfire, Joe had finished another thirty-six of the diagrams on the stone tiles.

"Well? Are you just going to sit there all day?"

"I'm as ready as I can be." Joe looked up at the irritated Scholar, then his eyes flicked over to the horizon, where the sun had shifted upward a fraction of a degree since he had walked out of the gate. "If it's not too rude of me to ask, what's your Constitution Characteristic sitting at right now? Dexterity? Strength?"

"It *is* rude, but I suppose it's pertinent to what we're doing," Boris stiffly replied, tapping his walking stick on the ground twice. "I'm not going to give you exact numbers, but anywhere between thirty to fifty for each of those. Don't *wince* at me like that, young man! Not all of us are sitting at the mortal limit for Characteristics and therefore more than fifteen times the Earth-human limit. It's clear what you're getting at, and the fact is that I move at a *perfectly* reasonable pace."

Joe silently agreed to disagree. Even so, he got to his feet and began strolling alongside Boris as the man moved at what seemed like nothing more than a sedate, serene pace to the Ritualist. For the first ten minutes, the walk was very peaceful, if rather boring.

Hoppily, Joe soon saw fluffy creatures bounding along in the underbrush next to the road—a perfect test target for his new combat rituals if they decided to make a nuisance of themselves. With his Midgard-peak Perception, he was easily able to distinguish the twitching noses, wide eyes, and long ears from the bushes and grasses the rabbits were trying to use to hide themselves. It was fun to just watch nature, yet Joe eventually grew tired of the creatures and stopped paying much attention to them.

An understandable, if unfortunate mistake.

Completely by reflex, Joe plucked a leaping rabbit out of the air as it launched itself at Boris with a feral squeak, blinking at it in surprise as it struggled in his grip. "Celestial feces, did you see that *catch*? I wasn't even looking!"

"Joe..." Boris's eyes were wide, trembling as he stared at the rabbit frantically snarling and snapping at him as though it were a rabid dog. "You've been to multiple worlds, completed dozens of quests, and slain thousands of monsters... right? Please tell me that you've completed an escort quest somewhere in all of that?"

"Err..." Joe glanced around, the rustling in the underbrush reaching a fever pitch. "Not so much, no. Is that a problem?"

"So long as you can keep me safe, not a problem at all," Boris stated with a quiver in his voice. "It's just, you see, the first time someone does an escort quest, the difficulty of it scales to make it a challenge. At least, it tries to; I don't know what happens if you're at the maximum possible strength for the world."

Joe shook his head disbelievingly. "This isn't a quest, so that doesn't matter, right? I'm just bringing you over to my guild area to give you a job. If anything, *you're* completing a quest for *me*."

"I have reason to believe the system doesn't see it that way," Boris whispered as dozens of rabbits broke cover, bounding across the road toward them. Just then, a notification popped up, and the Ritualist was forced to agree with the Scholar's assessment.

Ding! Ding!

Mandatory Quest gained: Ringing the Dinner Bell. You have gained a dynamic difficulty quest, one which has been tagged as an audience favorite. As this is the first time you are escorting a singular, local entity to a new location in order to house them in a new area under your direct supervision —also known as an escort quest—you'll need to fight!

Future escort quest modifiers may be impacted by the manner of success or failure of this quest. Main objective: Ensure Boris survives the journey. Do not carry, launch, teleport, or otherwise induce Boris to move in a way not under his own power. He must remain above 50% health. Remain within 100 feet of Boris for the entire journey. Reward: Boris arrives in Towny McTownface.

Optional objective: Do not allow Boris to take any damage. Reward: Potion of tripled walking speed. (Boris only.)

Optional objective: Defeat 100 hostile creatures during your journey. Reward: Amulet of Damage Immunity (Boris only, 10 minute effect), for each 100 additional hostile creatures defeated, increase the effect by an additional 10 minutes.

Failure: Boris dies or flees, never to attempt this quest again.

Activating three of his new rituals, Joe watched as a trio of cones of sharpened rock manifested and launched into the ranks of rushing rabbits. Each of the rituals generated a burst of shards every second for ten seconds, dealing a paltry eleven and a quarter damage each. It was not enough to scratch Joe's health regeneration, but more than enough to obliterate every last one of the fluffy creatures. The Ritualist glanced over at

Boris, who had gasped at the wave of crimson mist spraying into the air.

Squeezing down on the skull of the final rabbit, still squirming while clutched in his hand, Joe officially ended the first wave of attacks with a light *crunch*.

"Don't worry. I've got this."

CHAPTER SIXTEEN

"Seriously, just focus on walking as quickly as you're able to do."
Joe murmured in what he hoped was a reassuring tone as Boris
flinched away from yet another soft rustle in the underbrush. "I
feel like, after that absolute bloodbath of rabbits, you'd feel safer
around me."

"Was *that* supposed to be my takeaway?" Boris snorted as he
stepped sprightly, at least for him, his walking stick coming
down and tapping in time with his right foot. "Every animal in
the area that can possibly come after me is doing so, all because
my traveling companion is far too strong for the area. This is
the system trying to balance the quest by sending *all* of them.
But I should feel secure, because he can slaughter them en
masse with a smile on his face! Yes, I'm feeling *very* comfortable
in your presence right now."

Joe could only chuckle softly, practically whistling as they
creeped along the road through what had become a well-tended
section of the woods after the Wolfmen had been forced to flee
deep into the Forest of Chlorophyll Chaos. "I don't mean to be
so cheerful about it all, it's just... I guess it's kind of nice to see
the results of all my effort? I've been constantly pushing

forward, going up against stronger and stronger enemies. Sometimes it's hard to see exactly how far I've actually come. It's just that I remember how much trouble even these rabbits used to give me, and now I can just-"

He tossed out his intelligence-bound Ritual Orb, and it spun in place like a drill before shooting out with pinpoint accuracy, bursting through the canopy to nail a slithering snake to the trunk of the tree it was winding along. "Not exactly sporting, I suppose, but still pretty neat. I was worried when I came here that being capped would mean I was a lot weaker than I had been, and for good reason, after fighting that Battle Scholar."

"He was sent down from Alfenheim to make sure you couldn't casually come back to your old haunts," Boris stated shortly, shivering as Joe lifted a hand and casually drew in the air using Somatic Ritual Casting—allowing him to save his premade ritual diagrams, now that he was more familiar with them—only for a series of sharpened wind blades to whistle out and cut a trio of rabbits into skewer-sized meat chunks. "He's facing the same restrictions you are, but, as you noticed, is far more aligned with *combat* studies. Err... a question for you: is battle against these petty nuisances at all helpful for you?"

"Mhmm." Joe glanced to the side, looking at his quickly piling up notifications. "I gain no experience from monsters this weak, but I'm certainly feeling more confident in using these. I gain a point of specialization experience, since I'm using Novice rituals, all but a drop in the bucket. Mainly, it's just a way for me to sharpen my skills and complete a quest I have. Still, it's working out well, as most of my other combat abilities are a little... shall we say, *much* for this area."

He waved vaguely at his body, which was still flickering behind a slight distortion, though the turbulent mana had at least calmed down somewhat over the last hours. Joe was glad to see that the effect was fading instead of remaining at full strength the entire time, only to click off like a switch was thrown at the twelve-hour mark.

"Foxes!"

Boris barked as he shoved a finger to the left of Joe, pointing just out of his line of sight. Although the Scholar was worried, the Ritualist had long since been able to find the red and orange varmints that had been trying to sneak up on them. Activating yet another Ritual of Elemental Burst, Joe watched in satisfaction as the grass and leaves were shredded by the sharp wind, and the ground was watered with a splash of fresh crimson liquid. The creatures had more health than what a single burst from a Novice ritual could deal, but were in no state to dodge away as the mana gripped the air once more and sent it toward them as softly whistling death.

"Like I said, Boris. I've got this. Looks like I should start preparing the next round of rituals for when we run into wolves." The bald man began muttering to himself as he pulled out individual tiles, uncorking a vial of elixir and flipping it over to press the opening against the center triangle of the ritual diagram, where it stuck as though held fast by glue.

It took very little of his mental focus to use his Mana Manipulation and hold the elixir in place, suctioning the air out to make sure none was wasted, while keeping it firmly connected to the input space. One after another, he pulled tiles out and applied the elixir, preparing a dozen before he decided to hold off in favor of seeing how well they held up in combat.

The seemingly endless swarms of rabbits finally vanished entirely, only to be replaced by far fewer foxes, though they were a far more wily foe. Instead of rushing headlong at the humans, they tried to hide, ambush, or take advantage of a moment of distraction to rush in.

Unfortunately for them, Joe may as well have been an optimized fox-felling machine. By the time they reached the wolves' territory, he was starting to feel bad for how hard the small creatures had tried to chomp into the Scholar, only to fail every last time.

So, it was with great relief that he looked at a dense *wall* of wolves staring at him through the gloom of the early evening, hundreds of eyes reflecting the last photons of daylight able to filter through the now-thickened canopy above. Joe was more than ready for a change of pace, for enemies that would last longer than a breath's worth of time in a fight.

Pulling out his tiles, he allowed the elixir he had prepared to *drain* into the grooves his inscription tool had cut into the diagram. The goopy, Novice-ranked liquid touched the lines, hissing and rippling as it was sucked eagerly into the pattern like dry dirt drinking in water. The basic circle pulsed, and a tenth of the fluid in the vial vanished—but the lines began glowing brighter, the elemental symbols lit up like the final coals in a dying fire.

Instinctively tracing the ritual diagram with a thin line of mana, Joe smoothed out the imbalance between the different energies, allowing them to fuse into a cohesive whole. Then, with a flick of his wrist, he tossed the ritual forward like a frisbee, another appearing in his hand as he repeated the process twice, *three* times in as many seconds.

Shards of stone, nearly invisible in the fading light, erupted from the tiles each second. Instead of the unidirectional cone burst, which would continue on until the rituals burned themselves out, this time the rituals tracked what was around them, launching stone, or in one case, super-compressed water at the nearest, hottest body. The rituals perfectly tracked the creatures as they moved, scoring deep lines into the creatures' flanks, breaking bones or sending deep, painful lines of penetrating water through entire torsos.

Joe's hand flicked out, catching a chunk of rock just before it would have slammed into Boris. "Note to self, throw those ones farther. No way for me to whitelist the two of us with such a basic version of this spell."

"You don't need to make a note of that; I'll make sure to remind you." Boris hoarsely whispered as the ranks of wolves were devastated by the half-dozen rituals Joe had tossed into their midst already. "I believe we've moved into a new territory, and I was going to request that you find a suitable sleeping location, but... if it's all the same to you, I think I'd rather prefer we push on through the night."

"Probably for the best," Joe agreed as he started dropping tiles along the edge of the road on either side of them. "Don't get too close to these; I can keep them suppressed until we're far enough to not set them off... but it's probably best not to test that."

"You're just going to leave them on the road behind us? What if there's other travelers-?" Boris flinched once more as a sharp yelp came from behind them, glancing over his shoulder and trying to see what had been struck. "Never mind. I suppose anyone traveling this road probably has enough wherewithal to run away from a repetitive magical emplacement."

"Boris, these things *really* want you," Joe casually mentioned as the wolves that were flanking them shifted directions and lunged from three different directions, as if coordinating their assault. "I get that you're a squishy old guy, but why does it feel like you're wearing a necklace made out of fragrant meat?"

"I'd rather not speculate at the moment, but perhaps you should have spent your formative months on Midgard completing each type of basic quest," the elderly man snapped at him, clearly taking his fear out on his bald traveling companion. "Just... stay focused, and keep them off of me!"

Joe shrugged and began laying out a staggered line of rituals along the road, each of them with a small elixir balanced on their flat surface. "Probably for the best. I don't know when they're going to shift into their big, bad, nasty version, now that night is falling."

"That's not happening anymore. Whatever magical effect was twisting creatures during the night time failed long ago, hopefully because whoever was maintaining the spell was slain." At Boris's words, the Ritualist perked up, remembering the strange altar from long ago he had barely understood well enough to make a single, dangerous change.

"Fantastic!" Even with the potentially deadly situation happening all around him, Boris maintained the same slow, consistent speed he had been walking with that entire time. While it was somewhat frustrating, it also gave Joe plenty of time to move up the path, set enhanced rituals off to the side of the road, then rush back to pick up the ones that hadn't been used. Soon, he was sprinting back and forth, grabbing non-triggered tiles before Omnivaulting over Boris to get ahead of him and reset them along the path.

"Are you having *fun*?" Boris inquired with extreme exasperation as Joe did a flip directly above his head.

"Just staving off both boredom and wolves in one fell swoop, buddy," Joe deadpanned as he used a Ritual Orb to smack down a wolf that had managed to evade the Elemental Bursts. "If we need to complete this mission this way, I may as well push myself to do it in *style*. There's something about protecting a slow-moving VIP with a handcrafted minefield that is just... it feels *good*, you know?"

"No. I. Do. *Not*," the Scholar grumbled, though he lapsed into silence as he got more comfortable with the constant metronome of *boom, thwapp, yelp* that seemed to be on repeat. For the next few hours, Boris continued walking along in silence, merely glancing at the glowing circles Joe formed in midair or carefully edging past a tile that had been innocuously set up alongside the road.

Eventually, the wolves were left behind. Just as the elderly man started to let out a sigh of relief, a bear reared up over him, standing on his hind legs as it lifted a paw to swat him like a fly. He stumbled backward, falling on his rear just as Joe leapt over him, swinging a fist directly into the bear's snout. The creature went flying, rolling half a dozen times as it bounced along the ground before woozily starting to get back on its feet.

Joe let it do so, fully focused on collecting the scattered droplets of blood that had sprayed from its nose with a strand of mana then directing them into the prepared ritual. "Good thing I saved some of these. Bah, too bad I ran out of extra elixirs at sundown."

"You ran *out?*" Boris' words cut off as the tile in Joe's hands glowed with a dull, brownish-orange light.

As the blood was collected in the third triangle on the ritual circle, it sank in and anchored the spell to the already wounded bear. Though the creature likely couldn't feel it through the concussion it almost definitely had, the stone beneath its feet shivered for a fraction of a second before erupting into a single, sharp spire of stone which dug into its chest, impaling it and lifting the beast ever-so-slightly off its front paws.

"No travel time, though it seems to have still used the element that is most prevalent around *me* as the basis for its effect." Joe noted offhandedly, easily keeping track of the creature as it slapped its paws into the stone sticking out of it, shattering it and taking only a single step before yet another spike erupted from the ground and impaled it, this time pinning its leg in place. Eight more spikes appeared and slammed home, though the bear had gone still by the fifth. "Looks like one ritual at a time won't be enough to finish these big boys off. I guess I'll have to put in a bit more *direct* damage."

"That was quite gruesome, Joe," Boris stated as he came alongside the bald Ritualist. "Yet, I find myself surprised there was only one bear after all the swarms and packs I've seen you slap down over the last few hours. Certainly, there are fewer predators of that nature, but—ah, that explains it."

Their gazes had snapped to a sudden bright spot in the darkness, where a new creature had appeared: a rabbit the size of a coyote was staring at them, baring its oversized buck teeth as it let out a low *hiss* of anger. Its eyes were glowing with light, not merely reflecting it as wolves did. A heartbeat later, the creature was bounding toward them, easily twice as fast as the quickest canine they'd needed to deal with that day.

Deciding against playing around, Joe sprinted forward to meet it, grasping his Strength-bound Ritual Orb, which was shaped like a small dumbbell and therefore offered a perfect handhold, and *cracked* it into the side of the creature's head.

Damage dealt: 345. Oh-Oh-Overkill!

"Well, that was new. The question is, is it a new monster for everyone or just because of the quest?" Joe picked up the creature by the scruff of its neck, turning around and shaking the corpse at Boris as if its appearance was his fault. "What is this, and why is it in the bear section of the woods?"

"Am I supposed to know everything that's been going on while you've been gone?" Boris huffed haughtily as Joe rolled his eyes. "Fine, I won't pretend to be ignorant. Even as a sad hobo living on the street, I never stopped paying attention to the goings-on. This can be attributed to a power vacuum created after the Wolfmen were pushed out of this area. Midgard did its best to balance by allowing other monster types to fill in the void. Stronger ones. More intelligent and certainly more potent. Now there are regularly monsters about which can use magic, whereas before you would only run into that type once you were far afield, greatly distant from Ardania."

"There's the Scholar I've been missing. Tell me, Boris, before I came along, when's the last time you were able to use 'whereas' in a sentence without getting a blank stare in return?" Joe's quip fell flat as Boris raised an eyebrow, subtly reminding both of them how the Ritualist had been instrumental in his lack of recent intellectual conversation.

"Well, I suppose there's nothing to do but keep going." Joe awkwardly shrugged as he stored the creature away for further study at a later date. "Are you getting hungry? I think it's time to break into the travel bars, and I want to see if this creature has a core in it."

CHAPTER SEVENTEEN

Nearly a full day passed before Joe finally spotted a sign they were nearing the guild's town. It wasn't marked by roads or banners, just a subtle shift in the forest.

The ancient trees with their thick underbrush and shadow-drenched canopy gave way to a younger grove, one clearly shaped by human hands. The trunks stood in a neat grid, sunbeams spilling down on the blooming ferns, nettles, and countless varieties of bright, sun-hungry greenery stretching endlessly in all directions.

"Not long now, Boris." Joe turned to the Scholar, who looked like a stiff breeze might knock him out. After a night and almost full day of continuous traveling while pushing through exhaustion and muscle fatigue, his legs were trembling, and his face had the haunted, wide-eyed stare of a shell-shocked man. The walking stick he had clutched in his hands like a lifeline was being leaned on heavily, and each step came incrementally slower than the previous. "Hang in there, buddy. We made it. The town is right around that bend; you can see it through the trees."

Conversely, the Ritualist had a spring in his step. Not only had he been having a *fantastic* time pushing his skills forward, he had also been feeling gratified at the sheer power disparity he had been able to bring to bear. Still, he was feeling a bit reflective, and not just because of his Exquisite Shell. The trail behind them was covered in blood, bone shards, and scorched fur, stretching from the start of the forest 'til its end. The two of them were perfectly clean, any gore which had managed to land on their bodies having been long-since whisked away by the gentle cleaning effect of Joe's Neutrality Aura.

"I've been thinking, Boris. It's really interesting to see how far I've come, but there's absolutely no challenge with these creatures. Even the strongest of them only break down into Common material, which isn't really worth collecting." Still, there was no response, other than a nonverbal grunt as they continued trudging forward. "I guess what that means to me is, after I finish up the last few things I have to do on this world, the only reason I would come back is to visit my mother. Strange to think how an entire world can hold almost nothing appealing for me."

"Then you're just not looking hard enough," the Scholar finally spat out, earning a surprised glance from Joe. "Don't be so quick to write Midgard off. Every world has its secrets, its immense potential hidden away until someone discovers it. I'm certain there are places of power which would give you far more than a run for your money if you were to seek them out."

Joe begrudgingly bobbed his head in understanding, biting his lip as he realized he had misspoken. "I suppose speaking in such broad generalities in the presence of a Scholar was bound to backfire."

The elderly man wheezed out a soft laugh... that, or it may have been a soft plea for rest that never made it past his lips. Either way, Joe decided he was going to assume it was appreciation at his willingness to admit when he was wrong. They lapsed into silence as they finished the final short stretch, the open gates of the town finally looming large. The moment they stepped through, a deluge of notifications washed over Joe, freezing him for a few seconds as he quickly scanned through the information.

Mandatory Quest complete: Ringing the Dinner Bell. You successfully escorted Boris the Shamed to Towny McTownface! You did nothing to induce him to move faster, allowing him to make the entire journey under his own power.

Reward: Success is its own reward.

Optional objectives completed: 1) Do not allow Boris to take any damage. Reward: Potion of tripled walking speed. (Boris only.) 2) Defeat 100 hostile creatures during your journey, completed ten times! Reward: Amulet of Damage Immunity (Boris only, 100 minute effect).

Calculating... you completed the quest with a final rating of 'X'. Future escort quests on Midgard will be modified to the maximum possible difficulty, with rewards to match.

Quest update: Mastering Ritual Combat I.

Use 500 Novice ritual combat circles in live combat. 286/500

Use 300 two-discipline ritual combat circles in live combat: 36/300

Use 200 three-discipline ritual combat circles in live combat. 5/200

Skill increase: Alchemical Rituals (Apprentice 0 → Apprentice V).

Reductionist experience gained: 8,175.

You have reached level 11 as a Reductionist! 9,925 experience remains until level 12!

"Feces, it feels like years since I've seen that message. Oohh... that's nice." Joe caught two items as they appeared just above his hands, glancing at the amulet in the shape of a book —clearly representing Tatum—as well as a simple potion bottle.

Knowing these were both for Boris, he tried to hand them over, only for the Scholar to shake his head and wave him off. "Give those to me when you want me to use them; otherwise, I don't have anywhere to keep them."

"Ugh... quest items." Joe grumbled in annoyance as he tucked them away in one of his spatial rings. Feeling as though he hadn't gained anything substantial, seeing as his class didn't come with a bonus, and only one of his skills had advanced, the Ritualist decided to make his own rewards. He flashed around the corner using his high Characteristics and searched around to make sure no one could see him. "Knowledge! Alchemical Lore, Enchanting Lore!"

Seeing as his maximum mana was just shy of seven thousand, losing two thousand of it in an instant felt like more of a gut punch than usual. Joe winced at the instant heartburn, having the presence of mind to clamp down on the ambient mana around himself to reduce the 'noise' generated by activating such a skill.

Skill increase: Alchemical Lore (Journeyman V → Journeyman VI).
Enchanting Lore (Journeyman VII → Journeyman IX).

Blinking away the lingering pain of the massive mana channeling, he went around the corner and rejoined his scholarly friend, who was scanning the area with a slightly disgruntled expression on his face. Joe, still massaging his stomach and annoyed at how long it was taking the sensation to fade, decided to skip the pleasantries and get to the point of whatever was aggravating the man this time. "What is it? The town? I know it's not as grand as Ardania, but it's definitely on the way."

"Is it? I suppose you haven't been here in quite a while, but... this is... not what I was expecting." Boris waved a tired hand to indicate the settlement as a whole, quickly replacing his grip on the stick as he started to sag toward the ground. "Either way, I would be greatly appreciative of being shown to a bed."

Frowning, Joe had looked up and started inspecting the area on his own as soon as Boris began to speak, and he slowly felt his indignation creeping higher and higher as he looked around. "Oh, you have *got* to be kidding me."

As he turned a slow circle to take in the vast changes which had occurred in the town, the Ritualist couldn't help but feel as though he had walked, not into a town he had helped found, but instead had stumbled into a construction project funded by a strange combination of an overambitious merchant guild and a cinder block-obsessed bureaucrat. Long gone were the hodgepodge of buildings which had sprung up in order to meet the needs of the town at the time, and in their place were uninspired, squat slabs of stone and barely varnished wood.

Clearly, these had been turned out in bulk by the lowest bidder, at least… the structures meant to house people. Each of them were practically industrial in design, not quite identical, but certainly uniform—as though an overly strict HOA had been sitting on the zoning board.

Almost worse were the buildings that had a great amount of variety: chintzy, tourist trap-style buildings that looked to have been put together with duct tape, hope, and a deep whiff of desperation. Directly across from the open gate was likely the most put-together of them all, a squat building with the first floor made of stone, turning into a decent log cabin look on the second floor. A carved wooden plaque hung above the inviting doorway, proudly proclaiming the shop to be *The Path Not Taken.*

"Alternative class planning and life coaching—because not everyone wants to be swinging a sword for the rest of their lives." Joe felt his feet moving of their own volition, his mind as blank as if he had taken a blow to the head. He walked up to the building, peering through the windows directly into a gift shop. There he saw small depictions of the juggernauts which guarded the temple connected to the Pathfinder's Hall, reduced to overpriced action figures someone could bring home for the low price of one silver each.

But the worst part was various baubles and items on the shelves with advertisements proudly displayed above them.

Fast travel individual pass. Finish your plan and get back to the city <u>now</u>, *not later!*

Career path crystals—why make it hard? Shake to see what fate says you should try!

Missed out on the corpse plague? Buy a snow globe and shake it to see the red mist rise again! Buy one, get one for a friend!

Wanderer's Guild leadership—bobblehead version! Buy nine, get A-ten free!

"Is that… me? Abyss. What's that sign say…? Second floor, career counseling?" Turning back to Boris, Joe barely managed to blurt out, "They've turned the Pathfinder's Hall into a tourist trap? But… this is the first new Town in the kingdom! A fortress against the monsters and Wolfmen! Where are the *Wanderers*? Why has no one shut this down?"

The only break from the conformist monotony or pastel sign-covered storefronts was the enormous Pathfinder's Hall looming over the other buildings in the area. The towering, egg-shaped building still looked as glorious as ever, its smooth surface covered in a soft glow Joe wasn't certain everyone could see—he had increased his skills far beyond what could typically be found on that world, after all. Still, one familiar building wasn't enough to push back the absolute dissatisfaction he felt.

"Boris, I hate to do this to you, but I'm going to put you up in a hotel for a little bit." Joe paused as he came back to the same uncomfortable realization he had gained back in Ardania. "Scratch that, I don't have any money yet. Why don't you hang out here for a little bit; I'll be back as soon as I can? No… actually, go up to the Pathfinder's Hall, and I'll meet you there."

Seeing as his friend was back to grunting, Joe could only assume they were in total agreement with each other. He began walking quickly, cutting through the redesigned roads which wound lazily through the town, as though attempting to force everyone to go past every store within the walls before getting to the center of the space.

A single Omnivault later, he was on top of a rickety shop proudly named *This Might be Important Later,* which appeared to sell all sorts of commemorative gear, such as blank class patches —only five copper to have your class symbol added!— keychains, and coffee mugs. From his new vantage point, he could see the Town Hall near the center of the town, only the second structure he had noticed which didn't have major architectural changes.

Just as he started to calm down, he noticed a huge gap. Like a smile where the front tooth had fallen out, it was all too noticeable by its absence. Adjusting his vector, Joe landed just in front of the sign posted at the empty lot, eyes twitching as he read over the Times New Roman font cleanly printed on the paper.

Notice of condemnation. Area declared haunted. Trespassers will be prosecuted to the fullest extent of the laws of Ardania, should they survive.

"It wasn't haunted, it was *cursed*," Joe kicked a rock into the space, where it bounced off the broken foundation of the building and rolled back almost all the way to him, "and that was a feature! People *fought* to sleep in the hungry apartment building! If it didn't eat you, the bonuses were *crazy* good."

Absolutely steaming mad, Joe marched over to the Town Hall and gave the door a polite little tug—just enough to confirm it wasn't locked—then stepped back and drop-kicked the thing like it had personally insulted him. It flew open, slamming into the wall with enough force to echo up and down the street. Bellowing to keep his momentum, the Ritualist followed the door into the building. "Bring me to the Town council room this *instant!*"

After his dramatic entrance, Joe found himself staring at a solitary secretary who was looking right back at him with wide eyes. The man sputtered in fear, before managing, "Uh... um... sir, I can bring you there, but there's no one in it. Today's everyone's day off, I'm only here because we need someone in case there's an emergency."

Letting out a long-suffering sigh, Joe let his head fall back, and he stared at the ceiling for a long moment. Returning his gaze to the middle-aged man whose hand was slowly creeping toward what he was almost sure was a panic button, the Ritualist snapped his fingers hard enough to rattle the windows of the Town Hall. "In that case, go ahead and declare an emergency. Get me anyone who has any authority over this Town. I want them here five minutes ago!"

"We have no one with any kind of temporal powers—oh, you just mean ASAP. Yeah, I'll... I'll get right on that."

Going into the large council room, Joe paced back and forth for a few minutes, his sheer speed allowing him to traverse the room dozens of times in that span. The long wait allowed him to start calming down, and Joe took a few deep breaths, trying to understand exactly what it was about the place that was infuriating him so much. At the half hour mark, he was able to sit down and remain seated for more than a few seconds, his mind turning the issue over and trying to view it from different angles.

"This world? It's not even viable anymore. I've basically already written it off. So why should I care that it's been sold out and stripped bare?" Even as the words left his mouth, logic telling him to let the anger fade... it surged instead. "But abyss it, I *do* care. I fought for this place. I bled here. They've turned it into a joke? After everything we survived? No. I'm not walking away-"

"Sir, I'm going to need you to come with—oh, hey, Joe." The bald Ritualist looked over to see a familiar face, watching with a raised eyebrow as Jay the guard sheathed his sword and carefully showed how neither hand now held a weapon. "We got a report of someone attacking the Town Hall and threatening the local leadership?"

"I brought it into this world; I can take it out," Joe grumbled darkly, earning himself an eye roll from the perpetually cheerful guard. "I called for the town's leaders. Where are they?"

"Oh, they're here, just in case this was a legitimate emergency. Most of them are waiting to take pictures next to whoever I drag out of here as a photo op, but I suppose I can go tell them to actually assemble." Jay waved over his shoulder as he stepped out of the room, only for a sea of greatly annoyed faces to come into view.

"Wait..." Joe looked at each of the men entering the room, each wearing a nearly identical suit and matching tie. "I know you. Aren't you all the original financiers of the guild? I thought you were all stripped of your guild authority?"

"Funny thing about that, Mr. Joe." The final man to stroll into the room locked eyes with the Ritualist and walked over with a hand extended. "What do you think happens when *all* of the guild leadership is entirely focused on progressing their power, skills, and classes? Let me answer that for you. As soon as they're over-leveled for the area, they skip town as soon as they can make it to the bifrost."

"Mr. Johnson." Joe reluctantly accepted the handshake, trying not to scowl at the man's limp grip as they exchanged pleasantries. He looked around the square meeting space lined with rows of uncomfortable chairs, the walls which had various motivational posters, projection charts, and even an easel with a half-formed potential advertising campaign written out on it. Then he looked at the people sitting in those chairs, low-level, dull-eyed bureaucrats who were assuredly *swimming* in coin. "So many of my questions were just answered."

Mr. Johnson unbuttoned his middle suit coat button and gestured to a seat at the front of the room as he took one of his own. "As I stated, most high-level members of our guild have moved on to other worlds. Luckily for us, we've been able to far more than recoup our losses from the early days of being in Eternium. I admit, at first, we were rather miffed when we were sidelined to fight a pitched war, but the sheer *audaciousness* of all of you? The fact that you brought us a type of advertising you simply cannot buy? You've spawned legends all on your own, and we've been able to turn that into some serious success for the Wanderer's Guild."

"Yeah, I saw my plushie. I'll be direct; this place is a tourist trap," Joe flatly stated, his words causing the others to shuffle in their seats ever so slightly. "As First Elder in Waiting, and to satisfy my own curiosity, I need you to tell me how this advances the interests of the guild?"

"There's an easy one for me to explain," Mr. Johnson immediately responded in a silky smooth tone. "Let's look at the facts. Anyone who wants to adventure, fight monsters, seek higher heights... they do. We've made our mission statement on Midgard as such: establish a stable intake platform for new members. Recruitment, orientation and training, then finally redirection to more *appropriate* destinations as needed."

"Midgard is now a feeder world for the guild," another of the bureaucrats clarified, obviously proud of how they were managing things. "We find the talent, get them the information and training they need, and if they are the rambunctious sort, like... well, *you*, we get them on the bifrost as soon as they are ready to go. It's a win-win situation for all of us."

"Okay..." Joe took a calming breath, but before he could say another word, Mr. Johnson spoke up once more.

"If it's the royalties you're worried about, don't worry, we've been putting aside an appropriate amount. Not only are you listed as the sole owner of the Pathfinder's Hall, and therefore entitled to a full twenty percent of the ticket sales, your bobble-head sells at a two-to-one rate compared to everyone else's!"

"Two to one? Why? Wait, you're saying I just have a pile of coins set aside for me somewhere?" Joe raised an eyebrow, not allowing himself to get excited, as he knew nothing would ever be that simple with a group of people like this.

"Well..." Mr. Johnson coughed into his fist awkwardly. "All cash sales are converted into guild contribution points. For your convenience."

"Useful across all worlds, and *you* don't have to pay out on this one." Joe shook his head in wonder at the convoluted means they were using to line their pockets. "Okay, I hadn't asked about that, but we'll definitely come back to it later. I suppose the next major question I have is... what happened to all of the buildings I put together?"

"We decided to go in a more thematic way," one of the bureaucrats excitedly interjected, clearly having been someone who was on that project. "You see, Joe, when people come to Towny McTownface, they don't want to see bristling weapons and the standard medieval-style charms of Gardenia-"

"Ardania?" Joe butted in, blinking in shock at how casually incorrect this man was.

"-Yes, that." The financier nodded patronizingly. "No, when they come here, they want an *experience*! This is the epicenter of the corpse plague! The red mist! The site upon which Humanity cast out the Wolfman contenders and became a Unified Race! Just like any other place of great importance, most of them want to bring something home to remember the visit, and we made sure to make available anything they wanted!

From simple commemorative options to career counseling or even guided safaris into the depths of the Evergrowth Greenhouse. They get to stand where the heroes of humanity stood, or even the Dread Ritualist himself-"

The man choked slightly at that point, eyes going wide as he realized he had said too much. Joe rolled his eyes. "Yeah. Again, I saw the plushie. Who did you get to do the design work on the eyes? I'd recognize a Ritual of Glimmering from a mile away."

"Well," Mr. Johnson shot a warning look at his contemporaries. "There's an entire herd of Ritualists still living in town."

"Herd Of Ritualists?" Joe tested the words softly, wondering if he was having a fever dream or if this was reality.

"Well, of course I have, there's one right in front of me!" The entire group of bureaucrats started chuckling at Mr. Johnson's joke, who beamed as if he had come up with something truly original. "Anyway, today was supposed to be our day off, so if there's nothing we can help you with...?"

"No, there's *plenty* to talk about." Joe offered a shark-like smile. "As the first Elder of the Wanderer's Guild, I'm immediately going to be declaring a state of emergency for the town, putting it under lockdown and martial law as we prepare for war."

CHAPTER EIGHTEEN

There was a long, awkward silence following Joe's statement as each of the people in the room thought through their options. Then, seemingly all at once, the council chamber erupted into horrified murmuring. Joe's eyes twitched slightly at the lack of patriotic fervor, concern for the residents, or the potential for destruction that a war would bring.

"Martial law? You must be *joking*." A man pulled out a pen and notebook, fingers shaking as he opened to a saved page and slowly drew a line through something. "Do you have any idea what locking the public out of the town will do to our profit margins?"

"Our weekender package includes a penthouse stay, a safari tour, skilled counseling, and a tour of the most important sites inside the city and out of it!" Another slapped his hand on an empty chair, a *thump* echoing through the room. "We are booked for the next six months; how long are you planning for this little tantrum to last?"

"No, cancel all bobblehead production immediately, we're going to short the-" the man talking quietly into a magical device yelped as a Ritual Orb pierced it and flung it across the room, where it shattered against the wall.

Joe let the panicked sounds wash over him like rain off a duck, finally feeling truly calm since he had entered the town. Slowly reaching out, he plucked the precious-metal-inlaid mandate from the crown out of midair with a flourish. "The king and queen of *Ardania*-"

He stressed that word in an attempt to help them remember where they were living. "Decided to give me some additional rewards for my service to Humanity, for my *guild's* service. We've been given full authority to increase the rank of the Town to tier five, which will allow us to transform the Town into a City and the Wanderer's Guild into the Wanderer's *Sect*."

Silence swept through the room, and he let it linger for perhaps a few heartbeats longer than totally necessary. "To that end, I'm going to upgrade the Pathfinder's Hall, which should kick all of this off."

He hadn't even finished speaking before the mood in the room shifted in a decidedly unexpected direction. All signs of panic vanished like cockroaches scuttling away as the lights turned on, but it was Mr. Johnson, leaning forward with a gleam in his eye, that drove home what was going on in their heads.

"You're telling me... the Pathfinder's Hall is going to get an upgrade? Fantastic! It's already our biggest draw. People come here from all across Midgard just to see if they are making the right choices with their classes. We've got it down to a science... which ones are dead ends, which ones are diamonds in the rough-"

"I can't believe it's finally happening," the muttering member pulled a second device out of his pocket, rapidly speaking into it before Joe could smack it out of his hand. "Pathfinder's Hall expansion—speculative. Abyss, today's like Christmas in a futures market!"

"The first Sect! I can think of thirty new merchandise ideas off that alone! I need to get my people working on-"

Joe realized his jaw had dropped slightly as he looked around with glassy eyes, fully uncertain if he should be impressed or appalled by the shift he had just witnessed. "You suddenly want this? You do realize that, when we push for a higher tier, there's going to be a full-scale battle here. That's not even counting what it might look like when we try to shift into being a Sect. Who knows what sort of reaction we will get?"

"No one! That's the entire point of it. Think of the profit on the betting pools alone-"

"The town is going to be under siege!" Joe bellowed over the excited hubbub. "Maybe none of you were here during the last upgrade, but there was almost nothing left standing. We are risking almost guaranteed devastation-"

Instead of eliciting concern, as he had been hoping, a gentle rustling followed his words as each of the others in the room pulled out a matching leather-bound book, unclasping them to reveal detailed calendars brimming with text. Pen quivering in the air just above the page, Mr. Johnson waited patiently for Joe to speak again, but when he didn't, bobbed his head and pointed at the page. "Were you thinking a summer monster wave or sometime this fall?"

"Oooh, if we did it with the leaves changing color, any blood on the ground would blend in nicely."

"End of autumn would be better, in case cleanup takes longer than expected. The cold would keep the smell down and give us a chance to clear the place out properly."

"That would give me time to work with the vendors and make sure we've ramped up our production on the commemorative-"

"Are you *seriously*," Joe took a deep breath in through his nose, trying to maintain his cool, "Scheduling out the best time to summon a massive monster wave in order to maximize your profits?"

"Not just that, obviously." Mr. Johnson flicked his pen. "We'll also need time to build up defenses, bring in combatants, and all manner of serious considerations. We need to make sure we are ready for this. If we do this right, we can brand ourselves as a true crucible, a proving ground that will pull in not just the tourists, but even the most serious of adventurers. Yet another world-shaking event happening right here... who *wouldn't* want to move here and be part of the next one? We are going to need to bring back every active member of the guild we possibly can, hire mercenaries, enlist Battle Mages from the college, and so much more."

"I survived the Sect upgrade, and all I got was this lousy t-shirt." The financier Joe was starting to truly dislike whispered into his device. "I want ten thousand at a minimum-"

With a truly begrudging sigh, Joe grit his teeth and relented. "I can't say you're wrong to put serious effort into planning this out, but please keep the sales talk out of this until I leave. If someone talks about plushies, I might burn this entire place down and start over somewhere else."

"Plushies? Of a potential monster wave? Certainly not, Joe." Mr. Johnson shook his head, though he looked sidelong at the man sitting next to him and hedged under his breath, "but I bet the *miniatures* market would really-"

When Joe left the Town Hall, it felt less like he'd wrapped things up and more like he'd barely managed to escape a PowerPoint session. The upgrade had been scheduled a month away, giving him an extra week's leeway before he had to get to his mother's wedding. Allowing himself one full-body shiver, he looked to the Pathfinder's Hall. "That was brutal. But at least it's on the books, and everyone's on board with it. Maybe I should go—abyss, *Boris*!"

Flashing down the road, he was soon skidding to a stop in front of the egg-shaped building, yet his friend was nowhere to be seen. At first, he thought the old man may not have arrived yet, but a quick Omnivault straight upward proved that to be false. Time seemed to hold still for a long moment as he reached the crest of his upward travel, and his eyes locked on a pair of guards marching down the winding streets, holding Boris in the air with a hand under each of his armpits.

"This has to be some kind of joke. I don't even *recognize* the guild here anymore." In a matter of moments, Joe was landing on the road in front of the guards, sweeping into an upright position and glaring at them with his arms crossed. "I'm going to need you two to let go of him right now. This is the new curator of the Pathfinder's Hall, and the way you are treating him is absolutely shocking."

"Sir. *Sir.*" As Joe took a step closer, extending an outstretched hand to the Scholar, one of the guards, a burly lady with a square jaw and an attitude to match, held up a cudgel threateningly even as the other reached for his own weapon. "We're dealing with a vagrant at the moment. I don't know what this man has told you, but we're the security force of the Pathfinder's Hall. We know everyone who works there, and he's not one of them. Actually, he's in violation of the town code of conduct. No loitering, panhandling, and certainly no napping on the town streets—especially right in front of our main profit center."

"He hasn't told *me* anything." Joe didn't back down an inch, keeping his voice even and his eyes focused on the sunken-faced Scholar. "I *own* the Pathfinder's Hall. I'm the first Elder of the Wanderer's Guild. Boris was hired *today*; of course you don't know him."

"Next thing you're going to tell us is that you're the Dread Ritualist Joe, just because you shaved your head this morning." The second guard snorted, reaching forward to try and smack Joe's arm away from where it was still resting in midair. To the man's dismay, hitting that limb was like punching reinforced concrete—going by the pained *hiss* he let out even while the arm remained in place as though it were in geosynchronous orbit above the ground.

"I don't care who you want to *pretend* to be," the first guard took over, though she cast a slightly worried glance at her partner's reaction. "You don't just get to ignore the town laws and keep hobos around because you're feeling generous. Unless you've got some documentation, you need to get out of the way."

Finally turning his gaze to the guard, Joe stared daggers at her, his jaw working until he could force himself to remain calm as he spoke. "I am the highest ranking person in the guild on this *world*. As much as any one person can, I own the entire Town, and the rules are what I *say* they are. Now... you are treating my guest poorly, and I'm going to give the two of you one last chance to go about your business."

Letting out a surprisingly deep snarl of anger, the square-jawed lady let go of Boris and stepped forward, taking a swing at Joe while tapping on the Wanderer's Guild logo etched in the buckle of her utility belt. It flared with light just as the strike came down, but as the cudgel landed... nothing happened.

As apparently only *Joe* expected.

"That... I struck you with the full authority of the council! You should have been thrown all the way out of town!" Her eyes went wide as she started to realize Joe may have actually been telling the truth.

But it was already too late.

Moving faster than either guard could react, almost too fast for them to see, he reached out and gently—relatively speaking —gripped her armored pauldron in an iron grip, twisted, and put all one hundred and fifty points of his strength behind throwing her. She sailed up and over the low building they were standing next to, vanishing over its edge with a startled yelp. Joe turned to glare at the other guard, who was now standing with his hands slowly raising in a surrender position. "Need any other documentation, or will that do?"

Clearing his throat, the guard quickly shook his head in the negative. "That won't be necessary, sir! It seems my partner and I have made an error, and you helped bring it to my attention! My apologies. We have our protocols and weren't updated about your... return. Are you really... are you the Dread Ritualist?"

"Before today, I've never heard anyone call me that," Joe replied dryly, offering a shoulder for Boris to lean on, as it seemed the guards had relieved him of his walking stick. Then the guard said something that made Joe physically cringe, pulling away from him.

"I hate to ask, since our first meeting was such an unfortunate interaction, but... could you sign my snow globe?"

Now under no restriction about moving Boris around, Joe scooped the man up and jumped on top of a building, then sprinted to the nearby Pathfinder's Hall before the Scholar could get out more than a surprised, "You set me *down!*"

"Sorry about all that, Boris. Are you okay?"

"Unfortunately... it's nothing I haven't grown all too used to." Boris tried to push himself away from Joe as the Ritualist set him down, only managing to put himself off balance for a long moment. "I was only trying to get a better look at the Pathfinder's Hall, and I must have nodded off. Next thing I know, I'm being hauled off and called a public nuisance."

Grumbling under his breath, Joe started walking toward the towering, egg-shaped building. "Come on, let's give you a proper tour."

Yet, as they approached the building, there was one final barrier to leap. A bored-looking man sat behind a rope strung across the road, clearly designed to funnel foot traffic through a small kiosk. As the duo came closer, he looked up at them then back down to the book he was reading.

Not even bothering to stand, the worker droned out, "Entry fee is a silver per visitor, but you missed the start of the last tour. Next one begins in fifteen minutes, to give our dedicated career counselors a chance to rest their feet. Please stay behind the yellow painted line."

By this point, Joe was absolutely, completely *done*. Not even bothering to respond, he simply continued walking in a straight line toward the open doorway of the Pathfinder's Hall, a good dozen feet from the stall. As he got up to the rope, he pushed forward, barely feeling any resistance as it went taut, then snapped, exploding into frayed ends as he burst through it.

"Hey! *Sir!* Excuse me!" the man called out in a half panic, scrambling to his feet too quickly and nearly falling as he clutched at his legs, which must have fallen asleep. "You can't just-"

"Getting *real* sick of people telling me what I can and cannot do today," Joe softly seethed under his voice. "This is *my* building, and I think it's time to remind people *why* they set up shop a good distance away from the entrance." Placing a hand on the side of the Pathfinder's Hall, Joe interfaced with its system, only continuing forward as he heard a thunderous, repetitive noise.

A glance over his shoulder revealed a juggernaut skidding to a halt behind him, weapon hoisted in the air to intercept any interlopers. The door sealed shut behind them without a sound, leaving the Ritualist and Scholar in total darkness for a bare moment. A few steps later, Joe felt his frustration melt away, being replaced by a spark of pride and happiness as Boris looked around and gasped in sheer wonder.

The darkness around them receded, light swirling up and around the walls and giving them the illusion of standing over a chasm of stars. Below, above, around—every last inch of the egg-shaped dome was filled with celestial motion. Galaxies spun, stars burned, and meteors flickered past. Now that he had a far higher perception than the last time he had been in this building, not to mention his Journeyman-ranked Celestial-Arcane Interaction Lore, Joe was able to pick out each of the planets he had visited so far.

His eyes wandered along the stars, easily finding patterns corresponding to his ritual diagrams and their exact placement. "It's even better than I remembered... this place is absolutely perfect for a Ritualist. I was *absolutely* underutilizing it before now."

"What... *is* this?" No longer seeming even the slightest bit sleepy, Boris walked along the interior of the building, his eyes drinking in the crisp details of the universe surrounding them. The caution sound of each of his steps was swallowed by the enormous space, but the Scholar's movements became more assured as he realized he wasn't about to drift off into the star field below them. He turned in place, following along with the slow drift of a constellation that flickered into place next to him.

When he touched the symbol, a soft ripple of energy pulsed outward, washed over him, then back into the constellation—which rearranged itself into a shape reminiscent of an unfurled scroll. Joe knew from experience that he was looking at his current chosen class path. Several sections of the scroll-like constellation were dark, hinting at unexplored options, while others were shining brightly, highlighting known class branches, with the brightest being the advancement path Boris had taken thus far.

"This is the ultimate class compendium, but is it only my own? Is it adaptable? Is this a full archive of all known classes, or is there a set upper limit?" Boris trailed his index finger along the brightest path of seven stars, only then seeming to realize it detailed his exact progression. "Does this… how does it know so much about me?"

Joe, having interacted with the building, had seen how close it was to sending out its next Knowledge Nova. He'd started feeding in his mana at a slow trickle since they arrived, and so instead of directly answering the Scholar's question, he topped off the well of collected power and waited.

The entire space pulsed gently in response, energy shifting around and collecting into a singular point. Moments later, there was an absolutely enormous, soundless, and painless erup- tion as a nova of mana detonated outward from the Pathfinder's Hall, leaving Joe tingling with the knowledge that he had just provided quite a bit of information on his own class that hadn't been there a moment before.

A slight frown touched his lips, as for the first time he began to realize why more powerful people may be uncomfortable with the invasive nature of the data collection. Touching the wall, he double checked that his personal class information was locked behind permissions. It was a relief, to be sure, but there was still the unsettling knowledge that he had just been *analyzed*. "Yikes, that has a bit more *kick* now that I'm stronger."

"Are we truly inside of a living archive of classes, fueled by ambient mana that has been collecting class progression data from anyone who enters it?" Boris yanked his hand away from the wall as if he'd been scorched by cursed flames. "This could absolutely revolutionize how Scholars approach class development theory! I could write a dozen volumes on the collection methods alone, not to mention the actual results! This is... is..."

Trailing off, Joe watched as a now-familiar bitterness settled over his friend's face. The elderly man let out a self-deprecating scoff. "Not that it will matter, unless you are able to get me reinstated. At most, I could hand the research off to a Scholar in good standing and have them publish it under *their* name, if they would even deign to offer me a meeting."

"I said I'll handle it, and I will." Joe gestured at a section of the floor, which shifted upward to reveal a stairwell descending into the depths of the building. "You're going to need lots of time to collect that data in the first place, so you shouldn't feel any huge rush. Come on, let's show you where you're going to live."

"You expect me to follow you into a hidden basement in a sealed building? This is how people vanish, Joe."

The Ritualist rolled his eyes at the half-joking accusation. "The only things down there are storage, a ritual design chamber, archives on the research anyone still actively doing things with my coven has been collecting-"

Boris was halfway down the stairs before Joe could finish.

"-and a bed or two." Allowing himself a soft chuckle, the Ritualist confirmed a few of the changes he had been working on, granting Boris nearly unrestricted access to the controls of the Pathfinder's Hall. "If I am going to trust him enough to grant him access to all these places anyway, I may as well trust him to take care of it when I'm not here."

He then happily followed his friend and gratefully sealed the stairs behind him. If there was one thing Joe wanted at that moment, it was to be away from the commercialized abomination of his once-beautiful home.

CHAPTER NINETEEN

Joe had fully intended to get Boris settled then vanish into the wilds around the town for a few weeks while they geared up for the upgrade. But the moment his feet touched the bottom step of the stairs into the secret chambers, he realized they weren't alone down there. Though the air was filled with a thin cloud of incense, the light haze wasn't able to hide the shocked group staring at him from across the room.

Taka. Kirby. Robert. Big_Mo, and… Hannah.

All five were gathered in the ritual chamber, clearly having been startled out of whatever they had been doing. Whether that was carefully reading through a book, hunching over an experimental ritual diagram, or tossing a stuffed version of one of the Wanderer's leaders onto a pile, each of them froze like they had been caught doing something unsavory.

Robert was the first to react, his jaw snapping shut before he lurched to his feet and took an incredulous step toward their one-time leader. "*Joe?* You're *back?*"

That simple question broke the ice, and the air was soon filled with the sound of chairs scraping as they were pushed back, an incomplete Novice circle popping into a wave of heated air after being ignored for too long, and four people closing in on the bald Ritualist and speaking in unison.

"I thought you'd never come back!" Big_Mo seemed almost overcome with excitement, appearing to need to hold himself back from lunging at his long-lost mentor. "I can't tell you how sorry I am about-"

"Abyss, feel the *power* coming off of him! How strong did you get, Joe?" Kirby loudly spoke over the others, reaching out and flicking his Exquisite Shell, which let out a soft **chime** as if she had tapped a crystal chalice. "I bet you've got all *sorts* of cool new things to teach us! Anything to get my army of minions up and running. This world needs an overlord, and it should be me."

Joe noticed the only one who hadn't come over was Hannah. She had stood up but was staring at the ground, shoulders trembling as she waited silently as though preparing herself for her funeral. Wanting to figure out what *that* was all about, Joe quickly smiled at the others and said a polite few words then stepped to the side and walked over. They, noticing his destination, vacillated between not saying anything or trying to stand up for the person who had inadvertently gotten him exiled.

Hannah looked up, and Joe had to work not to flinch away. Her skin was pallid, so pale that the individual veins under her skin were clearly highlighted as though someone had drawn on her face with a pen. Her face was gaunt, eyes sunken, with deep bags underneath them. Framing her face was greasy, filthy hair, a perfect match for her clothes.

Trying for a casual tone, he opened his arms for a hug, "So, it's been a hard couple years, huh?"

A scornful laugh popped out of her, but Hannah didn't refute him, only shaking her head before slowly meeting his eyes. "You don't know the half of it. I'm lucky I didn't get thrown out of the guild, because there was definitely nowhere else for me to go. Worst part? The only way I could earn money for this last year was to stitch Rituals of Glimmering on the plushies the guild is selling of you. Kind of hard to distance myself from all this when I'm seeing a tiny version of your face twenty times a day."

"Why did you stay on Midgard?" Joe half-turned to include the others in this question as his Neutrality Aura began breaking down the filth in the room, though he kept most of its power especially focused on his previous mentee. "That goes for all of you. It doesn't look like you've been able to make practically any progress since I left."

"Oh, but we have!" Taka's face lit up as he half gestured across the room. "We've been using the funds we've been earning from the guild by doing some ritual work for them to make all sorts of different stuff. Or, well, try to. I earned a subskill of Ritual Magic thanks to all the calculations I was doing, but for the *life* of me, I can't figure out how to teach the others how to get it."

"Before I forget, again," Joe stopped the enthusiastic young man before he could start a formal presentation of his work and gestured at the Scholar in their midst. "This is Boris. I've hired him to be the official curator of the Pathfinder's Hall, so you'll see him around. If you don't bother him, I'm sure you'll all get along just fine."

"Nice to meet you, Boris. Spare bed is over there." Big_Mo gestured to a doorway just to the side of the stairwell back up to the main part of the Pathfinder's Hall. "You look like you're about dead on your feet."

The Scholar simply nodded once and shuffled away, vanishing into the bedroom. Kirby leaned close to Joe, her wide eyes narrowing as she looked at the details of his Tower Ritualist robes and gloves. "Looks like you've been busy and some kinda crazy successful. I want to learn everything I can about what you've been up to; how about we all relax and do some catching up?"

A few hours later, they were chatting and laughing, having been able to recapture some of the comfortability they once had. Finally, almost seeming like he were going to explode if he didn't get it out of him, Taka pulled out an iron key covered in dense calculations at the tip, which Joe recognized as forming about one-tenth of a completed circle. "Can I show you what I've been working on?"

Joe's eyes lit up with excitement for the sheer fact that he had not a single idea what he was looking at. "Absolutely. I wasn't trying to stop you; there was just a lot to go over."

"Probably could've written two trilogies out of all of that," Kirby grumbled incredulously, thinking over the tale Joe had spun about his time since leaving Midgard. "Here I've been plodding along, only able to research rituals after standard working hours."

"Yeah, what *is* up with that?" Joe inquired of the group as a whole, who shifted into an uncomfortable silence once more. "It's been two years, and this place is basically a clone of a town back on earth, complete with work shifts and random trinkets for sale."

"A *billion* people happened, Joe," Hannah chimed in glumly. "You don't understand what it was like. I don't want to say that being exiled was awesome for you or anything foolish like that, but the fact is… when you need to compete with that densely packed of a population for resources—everything from food to hunting spots—progression grinds to a halt. Things have been getting better recently, but only because people have been able to rapidly expand out. There's *dozens* of new towns every month, pushing all the way out almost to the edge of Ardania."

"Not to mention, ritual magic isn't exactly cheap. I can't think of any single discipline that is *more* resource-intensive." Taka's words made Joe wince, and he resolved right then and there to figure out how to open the path forward for being a Reductionist for all of them.

"Well, I'm back, and we're gonna get all of you power leveling with me, so that's a thing of the past now." There were a few moments where the others seemed surprised, then they quickly started to get excited. Joe wasn't one for making idle promises, and they all knew that.

"That's cool and all, and I'm totally on board, but let me

show you this!" Taka waved his key back and forth to draw their attention back to him. "I call it the 'remote access key'. You start by making any other ritual, then, in place of the standard activation sequence, you overlay it with the Student-ranked ritual I designed, which acts as a unique identifier and allows you to activate the first ritual from a distance."

Joe politely murmured a few words of encouragement but wasn't fully sold on its utility. "So... don't take this the wrong way, but I've found at least four different ways to activate rituals at a distance; what makes this different?"

"The difference is that the ritual is *already* primed." Taka grinned as he saw Joe begin to understand. "Meaning anyone holding the key can activate it... *and* I haven't found an upper limit on the distance yet."

"So, anyone who has the key can use the targeted ritual, without any need to figure out how to activate it on their own? No need for a good grasp on the fundamentals of Mana Manipulation? Training?" Suspicion flashed across Joe's face. "Did you figure this out so you could find a way to sell rituals anyone could use?"

"I absolutely did," Taka rubbed his hands together gleefully. "You should see the profit margin on even Beginner-ranked rituals. I can't imagine how much you'd be able to generate with... how powerful can you make them? Master rank? That's comparable to an Artifact-rank building, like the Pathfinder's Hall we're standing in!"

"I love the concept, and fantastic work coming up with this! As for selling, that just isn't all that important to me anymore. I can't even tell you how happy I am to say that." Joe offered a crooked smile. "Money is great for buying things I can't make myself, but that's pretty much just food and clothing at this point. Not much on Midgard is worth bringing to higher worlds, and I can tell you that gold and silver only matter as crafting materials up there. On that note, who else has something neat to show?"

Hannah half-heartedly raised a hand, looking like a functioning member of society instead of a crypt dweller now that Joe's auras had brought her up to peak health and cleanliness. "I wasn't going to bring this up, but since you mentioned you couldn't generate food with rituals... don't laugh, okay? But sometimes it was easier to get my hands on ritual materials than it was to go grocery shopping. Here, this is a copy of what I called the 'Ritual of Marching Fishes'."

"Plural of fish is *fish*," Taka muttered under his breath, clearly annoyed at how quickly they had moved on after talking about his contribution.

"It lets me summon a large number of regular fish, and they stick around after the ritual ends, if I start to butcher them." Even as Hannah spoke, Joe's eyes were drinking in the ritual diagram she had provided.

He tapped a small section of it, but before he could ask what it meant, she brightened and explained, "I was using it so often that I got bored, and I found out that, if I add in a piece of metal I've been carrying around—doesn't matter if it was something like a ring or just a copper coin that had been in my pocket for a while—I could add a secondary effect. In this case, it lets me kind of command the fish. I can make them move in a certain direction, stuff like that. Not super useful unless there's water around, but... still kind of fun."

"Sounds like you're on the path to figuring out either some kind of rudimentary version of Ritualistic Enchanting or Ritualistic Forging skill," Joe murmured as he handed the ritual diagram back to her. "Frankly, it could go either way, especially if it's only metal that it works with. I'm sure we're going to get a lot of use out of this, or a good meal in a pinch!"

Clearly wanting to be a part of the conversation, Kirby leaned forward and handed Joe another document with an exasperated look on her face. "Here. I was trying to figure out a way to leave a trail of darkness where I walked, to give me proper evil overlord vibes. Somehow, I made this instead."

"Ritual of Cloud Step." Joe read out loud, his eyes flicking down to start going over the details of the circles. "Student-ranked? Impressive. Produces a rainbow fog under the target's feet each time they fully extend them or take a step. Okay... I'm looking for what it is that makes this Student ranked. It's really well put together, very tight design, and I don't see many ways to improve it or let it be a lower rank. Why then...?"

"It lasts *so* long. A solid six hours, at least." Kirby's lips pulled back in a sneer as she stared at the document. "Not to mention, it fails to describe exactly how large that 'puff' of rainbow fog is. You're basically making a decent-sized cloud with each step, and it holds together for several minutes at a time, shifting through the colors of the rainbow, until it finally bursts into sparkling raindrops that fall to the ground. Not exactly the vibe I was going for."

Unlike the others, Joe didn't immediately hand the diagram back to its creator. Instead, his mind was spinning with ideas as he stared at the magical symbols. "Would you mind if I kept this for a while? I was able to memorize the other two right away, but I might need a little while with this one. It... this could be really useful to me, pretty much immediately."

"Keep it," Kirby waved flippantly. "I've moved on to barrier-type rituals anyway."

Big_Mo eagerly shifted forward, pulling out his own docu-ment, but a single glance had Joe shaking his head. Instead of accepting the proffered item, he extended his hand and mani-fested several copies of the Standard Ritual Combat manual. "Sorry, buddy. I already have an enhanced version of that one for you. Actually, these are for all of you. I finally found other Ritualists out there, all the way up on Vanaheim. Turns out they've been working on becoming high-level combatants for a long time, imagine that. But, if I'm not mistaken-"

Joe clapped a hand on the dejected Big_Mo's shoulder, a wide smile on his own face, "-creating that should have at least given you the first level in the Enchanted Ritual Circles skill. Am I right?"

"You already know about that?" The surprisingly muscular

man reluctantly grinned. "Never mind, who do I think I'm talking to? Do you know how I can improve it?"

"As a matter of fact, I do." Now, the bald Ritualist turned to include each of the others in the conversation. "Like I said, now that I can come back here as needed, I can offer advice, goodies from other worlds, and bring your baseline power up to snuff. I'll walk you through all of this, but the best thing for us to do is get you out there practicing ritual combat. There's an entire quest line for it. How about all of you get geared up, and I'll take you hunting for a couple weeks?"

"Right now?" Kirby blinked rapidly in surprise at the sudden shift in conversation. "Joe, we can't just walk away. We have jobs."

Giving her a few moments to think about the words she had just said, Joe patiently bobbed his head and waited. Then, clearing his throat, he raised an eyebrow and replied, "That doesn't sound like something an overlord would say... that's minion talk."

Her response was completely over the top. Kirby let out a sharp gasp, blanched, and stumbled away looking as though she were about to faint. "W-what? *No*! You're right! I'll go get packed!"

Any of the arguments the others were going to voice faded as the delicate-looking Ritualist ran off to her room. Big_Mo shot Joe a questioning look. "Are we leaving right now?"

Joe started to respond, but before he could get a word out, he felt a sharp tug on his mana. Before doing anything else, he summoned his notifications.

Query has activated! No reply.

Skill increase! Query (Student 0 → Student 1).

"Let's call it *soon*." Joe allowed his eyes to roll upward slightly, fixing on a point above them where the temple attached to the Pathfinder's Hall. "I have a meeting with my faction leader. A long overdue conversation. Get ready and plan not to come back into town until we're done."

They parted ways, and in a moment, Joe was alone in the

underground chamber. Taking a deep breath, he steeled himself for an in-person meeting with Tatum. "To the temple I go-"

Joe froze, his foot halfway to landing on the first step, as the hidden portion collapsed, the stairs dropping into the floor and forming into a long tunnel with a gentle curve. "No. This isn't... is this a secret passage between the Pathfinder's Hall and the temple? Celestial *feces*, I love this place."

He ran his hand along the newfound rough stone wall, fingers following a slight groove which had formed in the masonry as it had been created. Even though he'd technically been the one to construct the place, it was clear that the powerful Artifact had gained awareness and begun adjusting itself to better suit whatever personality it had started to develop.

Seeing as the construct was directly influenced by Occultatum—better known as the 'Hidden Deity'—Joe wouldn't be surprised to find all sorts of new outlets and tucked away corners. It didn't take long to reach the end of the tunnel, and as the floor began sloping upward, the ceiling began to crack. Warm firelight washed over him, and the stone moved out of the way as dark water began pouring in.

Instead of soaking him, the fluid he recognized as coming off of Tatum's shrine instead ran down the slope, only to be sucked into the same channels cut into the tunnel he had been running his fingers along. As he ascended into the temple, Joe found himself pausing as he looked around. Even after everything that had happened to him—moving between worlds, wars against monsters and Elves, gaining an immense amount of power—the Pathfinder's Hall was still the first truly *powerful* permanent thing he had created.

The room had expanded further since the last time he had been there, as though the world were slowly being persuaded to allow the space to warp slowly over time. The book-shaped altar in the center of the pantheon display stood proudly, ink-like water pouring from its stone pages and into the stream which ran around the room. Thick shadows played across the wall, only made darker by the strong flames flaring from the shrine of Tommulus and the matching sconces that had sprung up around the area.

Yet, there was a surprising amount of greenery in the space as well. A full-blown miniature, delicate forest flourished along the edges of the stream, looking more like an illusion than reality as the roots of trees dipped into the black water, and tiny deer no bigger than his pinky peeked out of the underbrush, only to vanish into the miniscule forest.

Wooden bridges spanned the water, clearly having grown alongside the room as it expanded out, to create either a direct path to each of the shrines or a pleasant indoor park someone could roam around to allow their mind to calm. Taking the direct path, as he was known for, Joe strolled to the central altar, allowing his palm to land firmly on the surface of the book.

In an instant, he was somewhere *else*.

The stars seemed different overhead, long streaks of light instead of far-distant pinpricks. Blinking a few times, he looked around, finding himself atop the peak of a mountain in an open-air temple once again, with only shifting clouds hiding the world below and strange, impossible lights flickering far, far above.

"Joe." The warm voice wrapped around the Ritualist like a hug, and Joe looked up to see Tatum in his gigantified form sitting in a contemplative pose as his gaze shifted to his first-ever follower. "It's good to have you back."

"Same," Joe murmured, and for a long few minutes, neither of them spoke another word. Instead, they shared a moment of quiet recognition, gratitude, perhaps even relief. Then the Ritualist tilted his head back, his gaze drawn upward to see what had been holding Tatum's attention. He felt a shudder go through his muscles but found himself unable to tear his eyes off the sky.

What he had mistakenly taken as some form of distorted view of the stars was instead an impossible canvas of shifting, crackling lines of power and meaning stitched together on an impossible canvas of black lavender. His eyes widened as shapes began to take form—symbols, ideas, hints of inspiration he didn't fully understand, but *desperately* wanted-

Then it was gone, and he felt a deep sense of loss as his eyes darted around, seeking the odd snaking ouroboros wrapped around a world—no, it *was* a world, or was it-

Darkness filled his vision, and for a moment, Joe was concerned that he had been struck blind, only for his other senses to kick in and inform him that there was a hand draped over his eyes. "Joe. Don't do that. Even I don't dare stare into the void for too long. When a truth has been lost, passed entirely out of living memory, it falls into the void. But deep truths like that don't like to be hunted. They unravel if you seek too much, and a mortal mind will go mad trying to force it to stay. Whether it is ancient wisdom, inspiration, or even a glimpse into the future, none of that is something you are meant to find *in that way*."

Joe exhaled sharply, realizing that the pounding pain behind his eyes, which had gone unnoticed until now, was already beginning to fade away. "Noted. Yeah, not sure what that was, but... it was *so* interesting."

"You know what else is interesting?" Even though it was clear that Tatum was simply trying to redirect Joe, the Ritualist couldn't help but get excited as he saw the sly smile on Tatum's face, and the broad wink he sent his way as the deity loudly proclaimed, as if there were someone listening in:

"You've been a loyal follower of mine from the start. Faithful, even when the path was hidden. Finally, *finally*... the time has come for you to claim some of your rightful rewards."

CHAPTER TWENTY

Tatum waved his hand dramatically, a soft shimmer of lavender light warping the space his fingers passed, symbols and glyphs unfolding like a lotus blossom blooming, forming into perfectly shaped letters which hung in the air. As he read over the densely packed words, the deity spoke with his normal smooth rhythm. "Busy, busy indeed. You are currently tied as the forerunner of humanity and have been recklessly charging forward, which I have greatly appreciated as your sponsor. Still, you've *really* let things pile up."

The words came out harsher than Joe expected, and it was only the smile the deity couldn't hide that let Joe maintain his cool. "First and foremost, as they are already attached to your Akashic record, you have spell upgrades which are long over-due. Several are queued for evolution, some with distinct branching paths, such as Exquisite Shell. *With these*, there is no other option but to upgrade them."

The Ritualist didn't miss the extra emphasis Tatum had been adding to his words, though he made sure to keep his mouth shut as the intensely powerful entity shifted to a different topic. "By the way, I'm very pleased to see that you have made it all the way to Vanaheim so far and have found powerful and wise mentors to give you guidance. This reminds me, you're also due rewards from the quest I gave you on Alfenheim to make sure Gaia didn't remain the sole deity on the planet. Problem is, that was mainly meant to be a daily reward you earned by coming back to one of my shrines, and it's been a long, *long* time since you visited."

"About those spells-" Joe *definitely* didn't let out a nervous chuckle at the thought of having been missing out for so long. "-An upgrade, you say?"

"Mmhm." Tatum's lips were twitching, and Joe didn't miss how his eyes flicked up over his shoulder, as if locking onto someone standing there and carefully monitoring the conversation. "But let me finish. You're also meant to get new spells, *very* powerful ones at that. Another thing, you've earned a reward for your Reductionist specialization. *Fantastic* choice to specialize in that, by the way. Don't think I ever got to tell you that in person."

"Not too shabby-"

Joe was cut off with a hurried, "Hold on. Lastly, the sheer number of followers you've brought me is closing in on, well, let's just say every Dwarf on Jotunheim, plus a good chunk of Humanity. Now, since you have long since reached maximum reputation with me, that's going to be rolled into a major boon from me."

Heart pounding in his chest, Joe didn't bother to hide the wide smile from his face as he took in all of the information. Still, the subtle signs Tatum had been giving him kept Joe from simply taking all of this at face value. After so long working together with the deity, he had learned that sometimes there was more to be gained from bargaining than simply accepting what was offered.

"That's amazing, and thank you so much! Look... I'm really happy with what I have now, and frankly am looking to build up my foundation more than I am looking to add more to the pile of things to learn and spend time on. Is it possible, and again, don't think me ungrateful, but is it *possible* that there's an option other than taking all of that individually? Spell upgrades aside, as you mentioned those are already part of who I am."

Tatum looked up and scratched at the stubble on his neck casually, too casually to be real, going by the trembles of excitement he was trying to mask. "I mean, I completely understand where you are coming from. I guess I'm not sure what you are asking for *specifically?*"

"It might not be standard, but, could you just kind of... roll all of it together? Give me a nice, consolidated reward? Even if it's a little less than all of the other stuff would have been worth in total, I don't mind too much." Joe splayed his hands to the side pleadingly, trying not to overact and give the game away but still trying to show that *he* was the one requesting this.

"I mean, I have no preference whatsoever, and certainly wouldn't want to advise you to take anything less than what you're owed." Tatum shrugged his shoulders slowly, pulling a face and holding the gesture just a *fraction* of a second too long to be anything other than feigned disinterest. "But, I mean, if that's what you really want... I'm sure we can consolidate things down to a clean, elegant solution for you. But only if you really want-"

"Yes, that." Joe nodded so fast that the sheer speed would have snapped his neck were he a baseline human. "My current mentor is a Class Sage, and both he and Grandmaster Pete recommended I figure out some way to trim down my skills to make a foundation I can really build off of. While I understand I could gain powerful skills or spells, I wouldn't want to look like I'm throwing his advice in his face. Really, you'd be helping me out, not to mention I'm curious to see what that would look like."

"Well, I am known as the Hidden God for a reason. Curiosity is practically a moral imperative of my faction's followers." Tatum held up one hand in warning. "Still, there's no going back from this; you can't try to undo the deal after it has been made. Part of the power of the rewards will be consumed simply in the consolidation."

"That's what I want," Joe stubbornly insisted, earning himself a faint smile from Tatum as dark electricity crackled around the deity's eyes. "Err…. you okay there?"

"**Accepted**." Tatum boomed out, his voice rolling out and echoing oddly off the cloud layer surrounding the mountaintop temple. "First, though you have previously spoken aloud that you wish for me to offer you ways to shield your rituals, with your current skill levels, it is outside the bounds of what I may offer to you."

Joe immediately realized what the deity was trying to tell him: only as a Grandmaster, or perhaps even as a Sage, would he be able to put such protections in place directly into rituals. A part of his mind immediately began wondering if there were ways to get the same effect using some of the other Ritualist class skills, but he refocused as Tatum spoke again.

"The power of each of the minor boons shall be funneled into the specialization reward you are due." Tatum's hands moved with deceptive swiftness, leaving afterimages in the air which made him appear to have five, fifty, then hundreds of arms before slowing and leaving traces of power behind.

Each of these consolidated as tiny constellations Joe just somehow *knew* were the representations of the skills grafted into his soul. Remaining silent, he looked on in awe as Tatum continued his working. "The inherent power of that specialization is to take many different things and distill them. Through this, I offer you the chance to take any of your skills or spells and condense them into a distilled essence of skills, which will be used to directly empower or slightly alter the skills you choose to keep. Choose now which of your skills you will sacrifice for this process."

"An inch wide, a mile deep. No need for me to keep any spells… I sure hope I understood what you wanted me to do,

Mirascible." Luckily for him, Joe had already spent quite a bit of time going over his exhaustive skill list and knew exactly what he wanted to keep and what he was willing to give up. Even so, with the plethora he was about to sacrifice, he knew this wasn't going to be a pleasant experience.

Taking a deep breath, the Ritualist quickly intoned, "Acid spray, Cone of Cold, Dark Lightning Strike, Mend, Planar Shift, Wither Plant... Infernal Conflagration."

"Dark Lightning Strike and Planar Shift cannot be removed in this way, as they aren't something you generated on your own. They were given to you by me. Mend is similar, but I think I can... yes, so long as you keep a version of it in the Lay on Hands spell, that's fine." Tatum was consulting some information Joe didn't have access to, but now wasn't the time for him to ask more questions. "Go on... what else?"

"I definitely want to keep my Artisan Body and the skills that help me control my Ritual Orbs... but some of the rewards I've gotten, even from the king and queen, just aren't as useful anymore." Though he had to force the words out of himself, Joe understood the implication that whatever power he gave up would be returned to him, at least in some manner. "Essence Cy-"

Hack. Tatum loudly coughed into a closed fist, then looked at Joe as if startled that he had done so. "Sorry, don't mind me! Go on, anything you want to be rid of, it's your right to do so."

"Uh... right." Joe spoke slightly slower, and to his great relief was not shown even a twitch of displeasure as he stated, "Magical Synesthesia? Oh! *Oh*! Mental Manipulation Resistance! Can I get rid of that? Please? It directly states in the skill that, at the Beginner ranks, I'll start to go insane if I die, and I've already gotten it almost halfway through Journeyman!"

"You have earned the right to get rid of any skill you have at this moment," Tatum repeated in an *extremely* neutral tone.

"Great, then, Polearm Mastery." Thinking for a moment, Joe moved to the next section of his mentally partitioned skills. "Words of Power, Written. I'm just not creating talismans or spell scrolls, and I'd love to see what I can get from this. Message? Yes... I can achieve the same effect with rituals without scraping someone's brain raw or making my ears bleed. I use Natural Magical Material Creation to create Aspect jars, so not that. Spellbinding... yes. I want to keep all of my Lore skills, so... I guess that's it. Huh. When it's all put down like that, it somehow doesn't seem as bloated as it did before."

"Losing ten powerful skills is nothing to sniff at." Tatum tilted his head to the side, just before making another offer that was like a bombshell in Joe's brain. "Is that all, then? I notice you are not using several of your titles, and those are functionally the same as externally applied skills. Would you like to combine them in as well?"

Trying not to hyperventilate at the sudden knowledge that such a thing was possible, though he *fully* understood how much this would change how titles were viewed if it got out, Joe swallowed and managed to squeak out through a suddenly very dry mouth, "Sure. Take Superhero Lander, Pierce the Darkest Night, Anti-mage, Immovable Object, and Councilman Of Novusheim."

"I can do all except the last, as that is not yours to give away." Tatum frowned ever so slightly. "In fact, when you return to Jotunheim, I believe it won't be yours at all."

"What are they doing over there?" Joe inquired with sudden dark suspicion. "It's Stu, isn't it?"

Tatum's lips pressed firmly shut, so the Ritualist just tossed his hands in the air and confirmed his choices. Still, the deity didn't do anything with the tiny constellations hanging in the air, instead moving on to a new topic. "Now, as for the power of the major boon you are due for bringing so many followers to me, would you like to manually decide how to distribute that in the same manner, or would you like me to apply it in the same way? Following that, would you like to go through each of the possibilities for changes in your skills, or would you like me to apply this all according to your subconscious preferences and how you use your remaining skills?"

Joe was just about to commit to however long it would take to go through and fine-tune each of his options, but the way Tatum licked his lips—and how a haunted look appeared in his eyes—convinced the Ritualist to simply trust that the deity who had always been working behind the scenes to help him out wouldn't be doing anything to harm him at this point. "I trust you, Tatum. Do what you think is best."

"Ah... in that case..." The clouds around the temple began to roil, lightning flashing among them and crackling into the open air in a bizarre reversal of nature. "The areas I have the most sway in adjusting are the skills directly under my purview. Only because you have a truly *impressive* amount of options available to you will it work to adjust things in this way. Don't be too concerned with what I'm about to tell you, but I hope it's understandable that, generally speaking, changing class skills directly is seen as a terrible idea."

Not letting Joe's imagination run wild, Tatum followed up his previous statement with, "Yet... in your case, your special-izations create useless redundancies. Before I go any further, know that allowing me to adjust them as I see fit will *reduce* some of the prestige options that will be available to you the next time you choose a *specialization*. Yet, those that remain will be more well-tailored to your situation-"

"Just *do* it, Tatum," Joe spat out, not sure how much longer he could brace for the incoming changes before he pulled a muscle in his neck or something. "I said I trust you, go ahead and believe me."

"Then it shall be done."

The very mountain the temple was situated on began to tremble as Tatum slowly lifted his hands. Dense power filled the air, which folded in around the duo until it was as solid as layered silk. The constellations representing Joe's skills began to move slightly, as though he were on the surface of a planet slowly rotating. One by one, the skills and spells he had chosen to sacrifice began to grow brighter, as power began to gently swirl around and into them.

As soon as he was ready, Tatum sent Joe an apologetic look that both beings were fully aware that this would be a painful process—they were essentially going to be performing surgery directly on his soul without the benefit of anesthesia. To his credit, neither hesitated. Joe merely clenched his fists and took a deep breath while Tatum flicked his fingers and tapped one of the constellations.

Pop.

The tiny constellation vanished, collapsing in on itself before breaking into millions of glowing particles which fell to the bottom of the bubble in the air it had been suspended in, still dragged along as the rest of the star clusters spun around Joe's spasming body.

For his part, the Ritualist's knees buckled, yet he didn't fall. Veins of light spider-webbed across his body as immense power flowed through him, lighting up the ritual that had been etched into his body upon choosing the Reductionist specialization. He could *feel* Tatum working, how the visual representation was simply to give him a view at what was truly happening deep within himself.

Pop.

Pop.

Pop.

Each burst of light made the human want to lash out, to fight against the process, but at that point, there was nothing to be done. He was held in place as firmly as if a mountain had landed on him, and even his mana pool was being suppressed and directed by the deity flooding him with what could only be called divine power.

Stardust poured from the ruptured constellations, the glitter now moving counter to the constellations, drifting downward until it had collected above Tatum's outstretched palm. Energy gathered then, making the previous potency seem like a trickle dripping into an ocean. The stardust began to be imbued with a heady cocktail of soul-stuff and primordial power, then the energized particulate swept away, flying through the air like a billion meteorites and vanishing into the heart of the other constellations, some far more thickly than others.

The clouds around the open-aired temple tore apart with a roar, spiraling upward as tornadoes which reached toward them like grasping tentacles. The moon appeared in the sky above them, looking as though it were falling out of the heavens as it expanded to cover nearly half of the entire void—only to crack like an egg and release a roaring dragon that froze in place. It then began to dissolve, as though it had been a projection on a cloud bank that was being blown away.

Comets streaked backward across the heavens, trailing shimmering lines which left behind visions of mythical creatures galloping or flying across them.

Even so, Tatum never bothered to so much as *glance* at the phenomena, fully intent on his task.

Joe's remaining skills began to shine, flaring with newfound purpose as they were changed, evolved, or adjusted. The Ritualist trembled, was thrown about mentally, crushed a thousand times... then he was simply standing, locking eyes with a concerned looking deity who immediately let out a sigh of relief when awareness returned to his eyes. "Did I pass out?"

"No. That would have been quite the mercy though, wouldn't it?" Tatum chuckled under his breath, gently placing a hand on Joe's shoulder and taking a slow, shuddering breath.

"Should I be worried at the sheer amount of relief flowing off of you right now, Tatum? If you weren't confident in me coming out of this, I would have liked to know that ahead of time." Joe tried to smack the hand off of him, but might as well have punched an Ebonsteel wall.

"But then you might have said 'no'!" Joe's jaw dropped, but Tatum only laughed and backed away. "Just kidding... mostly. Just a couple more quick choices, and I'll let you take a look at everything all at once. First, the spells I get to upgrade as a separate reward, then I'll explain what happened with... oh, nearly a quarter of the power I committed to this. Also, there were a few... *oddities* you should be made aware of."

"Oddities," Joe repeated in a flat tone. "Such as?"

"For one, 'Query' was shattered and added into the mix by —er… an outside source. Sorry about that; apparently you'll have to directly visit shrines to get advice from me from now on. On the plus side, that means I was able to devote its pending upgrade's power to the mix. Also, the process unlinked each of the skills bound in your Ritual Orbs, and a few of them gained levels because of that." Tatum winced and glanced at the sky. "I recommend looking over the entirety of your status carefully to see what all has changed. As far as I'm concerned, there's only one… *less* than savory change, but, again, this first."

Congratulations! Exquisite Shell is ready to evolve! Please choose one of the available options. These options have been generated based on usage and your desires.

1. *Exquisite Shell (Refined). This is a direct upgrade of the Exquisite Shell base spell. Effect: For every point of mana in this spell, negate .85 damage from primary sources of magic, .85 damage from primary sources of physical damage, and .8 damage from elemental effects. Increase conversion by .02n where 'n' equals skill level.*

2. *Exquisite Shell (Open Lattice). This evolution comes from your largest pain point of the spell, allowing the Exquisite Shell to be maintained and repaired with conscious effort. Effect: For every point of mana in this spell, negate .75 damage from primary sources of damage. Increase conversion by .02n where 'n' equals skill level. Mana can be added to the structure after damage is taken to bring it back to its full capacity. In lieu of elemental damage reduction, this spell instead provides immunity to non-magical sources of extreme heat or cold.*

3. *Exquisite Shell (Twin Shell). This upgrade allows the spell to be cast twice, where the first layer operates as normal, while a secondary shell is held in reserve. If the primary shell is destroyed, the secondary activates instantly. Both must be*

destroyed or deactivated to refresh the spell. Reserves an additional 5% of total mana.

"This isn't even a choice. Number two for sure. Next." A thrill ran down Joe's spine as he locked in his choice. "I can supply power while taking damage to make it last longer in the first place? Absolutely."

Congratulations! Dark Lightning Strike has reached a branching path! Please choose one of the available options.

A. *Dark Chain Lightning. No longer are you reaching up to strike your foes from on high. Instead, a consecrated bolt of dark lightning unleashes from your hand to your target. Effect: The lightning bolt deals 10n dark damage to all affected beings, where n = skill level. Each reputation rank with Occultatum allows the Dark Chain Lightning to branch one additional time after striking the initial target (Current rank: Extended family = 5 branches). Each tier in this spell increases the number of times the branched lightning can jump to a distinct target (Current tier: Expert = 6 jumps). Total possible targets struck: 31.*

B. *Light Chain Lightning. Under the influence of your Light Intelligence, you have severed the divine link required to cast this spell. The lightning is now yours to create and command, focused entirely through your Intelligence and the purity of your arcane endeavors. Effect: The lightning bolt deals 10n arcane lightning damage to all affected beings OR arcane lightning damage if impacted by the ground spread, where n = skill level. When striking only a single target, the damage of this spell is hyper focused on its target, piercing through 50% of resistances or immunity to lightning or magical damage.*

"Why is this an 'A' or 'B' when the last was numbers?" Joe's gentle complaint was only a passing thought, as this was a far more difficult choice. Glancing at Tatum revealed only a firm poker face, with no possibility of help or explanation for the very different options. "Essentially, this would have let me break it down to be added to the mix if I had chosen it ahead of time, huh? Well…"

Joe hesitated for longer than he expected of himself, but finally made his choice, locking in Dark Chain Lightning. "I see no reason to separate out further from you, buddy. If I want arcane lightning, I'll make a ritual for it. But even my new mentor begrudgingly admitted that I should keep a few powerful spells around, just in case."

Tatum nodded at him gratefully, still not meeting his eyes— probably because they both knew he had engineered the situation to make sure Joe kept the spell. There was one last notification waiting for Joe, but this time there was no choice for him to make.

Congratulations! Mass Resurrection Aura has been given a new effect: All damage taken by anyone who has been resurrected is reduced by 80% for 5 minutes.

"Okay, with that all out of the way…" Joe popped open his character sheet and decided to take a look at what had sent Tatum on a roller coaster of emotional responses. "…let's see how it went."

~ Joe's Current Character Sheet ~

Name: Joe 'Tatum's Chosen Legend' Class: Reductionist
Profession I: Arcanologist (Max)
Profession II: Ritualistic Alchemist (7/20)
Profession III: Grandmaster's Apprentice (15/25)
Profession IV: Ritualistic Metalworker (3/20)
Profession V: Ritualistic Numerologist Novitiate (1/5)
Profession VI: Arcane Enchanting Theorist (0/5)

Character Level: 30 Exp: 465,000 Exp to next level: 31,000 (Locked.)
Rituarchitect Level: 13 Exp: 87,450 Exp to next level: 3,550
Reductionist Level: 11 Exp: 68,075 Exp to next level: 9,925

Hit Points: 3,812/4,171
Mana: 8,888/11,933
Mana regen: 120.09/sec
Stamina: 1,331/2,233
Stamina regen: 6.85/sec

Characteristic: Raw score

Strength (Bound): 278
Dexterity: 277
Stoic Constitution (Broken!): 139
Light Intelligence (Bound): 283
Wisdom: 270
Dark Charisma: 229
Karmic Perception: 280
Luck: 223
Karmic Luck: 99 → 100

Traits:

- *Unsuppressed Growth. 10% of Mental Characteristics feed into the base value of their Physical Characteristic counterpart. You may now train each Characteristic twice per day.*
- *Karmic King: The secrets of Karmic Luck will be far more receptive to being understood by your fragile mind.*
- *Boon and Bane: You gave a dark spell an upgrade and now cannot wear hats.*
- *Stoic Enhancement (New!). 20% knockback and fall damage resistance. 10% magic resistance. 25% intimidation resistance. (Gained from the titles Anti-mage, Superhero Lander, and Immovable Object being absorbed by Stoic Constitution.)*
- *Synergist's Intuition (New!). Though the original reward for completing the challenge given by the title 'Never Satisfied' was meant to be a skill, it was destroyed upon creation, instead adding itself directly into your self-perception. You can now*

possibly detect and interpret synergy between skills you personally possess. The stronger the underlying connection between two or more of your skills, the more clearly you can sense the potential effect of combining them.

Equipped Titles:
Tatum's Chosen Legend. You are the Legendary Chosen of a deity and have earned his respect. Effect:

- +20% speed of learning any water or darkness related abilities.
- -10% learning speed of any fire or light based abilities.
- +20% favor gained.
- +30% damage against opponents who have a higher level than you.
- -15% Damage against opponents who have a lower level than you.
- Reputation gained at 2.5x normal rate, and lost at .25 the normal rate.
- Capturing places of power now proceeds 25% faster.
- You will be worth 50% more experience and favor gain to champions of other gods who manage to kill you.

Architect of Artifacts. Effect: Any action you take that will result in the construction of a new structure will boost the building's overall statistics and potential boosts by 10%!
Monarch of Mana (Upgradable). You are the Monarch of Mana, the first person to reach a mana pool so vast (10,000) that releasing it in one burst could permanently change a kingdom-sized portion of a planet.

- Effect: Once per 3 months (90 standard days or 2,160 hours) you are able to instantly refill the entirety of your mana pool.

Held Titles:
Councilman Of Novusheim (pending removal).

- *Privileges:*
  - *While in the area controlled by the Town of Novusheim, you have the authority to declare a state of emergency, requisition resources for purposes of bettering the Town, ordering members of the Legion to action, and pass judgment on crimes.*
- *Responsibilities:*
  - *Abusing your privileges can lead to being removed from the council. You must work for the betterment of the citizens of Novusheim.*
  - *You must be present for 8 of every 10 Council meetings if you are in the area. (Failed!)*
  - *Bonus: You are the first human on the council. All human citizens will be inclined to offer you discounts, work for or with you, and are much more likely to accept your orders without complaint.*

Combat Skills:

Corify (Student VII → Journeyman VI), improved by combining the infused deity-empowered remnant stardust from Cone of Cold, this spell now applies the 'Brittle' debuff when on hit. Effect:

- *Add 1n% chance that any creature killed within five seconds of Corify being cast will solidify a Core upon death.*
- *Applies 1 stack of Brittle to the target on impact, increasing the damage they take from blunt damage by 2%.*

Cost: 100 mana. Cooldown: 5 seconds.

Dark Lightning Strike (Expert III) → Dark Chain Lightning (Expert III). No longer are you reaching up to strike your foes from on high. Instead, a consecrated bolt of dark lightning unleashes from your hand to your target. Effect:

- *The lightning bolt deals 10n dark damage to all affected beings, where n = skill level.*
- *Each reputation rank with Occultatum allows the Dark Chain Lightning to branch one additional time after striking the initial target (Current rank: Extended family = 5 branches).*
- *Each tier in this spell increases the number of times the branched lightning can jump to a distinct target (Current tier: Expert = 6 jumps). Total possible targets struck: 31.*
- *Cost: 365 (100+5n) mana. Cooldown: 95 (360-5n) seconds. Each hand may cast this spell with its own cooldown.*

Exquisite Shell (Open Lattice) (Expert 0). This evolution allows the Exquisite Shell to be maintained and repaired with conscious effort. Effect:

- *For every point of mana in this spell, negate .75 damage from primary sources of damage. Increase conversion by .02n where 'n' equals skill level. Mana can be added to the structure after damage is taken to bring it back to its full capacity.*
- *In lieu of elemental damage reduction, this spell instead provides immunity to non-magical sources of extreme heat or cold.*

Mana Reserved: 10% of total mana used to cast.

Haunting Shadows (Master I). Empowered by a massive amount of divine mana.
What was once reactive has become relentless. Your connection to the shadow realm is no longer just a defense mechanism: it is a dark mirror of your intent, reflecting lavender light. Effect:

- *Upon any attack on the caster, a shadowy doppelganger appears next to the offender, dealing a retaliatory slap worth 1+n% of the damage of their attack, where n = skill level. Current (62% damage return, no maximum.)*
- *The shadow becomes a curse, intermittently materializing near the offender for 12 hours, dealing up to 1% of their total HP*

as dark damage per strike. Shadow echoes ignore 50% of all armor, magic resistance, and immunities, phasing through worldly defenses like mist through fingers.

- There is now no limit to the number of shadows that can be created on a single target. Upon the caster's death, all shadows are dispelled.
- When you attack or cast a spell, there is a 25% chance to generate a shadow echo—a spectral version of your action that strikes the same target for 50% of the original potency. This now includes group spells, rituals, and channeled abilities.

This spell is now a fully toggleable passive, and will only not activate on your behalf should you preemptively choose to turn it off. This will only turn off the active retaliatory effect, not the percentage-based chances of generating a shadow echo. You may also choose to cancel the haunting manually. Vengeance need not be cruel.

Lay on Hands (Expert III). Elevated by blending the divine residue left behind by Mental Manipulation Resistance, this spell now anchors clarity into the healing touch. Effect:

- Heals for $10n$, where $n = $ character level.
- Dark Affinity creatures receive double the healing effect.
- For 10 seconds after casting, the target gains a 10% chance per second to break free from mental effects (including but not limited to charms, fears, confusion, or hallucinations). This mental clarity effect is immune to suppression while active.
- Each hand can cast this spell independently, with each having its own cooldown.

Mana Cost: 5n. Cooldown: 3 seconds.

Mass Resurrection Aura (Student VII). This is a spell granted only to the champion of a deity, and only one follower may have this spell at a time. Effect:

- *Once per standard week (168 hours), you can channel the divine energies of Occultatum, bringing back to life any slain entities within n+5 meters that are within n+class level levels of you, within n+class level minutes of being killed.*
- *This spell will last 'n' seconds upon casting, reverting the deaths of any non-hostile entities in that range.*

Upon activation, you will lose access to all mana for 60-n minutes, where n = skill level.

Neutrality Aura (Expert 0). Improved to its maximum possible potency by combining the infused deity-empowered remnant stardust from Acid Spray, this aura now dissolves corruption, filth, and residue. A cleansing field of stability surrounds the caster, promoting equilibrium between self and environment. Effect:

- *Rapidly dissolves unclaimed trash-tier items or accumulated filth within its range.*
- *Removes all negative debuffs from friendly or neutral targets at double the rate of natural decomposition and strips positive effects from hostile entities within range at the same rate. Doubly effective against internal poisons, accelerating purging processes.*
- *Heals 1n HP/sec to non-hostile creatures within 5 feet (where n = skill level).*
- *Reduces incoming magical damage by 0.5n passively.*
- *Gathers moisture from the air, passively hydrating friendly targets over time.*
- *Acts as a gas exchange system, replacing blood gases with ambient air components, allowing for extended underwater or toxic-environment survival without breathing.*

Range: 0.25n → .3n feet by absorbing the Journeyman bonus. Mana Reserved: 10% of total mana used to cast.

Planar Shift (Journeyman IV). Awakened by the sacred stardust dust from

Mend to weave regenerative threads into the bond between summoner and summoned. Reach through the veil and call forth entities from beyond the known planes, bound by pact, intent, and ritual. Each summoned being is tethered to a living page within a divine summoning tome, detailing their nature, bindings, and dismissal rites. Effect:

- *Allows the summoning of a planar being of your choosing from the tome.*
- *Comparatively easy control over any creature of Journeyman rank or below.*
- *Summoned creatures now receive a passive minor Regeneration effect. This healing is permanent while they remain summoned, repairing injuries over time and enhancing longevity during sustained combat.*
- *Standardized skill progression: To increase the level of this skill, maintain summon control for one hour per current skill level.*

Body and Mind Skills:

Artisan Body (Refined) (Student VI). Your body is a canvas of progress, your mind a whetstone for potential. Every action, conscious or not, subtly shapes you. The path of refinement welcomes the steady hand and persistent heart. Effect:

- *All Characteristics gain a $1n\%$ increase in daily skill training efficiency, where n = skill level.*
- *Once per day, the first intentional use of a skill tied to a core Characteristic (Strength, Dexterity, Intelligence, etc.) gains a $+10\%$ bonus to training gain, as your body 'locks in' the movement or mindset more deeply.*
- *You are able to passively train a physical Characteristic at the cost of a portion of your Stamina Regeneration. Currently selected: Stoic Constitution.*

This passive bonus is automatically applied to the qualifying action and requires no activation.

Battle Meditation (Expert 0). A passive breathing pattern enhanced with the flavor of Mental Manipulation Resistance, which stabilizes thought and precision under duress. Those who wield exotic weapons find clarity in the rhythm of conflict itself. Effect:

- *Increases skill growth with exotic weapons by $2n\%$, where n = skill level.*
- *While in combat, this breathing pattern also grants $+.1\%$ resistance per skill level to disruptive effects like stagger, fear, or mild confusion—keeping your form intact under pressure. This benefit fades gradually over 10 seconds once the user is fully disengaged from combat.*

Coalescence (Journeyman VII). Through deep internal refinement, your mana becomes denser, more efficient, and easier to access. Effect:

- *$+1\%$ spell efficiency per skill level (up to a maximum of 50%)*
- *$+1\%$ mana regeneration per skill level*
- *Casting time reduced by 10%*

Combat Ritual Orbs (Journeyman VIII). Improved by combining the infused deity-empowered remnant stardust from Polearm Mastery, making the orbs more aggressive and responsive. Effect:

- *Each skill rank allows for the mastery of one Ritual Orb in combat.*
- *Each skill level increases damage dealt by $2.5n\%$.*
- *Durability of orbs tied to your Characteristics is increased by 25%.*
- *All active orbs gain a Psi Barrier that blocks damage equal to 25% of their max durability before degradation begins. This barrier regenerates fully after four hours of sleep.*

Essence Cycle (Journeyman IX → Expert IV). By powering your eyes with mana, you will be able to see the energy in all things. Practice will be needed in order to be able to ignore the ambient power in the environment. Higher levels of this skill will allow for more detailed studying of the energies. Masters of this skill are rumored to be able to perfectly learn spells simply by seeing them a single time. Effect:

- *$1n\%$ increased mana-visual sensation, where $n = $ skill level.*
- *You are now able to activate Essence Cycle without dropping into a meditative state. This allows you to follow mana emanations to their source, as well as moving between active and inactive states without an outside influence.*
- *While not being actively used, Essence Cycle gives a 5% boost to all attempts at Mana Manipulation, and increases your perception of mana by (Perception/4)%. (Current boost: 64.25%)*

Cost: 40 mana per second.

Magical Synesthesia (Student II). Infused with the collapsed brilliance of deity-gifted skill matter once held by Message <u>and</u> Hidden Sense, you have unlocked the voice of magic itself. Effect:

- *All items containing magic emit auditory signatures, now interpreted as descriptive words or emotive phrases, rather than abstract sounds.*
- *$+1n\%$ increase in mana-auditory sensitivity, where $n = $ skill level.*
- *Hidden entities, traps, illusions, or items hidden and forgotten now whisper softly to your senses. These whispers grow louder the more you focus on them, offering subtle clues without requiring visual contact.*
- *You now hear different types of mana in distinct tones or melodic textures.*

Mana Manipulation (Journeyman VII). You wield your internal mana with precision and intent, mastering its flow as both fuel and form. The bonuses you've earned have been made more cohesive. Effect:

- +0% total mana to skill level 30 (Apprentice 0), then an additional +1% increase per skill level.
- +25% spell efficiency.
- +10% stability to spells that cost more than 30% of your total mana pool
- Steady Flow: Increases spell stability by 10%, reduces casting time of all mana-using skills/spells by 10%.
- Can influence ambient mana in a radius of n/10 feet, where n = skill level.

Mental Manipulation Resistance (Journeyman III → Novice I). The skill you cast away returned on its own, slipping back into your mind like a shadow through a cracked window. It refuses to be forgotten. It grows in silence, returning stronger than ever. Some thoughts are hard to kill. Effect:

- Gains 300% skill experience until the Expert rank.
- Grants 10 + 1n% direct resistance to mental manipulation, where n = skill level.
- Protects against mental-impacting effects such as fear, mind control, magical seduction, and other intrusive mental influences.
- Grants 2.1n% reduced experience loss upon death.

Omnivault (Master IX). The ground has never been your friend. You have only ever seen it as something you must use as a launch pad to reach greater heights. Now, you are getting ever closer to a higher form of movement. Effect:

- You can now jump upward a distance of Strength/5 feet from a standstill.
- You can leap forward up to (Strength/5) × 3 feet while moving.

- *Your sense of balance in the air is unsurpassed, allowing for high-speed midair control.*
- *You may now reset your stance and use water in any state to Omnivault from.*
- *Each leap costs 1x% Stamina and 2x% mana, where x is the number of consecutive leaps.*
- *At double the x cost, you may leap or jump an additional time while still airborne.*
- *'Consecutive' means any jump within 3 seconds of the previous one.*

Teaching (Journeyman II). The ability to transfer knowledge is powerful, and you've slowly come to recognize its potential. Effect:

- *You can impart $(n - iT - s/2)$% of your skill level to those you are actively teaching. n = your skill level in Teaching. iT = inverse Tier of the skill being taught. s = number of students.*
- *In a public setting, bystanders may also learn the skill being taught at a reduced rate of: $n/2 - iT$*
- *Cost: $1n \times T$ mana or Stamina per second, where T is the Tier of the skill being transferred. No cooldown.*

Crafting Skills:

Alchemical Rituals (Apprentice V). Condensed by the sacred particulate which was all that remained of Ritualistic Alchemy, your alchemy has become purpose-bound to ritual casting. For you, alchemy exists to serve your rituals and nothing else. Effect:

- *Governs the ability to use alchemically enhanced components in rituals to alter, specialize, or broaden the effects of the ritual upon activation.*
- *$+1n$% to properly use alchemically enhanced components in rituals, where n = skill level. This applies to decisions like component selection, placement, and refinement. Bonus is also*

applied to skill checks when creating components meant for ritual use.

- *You now possess the knowledge to create alchemical items and reagents specifically for use within ritual circles. This means that all attempts to create alchemical items for non-ritual purposes **will automatically fail**. In return, when using your self-created alchemical components in your own ritual circles, there is a 10% chance that the item will neutralize all negative or unwanted side effects upon activation.*
- *All alchemical side effects caused during ritual use are 70% easier to understand, allowing for accurate recreation, manipulation, or mitigation in future attempts.*

Ascendant Matrix (Max). Your control over the reduction of mass to aspects has reached a precision so refined that even metaphysical loss is negated. Effect:

- *You are now able to create an Ascendant Matrix which retains all the previous properties of a Field Array.*
- *When an Aspect Jar is attached to the matrix, no aspects are lost during the reduction of an item.*
- *When the Ascendant Matrix is deployed over the entire project, all aspects are recaptured if lost when creating items.*

Beam to Bifrost. (Max). Divine mana has infused this spell with a touch of shadow. Using this spell sends you directly into the Bifrost, the cosmic crossroads, from which you may choose your next destination. Effect:

- *Instantly transports you into the Bifrost of the world you're currently on. From there, you may choose to travel to any previously accessible world.*
- *You may pre-bind the skill to activate as long as you're not in combat at the time of setting or activation using a delayed activation trigger. Triggers may include: Time-based (example: in 30 seconds.) Conditional (example: if I am silenced or*

imprisoned.) Sensory cues (example: when I say the word 'home'.)

- *Bound triggers persist until fulfilled, dispelled, or overwritten.*
- *Spell has no mana cost and no cooldown. Channel time: 10 seconds. (may be pre-channeled).*

Enchanted Ritual Circles (Student II) → *Empowered by stardust saturated with divine intent, reclaimed from your Enchanting (General), the base intent of this skill has been reimagined. Effect:*

- *Governs the use of enchantments in the creation and execution of ritual circles.*
- *Grants +1n% success and precision when using enchantments within ritual casting, where n = skill level.*
- *All enchantments created specifically for Enchanted Ritual Circles are now 100% more likely to succeed in both stability and compatibility. Example: If the use of the enchanted ritual circle bound the ritual to a target, it will be 100% more difficult for the link to be broken.*
- *The skill has become singular in focus. All attempts to create enchanted items not for the express purpose of ritual use **will automatically fail**.*

Magical Matrices (Journeyman V). Shaped by threads of deity-infused stardust, once core to Query, intuition has been threaded into logic, nudging your calculations toward brilliance. Math, the eternal adversary of adventurers, has become your silent ally. This skill enhances your capacity to integrate higher mathematics into magical diagrams and ritual-based systems, allowing you to design structures and spellwork with unparalleled precision. Effect:

- *+1n% effectiveness of the high-order mathematics Lore skills when applying it to the creation of magical diagrams which require any form of higher math, where n = skill level.*
- *Three times per day, while working through complex magical calculations or ritual construction, you may experience a*

'Query Echo'—a brief moment of insight that subtly nudges you toward a slightly more effective equation or structure. This nudge may manifest as an intuitive twitch of the hand, a visual overlay, or a momentary realization.

Natural Magical Material Creation (Journeyman 0). Infused with a hint of flavor from the saturated stardust of 'Pierce the Darkest Night', this is the perfect skill for those with a huge amount of raw mana and no real outlet for it, and it tends to lead to dangerous experiments! Sounds perfect for you. Effect:

- *Increases the density of the Mana matrix by 1n percent, where n = skill level.*
- *Denser matrices may allow for the spontaneous creation of magical materials at a higher than expected tier. (.1*n% chance.)*

Ritual Circles (Master II). The creation of ritual circles is a meticulous and tedious process that few have the patience or prowess to pursue. Having pulled the majority of the power from the 'Pierce the Darkest Night' title, you are now able to pierce the ownership layer and contest for control of active ritual circles. This is a subskill of the Ritual Magic category. Effect:

- *+1n% to use, create, destroy, or alter ritual circles, where n = skill level.*
- *By injecting 10% of mana of the original activation cost of a ritual, you will be able to directly put your power against the activator of said ritual. Should you succeed in the contest, you will be added to the whitelist of control for the ritual, and they will be removed. If no whitelist is included in the targeted ritual, you will automatically gain control of it.*

Ritual Duplication (Apprentice 0). This spell allows you to effortlessly clone an existing ritual with just a touch, transferring all of the magical symbology, geometry, intention, component requirements, and mana requirements to a new ritual circle. Skill Mechanics: Touch an inactive ritual. Use this spell. Done. Limitations: Only rituals of the same rank or lower can be duplicated. No edge-case nonsense, Joe. Effect:

- *Base mana and resource cost multiplier: (100 - 0.5n)%, where n = spell level (Max discount: 25%).*
- *Each additional duplication of a ritual or its duplicate doubles the cost. This doubling applies only to the specific ritual lineage—recreating it by hand resets the counter.*

Immutably Unique: Only one entity in existence can hold this spell.

Ritual Magic (Master VII). Reshaped by the flow of divine energy through the Reductionist class, this core class skill has been altered to better reflect your specializations. This is the cornerstone skill of the Ritualist class and is the thread that ties together theory, practice, and power. Effect:

- *-0.5% mana and component cost per skill level for all rituals.*
- *Governs the development of all Ritualist class subskills—each gains +10% growth until they reach the Master rank.*
- *Each core class subskill (Alchemical Rituals, Enchanted Ritual Circles, Magical Matrices, Ritual Circles, and Ritualistic Forging) gains an additive +1.5% passive bonus when working exclusively with aspects or aspect created items. (Example: Ritual Circles has +1n% plus a flat 1.5% bonus to use, create, destroy, or alter ritual circles, where n = skill level.)*
- *Exclusive bonus: -50% base mana and component cost for rituals.*

Ritualistic Forging (Expert II) → Infused with shimmering ashes of the sacrificed skill Infernal Conflagration, your forge no longer needs fire. Your hammer is the flame. Effect:

- *No external heat source required. Activating the forging process engulfs your hammer in infernal fire, fed by consuming impurities while preserving the usable material.*

- *1% chance to apply an Infernal Modifier to any item created —this may manifest as affinity, aesthetics, effects, or cursed qualities.*
- *3% chance to consume the supplied materials consumed entirely, taking as much as it can grab before being cut off.*
- *The associated hammering pattern 'Harmonics of Metal (Expert)' has evolved into 'Mantra of Metal (Master)'.*
  - *While chanting any mantra continuously during the forging process, a ritual circle of the associated crafting tier will appear over the correct striking point on the item, glowing in sync with your mantra's rhythm. Hammering accurately and in time with the mantra will provide a 10-100% increased chance of successfully creating items. Perfect success may increase the tier of the item. (Example: if you have a 1% chance of creating an item, the harmonics ringing through it will boost that chance to 1.1-2%)*

Somatic Ritual Casting (Journeyman VII). Bathed in the divine after-glow of stardust expelled by the collapse of both Words of Power (Written) and Spellbinding, this skill has been refined by Glyph and Bind. Effect:

- *You no longer need to draw ritual circles on the ground—you etch mana, component, and intent with practiced precision in the air itself.*
- *Stability of mid-air Ritual Creation is now set to Standard for any ritual at or below the tier of this skill. For each tier above, instability increases by +20% per tier (additive). Example: 1 tier above = +20% instability; 2 tiers = +40%, etc.*
- *You are able to create ritual circles up to the Apprentice rank in an instant if you have a deep enough understanding of them.*
- *Passive precision. Each completed gesture within a ritual leaves behind a brief visual echo, allowing you to visually verify positioning or trajectory mid-cast. These echoes linger for*

0.5 seconds, allowing for error correction with no loss of mana or material.

Lore Skills:

Alchemical Lore (Journeyman VI). Many are satisfied with the end result of their potions and simply follow the recipes to the letter time and again. You have started to dive deeply into the why of alchemy. Effect:

- *+1n% to the creation success and quality of alchemical items, where n = skill level.*
- *2% chance while creating any alchemical recipe to double the duration of the effect (+100% duration).*

Architectural Lore (Journeyman VII). Allows you to fine-tune architectural blueprints that you find or create. This will allow you to increase the quality of structures and decrease the cost of building them. Effect:

- *+1n% to the creation, enhancement, or reinforcement of architectural elements, structures, and magical buildings, where n = skill level.*
- *2% chance when constructing or altering any structure to add an inherent stability trait—doubling its resistance to damage, decay, or magical erosion.*

Calculus and Number Theory (Journeyman IV). The study of calculus and number theory is extremely useful in nearly all fields of magical crafting, ritual work, blueprints, and template design. There are very few areas within crafting untouched by this type of lore. Effect:

- *improve the rate of skill increase in nearly all fields of magical crafting by 1n +-T%, where n = lore skill level and T = Tier difference.*

Celestial-Arcane Interaction Lore (Journeyman III). You have taken a huge leap forward and understanding how the celestial bodies of the universe interact with the Arcane energies that you are tapping into. Increasing your understanding will allow you to increase your understanding faster. Effect:

- +.5n% faster skill gain for Celestial Arcane Interaction Lore, where n = skill level.

Enchanting Lore (Journeyman VIII). Your understanding of enchantments goes beyond function—you study the intricacies, the weave, and the purpose behind every layer. Effect:

- Allows you to fine-tune enchantments that you find or create.
- Can be used to increase the potency of enchantments and/or reduce the cost of creating them.
- All enchantments now require 5% fewer components to craft.

Knowledge (Journeyman VI). You tap into the Weave, searching for the secrets of this world. Patterns, insight, and structure unfold before your mind. Effect:

- When cast, choose two Lore skills to gain one level each, up to the maximum allowed by the tier of this skill.
- If either skill is below Journeyman, you may instead select the same skill twice to increase it by two levels. (Note: doing so replaces selecting two separate skills during that usage.)

Mana Cost: 2000. Cooldown: 18 hours

Ritual Lore (Journeyman IX). You don't just perform rituals—you dissect them, refine them, and reshape their very structure. Your understanding lets you manipulate the foundations of ritual magic with precision. Effect:

- Allows you to fine-tune rituals that you find or create.
- Can be used to increase the potency of rituals and/or decrease their cost.

Smithing Lore (Expert 0): There are depths to every craft which are difficult *to dive into, but as the skill progresses, you will not be hitting metal with a hammer; you will be forging. Effect:*

- *+1n% to the creation success and quality of forged items, where n = skill level.*
- *2% chance while creating any smithing template to increase the final quality or reduce the material cost of the item.*

CHAPTER TWENTY-ONE

"I can see why you were nervous about some of these, Tatum." Joe murmured as he finished reading over the dense information. "I think it's easier to count how many skills *didn't* change. Two? *Maybe* three? Also, what's up with Mental Manipulation Resistance? That skill is clearly out to get me, and if *you* can't get rid of it, what am I supposed to..."

Trailing off, he looked around himself, only to grumble in frustration at finding himself alone in front of Tatum's altar. "Why are you so weirdly stingy, system? He can alter the skills grafted onto my soul but can't have a conversation about it?"

There was no answer, which he actually appreciated. Typically, when he *did* get a reply, things got... concerning. Usually pretty quickly. Rolling his shoulders slowly, he lifted his Ritual Orbs into the air around himself out of habit—now long-used to training them almost unconsciously—only to flinch away as one of them clattered to the floor as broken metal shards. "Ah... right. I suppose I should probably fix that. Good thing I hadn't before meeting with Tatum. Stoic Constitution already changed and would have just broken it all over again."

Still considering the changes, Joe turned away from the altar and waited patiently as the floor opened up, then he descended into the darkness of the tunnel hidden below, feeling like an old-school villain as he vanished into a secret lair. Minutes later, he walked into the open area under the Pathfinder's Hall and raised an eyebrow as he saw Boris sitting there reading a book.

Skill increase: Mental Manipulation Resistance (Novice I → Novice II). Your surprise has faded.

Joe's eyes went wide as he saw the notification, only for it to appear again, increasing the skill to Novice three. "Abyss."

"Where have *you* been all day?" Boris looked up at Joe's accidental cursing, snapping his book shut and getting to his feet. "You had people waiting for you here for hours."

"Really? I just stepped..." The Ritualist shook his head, cutting off his ramblings before they started. "Actually, that makes sense. I just had a rather severe soul scouring, and I'm not surprised I lost a few hours there. I'm not great with keeping track of time in the first place, so-"

"He's back!" Taka's voice sounded out from the other side of the room, followed by a few minutes of doors opening and people coming out carrying various-sized packs. Joe looked at their containers in confusion for a moment, only to remember that spatial storage devices were restricted goods on Midgard. "Are you finally ready to go? By the way, the town management board is having a *conniption* looking for you. Know how I know that? It's not because I went outside, because the doors are sealed, and I *couldn't leave*."

Joe could only offer an apologetic grin as he shrugged. "My bad. Everyone ready to go?"

"Pardon me, but I do have another quick concern to raise," Boris sounded absolutely *aggrieved*. "First, I assume I'm not going with you, which leaves me alone in this place. Secondly, if I am meant to do the job you say I have, how am I meant to stay in the building? I'm rather certain that, as soon as you aren't here to stop them, I'll be dragged out by my ear and tossed out of the town, let alone the building."

"Right, about that." Joe motioned for everyone to follow

him, turning around to find that the secret passage had shifted into stairs going up once again. "Everyone follow me? Boris, I transferred you super-user rights to the building. You can seal the doors, restrict information from being found, and generally have control over this structure, more so than anyone except myself. They try to get rid of you? Lock them out. They have a problem with it? Tell them to take it up with your guard."

"My what now?"

"Your guard." By the time Boris stepped out of the stairwell, Joe had instructed the Pathfinder's Hall to open up, and the Juggernaut posted outside of the door was stomping toward them. "Meet Juggs."

Boris blinked rapidly, appearing scandalized. "Say that one again for me?"

"This is Juggs the Juggernaut." Joe's cheeks tinged pink, but he refused to acknowledge the accidental phrasing issue. "Juggs, you are to keep Boris safe, following his orders unless he is under duress. If you are uncertain if he is under duress, clear the building, have him seal it, then ask for clarification."

"*Acknowledged,*" came the rumbling voice, deep from the depths of the empty suit of armor. "New designation received. Orders… acceptable."

When he looked over, Joe was glad to see that the old man had a smile on his face. Boris was stroking his beard, trying not to look pleased with himself but failing miserably. "You know, Joe, that is a delightful companion to have. Might I say, I feel safer at this moment than I have in the last deuce of years… emphasis on *deuce*."

"You've gotten crass in your time on the streets, haven't you?" Joe shook his head in mock sadness. "Well, if you're all set, I'll take this moment to bring my Coven members out of here. We have trainin' to do!"

The handful of low-skilled Ritualists let out cheers with varied amounts of enthusiasm in them. Kirby was easily the most excited, yet Hannah stared at the daylight streaming in through the open door of the Pathfinder's Hall with trepidation.

Giving each of them a reassuring smile, Joe straightened up and strolled out of the enormous, egg-shaped dome. When a half-dozen guards confronted him with drawn weapons, his smile soured into something more dangerous.

"Whoaa, there, guys." Immediately, the man in charge of them, Jay the guard, put his sword away and stepped back, grabbing onto the two people nearest him and pulling them out of the small group's path. "Clearly our information was wrong, that's Joe. Yes, *that* Joe. He owns the place. Don't mind us, Joe! We were told someone took the building hostage or something? I'll clear it up for you. By the time you get back from wherever you're going, you won't be hassled anymore."

"Thanks." Joe actively tried not to feel surprised at the treatment, knowing his Mental Manipulation Resistance skill was just *waiting* to pounce. "By the way, I put Boris in charge of the place. I hired him as the curator for the knowledge it's collecting. Please make sure he isn't given any trouble... I'd be *extremely* irate if I came back, and the man I worked so hard to convince to come here was removed."

Much to his relief, Joe wasn't stopped again as they left the town, leaving behind the souvenir shops and uncomfortable reminders of what parts of Earth used to look like. Soon, the replanted forest stretched before them, and his high-level perception allowed him to start picking out movement in the underbrush.

"Looks like we're not going to get very far before we get to start practicing!" Beaming around at the others, Joe marched them along the road, quickly leaving the walls of Towny McTownface behind. Once they were fully out of sight of the sentries on the walls, he waved Robert forward and pointed at the base of a tree. "Go ahead and try out Elemental Burst, you should easily-"

"Wait, which one is that?" Robert pulled open the Ritual Combat Manual and flipped through it, only to glance up in despair. "Joe, I don't have *half* of the things this ritual requires!"

After going very still and quiet, the bald Ritualist pulled out his own manual and flipped it open, reading over the materials list the others needed in order to cast the ritual. "Ah... huh. Right. A moment, please."

Turning on his heel, Joe sped back to town, quickly finding an actual shop hidden among all of the trinket stores masquerading as treasure. After making sure he could spend contribution points instead of coins, he loaded up one of his rings with enough components to make a thousand of the Novice-rank rituals for each of the others.

He considered buying alchemical ingredients as well but decided against it—there was nothing in his skills that said they couldn't use the reagents *he* created, and alchemy was a massive time suck already.

Minutes later, he was back to his group, walking them through the placement of the materials, the correct angle to tilt their hand when drawing the upper left quadrant of the circle, and watching with nostalgia as leaves, crystals, shavings of precious metals, and chalk all melted into each other to create a single, cohesive ritual diagram. Once each of them had ten of the Novice rituals prepped and ready to go—nearly an hour's work for the slowest of them—they were finally ready to set out once more.

After seeing how his coven members prepared themselves for a fight, then how they used their rituals to hunt the creatures they found, Joe was absolutely amazed...

... at how bad they were at it.

"Big_Mo." Joe stood with his palms pressed together, index fingers on his lips as he tried to carefully measure his response to the latest attempt at hunting a squirrel. "I don't know how to tell you this, but it is supposed to be an Elemental Burst of wind. That had all the force of a half-hearted sneeze. I legitimately have no idea how you did that."

"No, look!" The man in question gestured at the shrubbery he had minced with his ritual. "It did what it was supposed to do. I just didn't hit the squirrel."

"The squirrel didn't move, 'Mo." Taka cheerfully called

over, holding up his most recent trophy—a bushy tail, which was all that remained of his target. "You've gotten too used to the auto-targeting function of adding blood in."

"It's how they're *supposed* to be used!" Big_Mo belted back, glancing at Joe nervously, as though the bald man were about to kick him out of the group. "Right?"

"Not this version. When we're using circles only, it's a burst, not an inundation. We'll work on it." Joe turned his attention to Taka, who was still gloating at his successful hunt. "Speaking of, you know the ritual is supposed to last ten seconds at a time, yes? It activates in one-second bursts, but yours only lasted three."

"I think I might have modified it to let out more of its power with each burst?" Now that Joe's attention had landed on him, Taka wasn't nearly as exuberant.

"Are you asking me or telling me? Could you do it again, on purpose?" Joe pressed, only for the younger man to shrug nonchalantly. "Look, all of you... the reason I'm back on Midgard in the first place is because I'm lacking in fundamentals. I admit I have the advantage in Characteristics, and I can make up for some of my deficiencies with raw speed or sheer resources. Even so, here I am, just like you, trying to get through this Novice questline. Don't try to modify things, don't skip steps, and-"

A rabbit hopped out onto the path, only to be surrounded by a shimmering rainbow. The unfortunate creature let out a sharp squeal then burst like a hot dog that had been left in the microwave too long, a fountain of shimmering dust spraying into the air and leaving behind a piece of meat and a perfectly prepared pelt. Everyone looked at Kirby, who raised her hands helplessly. "I swear, I did it *exactly* how it said to do it!"

"'Kay." Joe tried to fight against the grin pulling at his lips, wanting to give his pupil the respect she so desperately desired. To cover himself a bit better, he snapped his fingers and manifested his inscription tool. "Watch."

A secondary function of Somatic Ritual Casting he'd never

considered before was the ease of visibility it provided. By drawing in the air, he was able to create the lines and sigils extra-large, leaving behind crisp sections which spun into place to create a textbook-perfect diagram.

The four elemental symbols appeared next, each glowing with their own characteristic light. Pointing at each of the different portions, he gave a brief explanation on its purpose, why it mattered that it was placed *just so*, and even hinted that it was possible to see the element it would be infused with by the brightness of the sigils. Not wanting to confuse them too much, he didn't bring up the interactions with the stars they could focus on—yet.

He flicked the activation sequence with a touch of mana, sending a series of faint, shimmering lines through the air. The first one passed through a tree growing alongside the path cleanly, and the second one did the same but at a slightly different angle, causing the tree to begin toppling over. The third and fourth tore out chunks that would perfectly fit in a campfire, while the rest simply ripped into the fallen tree and sent chips flying everywhere.

"As you can see, the more precise the lines are, the sharper the wind generated will be. Same with whatever element ends up being used—though, with the others, it might manifest as pointed rocks, dense flames, or hyper-condensed water. When you let them stay fuzzy-"

Continuing to lecture as they strolled along the path, Joe answered whatever questions the Coven members had. Adding in some blood, he walked them through each of the different reactions that were created and *why* they happened. "I'd show you what happens with alchemy, but I'm going to need some time to prep that. I ran out on the way here, and it shouldn't surprise you that I forgot to make more."

By the time he had finished speaking, and the questions had stopped coming, they were another hour down the road. The others began murmuring amongst themselves, looking as though they had stumbled upon enlightenment. A few of them bragged about skill gains, comparing notes to see if the others had unlocked Lore skills as they had or just gained skill levels directly.

The system took that moment to notify Joe of a happy change he had earned as well.

Skill increase: Teaching (Journeyman II → Journeyman III).

While he was pleased at the increase in a skill that *didn't* make him nervous, the Ritualist suddenly realized they had been walking completely uncontested for a *really* long time. "Hey, I know this is going to sound weird, but why have we been so safe for the last hour or so? I've kind of been expecting... I don't know, maybe a rabid wolf or something to show up?"

Hannah was the first to speak up, clearly working to be a part of anything she could. "It's been a regular problem around town! Since there's so much tourism, the roads are heavily trafficked. Pretty much any monster above level seven is hunted down immediately."

As if to punctuate her point, the next time they heard rustling in the foliage, a hunter poked his head around a tree. He gave them a once over then led his own group out of the woods and onto the road. Doing his best to ignore the small team casually walking around them, Joe directed his coven members to target a plump squirrel watching them from a branch—only for a sharp whistling to sound out just before the squirrel was pinned to the tree, going limp as the arrow vibrated to a halt.

"Okay, next time let's-" Joe was cut off as two men in damaged leather armor came stumbling into view, dragging a third person between them. A trail of blood led back into the trees, pouring out of the man's shredded leg.

"Coming through!" One of the men barked at Joe's group, only speeding up as they stepped onto the hard packed road and out of the underbrush. "Move aside, or I'll *gut* you on my way through!"

Seeing the bald man in front of him still not moving, the

hunter put actions to words by drawing his dagger and thrusting it at Joe without hesitation as they got close. Not even bothering to defend himself, the Ritualist stepped close, letting the knife stop dead against his Exquisite Shell. A gentle chop at the man's head later, Joe was shamefacedly pressing a hand against the nearly unconscious adventurer.

"Whoops… hang on, I can fix you both." Joe cast Lay on Hands, grunting in satisfaction as a giant lump on the aggressive man's head faded, and torn meat knitted together under the thin sheet of water washing over the wound on the originally damaged hunter. "Hey. What did this to you, and where can we find it?"

It was the third member of their party who answered, cautiously looking on but keeping his hands to the side to show he wasn't going to follow the example of the first. "It was a stone wolf. None of our weapons worked against it. Blades just bounced right off of 'im. Already down, though. As soon as Billy took a hit, another group stepped in and took the kill."

"All that effort just to lose it and almost get sent to respawn." The now-healed man snarled as he inspected his destroyed boiled-leather leg guards. "Thanks for the assist. Now I can at least walk back from here."

"No problem-" Joe started to say, only for Kirby to lean forward and let loose a brilliant smile.

"What he's too nice to say is that going to respawn is free, but healing costs money. Now, he's a kind man and isn't going to give you a set price for his services. He'll take whatever donation you feel is the right one. Just do what your heart tells you." Joe felt his jaw drop slightly as the tiny lady practically shook the men down for the last of their coin. Just like that, he gained a couple silver, a handful of copper, and-

A golden line appeared in the air between him and the man he had healed. For half a heartbeat, Joe could see as the light shifted, moving from the now-leaving hunters to the coins in his hand. Then the light burst like a soap bubble, fading away quickly enough that he wasn't certain he hadn't imagined it.

Not entirely certain what had happened, Joe pocketed the coins and began slowly walking down the road. "That was definitely my Karmic Perception coming into play, but what did it mean? For a moment, we were connected, but it vanished after I was paid? Have I been setting up karmic debts between myself and someone else when I help them out for free?"

Breaking himself out of the cycle of confusion and rumination, as there was no handy-dandy library nearby for him to pop in and do research in what was almost *guaranteed* to be a restricted topic, Joe glanced around and watched as more and more people poured out of the woods. Big_Mo glanced at the sky and scratched his chin. "Looks like it's almost sunset. Should we head back, or are we setting up camp? I think we all brought enough for a couple days?"

Joe didn't respond immediately, his mind on the fact that his coven hadn't had any real challenge yet, how this place was practically *crawling* with other people vying for the same creatures, and—to put it mildly—how he had plenty of other things that needed to be done. "No. No, we're not heading back. Didn't I already say that? We barely scratched the surface of what we can do, and if we keep bouncing back and forth between town and hunting, it's just going to be a few weeks of dodging tourists and trying not to accidentally send a wind blade into someone's face."

"What are you saying?" Robert spread his hands, reaching back to tap his small backpack. "I didn't bring enough for an extended trip, so-"

The bald Ritualist looked down the road, and then, just through the grid-grown trees ahead, he saw it: untouched, old growth forest. "We've got everything we need, trust me. We're here to learn how to fight and complete quests, and we're not going to do that by living a regular nine to five like these other hunters. If we want food, let's hunt it. You want to go back and be perfectly comfortable? That's fine… but the rest of us are going to go out there and get *good* at this. Buckle up, friends. We're going on a full-fledged expedition to the frontier."

CHAPTER TWENTY-TWO

Three days later, Joe stared hungrily at the slowly roasting meat he was twirling over the campfire. "Looks like it's just about done…"

Grabbing the stick, he began to pull it off the heat, only for it to instantly blacken and crumble into charcoal. Caught somewhere between hunger and betrayal, the Ritualist threw it on the ground and let out a frustrated snarl. "Why is cooking considered *crafting*?"

"Maybe you should stick to cooking up alchemy potions, like you have been the last couple of nights? Here, this was made by someone *not* hated by food." Taka handed over a pan of fried potatoes and wild onions. "How long have you *thought* you could cook? 'Cause I have to say, it's pretty obvious you can't."

"I have no idea!" Joe accepted the offer with a long sigh of defeat. "Do you know how often I've had to cook since I got my specialization? *Never*! I've either eaten only prepared foods, travel rations, raw ingredients, or bought food from restaurants or stalls. But I actually *can't* cook? I don't even know how I would go about *gaining* the skill using aspects!"

"Aspect of the burnt offering." Big_Mo elbowed Robert and jerked his chin at the smoldering remnants.

Taka rubbed his chin. "That could actually work as the name of a barbecue place. It would fit right in back in town."

Surprisingly enough, Joe's abject failure in this particular arena helped to put the rest of his team at ease. Although terribly frustrated, Joe appreciated how they immediately began to tease him—it was clearly meant in good fun, and it was nice to see that they were warming up to him again.

"Here, protein that doesn't puff away as powder when you go to take a bite." Hannah added a filet of smoked fish to the potatoes, sending him a winning smile. "Hey, want to know something interesting about human interactions?"

"Um, sure?" Joe responded around a mouthful of piping hot taters, trying to hide the chewed bits with a hand.

"Do you know that the best way to build trust with someone is *not* to do a bunch of things for them?" Hannah correctly interpreted Joe's raised eyebrow. "They say that allowing other people to do things *for you* is the only way to quickly build trust. When someone invests in helping you, they start to care more about what happens to you. It creates a bond... so if you want loyalty and trust, you don't need to only show strength."

She pointed at his plate. "Being able to hand you this fish? Do you have *any* idea how much I hate eating fish by now? But I've gotten really good at making it taste *awesome*. Now... I guess I am not as mad about it? I feel like I'm finally able to contribute to the group, even if it's only a little."

"Same," Taka called over. "I mean, except that I've never hated potatoes."

Not quite sure how to respond, but having an excuse for not speaking right away thanks to everyone quietly eating their meals, Joe dipped his chin in a thoughtful nod. The silence lingered, and though it was comfortable, he soon decided to pull open the notifications he'd been waiting to open until they were settled for the evening.

Once they had started hunting in earnest, the last traces of humanity left far behind them, the Ritualist had been pleased to find that some of his oldest quests had brightened and reactivated, no longer grayed out and all but invisible in his quest sheet.

More out of a sense of nostalgia than any need for the reward, Joe had at long last completed his 'Playing Your Fake Role III' quest. When they had been rushing by monsters, he had acted as a distraction, jumping out of the way of their swipes and chomps at the last moment, moving in unpredictable ways as he bounced around the small battlefield. With his capabilities, it was practically child's play to dodge the attacks or vanish into the canopies with a powerful Omnivault as his coven members finally activated their ritual circles and took the beasties down.

Quest complete: Playing Your Fake Role III. Reward: Null.

You are too powerful for any Characteristic points to be added with this low level of a quest. No experience can be awarded. The associated skill is too strong to be upgraded. Assigning follow-up quest... nope. You have surpassed the bounds of system-guided progression for this level of quest. The training wheels have long since come off. Here, have a cookie.

Joe glanced at the chocolate chip cookie which had materialized in his hand, blinking a few times in consternation as he felt a hint of disappointment. "Abyss, I thought it might scale up and help me push further."

Another glance at his quest sheet showed that almost all of his quests for Midgard had just vanished, leaving behind only quests which gave reputation upon completion, as well as 'The Other Three', which had been denoted as extremely high difficulty when he had first gained it.

Trying to shake off the feeling, he glanced around at his small group, who were now chatting animatedly. Wanting to have something noteworthy to contribute to the conversation, he checked the next notification and allowed himself a moment of triumph.

Quest complete: Mastering Ritual Combat I.

1. *Use 500 Novice ritual combat circles in live combat.*
   (500/500)
2. *Use 300 two-discipline ritual combat circles in live combat.*
   (300/300)
3. *Use 200 three-discipline ritual combat circles in live combat.*
   (200/200)

Reward: +6 to skill: Enchanted Ritual Circles. +50 blank Tokens.

Ritual tokens: These blank tokens are each a perfectly round, 1 inch in diameter smooth stone, with an internal crystalline structure which makes them ideal for enchanting.

Quest gained: Mastering Ritual Combat II. This is the second of five Ritualist-tower generated chain quests consisting of increasing difficulty, which will help you determine your final specialization for combat-based rituals.

This first quest was meant to help you gain an understanding of your personal combat prowess, and teach you the tools required for fusing the various sub-disciplines of ritual magic for the purposes of combat. This second quest is meant to widen your horizons further.

1. *Use 300 two-discipline Novice ritual combat circles in live combat. (46/300)*
2. *Use 200 three-discipline Novice ritual combat circles in live combat. (2/200)*
3. *Use 500 Beginner ritual combat circles in live combat. (72/500)*
4. *Use 300 two-discipline Beginner ritual combat circles in live combat. (33/300)*
5. *Use 200 three-discipline Beginner ritual combat circles in live combat. (0/200)*
6. *Use 100 four-discipline Beginner ritual combat circles in live combat. (0/100)*

Reward: 1) Upon completion, choose one of the skills used in the creation of any of the rituals you created to receive: +10 to the skill if it is currently in the Beginner rank OR +8 to the skill if it is in the Apprentice rank OR +6 to the skill if it is in the Student rank OR +4 to the skill if it is in the Journeyman rank OR +2 to the skill, if it is in the Expert rank.

2) Gain a two-circle flourish along the cuffs of your Ritualist Tower robes, denoting you as a Beginner combatant. The circles will be embroidered in silver thread and will shimmer faintly in direct light. Though almost entirely ornamental in design, your portion of the spoils increases by 1% from successful combat challenges on behalf of the Ritualist Tower.

Progress toward the next quests in this quest line, such as using higher-ranked rituals, will be tracked but locked until the current quest is completed. Additional rewards and profession opportunities may be unlocked based on your performance.

Joe glanced at his gains, which had been slowly yet steadily increasing—especially since he had been making sure to activate his Knowledge spell the instant it came off cooldown. There was only one major problem...

Alchemical Rituals (Alchemical Rituals Apprentice V → Apprentice IX).

Enchanted Ritual Circles (Student II → Student VIII).

Alchemical Lore (Journeyman VI → Journeyman IX).

Architectural Lore (Journeyman VII → Journeyman IX)

Calculus and Number Theory (Journeyman IV → Journeyman IX).

Celestial-Arcane Interaction Lore (Journeyman III → Journeyman IX).

Enchanting Lore (Journeyman VIII → Journeyman IX).

Knowledge (Journeyman VI → Journeyman IX).

...He had managed to bring all of his current Lore skills up to the peak of the Journeyman rank, but his Knowledge spell hadn't rolled over into the Expert ranks. In other words, unless he gained additional Lore skills or had a moment of enlightenment that pushed the individual skills up a tier, he was stuck. Still, there was no need to be down about it, at least not at this moment.

"Good news, everyone!" Joe firmly placed his fork on his plate, which was already sparkling clean, thanks to his Neutrality Aura getting rid of the final few scraps. "I have the details for the next quest in the line, and you'll be pleased to know that, while it *is* a lot more difficult to complete, there are still a ton of Novice rank rituals you need to complete. In other words, don't feel wasteful because you're overdoing it with one version right now. It'll still be tracked, counted, and useful for the next one."

Big_Mo seemed especially relieved, as he had been practically unable to hit his targets to this point without first adding a drop of their blood to his rituals. It was only after Joe had seen how the alchemical reagents seemed to slip off his circle, or a gust of wind would cause him to miss perfect placement of it that he had started to appreciate what it meant when his alchemical rituals skill stated that it gave him a 'twenty-nine percent chance to use alchemical components correctly in the creation of ritual circles'. Until now, he had assumed that meant something along the lines of creating the potions and such themselves.

Frankly, it made Joe question each of the times he had failed dramatically with his own ritual diagrams—was it truly *his* failure, was the world conspiring against him because his skill levels hadn't been high enough, or was it somewhere in between? "We've been pushing hard the last few days, and I'd say we must be getting pretty close to the edge of the kingdom."

"Probably." Robert pointed in the distance behind them with his fork. "Haven't seen so much as a *trail* in the last hundred miles or so, let alone a proper road. Gotta love that mobile barrier you walk around in—you running face-first into stinging nettles is better than a machete for clearing a path."

"It's because the hole I make is person-shaped," Joe offhandedly explained, the corners of his lips twitching as the group shared a laugh. "Look, I'd appreciate it if everyone would keep an eye out for anywhere out here you think would make for a really good... let's call it a town. A big town. Natural resources, water, whatever. I've got a land claim token I'd like to use, and if there's something that's just perfect, I'd love to lock it down before someone else does."

The night passed quickly, with Joe focusing his efforts on

creating Novice substrates in his cauldron while simultaneously devoting some of his mental energy to keeping his Ritual Orbs floating around the camp full of his sleeping coven members. Whenever a creature came too close, one of his floating weapons would seek it out and leave behind a flattened mess before resuming its orbit. A few hours after midnight, he finished for the evening, woke Taka and Kirby up to have them keep watch, with bleary instructions to trade off with the others each hour until dawn.

The following morning started gray and quiet, the canopy above their heads gently allowing the light drizzle falling from above to drip through. They sat by the fire for a short while, each person warming up and enjoying a hot cup of coffee, thanks to Mate, who was absolutely *thrilled* to provide a great start to the day for as many people as possible.

"Num-*nuum!*" the elemental spoke in a sing-song voice when Kirby tried to turn down the mug being offered to her. When the elemental started waving its arms back and forth, dancing in place, her willpower failed. Seemingly quite proud of himself, Mate looked around with a pleased expression before sinking into the Ebonsteel mug tethered to Joe's belt with a happy **burble**.

The group had grown used to early starts, and now their movements were confident as they packed, put out the fire, and followed the path Joe generated by sprinting through the long grass and shrubs. No longer was anyone complaining about leaving behind their routines, as the allure of once again gaining levels and completing quests broke through their passive contentment with the status quo.

"I think I figured something out," Taka called to Joe as they caught up to him. "You know how I like to push the limits of the rituals?"

"You mean how you like to introduce unknown variables but try to console yourself by doing math before you activate them?" The bald Ritualist motioned for his coven member to continue, even as rain sloshed off of his Exquisite Shell and as-ever failed to wet his skin.

"Yeah. Check this out. Remember how you asked if I could make the overcharging of the Elemental Burst repeatable?" Lifting the ritual diagram they had all grown intimately familiar with over the last few days, Taka pointed at a slight alteration he'd made. "Look, if we make it so this sigil is serrated instead of a smooth curve on the circle-"

He explained the formula he'd come up with, using the words 'cosine' and 'tangent' far too many times in quick succession for comfort. "Then what we *should* get when we add the elixir is a burst of energy, the first acting like normal, while the second shifts in on all sides like a piston to compress it further. That should increase the range fairly significantly or deal a *lot* more damage if the target is in regular range."

Instead of pushing forward with the conversation, Joe did what he had wanted to start making into a habit—he gathered the other coven members around and had them look for issues on the circle. At a glance, he could see at least seven areas which could be improved immediately, but he held his tongue while the others offered their own critiques. After all, there was no way they'd be improving their Lore or Class Skills if they had him solve everything... not to mention, what Hannah had said to him the night before had really started to sink in.

No one brought up anything he hadn't thought of, so after Taka added in what he wanted to change, Joe simply handed over an elixir and let him give it a try. Mana poured into the activation section, and the air around the circle compressed quickly enough to cause a gentle wind as it was pulled to a singular point. An instant later, the air lanced out, spiraling as it sunk into the trunk of a tree. Bark blew off, and sawdust filled the air as the powerful attack drove through the wooden barrier, leaving behind a perfectly clean hole filled with gently curving grooves.

After that singular attack, the ritual circle fractured, letting out a high-pitched whine before detonating with a rush of mana and air. Taka *screeched* as his hands were flayed by the lashing winds, his hair starting on fire from the intense friction and rampant energy. Joe *moved*, patting out the flames at the same time as he cast Lay on Hands, instantly reversing the damage that had been done to his mentee. Taka took a deep inhale to scream, only to let it out in a long, shuddering exhale when he realized the pain had vanished.

"My bad, Taka." Joe immediately apologized, before anyone else could say a word. "I saw a few flaws, but I didn't think they would be enough to cause it to explosively rupture like that. I thought, at most, it would burn itself out, maybe be a waste of resources, but *completely* forgot to account for how the elixir overlay would shift the end result."

"Uhh..." Taka still stared at his hands, his mind still stuck on the mess he'd seen just moments before. "I guess we're good? What went wrong?"

"I'm still working on figuring all of this out, but I think we need to start adding in other implements and such that help to balance our class out." Joe gave a brief explanation on stabilizers, which could be made with Ritualistic Forging, and how each of the class skills seemed to offer something which would make the others more efficient and deadly yet safer for the caster. "Every other class uses tools, so why are *we* the only people that seem to think we need to brute force everything? I'll look into it on my end."

The day proceeded normally after that, the only real standout being whenever it was Kirby's turn to attack whatever creature had come in range. Somehow, the Elemental Bursts generated by her rituals took on more rare variants—capturing light, fog, and other effects that could still technically be considered 'elements', even when everyone else seemed to only have a singular effect.

A burst of compressed water from Hannah's ritual would be followed by a soup-thick cloud which manifested around a creature's head and gently suffocated the animal when Kirby took her turn. Stone bursting through the underbrush from Robert would be followed up by the dainty Ritualist's exact duplicate somehow interacting with the minerals in tree roots and causing them to stab out of the ground and into an unfortunate porcupine.

The bizarre effects irked her to no end, but were a source of intense scrutiny for Joe: if he could figure out her tricks—or as she called it, her 'curse'—he might be able to generate an entirely new subskill, or...

"Hold on a moment." The bald Ritualist whirled around as he firmly put his academic interest to the side, fingertips tapping against each other as his thoughts spun. "Before I go searching through the weeds for an answer, is it possible that you have any traits? Failing that, any active curses or blessings?"

All he got in return was a blank stare. "Is that supposed to be on my status sheet? I can't see any of that."

Face falling, Joe remembered that his close ties to Tatum allowed him to see portions of his status sheet, or combat logs, that were generally hidden from other people, unless they had specialized skill sets. "Ah. Right. Maybe we'll find someone with a high-level inspection spell that can help you figure that out."

Surprisingly, after Kirby, it was Big_Mo's rituals which remained wildly inconsistent. With Joe's steady guidance, and the support of the others who were also struggling with new aspects of their class, his aim quickly grew steady. Soon he was hitting the targeted monster more often than not, and when he *did* succeed, the power he brought to bear was an order of magnitude above the others. Somehow Big_Mo's diagrams squeezed out every last *drop* of mana he put into the ritual and hit just *that* much harder.

As they became more confident, Joe began to step back and let them figure things out. The coven began to function as a unit, each of them covering the others with their own strengths. They were learning and growing in power quickly; by the end of the first full week, each of them was at least in the Student rank.

Joe's teaching skill had really started to show its usefulness, especially when combined with his Master rank in Ritual Circles. For his part, the Ritualist had been planning to work on his Beginner quest line for ritual combat but had gotten completely sidetracked with a passage he had found in the dividing line while reading up on the differences between the tiers in the manual.

The transitional threshold: what does it truly mean to go from Novice to Beginner?

Novice rituals capture structured mana within the framework of mana-reactive materials, then release it as a singular expression. Each Novice ritual allows for three branching instructions: convert, target, release. It should come as no surprise, then, that the Novice combat questline only extends to three disciplines being used. While it is possible to push past and forcibly add additional inputs, the stability of the ritual diagram will rapidly degrade.

While some, especially utility rituals, are adept at rapidly switching targets, you will still find that they are following a singular set of instructions.

The core distinction of going from the lower rank to the higher is instructional complexity. The three instructions allowed to Novice rituals is raised to eight at the Beginner rank. This increase is not linear throughout the ranks, as you will see in later chapters, but expressly exponential, then, as the new generation says these days, quantum.

Let's have an example. Where a Novice ritual may capture mana, then slowly decompose into wavelengths to generate gentle light or rapidly consume it to focus it into a low-damage beam attack, a Beginner ritual may cause that light to split into more dangerous wavelengths, avoid the eyes of allies, or add on additional effects, depending on the design of the ritual —only to be further stretched with the inclusion of additional disciplines of Ritual Magic.

At that point, the author turned to esoteric ramblings, trying to sound wise with the analogy he created, but only managing to greatly confuse the topic.

—Remember, oh ye Novices, as you push forward into the mysteries of magic. The second circle reaches backward as it moves forward, a mirror of greater intent of the first. One speaks, the other listens, but in reverse. To

bind a fluxline across sympathetic sigils via early stage array math is to convince mana it has always been two things, not just one. To create a Beginner circle is to make the echo before the sound-

After reading only a few lines, Joe quickly set the manual to the side and reached for his coffee mug. "Ugh. When are people going to realize that the smartest people out there are the ones who can take a complicated topic and explain it clearly and succinctly? It's only when you don't know what you are talking about that you speak *around* the subject."

Taking his first sip on the ninth morning, now absolutely certain they were either outside of the kingdom of Ardania or right on the edge, Joe looked into the distance and choked. A splash of coffee shot out of his nose as he saw an enormous column of black smoke rising into the air, surrounded by smaller, wispy pillars which he had only ever seen come from campfires... or perhaps chimneys.

"Wake up! Someone's under attack, and *we* weren't invited?" He managed to force out of his throat, his aura helpfully removing the sloshing liquid from his lungs. "Let's go crash that party."

CHAPTER TWENTY-THREE

The black smudge in the sky quickly grew to a towering cloud filling Joe's view of the horizon as he and his coven rushed across the untamed landscape.

As they got closer, Joe's aura started to clear out the noxious fumes in a sphere around him, but the sheer density of the smoke made it impossible for him to dissolve everything before it got to the others. By the time they were close enough to see what was happening, he was the only one not intermittently coughing or wiping at reddened eyes.

Between one step and the next, they went from chaotic, wild growth to clear lines of sight across massive, cultivated fields. After bursting from the tree line, Joe held out his arms to stop the others, quickly scanning the huge open area and picking out a few distressing facts. One, they had once again stumbled upon humanity, at least an enclave of it. While at first he was concerned that they would need to move again, so as not to interfere with the local hunting parties, the second thing he saw made that point moot: hundreds of monsters were swarming across the fields, destroying crops as they slowly made their way toward the central area.

As his attention was drawn to the people defending their homes, Joe found himself decidedly unimpressed with their formation. Instead of swords or spears, the majority of the people were hefting pickaxes, pitchforks, or other farming tools. Only perhaps one in five had a proper weapon, and just a small percentage of *those* seemed proficient in them. While he hadn't been entirely certain if he should get involved, he felt his resolve firm up as his eyes landed on a banner fluttering above the central tent, picturing three stalks of golden wheat on a background of green grass.

"Is this where the Golden Greens Guild ended up? That's gotta be them. Pretty sure," the Ritualist murmured to himself, trying to recall if he had ever gotten a proper view at their guild heraldry. "Eh, only way to know for sure is to get over there and ask them, and I don't think they'd mind the help. Listen up, everyone! Try not to damage their crops; it looks like they're already taking a beating. If you can't help it, don't worry too much. I'm sure it's easier for them to plant new vegetables than it is to find their way back here if they're sent to respawn."

As they rushed forward once more, Joe realized what had been making him so uncomfortable about the situation. It wasn't the smell of ash, churned earth, or the odd fungal musk coming off the humanoid monsters. No, it was the fact that he hadn't seen anyone in this guild for literally years at this point, yet the farming guild seemed to still be living out of tents. Sure, they were oversized and probably luxurious for what they were, but the simple fact that they hadn't been able to move up from there didn't paint a pretty picture of how things had gone for them.

There *were* a few permanent buildings, but they were scattered few and far between, with smaller tents clustered around them. As far as he could tell from that distance, Joe could only assume the few brick and mortar buildings were barns, grain storage, and perhaps livestock pens.

Getting in range of the first of the monsters, Joe stared it down and—to his surprise—got a system notification.

Skill check failed! Perception check success!

Creature name: Tillbane Wretch. A twisted guardian formed of untamed soil and held together with a wild root system, the Tillbane Wretch is grown rather than born. These creatures rise from the earth only when the land is disturbed—forest being cleared, previously untamed fields being plowed, or when the energies of the land are redirected into the growth of herbs or produce. Where Tillbanes walk, cultivated lands are destroyed and reverted to their wild state.

"Coming back to how *that* was a possibility all along at another time," Joe huffed in agitation. "I guess this explains why I've never seen or heard of these creatures before. I'm not exactly the patient type that can turn sunshine into sustenance."

As they closed in on the Wretches, Joe's nose wrinkled, and he tried to focus his Neutrality Aura more intensely around his nose. The Tillbane stood a full head taller than him, its loamy body covered with tiny mushrooms that shed spores with every movement. The musky odor had become far more intense, with a sharp tang of natural fertilizer, feces, and rotting vegetation shining through.

Hannah gagged as they came within touching distance, reminding Joe that he should actually *do* something about this monster. His Ritual Orb of Strength launched off his chest, crashing into the monster then through it. The huge entity fell to the ground as a pile of fresh manure and crumbled dirt. "Okay, *that* was overkill. Hey, that just means they should be good targets to practice our rituals on! Spread out and start cutting your way through. Try not to get surrounded, but get up to the farmers and support them if you can."

"What are *you* going to do?" Robert shouted over the noise of wet compost splattering to the ground.

Joe shot him an excited smile. "I'm going to do the same thing, but *faster*."

With that, Joe shoved off the ground, causing it to tremble as Omnivault launched him over the sparse grouping of Tillbane and deeper into the sludgy mass of monsters. Even before his feet touched down, he had his inscription tool in hand and began sketching out a quick, compact Ritual of Elemental Burst. Allowing it to hang in the air, he turned sharply to the left, creating a second one at a ninety-degree angle to the first.

Twice more, he drew out the Novice-rank ritual in the cardinal directions, before touching each in turn with his left hand and duplicating them in front of his right in the ordinal directions. Finally, he activated them one after another, sending cones of sharpened stones blasting out of most of them, though two of the rituals cut through the Tillbane Wretches with sharpened air.

Just as Joe was preparing to move, a ninth, shadowy ritual appeared, stacked directly above one of the sharpened wind versions and activating on its own. Even without checking his combat log, the Ritualist realized it was the new, Tatum-enhanced effect of Haunting Shadows at play. In all directions around him, the monsters staggered under the sudden, unexpected elemental assault. They weathered the first blow of the ritual easily, every last one of them surviving until the final blast. Then, as the rituals collapsed, so did the nearest ranks of Wretches.

Something about that didn't sit right with Joe, and as he Omnivaulted to a new spot, he quickly glanced at his notifications to see why they had been able to hold strong against the entire hundred points of elemental damage the rituals could output.

Ritual of Elemental burst deals 10 damage. Tillbane Wretch resists 25% of the elemental earth damage!

This creature is significantly lower level than you. It takes 15% reduced damage from all attacks. Source: Title (Tatum's Chosen Legend).

"That's it, you're going into a pearl!" Joe flicked the necklace he had been given from Grandmaster Pete, assigning his title to the pearl and immediately feeling as though a tightness around his chest had loosened. "Nothing to do about the elemental resistance—or *is* there?"

As the ground rushed up at him, he stomped down as hard as he could on a Wretch's head, shoving off at an oblique angle and creating an opening with a Ritual Orb so he could land next to a swath of burning crops. Once again, his inscription tool traced out the ritual in midair. His hands blurred as he finished three more then duplicated them, only to pause in surprise as an inactive ritual appeared stacked with the most recently created one. "It can duplicate the effects of *Ritual Duplication*? Celestial feces, that's..."

All but salivating, Joe began quickly activating the nine ritual circles, and to his delight, two more sprang into existence, one a shadowy version of the already-duplicated-by-Haunting-Shadow ritual. "I wasn't complaining before, but now I have *nothing* but positive things to say about how that all went down, Tatum!"

Flickering light appeared in front of the majority of his rituals. Between one breath and the next, heat collected into shimmering orbs and was launched out to detonate against the Tillbanes, blowing large chunks off of the monsters. Joe was far more concerned with keeping a close eye on the duplicated rituals than the effects they achieved. Since all three of the intentionally and unintentionally duplicated rituals were stacked atop each other, it was clear to see how they... stacked up.

The flames produced at the bottom were the most intense, on par with any of the original creations. This made sense: it took in additional resources to generate the exact same effect. Explosions generated by the middle circle were half as effective, while those on the top barely dealt any damage at all. Still, the proof of concept had Joe rubbing his hands together in sheer excitement—barely any damage *was* still damage. If he could get the effect to activate when he was creating Master-ranked rituals...? Well, in that case, being less effective wouldn't matter *nearly* as much. Though he wasn't exactly certain how the math would work out, it still should hit with immense power.

A shower of dirt washed over him, blocking his view for a moment as he blinked in confusion at being pulled back to the situation. Turning around, he immediately identified where the substance had come from, as the Tillbane who had attacked him was staring at its destroyed arm in what the Ritualist could only assume was confusion.

"Friend, you've made your last mistake. Already disarmed? Then prepare to be de-feet-ed!" Sweeping his Ritual Orb low to the ground, Joe popped the creature's legs, sending raw earth spilling as though he had torn into a sandbag.

Drawing out a Novice ritual diagram, Joe found himself holding still longer than he wanted as he surrounded the first with a *second* circle, activating the Beginner-ranked version of the Ritual of Elemental Burst with a flash of intent and a hint of mana.

Stone arrows, nearly fifty percent larger than the Novice versions he'd been seeing, launched from the center of his ritual. The only other noticeable difference was how they shot in a spray that seemed directed, unlike the haphazard eruption of fragments of the lower rank. Each of the thickened stone projectiles struck a distinct target, making Joe murmur in appreciation before going silent as it repeated the attack, only to send the rocks into mostly new targets.

"Hmm, that's actually less effective. Looks like the Ritual Circle without any enchantment or alchemy added just picks targets at random. Or is it by proximity? Maybe that Wretch was slightly closer than the other after it had been pushed back? Need more data points!" Between having a near-endless supply of Common-ranked aspects, the ability to draw his ritual diagrams in the air, and a massive supply of targets, Joe was quickly able to deduce the answers he had been seeking.

Even with as quickly as he could destroy them, the monsters seemed nearly endless. As he was able to take them down with relative ease, he soon found himself in the center of an inverted crater, with a thick wall of dirt and vegetation having practically grown around him as the creatures were felled. "Time to move to the next spot!"

A quick glance around informed him that the monsters he had been destroying were nothing more than a drop in the ocean. Checking on his coven members, he was pleased to see that they were almost to the inner defensive line, having worked together to clear a shallow channel through the slow, shambling Wretches.

Just as he was about to return to his studies, the line of farmers slumped, a wave of the Tillbane moving through the breach at a slow yet steady pace. "Ah, seems playtime's over. Let's save these farmers, and... yeah, just have to watch the angle of my rituals. No way to *not* target other people yet, if I want to keep going with Beginner rituals."

The only saving grace was that the ritual circles were still *directional*. Moments after he had first witnessed the defensive line collapse in, Joe was landing, sweeping his two remaining Ritual Orbs around him to quickly destroy the monsters that had pushed through. "Abyss, I *really* need to take some time and make more of these. Note to self, after destroying your weapons in an Alpha Strike, *go make more weapons*."

With a swirl of his hand, a Beginner-rank circle was drawn in the air. "Got that down to eight seconds, nice. *Ritual Duplication*! Let's call it four seconds each on average—no, that makes it sound faster than it is. Two for the price of one is *not* the same as fifty percent each, in this case."

Activating both of the magical weapons, he moved on to the next, leaving them hanging in the air unattended. Just after he completed the next duo, the first two sputtered out and vanished, having used the entirety of their payload. Joe grunted as he pushed himself to work faster but was fully unable to shorten the time between creating them any further. "This is why... we are supposed to... make all of these *before* going into combat!"

His efforts were paying dividends—Joe was able to hold the empty section of the line all on his own so long as he maintained his current pace. Between the two rituals he was able to generate with each iteration, he was able to fight on par with what approximately twelve of the farmers could manage. Beyond that, the passive healing effect of his Neutrality Aura was bolstering the humans he had come to rescue, quickly knitting their bruised and broken flesh back to full health and letting them get back into combat.

Soon, even the people who had been driven away quickly stepped forward and reformed the line, reducing even more of the pressure the Ritualist was under.

"You!" Joe called to a random farmer. "What's the plan here? Are we going to have you all fall back so it's easier to defend this place, or *what*?"

"Already did that three times, mister," came the brusque reply. "We fall back anymore, we're going ta' lose the whole farm."

Nodding to show his understanding, Joe continued with his ritual creation, focusing carefully on each of the details as his hands flew. Another appeared in the air, followed by another and another almost instantly. Then again, and *again*. He heaved a sigh of relief as each detail of the ritual appeared clearly in his mind—bringing into play Somatic Ritual Casting's effect of allowing him to generate the diagram instantly. Immediately he began moving faster, creating a circle in the air and recreating it with ritual duplication, only because he wanted to level up the skill as quickly as possible.

Thanks to his capped Dexterity, he went from creating two circles every eight seconds to generating four of them *per* second. Moving down the line of defenders, he made a veritable wall of magic, sending hundreds of Elemental Bursts each second. In under ten minutes, he had circled the camp fully, and his efforts provided relief both from the encroaching monsters as well as rapid healing and rehydration wherever he went. By the time he reached his starting position, the farmers were putting up a *much* less one-sided fight.

Even so, more of the Tillbane Wretches were growing on the outskirts of the farm constantly. Joe ran forward a dozen steps, his orbs swirling around him and pulverizing any of the monsters that came close. Then he repeated his instant creation of rituals, creating a one man defensive line. Still, it wasn't enough, so he dropped his hands and focused on his Ritual Orb of Intelligence, taking a deep breath and sending it spiraling out to its maximum range, piercing through dozens, scores, then *hundreds* of the creatures.

With one portion of the perimeter suddenly cleared of monsters, he turned his efforts to the next. Reaching the third side of the camp, Joe found that the farmers had joined forces with their friends and were hacking their way through all on their own. Instead of taking over, Joe let them secure their victory, quietly ensuring each of them stayed at their peak health.

His heart was thundering from the sheer adrenaline of the fight, yet at the same time, he felt a deep sense of dissatisfaction with himself. "No experience, probably no loot. Oh, a couple unread notifications, so I probably gained some skill levels... otherwise this entire thing would have been completely pointless for me to do. I mean, besides saving all the people. Still..."

He rubbed at the back of his shiny head as he noticed a few people in official-looking garments hurrying toward him. Staying where he was, he glanced around the area and found only low-leveled people everywhere he looked. "No wonder no one else from the guild that has gone to a higher world has come back yet. Skill grinding is great and all, but-"

"That's *twice* now you've saved our butts, Joe." The Ritualist blinked, forced out of his inner turmoil as a woman with almost every inch of skin covered by her robes held out a hand as she approached him. "First time poison, second time monsters. I'd say I hope there isn't a third time, but I feel like that would be practically cursing myself. If you see us in trouble, I hope you *always* feel free to pull us out of it!"

The outstretched hand was grimy, absolutely coated in mud and pulped vegetation. Instead of being icked out by that fact, Joe grabbed the palm carefully, making sure not to accidentally crush the Guildmaster's hand. "It's been a while. Teddy, right? The rogue?"

"Close-range mage," she countered with the speed of someone who was long-used to having this exact conversation.

"And yes. Welcome to the Golden Green's main farm. We're, uh… having some troubles at the moment, or I'd invite you in for a drink."

"I wouldn't mind hosting him for a little while, while you clean up."

Joe froze as the familiar voice washed over him, and he turned to glance at the newcomer with a huge smile on his face, practically shaking in delight as he accepted the offer. "Never expected to find *you* here, Papadopoulos Whisperfoot."

"You should know this better than anyone, Joe—" The two of them bumped fists, and the dashing figure flicked his wide-brimmed hat up and out of his eyes before gesturing for the Ritualist to follow him. "—I expect my *friends* to call me Poppy."

CHAPTER TWENTY-FOUR

"Please, take a seat." The Duelist had a smug smile on his face as he waved at a couch with plush, golden, overstuffed cushions. "Most comfortable place on the frontier, guaranteed."

Joe stared at the couch, taking a long, deep breath as he shook his head. "You think I don't know why you want me to sit here? I can't believe you managed to steal these from the temple in the first place, let alone hold on to them this long."

"*And* keep them in pristine condition," Poppy primly finished for Joe. "So… not that I'm trying to hide, but how did you find me?"

Coughing into his fist to buy himself a moment, Joe felt his ears heating up as his face flushed. "Uh… yeah, about that. I was taking a group of trainee Ritualists on a very enthusiastic walk. We weren't expecting to find *anyone* this far out."

"Hmm. Still not paying attention to current events, I see." Poppy's words didn't have any heat in them, but Joe still tensed up. "The sheer population density has made it nearly impossible to go too far without finding people. Even all the way out here, I think there's a proper Town only a mile east? Their population was closing in on fifty thousand, last time I swung by. Not many people managed to get strong enough to survive the bifrost yet, and if they weren't here before it opened… I'd say it got at *least* five times harder to meet the requirements."

"I suppose that makes sense, what with everyone fighting for the same resources, training, and whatnot," Joe agreed with his old friend, lapsing into silence as he stroked his chin.

"Please stop touching me." Poppy slapped Joe's hand away. "I'm not a dog. If you want to pet an animal, you're going to have to go out there and meet Kenny. I'll warn you right now, though; doesn't matter what creature you *want* to see, you're going to end up playing with a goat."

"Why would I ever want to do that?" Joe blinked at his friend uncomprehendingly. "Farm life has really gotten to you, hasn't it?"

"You don't know the half of it." The Duelist's rigid posture failed him at that moment, and he slumped back into the couch. Waving down at his clothes, which were perfectly clean, not a speck of grime on the well-fitted vest and shirt combo, he lamented, "Just look at me! I'm basically wearing whatever I can find laying around these days. Don't get me wrong, I chose this life, but… it's been harder than it was supposed to be."

"I'd tell you what I've been up to, but I'm sick of going over it," Joe spoke into the lingering silence as Poppy's eyes went distant. "Farm life is what you chose? I was pretty sure you didn't come with me because you were planning on laying down roots, making sure you had a house for your daughter to land in when she was admitted to Midgard."

That perked the fighter up some, and he straightened out and nodded firmly, "*Absolutely*. That's why I'm here. I started out, wait, let me back up. I did a year with the Royal Guard, more as a gift from the queen than anything that I was really after. Got some great training, made good coin, but I'm meant more for one-on-one combat than large-scale group tactics. They got a bit *feisty* with me after I kept breaking their training scenarios."

"Took down all the threats by yourself?" Joe hazarded a

guess, getting a proud smile from the other man that all but confirmed it for him. "Took the money, decided to strike out on your own?"

"Not right away." Poppy's hand drifted to the hilt of his rapier, though he didn't seem to realize it. "Instead, I moved into the arena scene for a while, doubled my money, tripled it even, just by betting on myself. After I got past all the individual fights, the same thing happened. People wanted to team up, and I got grumpy when they didn't pull their weight."

"After that, I decided to go back to my old job, which is... I suppose non-disclosure agreements from all the way back then don't matter so much anymore. I don't owe them any loyalty." Poppy's hard tone put a small frown on Joe's lips, but he waited patiently instead of interrupting. "Anyway, I may have fibbed a little bit when I was telling you what I used to do a long time ago. Truth is, I worked as private security for the super wealthy and barely managed to get into Eternium before the monsters out there overran the private island we were on."

"*Abyss*, dude." Joe leaned back as he looked at Poppy in a new light. "Are you being serious right now?"

"Yep. Anyway, I made a name for myself in the arena and spread around that I was looking for work." Poppy waved around the large tent they were in. "That's how I ended up here. Technically, I'm the security consultant for the entire guild, but that just breaks down to fighting the monsters that are too strong for them to handle on their own and giving the members some regular training."

"But... farming? On the frontier?" Joe winced dramatically, a hand on his heart. "I'm just not seeing how this is getting you what you want."

"Need to build a home, Joe. Nothing available in the city, or not worth having, and I wouldn't want to raise her there, anyway," Poppy explained bluntly. "Money wasn't doing me much good, not with the price of everything going so far up. I like the freedom we have out here, and we have a bit of breathing room. Now..."

Joe stepped in to fill the silence left behind by Poppy's hesitation. "Now you just need to figure out how to build a house without those Wretches ripping it apart, yeah? What's up with all that, anyway?"

"Mind if I join you?" Teddy's voice was barely muffled by the fluttering tent flap, which she shoved out of the way as she stepped into the small space. "I'd invite you over to the main guild tent now that everything is taken care of, but…"

"-My couches are more comfortable." Poppy finished for her, earning himself an eye roll as Teddy pulled back her hood and flopped onto the cushions. "Not a problem; this is a conversation that should be more private, anyway."

"Straight up, what happened is we made a mistake." Teddy launched into her explanation with a long sigh. "We were turning a good profit and decided to expand the size of our guild. Joe, we are *great* farmers. Frankly, the amount of produce we're, um, *producing*, is absolutely ridiculous. Even so, every *scrap* of it is bought up at a premium before we can get all the way to market. So we decided to increase the size of our fields. Basically, just doubled the amount of land we were using."

Clenching a fist, she glanced out the ground and spat through clenched teeth. "We thought we were prepared for more Tillbane, but we assumed it would only be double the number of them. That makes sense, right? Double the land, double the monsters? I'm not crazy here?"

Already shaking his head as he opened his mouth to reply, Joe leaned heavily on his Calculus and Number Theory Lore to explain, "No, that doesn't sound right at all… Don't look at me like that. Did you add a second field the same size as the first? Or did you just push the boundaries of them back? Looks like you are cultivating all the land around you in a big circle with yourself at the center."

Vaguely motioning with his hands, the Ritualist did his best to ignore her stricken expression. "If you had, let's say, a hundred yards of farmland and doubled it to two hundred yards, you're going from thirty-one thousand, four hundred sixteen square yards to one hundred twenty-five thousand, six hundred sixty-four square yards of farmland. By doubling the amount of space you were using, you should have planned for a *quadrupling* of the monsters."

"Basically put a giant sign up that says 'come murder us' to the Tillbanes." Poppy grunted as he crossed his arms in annoyance.

"First, I *hate* the fact that you were able to do that math in your head." Teddy shook her fist at him, though it wasn't anger in her eyes, but despair. "Second... yeah, that tracks with what actually happened. I'm just not sure what to do. We abandoned the expansion, but they're still coming. I'm glad we kept this to just us because... I'd hate to have to admit publicly that, before you arrived, we were right on the verge of running."

The three of them sat in silence for a few moments, until Joe raised an eyebrow. "Now that you know this, what are you going to do? Is there anything that *can* be done to slow the monsters or make it so they stop coming at you? At least *as* much?"

"Not a clue." Teddy shrugged helplessly. "They show up anywhere wild land is converted, whether that's into towns, fields, whatever. At this point, we might have to get mobile again. If we scrimp a little bit, we should be able to set up a smaller farmstead a few miles-"

"*Wild* land, you say?" Joe's mind was churning along furiously. "Because we're on the frontier. This is starting to make sense, because I've messed with a *whole* lot of land in the past without ever once seeing one of these Tillbanes. What if I said we could help each other?"

"I don't have anything to pay you with, Joe, and I'm not sure what exactly you're offering in the first place," Teddy cautiously replied, obviously trying not to get her hopes up. "We've been stuck in survival mode for weeks, and even the food we need for ourselves is almost gone. Money? Forget about it. Even if we got the land up and running *today*, it's going to be another month before we are able to get out of famine mode."

"I can help with both of those. Probably." Joe waved a hand back and forth to show that the odds might be a *bit* more iffy than he was letting on. "Here's the thing, I have a land claim token-"

"Look, even if things are bleak right now, I have no interest in the Golden Greens becoming a subordinate of the Wanderer's Guild." Teddy's words came out sharply, but she bit her tongue as Poppy reached over and put a hand on her shoulder. Joe's eyebrows shot up at the interaction, and he began to think that maybe there might be a *second* reason Poppy had stuck around in this seemingly hopeless situation. "I just can't do that to my people."

"Good, because I wouldn't ask you to!" Joe cheerfully replied as he settled back in the plush cushion. "See, I don't need money, but I *do* need to use this land claim token. It's going to grab a pretty big chunk of real estate, since it's, um, a duchy-sized claim token."

"Feces on a stick, Joe, what did you *do*?" Poppy groaned on his friends behalf, but the Ritualist merely waved him off.

"I'm not planning to stay on this world, at least not for any real length of time," Joe informed him with pure conviction. "But I'd *love* to have someone I trust taking care of the area while I'm gone. Building it up, making farms happen, things like that. Maybe a nice house or two?"

This was directed at Poppy, who said nothing, but tilted his head forward slightly to acknowledge the point. For her part, Teddy seemed less defensive and more contemplative. "Sounds good, Joe. Too good. What's the catch?"

"I need *cheese*."

CHAPTER TWENTY-FIVE

"I'll claim the land, setting this as the center of my territory. To help you guys get back on your feet, I'll put together some rituals that'll make life easier for a while, as well as raise a few buildings, while I'm at it. You'll have all rights necessary to cultivate the area, exploit the natural resources, and have complete autonomy within your own guild. Oh, let's not forget an automatically renewing hundred-year lease on the land."

The quill in Joe's hand flashed across the parchment, leaving behind the words he was saying out loud in a neater, more legal-looking format. "In return, Teddy, and therefore the Golden Greens Guild, will act as my steward in my absence. Instead of collecting coins as my tax, twenty percent of all your profits will come to me as cheese. Stored, hoarded, traded or produced... I don't how care how you do it."

"Still not sure why you want cheese as your payment." Teddy glanced at the parchment questioningly, perhaps wondering if he was saying one thing and writing another.

"Shouldn't matter to you, as cheese is something I know you can get." Joe brushed off the question, not wanting to let out the secret of how it was the only currency of note a few worlds up from this one. As far as he knew, he was the first to return from Vanaheim, and by the *abyss*, he was going to get some *benefits* from all his hard work. "I want a fortune in fermented milk by the time I get back. Wheels ready to roll out, wedges stacked to the sky. Actually... here, I'll give you one of my storage rings after I empty it out, so you can directly store my cut."

"Cut the cheese," Poppy murmured under his breath, too quietly for anyone but Joe to hear. "Cut *of* the cheese?"

"Something you want to share, Poppy?" Joe let out a quiet chuckle, his eyes on the ink drawing on the parchment, though he was almost certain his friend's face was flushing. "No? Then, if this is agreeable to you... sign on the dotted line."

Teddy read over it then glanced up at Joe, a hint of concern still in her eyes. "This isn't a magical document. How do you know I'll follow through?"

"Same way you know I will." He shrugged nonchalantly, trying not to show exactly how badly he wanted this deal to go through. "Good, old-fashioned trust. I'm going away, who knows for how long. When I come back, I'll be even stronger. If I need to *flatten* this place and put someone else in charge of getting me the cheese I want, I could. Or, instead of going through all that rigmarole, why not just work with people I want to work with from the start?"

"Fair." Teddy signed the document, slightly rigid from the disbelief mingled with relief flowing through her. "Okay. You follow through on your end, and I will... gather cheese. Hey, I need to make sure to introduce you to our main animal handler, Kenny McGruff. Before that, how do you feel about goat cheese?"

"Baahh-ad," Joe bleated at her, only to immediately backtrack. "In a more serious way, I don't know. Feel free to include it, and if it doesn't work for what I need, I'll just ask you to stop. That fair?"

"Fair is a four-letter word in negotiations, Joe." Teddy scrawled her signature on the line. "But since it's in my favor, I'm not going to say no. Pleasure doing business with you."

"Great." Joe stood up, lacing his fingers together and cracking his knuckles. "In that case, let's get this show on the road!"

Stepping out of the tent, Joe glanced up at the sun, which hadn't quite hit its zenith yet. "Just before noon. I should have plenty of time to get all this done today. Two days at most. Hey, you guys want to help me work on some rituals?"

His question was directed at the members of his coven, who had gathered around to wait and see if they were going to be going back into the woods or could accept the local's hospitality and sleep in a proper bed for the first time in a week. Hearing that they'd be staying, likely overnight, specifically to work on rituals more powerful than they could generate themselves? Not one of them had a complaint.

"Fantastic. Just one thing I have to do first." He pulled the embellished land claim token out of storage and rolled it across his knuckles before flicking it in the air, catching it with a flourish, and activating it with a simple flash of intent.

You are attempting to activate a land claim token (Duchy). Please note, using this item will automatically grant you the title of 'Duke of Ardania', which comes with its own benefits and responsibilities. The location you choose to claim will impact the amount of land under your direct control. The farther you are from the capital city, the more land you will be able to claim. Would you like to use this land claim token now? Yes / No.

As he selected 'yes', the world paused.

Joe's eyes began to *itch* as his Karmic Perception forced his vision to tunnel onto the coin in his hands, widening as a pulse of ghostly golden light spread outward. The slow nova continued only a short distance before *poofing* into untold millions of golden filaments. They spread out and touched every blade of grass, tree, and person in the area before continuing onward like molecule-sized dolphins—sinking into something then erupting up before diving into the next.

The light moved faster than lightning, extending to the outer bounds of his newly claimed territory, which he somehow understood to be just barely more than forty thousand total acres—nearly *triple* the estimated area the king had given him.

Golden filaments collapsed back in on Joe, overwhelming him with sensations. He could feel the land, its wild, untamed places, how sections of it had begun to rot from too many monsters living in a concentrated area, how it was *angry* at the interlopers… then a more potent force slammed into his mind, and he felt his territory gasp in shock, the ambient mana shuddering in surprise as the full weight of Ardania's royal decree *crushed* the resistance of the now-claimed territory.

In the same moment, every Tillbane Wretch moving through the fields went still then crumbled in slow motion. A bond clicked into place, and a notification appeared.

You have claimed new territory. The size of the territory is large enough to confer a noble title. Checking against the registry of the kingdom you inhabit to see if you are granted this right, or are contesting their rule… congratulations! You have gained a title.

Title gained: Duke of Ardania. As a duly appointed noble, you have gained the right to:

- *Raise a personal army on your land. As a Duke, that army may consist of one thousand total individuals. If the kingdom is attacked, 80% of your personal army will fall under the command of the crown. If your Duchy is attacked by an army-sized contingent of enemies, the kingdom's military is obligated to send out a force to defend your land.*
- *There is an automatic 30% tax applied to all sales within your realm, but you have been granted a ten-year stay to develop and stabilize your territory.*

To expand your domain, you may:

- *Increase citizen morale and population.*
- *Improve quality of life and ensure access to natural resources.*
- *Create high-quality local services.*
- *Build high-quality dwellings.*

- *Ensure adequate food, water, and shelter across each of the settlements in your Duchy.*
- *Develop and secure infrastructure, which allows for trade routes and external markets.*

As Joe finished reading over the information, the land claim token shifted and flowed across his fingers, wrapping around his index finger and reforming as a golden ring. Immediately he checked it, raising an eyebrow in appreciation as he saw that the title he'd just gained had been automatically assigned to the newly created item instead of taking up a space on his character sheet.

Item created: Signet Ring of Duke Joe. This ring is soulbound to Duke Joe and can be recalled at any time with a simple desire to do so. When worn by Joe or his designated heir, this item automatically applies the title 'Duke', conferring all benefits and responsibilities the title generates. When worn by another party, this item automatically applies the title 'Duke by Proxy', granting rights and privileges for Duke Joe's territory.

"Neat." Joe turned and locked eyes with Poppy, who had just stepped out of the tent to see what all the commotion was about. Only then did the Ritualist remember that dozens of Wretches falling apart at the same time was cause for celebration, and enthusiastic cheering erupting across the farms was something normal people tended to be curious about. "Hey, I saw how you were looking at Teddy. Should I give this to her, or do *you* want to?"

Bobbing his eyebrows at the Duelist, Joe offered the golden ring, only for his friend to *harumph* and roll his eyes at the antics. "Don't worry, I can tell at a glance that *you* giving that to her offers no real permanence."

"Oooh, so you're thinking about *long-term* commitment," Joe teased as he swept past his now-sputtering friend, peeking inside the tent and flicking the golden ring over to a very surprised Teddy. "Catch! Congrats, it's official, you're in charge of this place, unless I have to take it back. I'm immediately abdicating this responsibility."

Returning to his coven, Joe clapped his hands together and looked around with a bright smile. "Now, shall we get to the fun part of the day? Who's ready to read through the Ritual Combat Manual and help me decide which diagram would be the best to design for defending this farm? I'm thinking it should take us no more than an hour or two to put together our initial ideas then compare notes and decide on an action plan!"

As every member of his coven threw their hands up, Poppy crossed his arms and sadly shook his head. "*This*, Joe. This is how I know they've been around you too long. Why not just look into... you know what? No. I'm not even going to give you ideas as a joke."

"And *that's* how I know for sure we used to be party members." Joe slapped his friend on the back and grouped up with his coven, already feeling a little behind, since they had each pulled out their own book and were quickly paging through it.

Trying to get ahead of them, the Ritualist opened his own heavily annotated manual and flipped to the back, finger lightly trailing along the embellished text as he read. "Master-rank rituals and introduction to war-scale magic. Oh? They only have a few actual ritual circles and no multi-discipline ones? I *suppose* that makes sense. It's not like Artifact-rank cores are so common they can create a bunch of variants and test them exhaustively."

A tiny moment of panic overcame him, and he quickly checked his storage devices, relaxing as he found a small hill of every core from Common to Unique rank practically filling the space in his codpiece. "I've only had one Artifact-rank core in the last few months, and I turned that into an aspect jar. Gonna have to get out there and hunt some big monsters soon..."

"*Gah!*" Big_Mo leaned away from his manual, eyes clenched tight as he rubbed at them furiously. "How does someone even get that many sigils packed so tightly? What are we supposed to be, *machines*?"

"Just read the descriptions. I was trying to force myself to study that same one and," Kirby pointed at her face, where tears of blood were dribbling from the corners of her eyes. "Let's just say Joe's passive healing came in handy."

"If it helps, that's a good start to your evil overlord look," Joe murmured, unintentionally causing the young woman to brighten considerably and return her attention to the book.

"Ritual of the Root Dominion?" Hannah offered an actual option, the first to do so. "Anyone not included in protection from the ritual has any roots in the area burst out of the ground and wrap around their feet, reducing movement by up to seventy percent. Looks like it'll also cause difficulty using movement spells, even teleportation, since they'd basically be trying to move a couple hundred extra pounds of dirt and plants."

"Mmm..." Joe thought about it but eventually shook his head in the negative. "While that does fit the aesthetic of the place, and there's plenty of plants, most of the monsters they would be fighting as farmers are already moving pretty slow. On that note, avoid fire. *Taka.*"

"I already turned the page!" Taka replied in an aggrieved tone. "I was just reading the description."

"I've got one!" Big_Mo turned his book around. "The Ritual of Predatory Earth. Anything moving through the area that shouldn't be gets stabbed by instantly growing earthen spikes. It would have a secondary effect of aerating the soil, which is great for irrigation and growth, right?"

Taking a deep breath, Joe considered how to best phrase his next statement. "I can see why you'd go there, but remember, this is a farm. There's going to be domesticated animals and hopefully people coming in to trade with the locals. Merchants, random civilians, stuff like that."

"In that case, why not use this?" Robert showed his find. "Ritual of Reactive Shielding. Puts a barrier around anyone keyed to the ritual who's about to take an attack, kind of like a basic form of Mage Armor. Only problem is adding people to the protected list, but there's a note here about making a taglock tree."

Each of them flipped to the same page. The more Joe read over it, the more he liked it. "It has five total effects, with the main one being a shield that absorbs five hundred points of damage when someone is about to be attacked. Taglock tree, huh?"

Flipping to the page referenced by the manual, Joe's lip curled in disgruntlement as he saw a drawing of the item: it looked like a miniature pine tree formed out of a thousand needles attached to a central cylinder rod of steel. "Student ranked? I *suppose* I can make that, but it's probably right on the edge, unless there's a forge in town. My anvil only lets me create things up to the Apprentice rank."

"Why in the world would *that* be a limitation?" Taka sent Joe a look that suggested he was making something up. "It's just a chunk of metal, isn't it?"

"Most likely something to do with not being able to handle the flow of energy, combined with the hammering." Joe couldn't offer a better explanation than that, so he returned to the main page. "Main effect is the shield, but it releases a short-lived cloud of... *poison*? I suppose that's to deter the attacker from coming after them, but how does the person—oh, I see, it also teleports them about twenty feet closer to the epicenter of the ritual at the same time. Got it. Block, cloud, vanish."

Kirby took over, reading the next section Joe hadn't gotten to yet. "What are the other functions, if it's supposed to have five? Oh. Constantly tracking each of the people, and calculating the power requirements to bring them in closer? Ick, that's probably a couple tens of thousands of calculations every time they move."

"It lasts a month, unless it uses all its power up," Hannah hopefully pointed out. "Pretty good efficiency, for what it does, and it's something any of us could come back and maintain."

"Look at what it can do if you add in alchemy!" Robert excitedly pointed to the variation written out on the next page. "It's a shield-to-payload transmutation and creates a different effect when the shield breaks based on the state of the person who was attacked. The puff of poison turns into a thick fog of acid if they are already bleeding or explodes if there was fire damage... *or* adds in a static effect that will shock and paralyze the attacker if it's raining. Otherwise, it just explodes in a sonic burst that deals damage and blows the poison toward the source of damage. That's pretty cool."

"I'd rather add in the amplifier; look at this." Hannah tapped two different implements, which had been added to otherwise-identical versions. "This is an antenna that increases the range of the ritual by nearly half, but the other one is a cascade trigger. If a shield breaks, and there's three or more people nearby who are also shielded, the breaking shield explodes into shards of force that deal three hundred percent of the amount shielded to the attacker."

"All of that is great," Joe agreed with them before they could start bickering. "But the fact is, I can only make the circle at the moment. I'm still an Apprentice in Alchemical Rituals, and like I said, I can only make up to Student-ranked forged items, unless I go into a proper smithy. Everyone feel good about this ritual? Want to help me design it? Actually, where should we...?"

Poppy swooped in at that moment, before they could start randomly creating intensely magical and possibly dangerous rituals out in the open. "If you'll follow me, I already had Teddy talk to some of the farmers. They're putting together a good spot for you to do all of this."

Moving past the tents and closer to the solo grain silo that had the guild's flag flapping off of it, the coven soon came upon dozens of farmers who were hauling rocks. They carried huge slabs around handedly, and carted piles of gravel in wheelbarrows. All of it was being dumped into a central area, large enough to be called a Town Square.

Poppy explained before Joe's curiosity could get out of control, "They're using all of the stone pulled from the fields to make a huge square surface. A few of them have stone merging abilities. Once everything is piled up, they'll turn it into a single block that you can draw stuff out on."

"Oh..."Joe winced as his friend shot him a sharp look. "Yeah, that was super proactive of you. I totally understand where you're coming from. Unfortunately, at the Expert rank, I have too many circles rotating for them to just be flat. We either need an actual ritualistic gyroscope—the template is on page one hundred and ten, in case any of you are wondering—or I need to draw it out in the air."

"Ow! My eyes!" Robert clutched his face as blood streamed out of the sensitive organs.

"Journeyman ranked template, whoops!" Joe grimaced until the sloshing stream of blood faded away, his skills passively healing and cleaning the man up. "In other words, none of you need to worry about that for now. I'll need to draw the actual ritual, since I don't have a way to make anything that high level."

Then Joe double checked his skills, fretting slightly before shooting an apologetic look at Poppy. "Then again, I might also need a couple of tries to get it right. My Somatic Ritual Casting is only Journeyman-ranked, so…"

"Do what you have to do; I'll evacuate the area in preparation for you exploding," Poppy responded with a heavy sigh. "Big stone slab first, or no?"

"Nnn—yes. Slab first." Deciding against wasting any more time, Joe pulled out his anvil and let it *thump* to the ground. "I guess we have time to start with a lesson on Ritualistic Forging."

CHAPTER TWENTY-SIX

"I'm starting with stabilizers, which even someone with a Novice-rank forging skill is able to make." Joe grasped at the air, his aspect hammer manifesting in his hand as he settled in next to the anvil. "Since I'm going to be creating an Expert-ranked ritual, and I don't actually have the required skill level to do so, adding in stabilizers and such will *probably* help me keep it from exploding long enough to actually complete the diagram. Now, that means I need stabilizers at the rank of each of the circles, starting with three at the Novice, five at the Beginner..."

Carefully explaining each step of the process to his coven members—who to their credit listened with rapt attention while taking notes—Joe worked both on completing the task as well as boosting his teaching skill. He could practically see the moment each of them either earned Smithing Lore or leveled it up; something about the way they shifted in place, or maybe there was an echo of the energy of the system infusing their eyes for just a moment.

As he lifted his hammer, his mouth constantly spouting information, Joe remembered how generous the system *used* to be when leveling up or gaining skills. It had been a *thrilling* experience, *really* sending electric, addictive tingles through the body. "Musta patched that. Too bad."

"Wait, I missed what you just said!" Kirby looked up rather frantically from her notepad.

"Eh…" The Ritualist pretended to be very focused on his anvil, where a glowing blob sat in a cage of a perfectly aligned Ascendant Matrix. "Just that this will be somewhat different when you do it, since the materials you'll use are actual metals and the like. Now, I *could* just make this according to the template, but I have a Hammering Pattern that lets me boost the chance of success, so long as I'm saying a mantra. According to the description, I can use *any* kind of mantra. It just has to have some kind of repetitive beat, but since this is the first time I'm using it…"

A farmer stumbled at that moment, almost losing his balance while taking a few sharp steps toward Joe, the hundreds of pounds of stone he was hoisting on his shoulders danger-ously close to falling on to the kneeling Ritualist. The bald man stared up at the too-close rock, which slowed and changed course as the farmer managed to regain control.

"Uh… never mind. I'm going to repeat something probably not as *dignified* as I had planned." The others chuckled nervously as Joe took a deep breath and began to chant, a single, slow-moving ritual circle appearing in the air above the blob of aspects and slowly shrinking, brightening for half a heartbeat at the same moment as Joe's hammer came down on it. *"Don't move too fast, I like my head. Dropping rocks that big makes people dead."*

It only took a few minutes for the first stabilizer to fully form out of the aspects, and by then, everyone was already sick of the mantra Joe had made up. Feeling he had made his point, the Ritualist casually tossed the triangle-shaped stabilizer to the side and started on the next one. "The metal is strong, a triangle feels right. Wide little base, pointy and light."

Technically his mantra didn't *need* to rhyme, but it helped the words flow off his tongue effortlessly, letting him keep a steady beat as he slammed his hammer down in the center of the glowing circles that appeared, pleased that the Mantra of Metal had essentially turned his forging into a minigame.

After a while, he was getting too into it, especially now that he was able to compete against himself, and this felt more like fun than work. It took Robert gripping his wrist as he was about to start on another triangle to make Joe blink and snap out of the trance he'd fallen into.

"Sorry, it's just... how many of these do you really *need*?"

Joe followed Robert's pointed stare, a weak smile appearing on his face as he saw dozens of tiny triangles stacked neatly next to each other. "Ah, yeah, that should be plenty for all of us as we get used to using them in conjunction with our ritual combat quests."

The Ritualist blustered, trying not to lose any face in front of his trainees. "Why don't all of you take six of those to get yourselves started? You only need three when you're casting a Novice circle, but *two* sets will let you leave one functioning as you get ready to activate the next one. Yeah... while you're doing that, I'll start on the Beginner-ranked version, and please feel free to stop me once I have fifteen or so. Ya know, since you guys don't really need those yet."

Having made these extremely regularly on Jotunheim, Joe was familiar with the process of creating the forged item, so he powered through them for each of the ranks he needed. The triangles were replaced by flat squares for the Beginner-ranked version, then pyramids for the Apprentice, and finally cubes— Student ranked, and his current limit with the equipment he had on hand. "Eleven Student versions... should I make a second set, or is this good enough for now? Maybe just one or two more? In case one of them breaks and needs replacing?"

"Do you know your eyes are dilated?" Kirby breezily pointed out as Joe licked his lips and started forming another blob of aspects to hammer. "I have to ask... since you left Midgard, when's the last time you did something that was just *fun*?"

"Oh, constantly." Joe stared at his infernal flame-wreathed

aspect hammer, staring in wide-eyed excitement as four ritual circles appeared above the blob of aspects resting on the anvil. "Hang on. Just *one* more, then I'll work on the tree."

Each circle drifted independently, rotating in lazy orbits that only aligned for the briefest of moments. His pupils darted back and forth, tracking each of the circles as they came together. The hammer dropped, passing through each ring in unison, only to *slam* into the blob of aspects. It was obvious that this would be a serious challenge for someone with far lower Perception, Constitution, and Dexterity. But for Joe?

It was just *fun*.

Perfect strike!

Each time the tiny system message floated up in the corner of his vision, he felt a little thrill. When the ritual circles vanished, he immediately frowned and tossed the cube to the side, ready to start again, only for two of his coven members to grip his wrist and pull him to a stop.

Before he could complain, Hannah was standing in front of him with an excited look that gave him pause. "Joe! Now you get to make the taglock tree, and that should get you working at this for a long time, right?"

His lips parted in a tiny 'o' shape as he nodded along, turning the page of the manual over to where the little tree was waiting for him. He barely even heard Kirby mutter to the others behind him, "If I hear 'Cubes, cubes, for these rubes, cube, cube, square forge bloob' *one* more time-"

"The worst part is that it's *catchy* when he's hammering at the same time," Robert was complaining as Joe began swinging again. "Cube bloob. Rube cube. Slippery-"

"Let's stop rhyming and go get these set up. Looks like the platform's ready." Big_Mo firmly interrupted, dragging the others out of Joe's immediate vicinity.

Now firmly in the grip of his efforts, Joe rapidly constructed the central pole of the taglock tree. There was a momentary disappointment as he started working on the first needle, only for it to form on the first perfect strike. But then he realized there were nine hundred and ninety-nine more, and his excitement returned in full force...

...and his mantra shifted to 'needle deedle dee-dle' to the beat of a turtle-stomping plumber.

These strikes were more about finesse than they were strength—gentle taps that resulted in a needle somehow manifesting with the strike, instead of needing to be pulled from molten metal and shaped. In under ten minutes, he was finishing the tree, debating internally whether he should intentionally smash it with the hammer so he could start again or just move on to the next step. Hearing his coven members returning, he reluctantly finished the project and pushed back from the anvil, promising himself some more relaxing work in the near future.

"The tree is done, the stabilizers are... set up? Great work." Joe stood, grabbing the tree at the base and carefully avoiding each of the needles as he whispered under his breath, "Needle deedle- *Ahem*. Let's get going!"

Going to the center of the new, near perfectly smooth platform, the Ritualist crouched down and created an Ascendant Matrix, dissolving the platform and creating a perfect square underground where they could place the ritual while leaving it in an easily defensible spot. Thankfully, he only had to adjust the positioning of the Novice and Beginner stabilizers, as the ritual didn't care if they were in the same 'Z' plane, only the 'X' and 'Y'.

At least, it didn't matter at *this* rank, as they didn't have stabilizers for the higher-rarity circles they would need to take into account. Gathering his coven members in a horseshoe pattern around himself, Joe began drawing in the air, painstakingly slowly—for him—as he verbally explained his reasoning for their benefit.

"Believe it or not, even if the Novice circle is the simplest of them all, putting it *just so* is critical for the functionality of the others. Technically, it doesn't matter so much until you get to the Journeyman rank, but why form bad habits?" The first circle formed without almost any effort on his part, and he pointed out the exact alignment he needed them to focus on.

He did the same for the second, third, and even fourth—where he paused to explain more than the math. "Now you can see why we need space. Look at this, and it should be obvious how the ritual rotating around itself is critical."

With his off hand, Joe traced the sympathetic links between the sigils and equations packed into each and every one of the ritual circles. "Look at how these connect. If I go from out to in, it's a clear, linear set of instructions. Do this, then this, then this, followed by this, *or* do only this, if that fails. Tell me, what would happen if we bypassed *this* sigil, and instead connected to the alternate line of instruction?"

The others, though trying to follow the logic behind what he was saying, eventually had to give up—the circles quickly became too advanced for their skill levels. Kirby tried for the longest of all of them and had the blood flowing from her ears, nose, and eyes to prove it. She pushed on so long that Joe started getting seriously concerned for her and decided to interrupt her thinking and just explain.

"Here's the thing. Think of these sigils as either a set of instructions or perhaps a couple of words, if you don't want to think in math terms. But! If I spin the ring and flip it around, not only does it invert the sigil in relation to the others—making the outer ring have a different meaning all by itself as it connects to the others—it also generates a completely unrelated effect."

He moved to the next ring in. "Look here. Putting this on a tilted axis creates an abbreviated set of instructions meant to decipher these two rings, allowing them to skip a step in the process, if it's required at the moment. It's mainly a power saving feature, at least for this particular line. At five rings, these words and conditions intersect and combine in new ways, not forming magical commands but sentences and conditional logic."

Flashing a smile at them, Joe casually added, "I know that

it's a long way off, but At the Master rank, getting this in place is essentially as complex as writing out the entire instruction manual of getting a rocket off the planet and landing it on the moon. Then bring it back. As for Grandmaster? Well. Even *I'm* going to have to wait and see what that looks like."

He took the time to answer their questions for a few minutes then held up a hand. "Since none of you are able to create Journeyman-rank diagrams, I'm going to focus on just finishing it and the next ring as quickly as possible. Try to keep an eye on what I'm doing, and I'll try my best to walk you through it as I'm going."

After another hour of grueling focus, Joe completed the final Sigil of the fifth ring with a flourish. Giving himself a momentary breather, the Ritualist did his best to ignore the sweat trickling from his temples. Thanks to Stoic Constitution, his hands remained firm and steady, and his Neutrality Aura took care of keeping him hydrated while healing his cramping fingers.

Steeling himself, Joe got back to work and pushed into the next ring. Almost immediately, his inscription tool shifted ever so slightly out of position as a strong gust of wind blew through the area, and the newly forming circle began to whine. Mana surged, welling out of the broken line at a frequency that warned of impending meltdown.

...*Bang. Blast. Detonation. Eruption.*

Joe jerked his hand in the other direction as the magic whispered into his mind, his inscription tool drinking in the mana and aspects he had just written out—the new effect of his Somatic Ritual Casting skill coming into effect for the first time. It allowed him to undo a line he'd drawn within half a second of putting it down, and the ring restabilized, crackling pressure smoothing away as the noise faded, and the magic harmonized with itself once more.

Magical Synesthesia (Student II → Student III).

"System," Joe ever-so-calmly stated as his hands continued tracing lines through the air. "You know better than to interrupt me in the middle of something like this. That was very rude of you."

The notification faded away, replaced by a faint, non-distracting light in the bottom-right corner of his field of vision. Joe continued working, twice more needing to undo some line he had just drawn or recalculate an equation he'd incorrectly input a variable into. But, as the fourth hour since starting the layer came to a close, the Ritualist completed the circle and stepped away with a sigh of relief. He watched with great pride as it stabilized and remained in place without his will holding it there. "Got it in one."

The system also noted his success, rewarding him lavishly. Joe could only think that perhaps it was feeling guilty.

Somatic Ritual Casting (Journeyman VII → Journeyman IX). Wow! You created a ritual an entire tier above your skill level. Keep at it, and you'll be an official Expert in no time!

"Now we just need to power it up." He froze in place, eyes flicking to his heavily capped mana pool. "Know what? Before we do that, maybe we round up some volunteers."

Seeing as they needed everyone in the guild to come and prick their finger on the tiny pine tree anyway... as people formed a long line to poke the tree and get poked in return, it was easy enough to snag seventy-one people—including himself and his coven—to act as power sources. Together, they spread out the mana draw of activating the ritual, and soon it was humming along, the rings rapidly building up speed.

While Big_Mo supervised the remaining guild members to make sure they actually bled on the taglock tree, Joe and the others stared at the active ritual, trying to see if they could learn anything else.

To help them along, the bald Ritualist did his best to point at interesting features. "There! See how the third and fifth rotated at the same speed for two full seconds? When they do that, they never form more than one phrase. Seems stagnant, yeah? But right after that, the fifth shifts to moving just a *hair* faster. Because of that, they're composing new instructions with each pass and stabilizing every seventh second as they come into alignment."

Letting out a low whistle, Taka stared at what looked like nothing more than a floating ball of glowing energy to his senses. "Going to have to get a whole bunch more levels before I see what you're seeing, Joe. That's not just math, it's magical math. *Angry* math."

Just then, another person bled on the tree, and the entire configuration shifted in a way that was so subtle even Joe almost didn't notice—only the golden line of light that suddenly extended from the orb to the farmer letting him track it. "This is so cool... I can't wait to get you guys to the level where we can theorize on this together."

Quest updated: Student Reductionist II. Unique crafts created: 4/5.

Class Quest complete: Apprentice Reductionist V. You didn't just complete this quest, you did it with Verve. *Sorry, no extra benefits just because you're being extra.*

Reward: Ritual pamphlet of Area Defense (5 rituals).

Glancing down at the five ritual diagrams that had just appeared in his hands, Joe double checked to make sure that was the end of that particular quest line, then allowed himself a moment of relaxation and triumph. "I *love* it when I get rewards for things I'd completely forgotten about."

CHAPTER TWENTY-SEVEN

Seeing as he was waiting on each of the members of the Golden Greens to finish their finger-pricking goodness, Joe decided to take a moment and rifle through the small pamphlets he'd earned as a quest reward.

Strangely, he had to accept each one individually, so as each appeared, he glanced at the name and description before storing it away and pulling the next.

Ritual of Blunted Wrath (Student). Causes all bladed weapons used by those not keyed to the ritual to rapidly dull over time. With each attack made in the boundary of the ritual, weapons will chip, points will bend, losing 2% damage, to a maximum of 40% reduced damage, dealt by slashing or piercing weapons.

Ritual of Elemental Ineffectiveness (Student). All elemental damage received by individuals keyed to the ritual and within its boundary will be reduced by 20%. This includes spell effects, enchantments, and terrain damage.

Ritual of Stutter Step (Student). All teleportation, forced displacement, or other means of instant travel within the boundary of this ritual will fail, lest the user of the spell, scroll, item, or ability is keyed to the ritual.

Ritual of Regenerative Denial (Student). All incoming healing, magical or otherwise, for individuals in the area affected by this ritual, and not keyed to it, are reduced by 25%.

"All of these are pretty useful, especially on Midgard," Joe murmured as he selected the final reward, only for his eyes to widen as it appeared in a burst of purple light along with a soft fanfare resounding through the area.

Congratulations! You've succeeded in a lucky draw! The rarity of your quest reward is increased by one tier.

Ritual of the Bugzapper (Journeyman). Upon activation, a radiant pillar of light will erupt from the center of the ritual, forcing all entities not keyed to the ritual to halt their attacks and make a Charisma check per second or be compelled to stare into the light, moving toward it at half their normal walking speed. Any damage dealt to affected individuals will break the compulsion and give them a doubled check to resist for the next three seconds.

Reading over the rest of the ritual's information greedily, Joe couldn't help but grimace at the alchemy requirements of the diagram. "Abyss, I really need to figure out a way to boost my alchemy soon... especially since I *regressed* in what I can make by absorbing Ritualistic Alchemy into Alchemical Rituals."

Reluctantly putting the pamphlet away, as there was no way for him to use it currently—even if he couldn't wait to try it out—the Ritualist looked around, only to lock eyes with a man staring at him. "Big cowboy hat, three different colorations of what I hope is mud on his boots, long piece of grass in his mouth that he's chewing on, matched almost exactly by the goat he's using as an armrest. You must be Kenny McGruff."

"Yawp," came the reply in the affirmative, the farmer tilting his head forward incrementally. "'Choo want?"

Only Joe's high Perception and Intelligence allowed him to instantly translate the thick accent into understandable conversation. "First, I wanted to meet you. Heard good things about how well you take care of your animals. Second, I was hoping to put together a few buildings. Thought I'd start with some stables, stuff like that. Figured you might want to have a hand in picking where they go."

"Yawp." Kenny slapped to the side of his goat, who bleated and meandered away from them, the oversized bell hanging off its neck clanging softly with each step. "O'er'ere's good."

As they started to walk away, Robert called after Joe, "Hey, what should we be doing?"

"They're having a food shortage," Joe glanced back, meeting eyes with Hannah and nodding at her. "Fish is easy to smoke and store, and anything left over makes a good fertilizer, I hear. Why don't all of you start summoning as much as you can for the next few hours, and I'll meet up with you after that?"

"I *love* fish!" an eager farmer called out. "Haven't had a taste since we got into this area. Only groundwater in the area, no rivers or lakes in easy walking distance."

"Did someone say fish? I'm *so* ready to have something light-"

"How fresh is it?"

Rumors of a new type of meat arriving shortly made the rounds, drawing a crowd as the coven quickly sprang into action. Right away, Hannah was positively beaming at the excitement her self-created ritual was generating.

Following McGruff, Joe cast his gaze around his newly claimed territory, watching as a huge swath of people moved through the destroyed fields, leaving behind dirt mounds in neat rows, which he assumed contained freshly planted vegetables. Now that the monster threat had been dealt with, the area was absolutely bustling with activity as the Golden Greens Guild tirelessly threw themselves into their chosen profession. Watching them work, lines of tension etched in their faces, Joe started to feel the weight of his unfinished tasks pressing down on him.

Yet McGruff continued to move at a sedate pace, his languid motions only further heightening the Ritualist's sudden desire to get back to progressing. Opening his mouth to push the man to move faster, Joe forced himself to bite his tongue and take a deep breath. "I've still got a solid four-ish weeks before I have to get back to the town and upgrade the guild. No need to push people unnecessarily."

Still, his plans for personal advancement, as well as power leveling his coven, needed to remain his top priority after this *short* diversion for developing infrastructure.

Just then, Kenny opened his mouth and let out a sharp bleating noise, startling Joe out of his thoughts as he stared at the man, completely nonplussed. The ambient mana in the area reacted to the noise, congealing and swirling into a tight pocket in front of the farmer. It burst with a final outpouring of energy, leaving behind a freshly-summoned goat.

"I thought you were a farmer?" Joe's rhetorical question earned him an amused glance, but Kenny didn't deign to answer, instead slapping the goat on the rump and sending it off, just as he had the previous one. Pulling a pair of long sticks off his belt, Kenny locked them together and twisted, then used the nearly nine-foot long pole to make an 'X' in the dirt.

"Mid' billin' right there."

"All right, let me make sure I got that... you want me to put the middle of the building in that spot?"

"Yawp."

A stack of documents came out of the satchel the farmer was carrying, and Joe didn't miss the official guild emblem etched into its leather surface. Clearly, this was something he'd just been given and wasn't his normal daily-wear bag. The man flicked the top page then handed the whole stack over.

Immediately recognizing the blueprints for what they were, Joe lifted the top paper and allowed his eyes to devour the contents. "All of these are Common rank? Corral barn, huh? Consists of a single structure that includes an enclosed shelter, with a heavy focus on the exterior pen as the key feature. Makes sense. I wonder if I could even make just a fence... well, I can do a wall, so a fence..."

His murmuring grew softer as Joe pulled out a tile and began quickly etching the required ritual, linking it to the blueprint and finding himself ready to activate it only minutes later.

"Hey, I need some volunteers to help with the mana require-ments of-"

Kenny let out a sharp whistle, and moments later, the pounding of hooves filled the air as dozens of goats raced in from every direction. "Got 'em. Magic goats. Don'cha worry 'bout it."

"…Sure." After thinking over the requirements of the ritual for a few moments, and realizing he'd never found a stipulation that he *couldn't* use animals as assistants, Joe directed the crea-tures to the appropriate spots and started preparing. He soon found himself clenching his jaw and twitching at the soft smacking sound of dozens of animals, and Kenny, chewing on grass as they faced him.

Without warning, Joe activated the ritual. Aspects flowed freely from his codpiece, the Ritualist not worrying about the minimal loss he would take by not using aspect jars. Only a few minutes later, Kenny and the goats were staring up at the newly created structure, each of them sharing the same expression of slack-jawed astonishment.

Rituarchitect experience gained: 50

"Purty neat trick." McGruff bobbed his head in reluctant acknowledgment. "Nex'un right away?"

"Yawp." Joe grinned at the farmer as he stole his word. "If your goats can handle it, we can probably get most of these up and going. Question for you while we work, you've got a lot of goats, but I need cheese. Do you have cows as well?"

"Mos'ly goats. Got a *couple* caws. Might git more soon, 'f folk quit chawin' the blasted beasts. Done hadta set mah goats up like lil' guard dahgs 'round the last of our stock. That's jus the poachers, not'ta mention the Wretches. Nah, you want cheese? I can getcha all *sorts* of cheese. Goat cheese, caw cheese, hoss cheese, dahg cheese, cat-"

"I get the picture." Joe hurriedly cut the man off before the conversation could devolve any further. Already, his ears felt like they were going to start bleeding if he let Kenny ramble on any longer. "If it can curdle, you can make it, yeah?"

The farmer tapped his nose twice, then pointed at Joe with a wink. It seemed he was warming up to the Ritualist, probably thanks to his goats rubbing up on the newly created corral as if they recognized it as their new home—which they likely did, being not only goats, and therefore fairly smart on their own, but clearly a magical variant.

"Trick's to make 'em like ya. Treat ya' buddy right, they'll getcha all the milk ya'd ever need." Kenny gestured for Joe to follow after him, not noticing how the bald man was shaking his head.

"I'm not much for animals. Well, no, that's not quite right. I like them just like I like going to a zoo. It's great to see them, know they're being taken care of, but then have someone else feed them, clean up after them, and make sure they're healthy."

"Huh, took ya fer one of them types that had an 'motional support animal." The way the farmer chuckled as he spoke finally pulled a laugh out of Joe.

"No, not so much. If I were going to get an emotional support animal, it'd be a pig. Well, not the whole pig. Okay, *fine*, it would just be bacon." As his temporary companion chuckled, Joe realized the man was actually rather easy to get along with. Soon, they were putting up a set of six silos, four barns, two warehouses, and three longhouses to replace a few of the sleeping tents. Before he could go any further, a notification popped up that gave him pause.

Rituarchitect experience gained (Summarized): 750.

Congratulations, your unincorporated field camp has risen to the level of a Hamlet! Before creating any other additional buildings, please place a Town Hall. As a note, further development will elevate the Hamlet to 'Village' status. As this is a farming-focused Hamlet, it will face unique challenges such as starved bandit raids, animal stampedes, and grazing beast hunting requirements.

"Looks like that's going to have to be all we do for now, Kenny. It was a pleasure meeting you." The two of them shook hands as Joe spoke, and without another word, the farmer turned on his heel and walked away, his herd of goats trailing after him to the accompaniment of dozens of cowbells announcing their presence.

For his part, Joe returned to his coven, only to stay on the sidelines and watch in great amusement as crates of flopping fish were loaded up and carted away—the lower-level Ritualists working frantically to draw out the next one as the hungry locals clamored for more.

When one of them got a bit too pushy, demanding they work faster, the smile fell off Joe's face and he stepped forward and clapped his hands together hard enough to make a small shockwave. "That'll be all for today, everyone. Group, pack up, we're going to be doing preparations for travel. Members of the Golden Greens Guild, it was a pleasure working with you, and... perhaps the next time we're here, you will police some of your more... *rowdy* members?"

They were all good people, and even the offender had the good sense to blush shamefacedly and quickly apologize, but Joe stood firm that they had other things that needed to be done. Still, he was greatly mollified and made a note to come and check on them, even before his cheese would be properly aged. "Right! I should make a shrine here; it'll be a pain in the *butt* to find the place otherwise."

After setting his coven members up with orders to start preparing their rituals for another extended excursion, he hurried out of the boundaries of the town, finding a clear space just past the tree line and generating a small shrine. After dedicating it to Tatum and priming it to connect to the Fast Travel system—which didn't reach all the way there yet, meaning he'd need to create a few of those on the way back to Ardania—Joe returned to the others and pulled out his cauldron.

As he slowly created Elixirs and Draughts, Joe ruminated on his growing frustration and decided to voice his concerns to the others. "Listen, with all of these external affairs taken care of, I'm really feeling the need to push my ritual combat skills further. On top of that, I want to get my hands on an Artifact-rank core. The only place I know for sure I'll be able to find one of those is pretty deep in the Forest of Chlorophyll Chaos. Thing is, the monsters there get pretty high level, and I can't guarantee you'll all be safe. Would you like to join me for most of the trip, then I can give you directions back to the guild?"

"Are you *kidding*?" Kirby answered nigh-instantaneously. "I'm going in there with you. It's dangerous, sure, but that's exactly what I need to push my skills. It's not like I'll get another chance to go in there anytime soon, and we'd be safer with you than pretty much any other guide, right?"

"You're all still using Novice rituals; I don't think-"

Joe's slow response was practically ignored as Taka took over the talk, "Ah, about that. I had a question on the Class Skills you'd mentioned. If someone wants to become a Sage, somehow they can do that in only one of the skills, right? So… right now, we have to create a ritual circle then modify it with the other skills. How is it possible that someone could become a Sage in, let's say Magical Matrices for instance, and *not* be at the same rank with ritual circles? Just doesn't seem possible."

"Same question, but Enchanting," Big_Mo tossed out with a sheepish expression on his face, practically shouting that he'd been thinking the same thing for a while.

"I'm really glad you asked. It's a great question." Joe slowly stirred his cauldron, extracting the Elixir and tapping the stirring stick on the rim before looking up to meet their eyes. "I don't know."

"Seriously?" Hannah rolled her eyes. "You drew it out just to tell us you didn't *know*?"

"Not just that," Joe replied offhandedly as he began scraping the sludgy remnants out of his cauldron. "Fact is, it really *is* a good question. I need to figure it out myself, because I'm sure it has something to do with leveling the individual skills up more rapidly. It's probably somewhere in my ritual combat manual-"

"I've already looked through it. Book doesn't have a proper explanation anywhere." Robert jumped in, only for Joe to hold up a hand to calm the frustrated man.

"I said, it's probably in *my* manual." Allowing his Neutrality Aura's new function to eat away at the last film of filth, Joe sat on the ground and pulled his tome out. "Why don't the rest of you keep working? I'll let you know if I find anything."

The rest of his coven had started circling around him, hoping to read over his shoulder, but at Joe's insistence, they reluctantly returned to their tasks. Allowing himself to sink into his book, the Ritualist's fingers flipped the pages of the manual with a sharp precision, his eyes rapidly scanning the dense writing. He wasn't searching through the regular contents of the book, only the annotations left behind by Grandmaster Pete.

If Robert said the information wasn't in the standard book, he was going to believe him.

Many sections were easy to ignore, such as alchemy symbols, dry instructions on altering the formulas in the book, and pretty much anything which started with the underlying of a passage and had an equation written in it. "Feces, all I know now is that he didn't learn it as an Apprentice, or Student... a~*and* officially not when he was a Journeyman-"

Joe flipped through the next couple pages, froze, and went back two. There, nestled in what had been a blank space between the Journeyman and Expert sections of the book, were words written so densely in ink that, at first glance, it had looked like someone had just painted it black. "*On ritual discipline specialization...* I think this is it."

"Read it!" Kirby immediately demanded, though, to her credit, she didn't drop what she was doing, instead splitting her focus while completing yet another Novice-rank circle.

Joe complied, hesitating only slightly since he wasn't exactly certain what he would be saying. If this spelled out an extremely difficult, hefty requirement, he didn't want to crush their dreams of following along this path. He knew firsthand that it was all too easy to crush someone's enthusiasm for progression if you let them know *exactly* how difficult it truly was going to be.

"He starts with alchemy, which makes sense, as this was the

Grandmaster of Alchemical Ritual's old book." He paused for a heartbeat, trying to give the ancient man a little more credit. "To be fair, it would also be the first alphabetically, so maybe he's just-"

"Joe! Read the book!" Big_Mo barked in frustrated exasperation.

"Right." Letting his gaze go back to the start of the passage, the Ritualist took a breath and started. "Alchemical Rituals are not simply chemically enhanced ritual circles, as I've known for a long while at this point. Mostly, I see the class skill of ritual circles as the entry point, but I can already see the path forward without needing to progress it any further than the Expert rank I've just achieved. Certainly the ritual diagram remains necessary, but I've finally-"

"Okay, I'll take it back. Maybe you read it first, then condense it down a bit? I don't need to listen to an old man's journal." Taka was practically vibrating with frustration as Joe read out the passage word for word.

"*Well?*" the Ritualist growled, annoyed at the constant interruptions. "I'm trying to make everyone happy here! Do you want to hear all of it, or a condensed version?"

"Condensed!" The group shouted practically in unison.

"*Fine!*" Furrowing his brow in concentration, Joe read through the entire novella worth of information, eyebrows going up in surprise, mouth shaping into an 'o' of understanding, before returning to contemplative reading. Finally, he looked up and met the searching eyes of his friends.

"I think I've got it down well enough to explain it, at least. Here's how it works-"

CHAPTER TWENTY-EIGHT

"I'm still going to read a little bit of what he says-" Joe pushed through the immediate groaning "-because it's important! Listen, he says in here that no one under the Expert rank in at least one of the disciplines, which is what they call the class skills, is given this information ahead of time. They don't want people to be too focused on any one thing, which I *actually* agree with."

Big_Mo lifted his hands defensively. "Shouldn't that be *our* choice? I know what I want to be able to do with these things, and I don't really care about the rest of it."

"Well…!" Joe started heatedly, only to trail off and cough gently into his hand. "Then you're in luck. As it turns out, it's not overly necessary, especially since you seem to be leaning heavily toward Enchanted Ritual Circles. I'm just going to start reading."

"**Ahem**. I've finally been told how the disciplines break their shackles—that is… how the disciplines outpace the original Ritual Circle skill. The simplicity annoys me to no end, as I feel that I've wasted many years as a generalist when all I've wanted to do is bring alchemy and rituals together to the highest heights."

The others grumbled softly in agreement, but Joe knew their curiosity would get the better of them soon enough. "While Ritual Circles are the bones of all of this, they are not the bottleneck I once thought they were, the hard ceiling against which all the other disciplines would press. Alchemical Rituals... in my mind, the most finicky, the most alive of the disciplines, barely needs the others. If I push this hard enough, my Ritual Magic skill lifts higher than I thought it should have been able to go. After learning a class-specific *methodology*—he underlined and circled that word, I don't know why."

"Methodology?" Hannah quizzed him, earning a nod of acknowledgment. "Well, if it's anything like forging, maybe that's its version of a mini game? Hey... seriously, don't grin like that, it makes you look really creepy."

"Like what?" Joe reached up and touched his lips, which were twitching in excitement at the thought of gaining access to another crafting 'game'. "Enough about me! Where was I... ah. Using my knowledge of Ritual Circles as a base, and my many years of work as an Alchemist previously, I'm now able to condense my reagents from the inside out, creating the diagram within the liquid itself—rituals in a bottle."

The Ritualist paused for a fraction of a second, his mind tripping over that concept, fully uncertain how it would work. "If I did it correctly, the simple act of uncorking or smashing the bottle will have the liquid shifting on its own to form the circle that's required. Gone is the tedious drawing of lines, placement of metals and stabilizers. Now, all of it, from Novice to Expert, can be completed within my cauldron."

"I like the sound of *that*." Kirby's mumble broke Joe out of his rapid reading, a reminder that he was supposed to be condensing *some* of the information.

"Me, too, if I'm being honest. Still, I think my mainstay is always going to be Ritual Circles." Joe tapped on the book. "By the way, it outlines the way to gain skill levels in each skill. For

Magical Matrices, the fastest way to advance it is by taking rituals and *simplifying* them. If you were able to get to the Master rank in that skill, it means you should be able to take any Master-rank ritual and simplify it down to the Expert level."

"Does it say how much you have to simplify something to gain experience?" Taka asked with a hint of desperation in his voice.

Double checking to make sure he wasn't giving the man incorrect advice, Joe responded, "Looks like you need to reduce the requirements of any given ritual by at least ten percent in order to gain some skill experience. Doesn't mean you'll be able to *create* it, but-"

"It's a start," Taka finished for him, satisfaction filling his voice. "I can do that. Especially if you can figure out how to help me get a couple extra Lore skills."

"Yeah, you know, I need at least one more as well." Joe grumbled as he sent a sidelong glance at his skill sheet, where Knowledge and all of his other Lore skills remained stuck at Journeyman nine. "Also, apparently, since forging has Hammering Patterns, and alchemy has Methodologies—if we got the context of that correct—then matrices has 'Sequences'. Don't know much more about them; Pete only added a slightly spiteful message about spatial reasoning and timing."

"What about enchanting?" Big_Mo interrupted, tired of having to wait his turn. "I'm assuming I don't need to keep grinding out my regular enchanting skill?"

"Sorry, yeah, you're right. Looks like almost all of these need Ritual Circles to hit at least Expert rank, but Enchanted Ritual Circles calls that out explicitly. Apparently, that's as far as you need to go in the skill, ever. Then the ritual tokens do the rest. Essentially, you're embedding the rest of the ritual onto those, then placing them within the circle. Theoretically, it looks like even a *Sage*-rank Enchanted Ritual Circle only needs an Expert circle as a base."

"Still." Joe paused for a moment, considering the other part of Big_Mo's question. "I'd keep going with the general

Enchanting skill; it's at least not going to *hurt* to have that higher. No notes on any kind of mini game, so that-"

"-Is fine for everyone except for your addictive personality," Hannah interjected under her breath, face shifting to apologetic as she realized she hadn't spoken quietly enough, as the others started to chuckling at her unintentional roasting of their teacher.

"*Lastly*," Joe glowered playfully, then glanced at the book. "Forging. It's kind of like a really bulky version of alchemy, from what I'm seeing here? Essentially, you'll be making stabilizers, amplifiers, redirectors, interchanges, and the like. All of it is supposed to be modular in design, then you combine it and... it *overrides* the need for a circle? He has a little diagram here, but I'm not sure what to make of it. Looks like someone throwing a grenade, but... I don't know how to describe it other than he's terrified he's going to have it go off in his hand."

"You said lastly, but what about the Ritual Circle skill itself?" Kirby pointed out. "What's the trick to having that one as the highest?"

"No tricks in that one, just making and activating ritual circles." Joe half shrugged, not at all disappointed. "I'd love to figure out how to gamify it, but... it's already pretty fun just by itself."

"Pretty sure it's what you were talking about yesterday, with the way the sigils and equations work together to form various syntax." Robert pointed out, making Joe freeze in place as inspiration struck. "Like you said, as you get better at it, you're able to pretty much read everything out, right? The symbols become a word, together they become a sentence, but it can be read as paragraphs, all the way up to enormous grimoires of information at the high ranks. Or, at least, I assume? Sure, it might not be fun in the traditional sense, but it would at least make *sense*."

"Huh." Joe turned his full attention to Robert, his eyes dilating as he read the system notification he'd just received. "Turns out you're a genius."

Congratulations! You have realized an underlying truth of one of your core class skills and have earned a reward!

Skill gained: Magical Syntax Lore (Novice I). You have begun to understand the linguistic structure of magic. As you analyze, construct, and destruct magical diagrams, you will find that the syntax of magic is more easily understood. Misplaced conjunctions, overloaded conditionals, and unbound clauses which cause instability or unintended effects will never be able to hide from you. Effect:

- *Allows you to fine-tune the sigils, placement, and better understand the context of the same within magical diagrams you find or create.*

"That's all I have for now!" Joe closed his book with a *snap*, storing it and retrieving his inscription tool in the same motion. Without any further explanation, he began rapidly drawing out the ritual diagram he was most familiar with: Architect's Fury. Novice, Apprentice, all the way to Student, he scribbled all of it out as quickly as possible, then settled in to study it.

Joe traced a finger along the glowing rings of the inactive ritual, even before the colored lights of the aspects faded away, leaving behind only black lines still shining with a gentle lavender light. "If blueprint is present, then parse structure."

Starting at the innermost circle, he read through the information and equations slowly, giving the system enough time to adjust for his current understanding of how the syntax worked. He'd been doing all of this *without* the associated Lore skill, so as he went, a rapid series of chimes sounded out. Joe ignored them for the moment, deciding against opening the notifications and just powering through, even as the sigils gained a depth and complexity of context he hadn't realized before.

The Ritualist came to one section and almost bypassed it, only to pause and go over it more carefully. "If load-bearing joist schema isn't rated for defined weight, *iterate*?"

He blinked a few times as he thought over that answer.

"Wait a moment. That's not right. It should check against the other positions set symmetrically with itself. This isn't a fallback, it's a *recursive* mutation. It'll just slap something there that eventually does work, but how much power gets tied up in it? Instead of *iterate*, it should be... *check against*."

Unable to stop himself, Joe drew out his ritual again, this time glaring at the simple nested loop and replacing a single symbol. As he finished, the ritual glowed with a soft golden light for a moment before a slightly louder system notification pinged and forced his attention to it.

Skill increase: Magical Syntax Lore (Novice I → Student V). Wow! What a jump! You must have been doing this for a while? Somehow, I don't think you've shown us what all you can do. Prove Mastery in this skill to rapidly advance it, or do whatever everyone else does and advance it slowly by learning on the job!

Variant ritual created: Builder's Intent. This is an optimized, specialized variant of the 'Architect's Fury' ritual. When activated, Builder's Intent scans the assigned blueprint, creating an exacting representation of the structure, with only the slightest flourish: when an error is found in the structural design, the ritual will check against a symmetrical portion of the blueprint and use those details instead, ensuring proper placement and load transfer.

The final structure's requirements are minimized through optimized placement, reducing the total cost of materials by 5%, as there is no longer a need to add in extra material to account for wastage.

"Huh." Joe looked at the newly created ritual, excited at the idea of creating variations using nothing more than a small shift in how the variables were read. Still, his mind kept coming back to one thought. "You know... I guess I never really thought about it much, but the blueprint reading and structure creation portion of the ritual never had its own name 'til now. Nice."

Looking up and around only to realize it was already late evening, the Ritualist felt a moment of great pride as he took in the sight of the members of his coven diligently producing ritual diagrams, one after another. Sure, the Novice-rank circles were fairly straightforward to make, but each one still represented a handful of minutes and a pocketful of copper or silver in components.

The fact that they were so willing to invest so much of their time and coin—Joe's thoughts came to a stop, and he narrowed his eyes. "Right... I bought all of that. No wonder they're willing to use it all without concern."

"Thanks for bankrolling our skill levels, boss man." Big_-Mo's lips curled in a knowing smile as he heard Joe's dark mutter. "Finally finished with what you were doing?"

"Yeah, just putting all this new knowledge I'm finding to work." Joe stood, glancing around until his eyes landed on the not-too-distant tree line. "Be right back; need to stretch my legs. Then I'll join you in building up our arsenal."

"You don't have to go into the woods, you know." Kirby jabbed her finger toward the tents. "They have a porta-potty tent right over there."

"That's not..." Deciding against explaining further, Joe jogged into the trees, made sure he was alone, and cast his Knowledge spell, selecting his newest Lore skill and gaining two levels. As Magical Syntax Lore hit Student seven, he waited with bated breath... only to have his hopes dashed when Knowledge failed to gain a level. "*Ahh*, too bad. Can't be too much longer though, right? A couple more days of this, and then I'll be able to push *six* of my Lore skills into the Expert rank."

Returning to the group and refusing to meet Kirby's twinkling eyes, he settled in next to the others and began quickly generating ritual diagrams. Once his stack rivaled theirs, he switched over to Beginner-rank versions. After those tiles began threatening to tip over with each gentle gust of wind, Joe changed it up once more and started working on *Apprentice* diagrams.

Only after he was sure he had a couple of days' worth of continuous hunting materials ready to go did he reluctantly put away his inscribing tool and pull out his Common-rank cauldron. After starting a fire, he settled in and began creating

Elixirs one after another, his speed of generation now ever so slightly slower than the other members of his coven could create a ritual diagram.

No matter how helpful his Neutrality Aura was, Joe was forced to scrape and scrub at his cauldron between each product he generated, greatly slowing his total progress. "Seriously, what *is* it about alchemy that frustrates me in a way that the other disciplines don't? Is it just that I can't use this in any kind of standalone way? Maybe it'll get better after I figure out a 'methodology'? I guess it certainly isn't going to get *worse*."

Right now, creating the required items for his Alchemical Rituals was done by rote memorization then following a preset formula that allowed for absolutely *zero* wiggle room. Everything mattered, from the placement of the reagents—in his case, aspects—to controlling the temperature to be *just* right, which he wasn't doing very well by using a campfire.

From there it was just timing, sequencing, and absolutely no instinct. It didn't feel magical: it felt like cooking a souffle with a head chef breathing down his neck waiting for any deviation from his explicit instructions.

"Methodologies… how does that come into play? Actually, someone had to be the first to make one, right? Maybe I should focus on that, instead of how this sludge needs to be scrubbed out from under my fingernails." As he made chemical soup over and over, he found his mind wandering as he became more familiar with the process and could complete it without needing to give it his full attention. "I was already using Magical Syntax by the time I figured out what it was. Does that mean there's something I'm doing, or supposed to be doing, that makes this more fun and interesting?"

His Hammering Pattern had been generated originally when he was working under an Expert—yet *another* indication that something happened in the Expert ranks which would fundamentally change the skills—and had been upgraded when he managed to absorb some of the backlash energy from Grandmaster McPoundy overusing his skills.

Then it had taken Tatum layering additional energy on it to forcibly upgrade the pattern yet another time—Joe pushed the thought to the side, returning to the inception of the skill. "It's got to be something at the Expert rank that makes this happen, but it's obvious it can be either brute-forced, taught, or learned by accident if I pay enough attention."

He sank deeper into his subconscious as his hands moved on autopilot, still adding aspects precisely, scooping out the results, and scouring the remnants. Only as he compared notes between his Hammering Pattern and his realization of Magical Syntax did he have a flash of inspiration. "Wait... it's all about studying and learning! I studied under that blacksmith originally, and I self-taught for Ritual Circles. But as soon as I realized what I was doing, I gained *the Lore skill*. Since I had learned the Hammering Pattern from the blacksmith, maybe that made me *not* gain its lore... but what if *Lore* is the key?"

His mind worked through his realizations, coming back to the same question over and over: what if improving one high enough *generated* the other? "If understanding can unlock the lore on its own, maybe pushing that to the Expert rank is what unlocks the—I guess in this case—Methodology? What if no one explains about this until that point, because otherwise you don't get a helpful boost alongside it? At least that would make sense why they don't spread the patterns or whatever around."

Frankly, it made perfect sense to him, enough so that he felt the spark of hope in his chest blaze up into a bonfire as he stared at his skills caught on the precipice of tipping over into the next tier. "Nothing to do but wait and see, I suppose."

It was at that moment that his cauldron shattered, dumping boiling sludge over the embers of his campfire and fully dousing them. He stared at the mess without comprehension, blinking a few times as the shards of his cauldron slowly cooled down from the brilliant white-hot coloration they had taken on. "Uh... what?"

Only then did he realize he'd made a small error. When he had been making ritual circles, he'd made three piles. His subconscious had been pushing him to replicate that with alchemy, and Joe had begun creating Vials—an Apprentice-rank alchemy product. "Abyss, that cauldron was only rated Common... I'm surprised I made even one Vial. Frankly, it should've exploded as soon as I tried to do anything above Draughts. Oh *no~oo*, I can't do any more alchemy. Nothing to do about it for now, so..."

The horizon was starting to lighten, false dawn approaching quickly. Licking his lips, Joe pulled his anvil out of storage and let it *thud* to the ground. "Looks like people have slept long enough! If we're going to go fight in the Forest of Chlorophyll Chaos, I need my weapons back. Let's see how well the Mantra of Metal works when making orbs."

Soon the entire population in the area was up and about. The farmers normally got up around that hour, whether to tend to the crops before the heat of the day or take care of uncomfortable animals. But for everyone else, it was the clanging of metal on metal and a sing-songy chant that roused them from their sleep with angry, crusty eyes.

"Spin and swing, float and fling!" *Clang, clang!* "Shiny balls are my new bling!"

"He's doing it again!" Taka moaned, pulling a pillow over his head. "Somebody hit *him* with a hammer and see how he likes it."

CHAPTER TWENTY-NINE

"When are you going to stop making those things?" Hannah's words caught Joe off guard as he tossed another Student-ranked Ritual Orb to the side.

"Huh?" blinking a few times, the Ritualist glanced at her in confusion, then realized he hadn't let anyone know what he was doing. "Right, those are actually my weapons. Most of them broke when I was on another world, and I needed to replace-"

"You've made about a dozen of them now, and I was just worried you were falling back into doing one thing too many times." Hannah interrupted, seeing that Joe was already returning his attention to his anvil. Yet again, her words gave him pause, and he slowly set his hammer down.

"Yeah... I think I might have a problem." Glancing up with a sheepish expression, Joe forced himself to step away from the anvil. "My cauldron broke last night... err, I suppose it was actually this morning, and I'd been saving forging for a reward."

"It's not wrong to have *fun*, Joe." Seeing that he was floundering for an answer, Hannah moved closer and rested a hand on his arm. "Just like anything else, it's when you get too invested in it. On the plus side, your hobby is something productive and generally useful. If you had to get hooked on something, being a crafter's not a bad way to go. Also, can't you just make a new cauldron?"

"Probably? But it's not that easy." Joe explained the restrictions on his skills, specifically how, if he were to make something not explicitly for the creation of rituals, it would fail. "Most likely, I'm going to need to go and purchase a new cauldron from somewhere or find someone who I can commission to make a cauldron specific for rituals and sell me the template they make for it. Not even sure where I would go for that on Midgard, which means leaving the world and trying with the Dwarves or something. But I'm not sure how long travel between worlds actually takes, and I have a couple major events going on here that I don't want to miss."

"Not to mention…" Hannah jerked her head to the side, silently drawing Joe's attention to the other members of the coven that were packed up, waiting patiently with their packs on and eager expressions on their faces. "We were supposed to leave half an hour ago."

"Right!" Joe swiped his hand over his stacks of goods, vanishing them into his storage device. As he walked alongside Hannah, he pulled out one orb after another, slotting the smooth metal balls into his bandolier and mutteringly inspected his gear. "Broke everything except the Intelligence and Strength-bound ones… now I have two at the Unique, and the rest are only Rare and deal a *fraction* of the damage. Only silver lining is that I don't need a control cuff anymore and can still use five of them skillfully."

Combat Ritual Orb (Rare). Each orb deals a base of 100 blunt damage.

Current Ritual Orbs equipped: 9. You will be able to create a ritual up to the Student rank with the current configuration and material makeup.

Not wanting to get caught up in any more of the local drama, the small group of Ritualists slipped away without saying goodbye to anyone or meeting the eyes of the farmers they passed who were already hard at work. Joe glanced back as he allowed the rest of his coven to step into the woods ahead of him: only to meet Poppy's eyes from across the distance.

The Duelist solemnly nodded at Joe, who returned the gesture before shifting deeper into the tree line and allowing the flora to obscure their line of sights. He let out a deep sigh, already missing his old friend, but he was decidedly pleased that the man had found a life he wanted to live.

Rustling in the underbrush reminded him that they were back in the untamed wilds, and he lifted his Ritual Orbs into the air around him, both to ready himself for combat as well as to simply continuously practice with them and grind his skill levels higher. "Careful, friends. That first step is a doozy."

"No joke." Robert's voice was a hushed murmur, and a quick glance showed that the man was tense and searching around the area too quickly to notice rapid movement. "One second we're walking across flat farmland, then, *bam*! Deep forest where everything wants to eat you."

"Take it easy, city boy." Joe elbowed his coven member play-fully. "First off, nothing's going to manage to take you down with me around. Second, even if something *does*, I can bring you back."

"Less helpful than you might think." Robert's words were harsh, but they left his mouth as if he didn't want to speak them —barely a ghost of a sound making it to Joe's ears.

Trying to ignore his overly tense companion, Joe spoke louder to include the rest of them. "Here's what we're going to —I said take it *easy*, Robert. Nearly knocked your head into that tree. Here's the plan. I've got a pretty good idea as to where the Forest of Chlorophyll Chaos is, but we're going to have to circle it for a while until we can find some Wolfmen."

"Are you *serious* right now? They've been even more hostile the last couple years than they were, even when they were trying to rip the kingdom apart." It was Big_Mo who had the strongest reaction, much to Joe's surprise. "I've heard of entire platoons being deployed against only a couple of human adventures. They've been using overwhelming force-"

"Probably a good idea." The firmness in Joe's voice left not a *hint* of doubt in his words. "Think about it, they're a Shattered race. If one of them gets cut down, they don't get back up. We do. Of course they're going to try and mitigate their losses as much as possible. Now, as I was saying, I want us to start getting into a proper battle mindset. Spread out, watch your zone, and I'll stand in the center and make sure none of you are taking any hits that are going to put you down for good."

Even if Joe wasn't as up to date on human-Wolfman interactions as perhaps he *should* have been, the intense reactions seemed overblown. The extreme anger in their eyes put him on edge, so it was almost a relief when the first attack came less than half a mile out of the fields.

The ambient rustling in the underbrush shifted into a crashing, the hallmark of a charging beast. An enormous stag burst out of the leaves, a hardened, mana-crazed monster. Its fur seemed to be made of stone, its hooves reflecting light like polished steel. Having already spotted the group, it released a grating bellow as it breached its concealment and lunged for them—antlers lowering in preparation of goring the team one after another.

Then Joe was next to it, gripping its antlers and twisting the creature to the side hard enough to send it to the ground.

It crashed and rolled, leaping up with a deep baying, which seemed out of place from such a creature. Whipping its head around, the stag looked for the bald man who had tossed it— but Joe was already far above, watching from the limbs of the trees. "Kirby, you're the closest; it's coming for you in the next two seconds. Get that ritual up between it and you, now! Taka, support her from the left. Robert! Don't just *stand* there, get a tile out!"

Deciding that they all needed a wake-up call, Joe let them fumble through the fight, for the first time not taking an active role alongside them by activating his rituals. A circle of bluish white spiraled into being just in front of Kirby, the Ritual of Elemental Burst blasting the stag with wind just in time to push it to the side. A second later, she would have taken a tine to the shoulder—dangerous, but not immediately fatal.

Sharpened stones began to sink into the beast's pelt, drawing out a fresh round of snarls, though still more fury than pain. It shifted slightly, crouching and springing to the side, putting itself out of the direct path of the two currently active rituals.

Joe's jaw dropped, not at the nimbleness of the stag, but at how the others simply stood and watched until it touched down, apparently having not even considered that their target might get *out of the way* of their attacks. Then the monster was among them, all coiled muscle and seemingly polished antlers.

Hannah went tumbling as the enormous weight of the creature slammed into her at an angle, only Joe pressing the stag back with a pair of his Ritual Orbs keeping the hit from being disabling. The frenzied animal reared up, a low sound vibrating out of its throat as it slammed down with its front hooves.

The ground buckled beneath it, and razor-edged stones flew like shrapnel—not unlike the ritual damage it had taken only moments previously. An oversized chunk flew at Kirby's face, only to *ping* off a glistening barrier seemingly made of bubbles interwoven to create some kind of ring mail. Half a dozen of the tiny bubbles popped as the stone impacted them, not regenerating, but somehow being enough to repel what had to be fifty pounds of sharpened rock moving at a high speed.

"No, don't activate-!" Joe cut off his shout with a *tisk* as Taka panicked, releasing a burst of sharpened wind blades from his ritual... which was aimed *into* the group. Immediately, the stag was on the move again, twisting around after the first slices drew blood, then throwing itself straight at Big_Mo.

The bald Ritualist didn't see what happened next, instead reaching out with a tendril of mana and directly interfacing with the rogue ritual. It was the first time he'd ever attempted to wrest control of one away, but with his newly enhanced Ritual Magic skill, it came under his power instantly. Joe deactivated it with a flash of intent, bursting the Novice-rank ritual diagram and causing a minor explosion of wind that cycloned upward before fully dissipating.

"Ten percent of the mana required to activate a Novice ritual? Didn't even notice it." Joe marveled at the ease with which he had taken over the out-of-control Elemental Burst, then remembered his people were currently fighting for their lives.

To his great delight, it appeared they'd risen to the challenge.

Big_Mo was standing shoulder to shoulder with Taka, at an intersecting angle from Robert and Kirby. All four of them activated a ritual near simultaneously, pulling out another and adding on a second layer, even as Hannah did the same from her own, freshly mud-churned position.

Joe looked on with a critical eye as dozens of wind blades and stone spikes pelted the area the stag had come to a rest in, then he lifted his hand and pointed at the deer, sending his Ritual Orb of Intelligence zipping through the air to cleanly penetrate through its hind leg just before it could jump away. "They earned this win. Sorry, stag, shan't simply stand still and so suffer your springy sabotage. A little confidence boost never hurt anyone... except this deer, I suppose."

He hopped out of the tree, and in moments, his coven members were sparklingly clean, even the most minor of bumps and bruises fading into clear, healthy skin. "That was good, there at the end. Something that we should all remember is that ritual casting is meant to be a group activity in the first place. Right now, all of us are using our own rituals, but eventually, for big stuff, you're going to need to lean on each other. If each of you specialize, one of you will be putting together the equipment, another the alchemy, and a few of you might be drawing out the circles together. It'd be pretty cool to see all of you working to activate and control something massive."

Against his expectations, no one was angry with him for removing himself, having clearly recognized the need they had for practice with... *less*... of a safety net. Joe started leading them away once more, and this time they made it nearly three miles before a lumbering, bear-like *thing* spotted them and began rushing over. "Looks like that's more rot than muscle. Nasty. Welp, looks like we found your next learning opportunity!"

Joe popped into the treetops once more, to the others' clear dismay. Worse, the creature didn't care at all about taking the attacks directly, simply running directly through the wind blades, water jets, and sharpened earth spikes. Each attack that opened a wound allowed dark sludge to squirt out, as if the internals of the beast were highly pressurized.

"*Joe!*" Hannah shouted at him as he watched from a comfortable position. "This is disgusting!"

"Sorry, I can't hear you over this fantastic *learning opportunity!*" Joe called from where he was safely watching, chuckling all the while as they danced around the awkward strikes of the extremely durable monstrosity.

As the number of active rituals continued to ratchet upward, the coven members also needed to dodge *those* on top of making sure not to interfere with their companions. Big_Mo was the first to realize they could use the toxic goo to target the bear—no surprise there—and in under ten seconds, all the remaining Novice rituals petered out, to leave only those directly striking at the bear-shaped cesspool.

"Only another ninety-five miles or so before we get to the forest!" the bald Ritualist cheerfully called as he landed on the ground with a **squelch**. "Hey, that thing definitely had a core. Are you guys going to claim it, or do you mind if I pull it?"

There was a literal green cloud of gas escaping from the wounds of the fallen beast. Unsurprisingly, not a single other person volunteered to go and collect loot out of it. After shoving his hand into a gaping wound and sloshing around for a few moments, Joe pulled out a core that quickly shined up as his aura got to work on it.

After hiking another six miles through the dense forest, Joe noticed that the others were beginning to show signs of deep fatigue. Calling for a halt, he had AutoMate tend to them during an over-long coffee break. Once they recovered enough to push on, the frontier was soon filled with flying stones, jets of pressurized water that misted into the air, or neat ribbons of cleanly sliced vegetation.

"*Oohh*, ninety miles to go on the road, ninety miles to go-"

"-take a rest, get back to your best, eighty-nine miles to go on the road!" Taka joined in, much to Joe's enthusiastic clapping and the others' dismay.

Several days passed like this, with Joe only calling a halt once he was *certain* his far-lower-leveled companions couldn't push themselves any harder.

By the time the almost-neon-green leaves of the Forest of Chlorophyll Chaos came into view, he was all but positive they were ready to give up and go home.

"Welp, we made it!" He turned to them, trying to maintain his false cheerfulness as the reality of venturing off on his own again began settling in. He cleared his throat and tried again.

"Now, I'd like you all to pay attention to what's been happening for the last few days. I've barely stepped in at all, and the strongest creature you've had to fight topped out at level fifteen. The weakest monster among those trees is at level twenty. Not only are you going to be fighting something better prepared, stronger, and more intelligent, there's also the fact that Novice rituals will do pretty much nothing other than tickle them. With that in mind... I think it's time for all of you to work together to bring yourselves back to Towny McTownface."

It was a testament to their exhaustion that the other members of his coven didn't react immediately to his words. But when they did, Joe was frustrated and surprised by their answers.

"Not a chance."

"At this point, I'm going in there with or without you."

"It just says I have to use the ritual in combat, not that I have to *win* or anything like that."

"If you think for *one* second-"

Letting out a heavy sigh, Joe ran a hand along the side of his bald head and slowly looked at each of them in turn. "Okay, enough, I get it! Look… I can't stop you—I mean, I can—but going in here isn't a great idea. I won't be able to sit back and take it easy in there, I'm going to be fighting in earnest. If you're coming-"

"Oh, they should *definitely* go with you, Joe the Ritualist." A growling voice came from behind him, and Joe spun around with wide eyes—his Perception hadn't notified him of any living threat in the immediate vicinity. "After all, it's *dangerous* to go alone."

When he saw a Wolfman standing nearly fully upright, he didn't exactly *relax*, but he did feel a little better. They were *famous* for being able to traverse the woods silently and stealthily, and that was without the odd, twisting rerouting of space the chaotic forest earned its name from.

"I'll be going alone either way, unless I manage to secure a few safe travel tokens." Joe carefully phrased his words to ensure he wasn't making a request, which could be taken as weakness —no different than baring his throat to the beastkin. "Don't suppose you've seen a few of those lying around, looking for new owners?"

"Hrmm…" The Wolfman growled out a laugh as it strode forward slowly, feet not making a sound though they landed on a carpet of leaves and dry twigs. "I can do a trade, perhaps? Safe passage for cleaning up a mess your *kind* are making."

"I'm definitely open to discussions," Joe replied neutrally, his Ritual Orbs forming into a cluster in front of him, just in case. "What did you have in mind?"

"One of your oversized groups of common purpose are intent on attacking a place of power," the Wolfman spat as if the words tasted foul on his muzzle. "They are trailblazing as we speak, and when they reach their destination… they will die."

"Seems to me," Joe did his best to keep the confusion out of his voice as he pressed for information, "that your problem is taking care of itself, in that case. Why do you want me to-"

"It is not *them* I worry about," the high-ranking Wolfman Scout snorted in derision. "But what they are unleashing. An endless swarm is sealed behind the door they seek to open. One which will blanket the land, leaving behind nothing but earth and stone where they pass. Their queen, the matriarch, will release hundreds of her spawn each *second* once she has been awoken, and there is enough space for her to do so. Say you will clean up their mess, and I will hand you the tokens right now."

"Hold on…" Joe saw no reason to mention that he was after a place of power himself. "If I clear it, I want it. Any problem with that?"

"Live… and let live." The Wolfman tossed over a clinking satchel before stepping back and fading into the forest. "Once the swarm is eradicated."

"Perfect." Joe showed a mirthless grin as he checked the bag. "Harmony through homicide. The proverb that practically writes itself."

CHAPTER THIRTY

"Okay, everyone, looks like we have some choices to make. Who wants to help me make some Expert-ranked rituals?" Joe handed a token to each person, fully aware the forest could expand at any moment and swallow them up.

"Do we have time for that?" Hannah questioned him in a faint voice.

"Sounds like an entire guild is trying to take over a place of power." Joe scoffed and started pulling out tiles. "If whatever is in there is powerful enough to wipe them all out, we're going to need all the preparation we can get. Let's start with... let's say twenty-five Rituals of Elemental Burst at the Expert rank, and go from there. Ooh, look! This section means the ritual is considering more esoteric elements as possibilities for use! Now, who wants to guess what this quotient means...?"

Joe paused from his work hours later, wiping at the tickle left behind as sweat dripped down his forehead, only to be cleaned away nearly as soon as it appeared.

The others were moving about nearby, working on their own projects, the only sounds being the scratching of inscription tools or a soft *pop* when a glass bottle was opened, and an

Elixir was added to a ritual diagram. Big_Mo especially was wrist deep in empty bottles, broad hands shaking ever so slightly as he pushed himself to apply it *perfectly*—only to fail more often than not. Still, going by the radiant smile on his face, he was gaining skill levels rather quickly.

Each other person was entirely focused, save for Robert, who continued to distractedly look up at the nearby forest fearfully whenever a squirrel so much as jumped from branch to branch.

Knowing nothing he said would alleviate the man's irrational fear, Joe turned his gaze to the others, sweeping over Kirby, who was sitting cross-legged and gently singing under her breath as she worked. Then he looked to Hannah, who was squinting at a ritual diagram that was becoming ever harder to make out in the low light. Finally, he returned his attention to the Expert-ranked ritual he had been working on.

Joe had just finished carefully nudging the syntax, though he hadn't been able to do much more than adjust how focused the bursting element would become. As it stood, he had been able to take the typical cone shape and focus it into a narrow beam or go completely the opposite direction and spread the damage out over an even wider area.

In the first case, it should increase the total damage or magical penetration of the ritual… but in the second, it would merely apply rather low-level damage over time to many things in a large area. Letting out a quiet sigh, he debated on which way he wanted to go with it. "Better do both, now that I think about it. This whole situation has me uneasy…"

"You mean the cryptic warning about an entire guild being wiped out by whatever they're about to attack, and how we— the *six* of us—are going to be trying to figure out how to win when a couple *hundred* people-" Robert's fearful attitude finally started getting to Joe as he ranted, and he turned hard eyes on the lower-level Ritualist.

"You know I meant it when I said you don't have to come in there, yes?" Joe's words were blunt, though he did his best to say them in a tactful manner. "Just because the others want to go doesn't mean _you_ have to. Dying hurts, and it pretty much sucks in every respect. I get it. It's a risk you don't have to take, but you're going to find it comes around more and more often the more powerful you get."

"_No._" Robert clamped his mouth shut and slowly lowered his eyes, until he was staring at the tile clutched in his white-knuckled grip. "I'm not going to get left behind again."

"Why don't we talk about what we can do to _mitigate_ that possibility?" Joe glanced around once more, making sure everyone was paying as much attention as they could afford to at that moment. "The Wolfman implied heavily that it would be a large swarm of creatures; to me, 'swarm' means bugs. If anyone disagrees, please offer alternatives, otherwise let's think about the best way to get rid of them."

"_Fire._" Kirby's eyes practically began to shine as she whispered the word reverently. "Wait! No, _poison!_"

"Both good answers…" Joe glanced around once more, but everyone actually seemed to agree with Kirby's megalomaniac tendencies for once. "Good stuff… let's make sure we have a ready source of flame next to our rituals when we get ready to use them. If they have an entire guild, I'm sure they'll have some Fire Mages with them, so we can just cozy up to them and, you know, borrow what they produce."

Thanks to the lingering scent of danger in the air, no one seemed to be in a chatty mood.

After a few moments of extended quiet, Joe returned to his project with a casual shrug. Gently tracing a finger along his notes, his lips moved ever so slightly as he parsed the syntax aloud, brow furrowing as he found layered context he didn't have a good reference for. But that was fine with him, as he was entirely focused on grinding the skill up far enough to-

Ding.

"Finally!" Joe pulled open his notification. Just as he had assumed, his new Lore skill had finally hit a bottleneck: Student nine. Dropping what he was doing, he pushed off the ground and jumped into a canopy, making sure his suddenly nervous coven members didn't have a clear line of sight of him. "Knowledge, Magical Syntax Lore! *Twice!*"

Skill increase: Magical Syntax Lore (Student IX → Journeyman I). Congratulations! As a Journeyman in this skill, you can expect to have a far easier time with all lower-tier syntax questions.

Skill increase: Knowledge (Journeyman IX → Expert 0). Congratulations! This spell will now be effective on all Lore skills up to the peak of the Expert rank, to a maximum of Expert level nine.

"There it is." Joe read the second notification greedily, barely able to contain his desire to use it, only to be stymied by the refreshed cooldown timer. "Eighteen hours, then the secrets hidden by experts will be mine. Oh... *and* I'll finish my profession!"

Dropping out of the tree, he landed back near his original seated position, only for Big_Mo to chuck an empty bottle at his head. "Naked monkey monster! Oh, wait, never mind. It's Joe."

"*Not* funny." Though it was actually quite hilarious to Joe, it was Robert who said these words in a sullen tone. "Look, can we just get this over with? It's going to take us a while to figure out how to find the guild in the first place, isn't it?"

"Robert, if you don't focus on building up your arsenal, you're going to run out of attacks way before anyone else does." Joe gestured at the others, who were even now frantically working on their next designs. Seeing their anxious dedication was oddly comforting, nostalgic even. "Look at your friends. They look like proper Ritualists: frantic, exhausted, pushed to their limits, but still going. Why are you so freaked out by the forest? You're usually competing with Hannah for most rituals completed in the shortest amount of time, but you've been flipping that tile back and forth for the last five minutes."

Once again the man glanced down, although this time, his grip on the tile increased to the point where it cracked. As he tossed the now-useless stone to the side, he finally looked up with a shamefaced expression. "They're better at this than I am. maybe I should just-"

"Finally!" Joe's sudden bellow startled everyone, to the point a couple of them needed to frantically adjust the lines they had just drawn to keep their rituals from overloading. "I've been waiting for you to get your gripes out for *forever*. Let me ask you this... how long have you been doing this? Making rituals?"

"More than two years now," the man answered slowly, not entirely certain what was happening.

"Good, good." Joe bobbed his head up and down. "Why are you getting all hung up on it *now*?"

"It's..." Robert hesitated, grit his teeth in a snarl then pushed forward almost viciously. "*I* was doing the best back in town! My projects sold for a higher price, and more of them! But now? We get out here, and I'm right in the middle of the pack at actually being able to use these in combat."

"Dead last, actually," Joe cheerfully corrected him. "Big_-Mo's really come a long way."

"Don't drag *me* into this, what the abyss, man...?" Big_Mo grumbled at the undesired praise.

"Look, here's the deal." Joe locked eyes with Robert, not letting the other man look away. "You were doing the best, now you're not. You're insecure about this, but what does that mean? I'll tell you right now... insecurities are just pride wearing a frowny face. When you're too proud to accept *not* being number one, this is the result."

Robert glowered at him, not sure how to respond—not that Joe would have let him.

"Are you actually nervous about the fighting? Not really. It's just that now you're realizing that other people have strengths that you might not. Well... get over it. We all need people with complementary strengths, otherwise we won't have all our bases covered. So how about you get your head out of your butt and start making rituals to keep yourself from getting nibbled?"

"Who do *you* lean on for 'complementary strength'?" Robert challenged the leader of the coven instead. "Looks like *you're* trying to do it all-"

"I have a few unique advantages, but you'll notice I'm also

putting in more work than all of you *combined*." Joe calmly picked up his own tile and put words to action, not wanting to lose too much of his preparation time. "If you're going to pick someone else to compare yourself with... definitely pick someone *else*. Now, you can either get ready so you can be an asset, or you can leave. Either is fine. I *will* say, if you rush off in a huff right now, I'm going to lose a lot of respect for you."

That stopped Robert cold, and though he stared at Joe for another few seconds, the bald Ritualist realized it was only because he didn't want to meet the eyes of his peers. Still, Joe only relaxed after the man grudgingly picked up a fresh tile and got back to work.

Now totally intent on his own work, Joe winced as he realized he'd finished only one ritual so far: a basic, if Expert, version of the Ritual of Elemental Burst. Grimacing at the thought of spending a huge chunk of his remaining time sitting still, Joe tried to embrace the suck and began drawing out the heavily focused version.

"Pull all vectors from the cone into a single line. Lots of punch, not so much coverage. Doesn't matter if the place of power is guarded by bugs or bats, there's going to be at least one of them that's a serious threat and needs the big boy weapon ready if I want to tap it." Pausing, the Ritualist pulled a face. "Not even here a full fortnight, and I'm using new slang. Bleh. Need the big 'un if I want to *slay* it. There. Better."

It took until a couple hours after midnight for him to complete the ritual and gratefully, carefully, store it away. "I'm on a roll with these, so I should work on the next one right away, but... a nap probably wouldn't hurt too much. I forget how much sleep I actually needed when I was this weak."

"You haven't slept in days, though?" Kirby, who had apparently been assigned to stay on the graveyard shift of watch, quietly joined into his previously solo conversation. "Hopefully this means you can imagine how exhausted the rest of us are? It's not easy keeping up with you. Not that we should *try*, if we listen to the advice you gave Robert."

"Oh, you should *try*. You might even surpass me someday, but there's just no need for *comparison*." Already, he could tell that his words rolled off her like water beading off of a duck. "I've heard it said that comparison is the thief of joy-"

"Whatever, just go get some sleep. By the way, you should check your bedroll for damage. The light reflecting off your shiny head attracts moths when you sleep." Kirby sounded completely serious, but it wasn't the thought of destroyed linens that made Joe's eyes go wide.

"What is *wrong* with me?"

"I've been asking myself that for-"

"No, stop. Not right now." Joe lifted his hand, pulling out each of the pamphlets he had gained as a reward for completing his Reductionist quest. "Regenerative Denial, Stutter Step... *Ritual of the Bugzapper*. Oh, Tatum, you sneaky, sneaky deity. So it'll be bugs for sure, then? Or, no, it doesn't really matter, either way. I've got to make sure to make one of these before we go in there. At *worst*, we'll have a perfect distraction if we need to use it. At best, I can't imagine a swarm of insects having high enough of a Charisma value to make a saving throw against this."

"Although..." A small thought niggled at the back of his mind. "Who knows what the boss monster will be like? What if it's some insanely charismatic summoner, instead of just another bug? Or some kind of hive mind that can use all of the... no, I have no way to prepare for that, so I just have to focus on taking down as many as I can and grabbing whatever rewards I can get."

Just then, the small hairs on the back of his neck arched, and he shivered as though someone had stepped on his grave. "I mean, I am going to grab some rewards, right? I'm sure whatever guild is fighting is going to be reasonable about us coming in and helping out... or more likely, they might attack us on sight, thinking we're trying to take advantage of their distraction to wipe them out. Abyss."

Trying to console himself with the thought that he didn't

actually *need* any material rewards—as simply dropping a shrine and claiming the area for Tatum would advance his quest—didn't work. "The whole reason I came here in the first place was to grab an Artifact-rarity core. I can battle other people for control of the place, but I need that core. If the Cult of the Burning Mind was any indication, the monster that shows up may not easily respawn."

Naturally, thinking about gaining monster cores had Joe glancing at his skill sheet, specifically Corify. His jaw dropped in horror as he realized the grave mistake he had nearly made: all of his skills had been unbound from his Ritual Orbs during Tatum's realignment of his... akashic records, as the deity had put it. "Mmkay, Not sure what I was thinking when I told the others I'd be making twenty-five Expert-ranked rituals. I don't have eight days to devote to this. How about... two? Then I'll recapture that spell in my orb and figure out what we're going to say when we show up on the battlefield."

Blinking tiredly, the ritualist slowly shook his head and settled in on his bedroll. "That's... that's a lot. First, a nap."

When he woke up, it was to a steaming cup of coffee right next to his nose and a cheerful elemental waving at him. "Mmfmm. Good morning, little buddy."

Wakey-wakey! The teeny tiny voice warbled back to him before the elemental settled slightly, pouring itself back into its cup and vanishing. As Joe sat up with a groan, not truly able to experience casual soreness from sleeping on the ground—not when his skin was at least as hard as the stones on this world—he still found himself thankful for the mug of sheer joy and happiness he was able to sip from.

"You've spoken more in the last week than the last few months, little buddy..." Joe mumbled as he drained the cup, only for it to be refilled in an instant. "Is it that you're more talkative after I sleep? Too bad you didn't come with a 'best way to care for your coffee' manual. Still, if you ever need something, try to figure out how to let me know."

As he idly considered searching for some form of lore book

that would help him learn more about the elemental, he noticed the others breaking camp and preparing to move. "Hey, don't worry about going anywhere. We're going to work hard today, but all of us should get at least one more good night's sleep."

Hannah exchanged a skeptical glance with the others, but Joe could easily read how exhausted she actually was by the slump in her shoulders and the wobbly bend in her spine. As he wondered whether it was his own Charisma allowing him to notice those details, she asked the question everyone was thinking.

"Shouldn't we head in? That Wolfman seemed pretty sure the guild was going to get wiped out if we didn't hurry. Seems kind of urgent?"

"Nah..." Joe's casual wave of the hand, coupled with sipping from his cup, didn't earn him any brownie points with the group. "Here's my thought. If it were something that we had to rush in for, he *definitely* would have told us. Believe me, another day of preparation and a solid night's rest is going to help us more than anything else. Not to sound callous, but I'm far more worried about the six of us than I am the hundreds of battle-ready combatants that whatever guild in there is bringing along. If they can't hold out 'til we get there, well... that's not our problem."

The day passed very similarly to the previous afternoon, with each of them preparing the most potent rituals they could manage. None of them were locked in on using Novice-rank rituals due to a skill issue; they simply had been doing so to progress the ritual combat quest as quickly as possible. Over the next few hours, Joe finished two Expert-ranked rituals, leaving him with a total of four ready to deploy as soon as he needed them.

After that, the remainder of the day was spent assigning his spell to his Ritual Orb of Strength then building out a series of mostly Student-ranked rituals, with a few Journeyman thrown in for good measure.

He had considered using some of his new area-defensive

spells and finally settled on putting together a Ritual of Regenerative Denial. At first, he had put the idea to the side, not wanting to reduce the healing his—hopefully—short-term allies would receive, but remembered just as he was about to discard it that he could add entire classes of entities to the whitelist. For instance, 'humans'.

"Abyss, I've been playing with Novice and Beginner rituals way too long if *that* slipped my mind." As evening shifted to twilight, the others reluctantly began to settle down, casting anxious glances toward the tree line, which had literally grown closer to them over the course of the day. Having already gotten his fill of sleep, Joe informed them that he'd be handling the watch tonight.

Then it was just a matter of waiting patiently for the last of them to succumb to slumber so he could cast Knowledge.

"Enchanting Lore, and..." Joe hesitated for only a moment, a glance at his skill list showing the clear choice. Still, even that heartbeat of time was enough for the welling mana to become painful as it began to pool, forcing him to gasp out the final words, "*Ritual Lore!*"

Immediately, he was flooded with notifications, as the power racing into his brain gushed through his spinal cord, cerebellum, and spread out to sink evenly into each of his lobes. Blinking away the tears that had sprung into his eyes unbidden, Joe began reading over them—his smile growing with each word he read.

CHAPTER THIRTY-ONE

Skill increase: Enchanting Lore (Journeyman IX → Expert 0). Congratulations! You can now officially call yourself an expert in Enchanting Lore, elevated beyond mere competence and marking you as a true authority in this field. Even more astonishingly, you have achieved this milestone without possessing an associated Mindset. As recognition for this remarkable feat, one will be tailored specifically for your highest ranking enchanting-focused skill.

Skill increase: Ritual Lore (Journeyman IX → Expert 0). Congratulations, you can now officially... wait, that's odd... call yourself an expert in Ritual Lore! Two at the same...? That's... congratulations on whatever inspiration you found that allowed you to achieve this impressive... success. Your advancement in this skill has triggered a powerful paradigm shift in one of your Core Characteristics.

Wisdom → Ritualistic Wisdom. As power flows and interacts in the world, you've found that it can be found in both structured spellcasting and spontaneous confluxes. You now possess a small chance to instantly conceptualize and generate complete or nearly complete ritual diagrams when resonating strongly with a location, significant event, or natural power convergence. Being able to witness the flow of power firsthand will signifi-

cantly enhance your odds of capturing inspiration and transforming it into practical application.

Mindset created based on Enchanted Ritual Circles: Tokenization Mindset (Expert). By gaining a deep understanding of Enchanting, you have learned to enter a minor trance and test your spatial awareness with rapid pattern recognition. While holding the planned enchantment firmly in mind, a shifting lattice of ephemeral glowing lines and blocks will manifest in the air before you. Effect:

- *By swiftly tracing these rapidly moving and disappearing patterns exactly with your inscription tool, inlaying them with aspects at the color-associated power, you can condense and imprint an entire enchantment onto a ritual token directly.*
- *Accuracy and speed in tracing the pattern and providing the correct aspect provides a 5-50% increased chance of creating and miniaturizing a viable enchantment on a token. Less than 90% accuracy guarantees instant failure.*
- *Flawless completion offers a 0.05% chance of directly enhancing the enchantment to a higher rank.*

Profession maximized. Arcane Enchanting Theorist (5/5).

I suppose congratulations are in order for managing to <u>technically</u> fulfill the requirements of your profession: Arcane Enchanting Theorist.

Despite your shortcuts and circumvention of proper study, which some may consider disrespectful to dedicated Theorists, you've achieved the <u>technically</u> stated goal of this profession.

I suppose you could even consider yourself innovative in how you went about it. Nonetheless, unorthodox though it may be, you've <u>technically</u> met the standard. As this profession is an elementary step stone toward more meaningful pursuits, you may now consider this profession as a fulfilled certificate of completion for <u>any</u> single enchanting-related profession which requires <u>any</u> enchanting prerequisite.

Please upgrade your profession as soon as possible, and don't recommend this path to any of your... friends.

"Say technically one more time," Joe rolled his eyes at the final message, immediately putting the backhanded-compliment-filled message out of his mind as he slowly rubbed his hands together in excitement at the thought of having gained access to yet another minigame. "Now I just need to figure out how to use it… and what's up with my Wisdom getting shifted? Not complaining, especially since it's the first one that seems directly associated with my class-"

"*Wakey, wakey!*" AutoMate's tiny voice interrupted Joe's intense contemplation, the words riding on a waft of delicious coffee.

"Thanks?" The Ritualist glanced down uncomprehendingly, only to realize that the sun was already starting to clear the horizon. A panicked check of the others had Joe heaving a sigh of relief—no one had been attacked while he had been otherwise occupied. Going by how they were sleeping as if half-dead, forcing them to wait another day had been the right call.

More firmly this time, he gripped his mug and got close to his little elemental so he could keep his voice down. "Thanks, Mate. You're great. Don't want to be late. Got a hot date."

Pew, pew, boom! Mate made various noises indicating battle, nodding sagely before swirling down and away. A short while later, each of the others were up and moving. Joe was pleased to see that they were far more cognizant and focused after a good night of uninterrupted sleep.

After giving them time to freshen up, checking that they had their rituals ready to go and were otherwise as prepared as possible, the Ritualist led them confidently toward the towering, neon green line of trees. With each step, the dense smell of the forest thickened until it was an almost palpable… he lifted his fingers and rubbed them together, grunting as the thick pollen coating his shell. "Actually palpable. Ick. Tree gunk. Last chance, everyone have your safe travel token equipped?"

They replied with tight nods, their eyes shadowed and sharp with apprehension at the prospect of pushing into an unknown combat situation. Joe allowed them to have their silent reflection as he pressed forward, and soon the forest had swallowed them into its underbrush, near-identical trees growing in all directions.

It took them all of ten seconds to become completely turned around, and they would have all been separated and deposited in random locations already if they didn't have their tokens equipped. Yet, only a few minutes after entering, the sounds of combat started to grow steadily louder—shifting from an indistinct clatter from only the strongest blows of being dealt and received to a constant, furious roar punctuated by shouts and screams of excitement or maybe panic.

Glancing at the others, Joe shot them a knowing grin as he saw their puzzled expressions turn on him. Big_Mo stared suspiciously at his too-happy leader. "They're just right here? Did you know that the whole time, or is this a happy coincidence?"

"It's the tokens." Joe tapped on the tiny metal symbol dangling a little below his pearls of wisdom. "Our friendly neighborhood Wolfman made sure they were keyed to the place of power—in other words, it didn't matter where we had entered the forest, we would have arrived here just as quickly."

No one seemed fully convinced, but that didn't bother the Ritualist one little bit. "That's part of the reason I made us wait. If we got here too soon, we'd have beat the guild here, and they may have seen us as competition. This way, they get to test the waters for us, we get to see what we're dealing with, and now we can brand ourselves as helpful passersby instead of a wandering threat."

Their skeptical looks rapidly faded, replaced by a mix of nervousness and excitement at the impending battle, as well as just a *hint* of respect in their eyes for how he had handled the situation so far. Robert cleared his throat, "We slowed down just now, but shouldn't we hurry up? Sounds like they're having a rough time."

"I'm sure they're fine." Just as Joe breezily pushed away Robert's concerns, the dense foliage suddenly thinned, depositing them at the edge of a massive clearing and allowing them to see the scope of the battle that had clearly been raging for hours at that point.

There was no way to describe the scene before them other than 'pure nightmare fuel'.

A massive cloud of insects carpeted the ground, buzzed through the air, and covered every available inch of the combatants—shifting, buzzing, biting, and stinging. It wasn't just one type of bug; practically every aggressive category had a representative present. Worse, the majority of the bugs weren't even attacking the guild, they were churning the forest around them into splinters as they voraciously gnawed on absolutely every scrap of biological material they could find.

What Joe had taken as the sound of huge weapons landing on shields was actually the trembling trees collapsing as the chitinous horde gnawed through the trunks like termites through plywood—in a few cases, the bugs in question actually *were* termites.

"Nevermind! They're not fine!" Joe felt his jaw drop as the grotesquely varied insects boiled together like an oily, creepy-crawly tidal wave. In the few moments his coven stood still out of pure shock at the edge of the forest, the trees they'd been standing next to vanished into hundreds of thousands of grinding mandibles, not even sawdust left behind as it was sucked down to feed the endlessly hungry pests.

"Shields on if you got 'em!" Even as he snapped the rapid order to the others, Joe tried to figure out what exactly was happening. Though he was only able to capture flashes of the action as the swarm shifted, he still managed to put together a picture of where they were coming from, what was being attacked, and where he and his team were most needed.

First, the battle was fiercely raging as the adventurers desperately tried to survive against the relentless assault. Warriors swinging ichor-coated blades crushed bugs by the hundreds, only for thousands more to push forward for their chance at chomping down fresh meat.

The combatants wearing heavy armor seemed to have the

worst of it, with the insects pushing through the gaps in their armor and sinking mandibles and stingers deep into now-unprotected areas. The tanky fighters screamed in helpless frustration as they attacked the endless enemies, even while slamming fists into their armor in an attempt to crush anything wiggling below.

The mages near the center of the battlefield were faring better, if only slightly. Enormous gouts of sustained flames, fireballs, and all manner of spells turned tens of thousands of the insects into charred corpses, but the crunchy tidbits that remained were even easier for the next wave to devour. The spellcasters seemed comfortable, magical barriers around their bodies doing a far better job keeping the writhing horde off of their skin than armor was doing for their fellows.

Just then, a large cockroach attempted to fly into Joe's ever-so-slightly opened mouth, only for his Exquisite Shell to stop it dead. It fell to the ground, landing on its back and furiously rocking back and forth as it tried to get up. Shaking out of his light trance, thanks to the sheer disgust of the moment, the Ritualist started forward.

"We need to find where they're coming from, then I want *all* of you to set up as many rituals around that spot as possible! Overlapping fields of fire, and I do *mean* fire. I'll try and get some of those pyromancers moving your way. Remember, right now their sheer numbers are their greatest weapon, and we need to disarm them as soon as possible."

Joe's throat clenched as he saw a few of the adventurers let out shrill screams and dropped to the ground, spasming a few times as they slapped wildly at the living carpet of insects... only to go still a few moments later, vanishing entirely almost immediately as the bugs consumed them. The only saving grace at that sight was how the horde turned on itself, fighting over the final scraps and self-destructing for a long few seconds.

In the lull, he finally found the source of the plague of pests.

A set of gargantuan doors, ancient in design, were jutting from the ground at a forty-five degree angle and constantly vomiting forth the seemingly endless stream of screeching, segmented minibeasts. The huge slabs of stone were banded with dull metal, which flickered intermittently with broken inscriptions that had either been warnings or the seal containing what had been trapped in the place of power.

Even through the sounds of combat, the drone of wings, the crunch of millions of tiny legs on every possible surface, Joe could still hear the soft notes of fading magic, thanks to his Magical Synesthesia.

Stop. Contain. Soothe. Hibernate. Passive. Stop. Contain...

Hearing the magic itself as whispers in his mind sent shivers along Joe's skin, "Yeesh, feels like I just stepped into a horror movie, and the walls are about to start bleeding. There's the doors! Get moving-"

"You're just going to *leave* us?" Hannah had to shout to be heard over the thunderous noise of buzzing wings and clicking legs. "Where are *you* going?"

"I need to go play politics so we don't get attacked when we try to help them!" Joe pointed in the direction of the guild that was entirely on the defensive at this point. "They've already lost people, so if we present ourselves as an enemy, they'll jump at the chance to have a target they can hit and actually take down. Get those Elemental Bursts in position, catch some flames, and burn those bugs! *Go!*"

Joe had only ever been as grateful for his Exquisite Shell as he was currently in one other situation: when he had been burrowing like a worm through a thousand years' worth of piled garbage on Alfenheim. At the moment, the perfect seal created by the magic afforded him a close-up view of the hissing, chomping mass without them actually being able to drive their stingers into his eyeballs like they were trying so hard to do.

The tiny limbs clicked futilely against his defenses, annoyingly loud, yet failing to deal even a point of damage to the high-level barrier. He surged through the swarm, steadily crunching critters below him as he moved toward the rear of the defensive line.

"*Outsider!*" a man snarled a warning, eyes narrowed in hate and suspicion as Joe came into view. "We've got hostiles coming up on the back line! How did you even find us? This raid was planned entirely in secret; even *we* didn't know where we were going!"

"Joe the Ritualist, from the Noble Wanderer's Guild." Joe's calm, confident answer gave the other man pause, though he was constantly shifting as he attempted to swipe away the insects skittering along his armor. "I'm here to help-"

"Yeah, *right.*"

"-since I got a request to put this swarm down before it gets out of hand and wipes out all the crops on the continent," the Ritualist finished, his words putting a light of understanding and fear in the warrior's eyes. Both of them could see how bad the situation was, so after only a moment of hesitation, the fighter motioned for Joe to follow after him.

They pushed into the center of the defensive formation, the warrior bowing and leaning forward as if walking against a powerful wind. He shouted into someone's ear then stepped aside to allow a tall, battle-scarred man to take his place. The pale, grim face was streaked with dirt, blood, and hand-length centipedes. "How are *you* going to help us?"

"I've got a small group of, uh, Mages that can set up spells that constantly go off in an area. I've sent them toward those doors; they should be setting up as we speak. They need fire in that area-"

"Not a problem, that's where most of our Mages are focusing their spells anyway." The man's mouth curled back in disgust, only for a gadfly to take advantage of the situation and buzz against his lips, causing him to sputter furiously. "We've already lost eight percent of our forces to what amounts to *mosquitoes.* Pretty bad for morale, so I can't promise we're going to hold out much longer. You want in, you're in. You're dealing with the Poor Lifechoices."

"Yeah, I get that a lot." Joe nodded at the pale-faced man, who looked as if he were about to say something, only to sputter as a cloud of horseflies swarmed his face. "I'm going to set up a large-scale magic effect; I need some volunteers to help me power it up."

"You show up out of nowhere, then tell us you need some of our people to... what, exactly? Sacrifice themselves for you?" The person Joe could only assume was the guild leader narrowed his eyes in renewed suspicion. "I think that what we're actually going to do is-"

A shout went up, jerking their attention over to the open stone doors. A contingent of large, clearly elite bugs had just burst through the tunnel. They looked to be some kind of warrior caste of praying mantis the size of large dogs. Their front limbs were metallic, shimmering razor-sharp blades... making them a great target. Joe lifted his right hand, pointing at the leading beastie with his index finger.

"Dark Chain Lightning."

As this was the first time he had used the upgraded version of this spell, Joe was nearly as agog at the effect as the guild leader, though he managed to keep his composure, the only sign of how thrilled he truly was showing in the form of a *slightly* too-eager grin tugging his lips upward.

For the space of a heartbeat, it almost seemed like nothing had happened. His dark lightning had always been all but silent, making no crackling or hissing along its path, no thunderclap as it whispered through the air. The line of paradoxically inky black light simply leapt across the distance and touched the leading bloated horror of a bug, coated its body, bounced between its blades, and *crackled* along its extending, translucent wings all at the same time.

Just after the moment of impact, the bug burst open violently, erupting in a macabre explosion of overheated viscera and putrid steam.

Joe was certain the stench billowing outward would be nauseating, but he was far too focused on what happened next, since the spell was just getting started. Before the elite attacker had even fully burst apart, the single thread of dark energy split into five then leapt to the contingent of elites behind the first.

Each of the tendrils found a target, sinking into the bugs and causing an identical eruption of viscous goo and fragmented chitin. The threads then jumped *again*, still in perfect silence, six times each. Joe watched as each victim detonated, liberally coating the ground around the entrance with sticky, smoking filth.

"You got every one of them at the exact same time?" The soft gasp from the guild leader recaptured Joe's attention, while also reminding him that not everyone had the same immense Perception as himself. Likely, he had seen Joe casually point, then a small platoon of elites went **pop**. "Ehh, as I was saying, what we're *actually* going to do is… give you every able-bodied person we can spare. Anything we should be aware of?"

"The more mana they have, the better." Joe began pulling out ritual stabilizers and carefully placing them on the ground. Luckily, as they were made of metal, the bugs completely ignored the items beyond using them as a clean new spot to land on. "You've got about five minutes, then I need to get started."

In truth, he could've been ready much faster, but setting a specific deadline usually helped get people motivated to make things happen. As Joe had hoped, as soon as the words were out of his mouth, the guild leader started howling orders for the Mages to rotate out and gather up. His words were punctuated by six huge bursts of flame which roared into position around the ancient entryway, followed a second later by yet another gout of fire converging on the escaping swarm.

"Time to *inflame* this infestation." Quickly positioning the volun-told Mages, Joe offhandedly warned them their mana would be draining momentarily, then returned to his central position. Taking a deep breath, he began pumping mana into the activation sequence.

Six magical circles expanded out, the bright lights casting

millions of shadows as they washed over the endless arthropods. As the mana in the air noticeably began to thicken, draining into the central part of the diagram, the droning insects intensified their assault—instinctually understanding something was amiss.

For his part, Joe hummed a cheerful tune as the process of the ritual activating dragged along almost painfully slowly, the tiny mana pools of those who had remained on Midgard barely enough to sustain the requirements of the ritual. "Almost done... just a few more minutes. Don't worry guys, those are screams of *excitement* coming from your guild members, since they know all these little bugs are about to go away."

He knew no one could hear him, but the little fib helped him feel a little bit better.

Finally, the last sigil began to glow with an intense, vibrant light as the world around them crackled with *potential*. Everyone, from the guild leader to the most basic ant, could feel the shift as the activation sequence reached a tipping point.

The world brightened up, a sharp intensification of the sunlight as though a magnifying glass held by a titan of immense proportions had suddenly been focused on the battlefield. Moments before, the daylight had been almost completely blocked out by the millions of bugs swirling around the battlefield as a treetop-touching column. In the next second, the smallest of bugs began flashing incandescently, igniting in a minuscule burst of flame before popping.

Only a dot of sizzling vapor remained to show where they had been only a moment previous.

As the ritual ramped up, the intermittent bursts became a relentless cascade of rapid-fire *popping* that filled the air. Over the next minute, bugs burst by the thousands, their already brief lives cut short and ending as foul-smelling splatters. Soon, the entire battlefield was slick with a thick, oily sludge that slowly oozed over the churned earth, splashing into the air as larger bugs fell from the sky.

Joe stepped away from the ritual, which was only doing ten

damage a second—no better than a Novice rank—except it was damaging *everything* not a human and covering nearly half a mile. Though there were plenty of larger bugs still fighting, the fact that the warriors could stand toe to toe with them and feel the satisfaction of their blade sinking into the beasts was an immediate morale boost.

Anyone *not* directly engaged in a fight was doing one of two things. Either they were staring at Joe and the shimmering dome of power his ritual had condensed into, or they were cursing and grumbling as they did their best to scoop the goo of a thousand bugs out of the gaps in their armor.

"Yuck. I do not envy anyone needing to clean burst thorax out of chainmail," Joe muttered, shaking his head as he saw a mess seeping along the legs of a warrior with haunted eyes, then forcing a grin onto his face as he noticed people staring at him. "I mean... *ya~ay*! It worked as intended!"

CHAPTER THIRTY-TWO

Quest complete: Student Reductionist II. Now that you have created a Unique (Expert rank) craft from aspects, do it again, but different!

Reward: A forging blueprint useful to your class. Access to Student Reductionist III.

Class Quest Gained: Student Reductionist III. A Reductionist is not a master of only one form of crafting. Create a Unique craft from a discipline other than [Ritual Circles]. Reward: A blueprint or template useful to your class, based on the discipline used to complete this quest. Access to Student Reductionist IV.

Knowing that looking at the forging blueprint at that moment would only make him despair that he could not go and use it, Joe tucked his rewards away without even letting himself read the name at the top of the page, then he looked across the grotesque battlefield to see how his coven members had fared.

He sucked in a sharp breath as he saw them battered and bloodied, staggering toward him with Hannah and Big_Mo being dragged back by the others, massive lacerations covering their bodies. The Ritualist began running toward them, eyes carefully inspecting the wounds which were still weeping blood, but nowhere near as fast as they should have been for the size of the injury.

As they crossed into the radius of his Neutrality Aura, their wounds began to knit themselves closed, and now-fresh blood began pumping onto the ground once more. Skidding to a halt beside them, Joe placed a hand on either member of his coven, casting Lay on Hands simultaneously on each. Dark water rippled out from his hands, flooding over their bodies and leaving clean, unblemished skin where it went.

In moments, the tension in their faces faded, and they managed to get to their feet under their own power. Waiting a few moments longer, Joe watched as the last of the blemishes faded, the filth coating them fizzing away. Soon, they were wearing clean, if badly damaged clothes.

"I remember when having big rips in your pants was fashionable." Joe motioned for the others to follow him as an angry buzzing noise emanated from the tunnel reaching deep into the earth. "Maybe you guys will bring it back?"

"I can't even tell you…" Robert took a deep breath, glancing back at the ancient doorway as goat-sized bugs began swarming into the open, "how *fun* that was! Seriously, what was I so worried about? Yeah, it sucked to get chewed on, but I gained two entire levels off of that already!"

"Skill levels?" Joe's confusion was met with an enthusiastic shake of Robert's head.

"*Nope*. One of my Elemental Bursts caught a larger bug just as it was coming out, and it detonated, killing a couple hundred more at the same time." There was a cocky grin on his face, and his eyes were burning with a manic light. "Got five entire points of luck at the same time."

Joe let out a low whistle as he looked over his shoulder. It was meant as a compliment for Robert, but at the same time, he was amazed by how quickly the dynamics of the battlefield had shifted. Huge waves of weak bugs continued to pour out of the tunnel, but upon reaching the surface, they popped and sizzled as they came under the effects of his ritual.

The members of the Poor Lifechoices were quickly regrouping, forming up into disciplined ranks as the skirmish began falling into a more-familiar format. Now that the only insects they had to contend with were at least the size of a forearm, the heavily armored warriors got into position, knowing that shields and plate mail would actually be useful once more.

Archers and Mages fell into position behind them, supporting the front lines as stronger bugs rushed them, mandibles clicking hungrily as the starving creatures attacked with feral rage. With the ritual in place, the chaos had been trimmed away, leaving behind a whiff of order and rapidly increasing morale.

Steel clashed against chitin as the Poor Lifechoices guild advanced step by grueling, gooey step. Shield walls pressed together, shoving in unison as one among them shouted a countdown. The wall of metal and muscle crushed the bugs against their own kind, neither side willing to back down an inch. Every lunge forward sent another spray of ichor into the air, dozens of the large arthropods popping like water balloons with every press.

Arrows endlessly flew from bowstrings, Archers not even needing to aim—other than not to hit their own people—and still all but guaranteed to staple handfuls of bloated thoraxes together. Behind even them, Mages were shouting incantations, hands moving in arcane patterns as reagents were sprinkled through the air.

The bugs attacked with everything they had, hissing, shrieking, chewing through their own dead in an attempt to reach the living. But finally, *finally*, they were losing ground.

Taking a break between calling a countdown, a ragged voice bellowed, "*Pu~ush*! We're gonna win this! Get them back to the tunnel, and we can stem the tide from there!"

"They're coming from somewhere deep underground; let's find out where… and *kill it with fire*!" This voice came from somewhere in the ranks, and the exhausted adventurers surged forward with renewed energy. Every foot of slick ground they reclaimed brought them that much closer to taking their revenge on the bugs for chewing through them and their friends —and they were *ready* for it.

"Should we... I don't know, go back to the entrance and set out more rituals?" Taka inquired uncertainly, glancing down at his freshly healed arms, which had been practically hamburger meat only a few minutes previously.

Kirby firmly shook her head. "Look, the bugs coming out now are level fifteen at the *minimum*. They were level four like two minutes ago. Not to mention, that's not even the elites, so who knows if they're going to get even stronger?"

"You are correct; we have better things to do." Joe made the call as he began pulling handfuls of stabilizers out of his storage rings. "Start setting these up; we need to be ready by the time the Boss Monster shows itself. I took care of the little annoyances, so they can handle standard combat. Still, we all need to be ready to jump in as soon as it gets dicey."

Not needing any further explanation, the coven members got to work, quickly placing the twenty-six stabilizers in concentric patterns, triangles, squares, pyramids, then cubes. As Big_Mo placed the final cube, words spilled from his mouth. "Random thought, what's next for stabilizer shapes? Does it repeat again, some kind of stack of pyramids, or is it a new shape?"

"Six-point-five degrees. Rotate the diagram, *abyss*, I'm still only halfway-" The bald Ritualist unhelpfully muttered, wiping his sweaty palm on his robes distractedly, not even noticing as the material failed to absorb the liquid, only for it to still be wiped away by his Neutrality Aura.

"Joe?" Big_Mo pressed, "What's the next shape? Also, why are you angling that? Shouldn't the ritual be level, or, you know, at least not pointed at *us*?"

"Parallel with the expected angle, just... hang on, you'll see." The ritual diagram began to shift, practically groaning to those with any form of magical sensitivity as the spin-axis aligned awkwardly. "It's just being stubborn, we should be able to... there!"

"I wonder what happens if we put in the stabilizers upside down." Kirby idly wondered, seeing as each of them was now standing around uselessly, unable to assist further with the Expert-level ritual circle Joe was preparing to activate. "Could we just flip that pyramid and stomp on it? Or would it count as a square stabilizer, at that point?"

Even through the haze of rapid ritual deployment, Joe shivered at the thought of having them mess with the stabilization process like that. "Guys, I'm almost done, don't do anything crazy-"

At that moment, the deep buzzing which had permeated the battlefield went deadly silent. No fluttering of wings, no clicking of chitinous legs. There was only a soft grinding of stone on stone, and everyone turned their full attention to the tunnel the bugs had been pouring from.

The doors, several tons of stone and metal, were bouncing ever so slightly, as if a strong wind were somehow managing to rattle them. Joe's eyes were drawn to the hinge pins only visible since the barrier had been thrown wide open, and he managed to see the exact moment they shattered with a high-pitched *ting*.

Then the opening deep into the earth vanished behind a geyser of dust and rock, an indescribable explosion of noise doing its best to blow out their eardrums as the ground heaved upward, something between an avalanche, volcanic eruption, and a landslide.

Moments later, the ancient doors made a reappearance, falling out of the enormous plume of pulverized rock and superheated dust and slamming into the ground hard enough to fully bury themselves. The resulting shockwave knocked the entire guild backward, and even Joe felt his robes flutter under his Exquisite Shell, though he was far more concerned with maintaining the structure of his ritual as the stabilizers were sent tumbling to and fro.

Barely managing to hold on to the diagram, Joe got it under control and ready to activate once more then turned his attention back to the spectacle.

The dust cleared unnaturally fast, the echoes of the explosion fading behind a deep, buzzing drone rattling the dust-thick air. He flinched back from what absolutely *must* be the Boss Monster protecting the place of power: an insect grotesque in both shape and size. Its body was covered in a patchwork of veined plates, as though the armor had been covered in long-dead bugs which had melted into mold along its surface.

The strange insect unfurled from the new crater, stepping out with a lithe grace before spreading a massive, fan-like structure into the air behind it—a tail any peacock would die of jealousy upon seeing.

Ding!

Perception check successful! You have encountered a Planthopper Nymph Matriarch! The Matriarch is a catastrophic result of centuries of being sealed inside a place of power filled with stagnant mana. While it has no direct combat capabilities, it endlessly generates swarms of juvenile spawn which consume organic or mana-saturated material to rapidly gain levels. Each time it reaches a 10% threshold loss of health, the insects it generates will increase by one level.

This mutated apex insectoid is a Master-threat Field Boss.

Joe's hands were moving furiously as he zipped back and forth, not bothering to hunt down the lost stabilizers, simply placing new ones in the necessary position. "This, right here, *this* is why we make extra combat rituals!"

Just as the Poor Lifechoices guild started to react to the appearance of the Matriarch, the gargantuan monster crouched down, the bottom of its thorax scraping the ground... then pressed upward, jumping high into the sky with a single bound.

It wasn't anything near as graceful as Joe Omnivaulting, more like a spring-loaded wagon breaking an axle and being *tossed* upward. The hunched form trailed curling spirals of bugs as they spawned along its path, and just as it reached the zenith of its leap, the enormous fan of a tail suddenly revealed its reason to exist: erupting outward and catching the air with a chest-thumping *wumph*, managing to slow the Matriarch's descent like the fuzz of a dandelion's seed pod.

As it ever so slowly drifted downward, smaller bugs poured off of it in a greasy waterfall of wings, legs, and gnashing jaws. The guild members shouted with dismay as the Planthopper immediately left their viable attacking range, but Joe was only concerned with the leading burst of bugs as they descended... finally hitting the top of the dome his active ritual created.

They splattered as if they had hit the windshield of a car going ninety miles an hour, the filthy rain they created sizzling away before making it halfway to the ground. "*Goo~o...d*. That means it'll still be in range of a focused version, but before that-"

Fireballs, lightning bolts, and chunks of stone raced up to meet the Matriarch as it descended, a riot of power smashing into the creature and forcing its health to plummet. For a moment, Joe's jaw dropped, and he was left wondering if he was even needed.

Then the Boss Monster spun in place, reaching out with long limbs that had odd, scoop-shaped ends. Dozens, scores, *hundreds* of smaller bugs were swept up as it rotated, only for the smaller creatures to end up in the Matriarch's mouth, swallowed like a handful of bitter pills.

Though the burn marks remained on the armored plates, the flesh below quickly boiled back into place, squirming into position and even regrowing the patches where the protective layer had been pierced. Worse, the creatures spawning next to the monster had increased in size across the board, and as the next volley hit the queen, they did so again.

"Feces!" Joe's eyes went wide as he grabbed his nearest coven member, "*Taka*! Get over there and warn them that each time they reach ten percent of the monster's health, the bugs increase in strength by a level! If it regenerates, and they hit ninety percent twice, three times, it'll level its spawn three times as well!"

He sent Taka on his way with a shove, then rushed to finish his ritual activation. "Everyone, get in position!"

"Joe, there's no way we can activate this with just the five of us!" Big_Mo nervously replied, even as he moved to the second circle and braced himself. "We need at least a dozen more people-"

"This will *have* to be enough!" Joe dropped a hand down in a cupped position, pulling a set of Mana Batteries from his codpiece and tossing them into positions volunteers should have been filling. "I've done more with fewer people, now get ready!"

His gaze flicked to the side, where the tree line had rapidly receded. There, at the edge of the bounds of his ritual, bugs were falling from the sky, unharmed and *hungry*. Already, they were swelling in size and danger rating as they chewed through any biological material they came across. Levels were ticking up quickly, even faster than those the Matriarch was generating.

"Celestial—*look!*" Hannah jabbed a finger upward. "It should have landed by now, even with as slow as it's falling, but do you see her tail? It's catching the updraft from the little bugs flying underneath her, so she's getting fanned upward."

"They'll never be able to deal damage faster than she can recover, unless we can force her to the ground," Kirby whispered in a practically awe-filled voice, which Joe felt was a little... out of sync with the reality of the situation. The Matriarch let out a shriek at that moment, a high-pitched dog whistle of a sound expelled from behind rows of bladed mandibles.

Joe grit his teeth as the sound crawled into his ears and coiled around his eardrums like a parasite. Forced to glance up, he saw how a chunk of its shoulder had been cracked under a coordinated barrage of spells, only for the Matriarch to discharge a supernova of insects that bloomed outward in every direction. Slightly larger, faster, and meaner... also perhaps *tastier*, going by how the Planthopper began slurping down her own swarm.

"Let's light this up!" The Ritualist grunted in familiar pain as a large chunk of his mana pool vanished in the next instant, beginning the activation of the Ritual of the Bugzapper.

The ground began to vibrate, and the luminescence in the area began to flicker in a hypnotic frequency. As a purely utility ritual, it was far faster to activate than its combat counterparts had been, merely requiring a few dozen seconds to spin up to full power. Once it was self-sustaining, Joe and his coven dropped to the ground, watching as a spiraling column of light erupted at the heart of the ritual, flowing from there and into the air like a quadra-helix.

An aurora of greens, blues, golds, and brilliant, *transcendent* energy-made images flowed upward for forty feet… then curved at exactly six and a half degrees. The still-extending tendril of light gently swirled down the mouth of the tunnel, the beam following what Joe could only hope was a gentle downward slope. Still, even if it didn't perfectly align, it did what it was supposed to do. Bugs stopped pouring from the depths, held in place by the compulsion the ritual *exuded*.

Insects everywhere froze. Even the Matriarch stopped devouring her own, turning toward the light and slowly drifting closer. In fact, *every* bug in visual range of the glimmering lights began crawling, creeping, or flying to the illusion.

Flares of incandescent heat popped along the edges of his ritual as the insects that had escaped were drawn back in. Gritting his teeth, Joe realized that the Ritual of Elemental Burst would be a problem if he allowed it to continue and reached out to pause it.

He barely made it in time before the Matriarch descended further, crossing the boundary where she would have begun taking damage over time and possibly breaking out of the effect of the bugzapper. Then he stopped and listened, allowing the magic of his ritual to whisper to him. Only then did he realize that the ritual wasn't forceful or coercive. It was *gentle*, inviting its targets with serene satiation.

Come closer. Rest. You are full, warm, safe.

As he focused on the whispers, they became louder and

more commanding, and his Magical Synesthesia overtook his good sense. Only Robert gripping his arms made Joe snap out of it, realizing he had almost been captured by his own spell. With a sheepish grin, he pulled out his next project and quietly but frantically motioned for the others to move to the next spot and start helping him set up.

"That's going to buy some time. If we're lucky, it should be just enough to-" Joe whipped around, eyes wide in horror as he saw an octet of flaming spheres racing into the sky and closing in on the Matriarch. Joe let out a strangled shout, his words already too late, the sounds being swallowed by the detonation of spells against carapace.

"No, no, *no*! I forgot to tell them not to attack the-"

Scre~e~ech!

CHAPTER THIRTY-THREE

Joe's mana moved faster than his thoughts, threading through the sigils and reaching for the activation sequence—

Forcibly pulling himself back, the Ritualist ground his teeth as he glared up at the Matriarch, who was already shifting her position. "Blasted bug... it's going out of range."

All around him, the battlefield was collapsing. The momentary calm offered by the zapper had mostly faded as bursts of spells and arrows landed on the boss monster. Clearly, Taka hadn't been able to impress upon them that each attack doubled the chances of the monster being able to resist the compulsion for the next few seconds. With each dog-whistle screech, half of the immense swarm was pulled out of their own dazed state and attacked the Poor Lifechoices Guild with renewed vigor.

In any other situation, it would have been almost fun to watch how the oversized wasps would land on a warrior, raise their stinger, only to then pause and casually fly away. But, as that was only happening approximately half the time, with the barbed blade punching into unprotected flesh the other half... it just wasn't as enjoyable. "It's an endless escalation. No wonder the Wolfman said they were doomed to fail without outside assistance. She's abusing that threshold power boost like *crazy*."

Stepping away from his ritual, Joe directed his people to stay ready and in position, then sprinted at the main group of warriors—only for them to tense up as if he were going to start swinging as he got close. Instead, he yelled directions at the top of his lungs, hoping someone would pay attention and actually listen to what he was saying.

An Archer stared at him for half a second then lifted an arrow threateningly, pulling back on the string and... *attacked*? Joe contemptuously snatched the arrow out of the air, snapping it in half and throwing it to the ground. For his part, the man who had attacked Joe simply scowled and slid back slightly, trying to hide among the ranks of his guild.

"I need *volunteers*!" Joe bellowed after the call went up to stop attacking the Matriarch. For a few tense seconds, it continued drifting away, then slowly spun in place and began floating toward the light once more. "If we don't take that thing down, *now*, it's going to make a break for it! Once it gets away, we'll never be able to catch it until it consumes the entire Forest of Chlorophyll Chaos! By then, it'll be an unstoppable scourge!"

Pausing for a long moment, Joe glared at the doubtful faces staring back at him, "Are *all* of you strong enough to hop on the bifrost and leave this world behind until every last one of those bugs starve to death?"

"Mages, put together a platoon and go with the bald one!" an authoritative voice called from near the center of the group. "He's officially an ally-in-combat, and if I see another attack on him or that big bug, I'm going to take recompense out of your paychecks!"

That got people moving, and soon Joe had a dozen people moving over to get in position with the rest of his coven. "We need to get that thing close, then—*are you kidding me*?"

With a sharp *twang*, an arrow launched up and into the Matriarch, pinning a dozen still-wiggling bugs to its outer carapace. Yet again it let out the sharp, whining note that caused goosebumps to raise along Joe's arms. Thousands of insects stuck in a trance snapped out of it all at once, turning and rushing toward the guild. The same commanding voice called out, though this time filled with heated anger, "Who was that? You! Wait... who are *you*?"

If he hadn't been staring at the Archer, Joe would have missed the moment he turned to glare at him. The man's eyes gleamed, and with a sharp motion, he reached up and swiped an open palm across his face... wiping away the guise of a rugged veteran and leaving behind a pale mask of crescent eyes and a cruel smile. With a snap of his fingers, the man vanished, a soft clap of thunder indicating he had teleported away, not shifted into invisibility.

Joe spat to the side, though his Neutrality Aura ensured the spittle never hit the ground, "*Jesters*. Why is the Zoo involved in this? No... not now. I'll cross that bridge when I get to it. Win the fight first, *then* worry."

For the first time since her first leap, the Matriarch touched down on the ground, dozens of tons of armored flesh hitting like a cruise ship being dropped with parachutes: gently, but only for its size. The ground cratered, and the insect shifted back and forth, trying to dislodge her bulk from its new resting place. Only after a long few seconds did it manage to lever herself up, the entire time scores of warriors swarmed forward and did their best to cut the beast apart.

"Stop attacking! It's not going to do anything!" Joe was roaring over the clatter of weapons on armor. "I said *cease fire*, you fools!"

It wasn't until the guildmaster mirrored his words that the barrage stopped, but by then, the Matriarch was already buzzing furiously as she sprang upward once more, out of range of the warriors while swiftly sucking down her spawn to begin recovering her dwindling health.

Joe sucked in a breath as he looked at the thick puddle of life fluids that had poured from the Matriarch, shifting his plan in a flash as he raced over to try and scoop some up, only to be met with disappointment as the first handful he collected had floating bits of bugs, bright red blood from where the humans had been hit, and all manner of impurities that made it almost impossible to use as a guaranteed targeting mechanism for his ritual.

"*Big_Mo~o!*" The Ritualist bellowed over his shoulder, sweeping into a crouch and tightening his core. "Get *ready!*"

Calculating his angle, Joe shoved off the ground, Omni-vaulting thirty feet straight up, crashing through hundreds of bugs as he ascended. As his upward momentum slowed, he found himself standing on a veritable platform of bugs rushing to stop him. Kicking up with a powerful **crunch**, Joe blew apart a dog-sized flying cockroach as he moved higher. The next time he landed, he held still, even as the flying carpet of bugs tried to shift up and attack him.

Swinging his Ritual Orbs back and forth, the Ritualist crushed a path out just as the third second of remaining in place came to an end. Repeating his macabre platformer game over and over, Joe slowly crept upward, a hundred feet, five hundred... finally meeting the Matriarch nearly a third of a mile up in the sky. For a long few moments, they were at the same height, and he could have *sworn* that his eyes locked with the Matriarch's hate-filled compound ones.

Then she drifted slightly lower, even as he pushed upward once more. The wind howled past his ears as he reached his highest point then started to fall once more. This time, he didn't need to worry about catching himself.

His Ritual Orb of Intelligence was directed to sit just in front of his hands, which were pointed directly downward at the top of the mega-insect, wrists together as the drill-shaped Ritual Orb began to spin. Holding it with his mind as long as possible, Joe finally released his weapon just before he crashed into the Matriarch. An eruption of ichor obscured his vision as his weapon drilled into the bug, only to vanish from his senses an instant later—the only warning he got that it was stuck deep inside the monster's flesh and now out of his reach and control.

Landing heavily on the floating creature, Joe lifted his fists and pounded on the edges of the open wound, forcing clean goo to collect in the small crater as the intense percussion forced it out into the already healing space. Scooping up a double handful, he turned to jump, only to slip as the bug twisted, landing heavily on his side and almost losing the precious ichor. For a stomach-churning moment, he slid toward the endlessly grasping limbs of the creature, only to shove himself just far enough away to avoid its last-ditch lunge by slamming an elbow into its side.

Then Joe was out and away, instantly in free fall.

Though the ground was rapidly approaching, and he was crashing through hundreds of bugs in his descent, Joe's only focus was on keeping the fluid contained in his hands and *not* letting his Neutrality Aura boil it away. "Come on… *come on!*"

Then the dirt was rushing up at him, and Joe kicked out with his feet, redirecting his path by kicking an eagle-sized mosquito and rebounding off its proboscis as if it were a tiny diving board.

Hitting the ground hard enough to make his teeth go numb, he tucked and rolled, bouncing twice before using the momentum to bring him to his feet, already sprinting at the ritual a *hint* of power away from activation. "Move, move, *move!*"

"We're all in position!" Hannah screamed back at him, "Go, it's *coming!*"

A creeping sense of dread overcame Joe, and he pushed himself harder as the Matriarch's scream came from far too close behind him. Thousands of bugs were crushed in its descent, generating a sound he had no words to describe. "It's not possible that it knows what I'm doing, I must have just really made it mad!"

Instead of trying to skid to a stop, Joe hopped, turning around to face the descending Matriarch and slamming his feet down. He came to an instant halt next to the central node of the ritual diagram. Pulling his hands apart, he watched with rapt focus as two shining droplets fell toward the targeting sigil… only to turn into steam and blow away with the wind as his aura finally finished with it. "Oh, that's just not-"

Burble! Buggy java? At the tiny voice, Joe reflexively looked to his hip, where his Ebonsteel mug was hanging. AutoMate was looking at him with its bright, coffee bean eyes, poking a brown pseudopod limb down at the interior of the mug, which was brimming with ichor.

"You're the *best*!" Joe hooted in excitement as he took the mug and upended it, pouring the precious fluid into the ritual with one hand while using the other to direct a stream of dense mana into the ritual.

The rings of the diagram suddenly extended, pulling each person into position out and away then up in the air as the rings began rotating around themselves. At almost the exact same time, the Matriarch slammed into the ground, *barely* missing the second circle as she made landfall. "Ha-*ha*! Coffee saves the day, yet again!"

Warriors were sprinting toward the unprotected ritual, throwing themselves at the grounded bug as she spawned wave after wave of chittering creepy-crawlies. Seconds ticked by as power rushed through the ritual, Joe channeling every bit of it into the activation sequence and feeling a pit of bile building up in his gut as the Matriarch shifted her position ever closer to being directly under him—preparing to spring upward and crush him with sheer momentum.

Joe had to tune out the noise around him as volunteers began to scream; the bugs being spawned tore into the tasty snacks that couldn't move for fear of disrupting the ritual. The bright sunlight began to ripple and waver as it was collected, redirected… *intensified*. "Ten seconds! Come on, we can make it! The target is locked, there's no guesswork, or assumptions, we just need to-"

Spatter.

The Planthopper Nymph let out a *screech* as she shifted her attention to the guildmaster who had just cleanly cleaved off one of her legs at the joint. Joe's eyes flicked to the grotesque view, only for the boss monster to be hidden by a wave of smaller arthropods spawning directly around the Matriarch—proving that attack had shaved off a good chunk of her health.

Every sigil on the ritual began to hum dangerously, bluish-lavender light locking in place as the mystic geometry actuated. Just as the last rune flared to life, Joe felt an impact in his chest, and his mana pool nearly emptied itself. Sucking wind, he started to fall as the ritual discarded him, no longer needing him to remain to complete its task.

For a moment, he thought that his vision was tunneling...

...then he realized the world itself had dimmed.

The early afternoon sun was almost blotted out, as though a solar eclipse had swept over Midgard. Then, the missing light was focused into a single radiant beam cutting down from on high.

Any lesser insects the light passed through simply vanished, vaporized in an instant as the superheated sunshine landed on the Matriarch as a physical blow. Letting loose her standard screech of rage, the creature abandoned her attempt on the guildmaster's life, shoving up and away in hopes of escaping this devastating magnifying glass of the gods.

Up she went, farther and higher than before... only for the sunlight to perfectly track her, bound as she was to the field boss by blood and enchantment. As she extended her tail, hoping to catch the wind and make an escape, the extruded wax the fan was made of melted almost instantly, sending the tremendous creature spiraling to the ground where she impacted hard enough to half-bury herself.

Clouds of bugs spawned around the Matriarch, crisping and popping wherever they touched the light. Her health plummeted, flesh boiling away, and for a moment, Joe let himself hope they had won.

"Taka and Robert got eaten!" Hannah's voice in his ear caused Joe to wince, suck in a sharp breath, and shake his head.

"I hope this is taken the right way," Joe stated with a heavy sigh, "but I kind of wish anyone *except* Robert had been eaten. It's going to be *impossible* to get him out and adventuring again."

Kirby came alongside Joe, holding her left arm with her right hand and waving the detached limb at him. "Can you fix this?"

"Wow, yeah…" Joe pressed the torn flesh together, casting Lay on Hands and making sure everything was working correctly before allowing himself to say what he had immediately thought. "Try not to let them disarm you again."

"You're *so* lucky you healed me first," Kirby growled at him as she tested her range of motion. "Don't worry too much about Robert; he basically threw himself head-first into a giant ant and set off a ritual inside of it before he was chomped through. Blew its mouth wide open, but it didn't save him. Still, pretty sure he knew he wasn't making it out of that—*gah*!"

KreeEEEeee!

The piercing whistle of insectoid rage echoed unnaturally across the battlefield, drowning out all sound for a long moment. In the distance, trees fell, and noise rushed back in as the battle recommenced. Joe glanced down at his hands, which were trembling ever so slightly from the skill-induced fear that had washed across the area. Then came a system notification, preceded by a slow, throbbing drum beat.

Doom… Doo-doo-doom. Doom… Doo-doo-doom.

Phase shift initiated! The Planthopper Nymph Matriarch has fully realized her power and is now a Planthopper Matriarch!

"I don't care what they call it, kill that monster!" The guild leader's voice howled over the commotion as he activated a skill that boosted his people's morale. In return, they screamed for blood and rushed at the Matriarch, a brightly lit silhouette in an otherwise darkened world.

Enchanted weapons began flashing, arrows slammed home, and a cacophony of spells tore chunks of flesh from the creature's body.

Big_Mo limped up next to Joe. "Looks like they're going to

finish it off. Time for level ups and waffles. What kind of loot do you think we're getting off of this?"

"That's-" Joe choked on his next word as he realized he hadn't made any agreement with the guild before diving in to save the day. His mind began racing, and looking around the battlefield, strewn with corpses, he knew what he, as a leader, would do. "We're not going to get *anything*. They're going to claim they need every last scrap of material to make up for the campaign coming here and getting partially wiped out."

"But..." Hannah bit her lip, going silent as Joe took a steady step forward.

"Start snagging the most interesting-looking corpses you can find. I'm going to make sure I get what I came here for." With that, Joe sprinted forward, threading through the ranks of guild members and quickly closing in on the evolved Matriarch.

Her body configuration had shifted, regrowing her lost leg while elongating significantly. Even as he got closer, the Ritualist could see enormous, translucent wings sprouting from her back, which tensed immediately as the Matriarch prepared to take her inaugural flight—only for the guild leader to once again leap at her, swinging his massive sword in a full circle before slamming it home against the side of the bug and cleaving an entire wing free with a roar. "Not a *chance!*"

Joe slipped around the bug to stay out of sight of the guild leader, swinging a foot out and around behind him to kick up a thick cloud of dust. He arrested his momentum as he blocked the view of the guild members then he focused intently enough to cause his left eye to start twitching. Lifting his Strength-bound Ritual Orb, he sent it flying at the Matriarch just as her health dropped below two and a half percent.

"*Deadlift Corify!*"

The dumbbell-shaped orb crashed into the carapace of the Planthopper, cracking through and sinking into supple flesh below. It glowed brightly for a moment, then Joe lost connection to the orb, just as he had the previous one.

"Son of a-"

CHAPTER THIRTY-FOUR

Eyes dilating, Joe barely managed to take note of a thin coating of golden light that wafted off of him, vanishing into the air, like a cloud of pollen being dissipated in the wind. At the same moment, an orb burst out of the side of the matriarch, shooting directly toward him and *thwapping* into his hand. He stared at the object for a moment, almost stupefied as he tried to understand why his Ritual Orb had changed shape.

"*Abyss!*" Joe hissed at his foolishness, stowing away the intensely luminescent core that had just shot into his hand— Deadlift Corify's special option had activated after all.

He whipped his head around, wondering if anyone had noticed his theft of the true prize from the monster, but to his great relief, everyone was still focused on the thrashing bug. "Thank goodness all the light in the area is being captured and dropped on that thing, or this would have been like a second sun rising!"

No one even *noticed* that the Matriarch was already dead, and her 'attacks' were just the creature spasming in death throes.

Snapping his finger dramatically, Joe cut off the directed

Ritual of Elemental Burst, and the light in the area returned to normal—just in time for the guild leader to leap into the air with a flourish, swing his sword up and overhead, and bring it down to directly cleave the body of the Matriarch into perfect halves. The man hit the ground, his sword and soles of his feet landing at the same time.

Then the Matriarch's corpse split, toppling in opposite directions.

Letting his head fall back, the guild leader howled to the sky, "Poor Life *Choi-ces!*"

His entire guild echoing him, the leader threw himself against the remaining bugs. Luckily for, well, for the entirety of Midgard, Joe's ritual bugzapper was still in effect, keeping the insects returning to the area, even as they tried to swarm away. The Ritualist took a few steps closer to the Matriarch, only to be blocked by a series of the guild's high rankers already setting up a perimeter around the fallen Boss Monster. All of them were eyeing him cautiously, weapons at the ready—yet pointed at *him*, not the monsters.

"Seriously? After all that, you're still acting like I'm an attacker?"

"We don't really know you, and it wouldn't be the first time someone has acted friendly just before trying to swipe all the rewards and run for it," one of the rankers stated in a surprisingly even tone. "Look, I'm sure our leader will reward you handsomely at the end of all this. But we need to think about the campaign costs, the death benefit fees-"

"Yeah, whatever." Joe shook his head in disgust then turned and began stomping over toward the half-collapsed tunnel the guild had unsealed. "I'll just clean up *your* mess and be on my way then, *I guess.*"

There were still thousands of fairly high-level insects to put down, though luckily it was more of an extermination than a fight, thanks to them being held in place by the hypnotic lights of Joe's ritual. While he allowed the Poor Lifechoices to deal with that, the Ritualist began putting together a rather simple diagram: the Ritual of *Builder's Intent*. Though he had created so many structures that he had lost count, Joe was still excited to try this new variant for the first time.

Not bothering to look for volunteers, Joe simply placed his Mana Batteries in position and began generating the ritual in midair using Somatic Ritual Casting. Finishing quickly, he applied the blueprint for a simple shrine and reached forward to activate-

A hand shot out and clamped around his wrist, not managing to slow his momentum in the slightest, much to the surprise of the random guild member who was trying to body block him. The startled burly warrior was dragged along like a toddler as Joe moved his hand back and forth, letting out a startled **squawk**.

"Do you mind? I'm just about done here."

"Stop whatever spell you are casting this *instant* and wait for the guild leader to inspect your intent!" the warrior blustered at Joe, who simply raised an eyebrow, lifted his left hand, and karate-chopped the offending limb, snapping the man's wrist with a single blow. As the huge man howled in pain, the Ritualist finished his crafting and sent a burst of mana through the spell circles.

Mana and aspects flooded out of him, coalescing into a small shrine.

Placing a hand on the blank altar, Joe dedicated the shrine to Tatum and watched with cautious optimism as it shifted its appearance to that of a giant stone book with a trickle of black water flowing out of its pages like a silk-ribbon bookmark.

"What have you *done*?" the hard voice of the guild leader sounded out behind Joe, and the Ritualist calmly turned to regard the nearly half of the guild that was currently surrounding him. "I can feel something changing in the air. After all that, why would you betray us at the last-"

A deep vibration rumbled out from deep underground, and moments later, a thick, concentrated cloud of energy that could only be called 'miasma' began pouring out of the entrance of the tunnel and being suctioned into the tiny shrine, which remained clean and unblemished as the seemingly endless tide of foul corruption poured into it.

Place of Power captured: The Slavering Crypts. A portion of all energy accumulated here has been shifted to your deity! Tatum has accepted your donation of the toxic, stagnant, corruptive mana permeating the crypts.

Hidden Quest complete: neutralize the crypts. For centuries, dark power has seeped into the slavering crypts, choosing the foulest of hosts to safe-guard it. Simply defeating the guardian of the crypts is not enough. Without having removed the stagnant mana, a new guardian would have been chosen and elevated.

Reward: The Slavering Crypts will not generate a new Boss Monster, so long as this shrine remains in place. +2 skill levels in a curse-breaking related skill if you have one, else a new skill will be generated.

Now that the danger had passed, at least from the monsters, Joe felt a flood of notifications swell up in him, like a sinus headache starting behind his eyes. Still, he simply stared at the guild leader opposite him, who was reading over his own notification and growing paler by the second.

"Ahem... stand down, everyone. Seems like he just saved our bacon... again." Rubbing the back of his head, the guild leader offered a sheepish smile to the powerful bald man now glaring at him with his arms crossed. "Hey, how would you like that wing I cut off the Matriarch? Should be about ten percent of the creature, and it's Artifact ranked. A token of our appreciation, and... unfortunately, all I can really spare, since it somehow didn't drop a core on death, like we expected."

Not replying right away, as he was trying to keep a straight face, Joe simply graciously bowed his head in acknowledgment. "Works for me. I'm feeling rather generous at the moment, having accomplished my goal."

"Oh?"

A hint of suspicion appeared in the guild leader's eyes, instantly vanishing as Joe finished. "Yeah. You know... keeping the swarm you unleashed from eating the world?"

"Right... right." The guild leader reached out of hand. "Sorry about that. It's been a really long day. Friends?"

"Acquaintances." Joe took the outstretched hand, giving it a firm shake as they both cautiously sized the other up. "Well. I'll take my wing, and we'll be on our way. Have fun exploring the crypts; I'm sure they're absolutely loaded down with treasure."

"You really don't want *any* of it?" The question was tossed out in a far too casual way, and the Ritualist could practically *smell* the distrust.

"What can I say?" Joe turned and began walking away, lifting a hand and giving a single wave as he shot his coven members intense, meaningful stares. "Like I said, I got what I came here for."

As he and his people moved away from the prickly guild, Joe took a moment to glance at his system notifications.

Two skill levels have been automatically applied to Enchanted Ritual Circles, as 'curse breaking' is considered a major component of its utility.

Skill increases:

Dark Chain Lightning (Expert III → Expert IV). Pretty fun spell, right?

Exquisite Shell (Expert 0 → I). Did you even notice that you took no damage after falling out of the sky? No, of course you didn't.

Lay on Hands (Expert III → IV). Reattaching limbs is a great way to rapidly increase this spell's level! Get your friends on board with it!

Neutrality Aura (Expert 0 → Expert II). You healed hundreds and removed over 5 tons worth of nutritious sludge the Matriarch could have used to heal through an immense amount of damage. Impressive.

Artisan Body (Student VI → Journeyman 0). This has been waiting for you for a while, check your notifications more often. Just for giggles, maybe try a Characteristic other than Constitution to passively grow for a while? Could even be fun.

Magical Synesthesia (Student II → Student V). You get to hear more voices around magic.

Mental Manipulation Resistance (Novice III → Beginner I). The voices entering your head now require proper authorization.

Enchanted Ritual Circles (Student VIII → Journeyman 0). Congratu-

lations! You are now technically a Journeyman, with almost no idea how to use this skill. At all. Frankly, it's impressive. Here, this should at least get you started.

Item gained: Ritual Tokens for Bald Dumb-Dumbs. This is a primer on the use of Tokens in Enchanted Ritual Circles and some common uses and applications. Technically it is a Lore book, but as it is designated for Beginner-ranked Ritualists and is single-use, you can have it for free.

Quest updated: The Other Three. You have captured a Place of Power in the Forest of Chlorophyll Chaos. There are two more around the center, and each of them can give interesting benefits. You've captured half, and concerned gazes are turning toward you. Grab the others! It'll be fun! Reward: Variable. Failure: None.

Recommended level: 30.

"What should we be doing, Joe?" Big_Mo murmured as he watched the guild members in the distance going about their business, though still casting calculating glances in their direction every once awhile. "Should we just… leave?"

Shaking his head, Joe directed the group toward the fallen Matriarch. "I need to grab the reward they offered us, and… I'm going to essentially destroy it, but I'll make it up to all of you in a manner of your choosing. Contribution points, personal lessons, whatever. While I'm doing that, I think the three of you should stick close to each other, but go and set off every last ritual you possibly can. There's still thousands of bugs under compulsion, and nothing says you need to use one ritual per monster, just that you need to use them in combat to finish the quest. Spam 'em. Get rid of everything you've got."

The trio nodded excitedly, their eyes lighting up with enthusiasm as they hurried to an unoccupied space under the scintillating light show. Alone once more, Joe slowly approached the severed wing, and the warriors guarding it reluctantly allowed him to pass. "Oh good, you guys already heard that this is for me? Cool, thanks."

He was only trying to lighten the mood, but from the tightening of their jaws and the twitching lips as they tried not to scowl at him, Joe could only assume he hadn't succeeded in a

Charisma check on them. Kneeling beside the multi-ton crescent of chitin, wax, and still-spasming connective tissue, the
Ritualist stretched his arms to the side and began directing his
mana out in long, perfectly straight filaments, slowly making an
Ascendant Matrix as large as he possibly could.

Although he did his best to cover the entirety of the wing, it
was simply too long to be reduced in a single attempt.

"Abyss, that's going to waste some of the material at the
cutoff point..." Joe glanced at his Mana Manipulation skill,
which governed his ability to control his mana well enough to
expand pure energy constructs such as this. "Still stuck as a
Journeyman... I need to do something about that soon, or I'm
going to start having a lot of trouble."

Once the glowing faraday cage of power was in place, he
pulled out aspect jars one after another, placing them at intersecting points along the lattice. Silver Uncommon, light blue
Rare, indigo Unique... and finally his newest, brilliant orange
Artifact-rank jar. As he knew he was being watched carefully,
Joe positioned himself to mostly cover the final jar. He didn't
want anyone to think they had an easy chance at snatching a
powerful, expensive item such as this. "Not that anyone other
than me could use it, as far as I know, but it would still *suck* to
lose it."

With everything in place, he allowed his mana to flow
through his body into the matrix, and immediately felt an
immense strain as his lacking mana density and manipulation
skills fought against the Artifact-rank item he was attempting to
reduce. Joe pushed more and more power into the matrix, and
ever so slowly, the wing began to dissolve, starting at the top of
the space and creeping toward the bottom.

Brilliant lights flared out as the wing slowly vanished, only to
be caught in the carefully built web around them and pulled
along the lattice until they were deposited in the correct jar. A
handful of minutes passed this way... then it was gone.

All of it.

Just as the chunk he was working on was fully reduced, the

remainder of the wing turned black, shriveled up, and blew away in the wind—completely lost. Joe's jaw dropped, his hands unconsciously reaching toward the chunk of wing that had been destroyed in the process. "*Feces*! I thought I was going to lose a *little* of it, not half a *ton* worth of material! Abyssal Midgard Characteristic cap! That was *way* harder than it should have been."

Still, it wasn't a complete loss, as evidenced by the notification which sprung up a moment later.

Aspects captured!
Artifact Aspects: 1,111
Unique Aspects: 2,222
Special Aspects [Spawn]: 3,333
Rare Aspects: 4,444
Uncommon Aspects: 5,555
Common Aspects: 6,666

"That's... an oddly linear spread." The Ritualist immediately stored the Artifact jars, marveling at the fact that he had already accumulated over five thousand aspects, thanks to its passive generation and this new influx. "Just about half full... guess I'll have to use some of those up!"

That realization eased some of his angst over losing such a treasure. As he calmed down, his eyes were drawn to the Special aspects he'd captured. "What do 'spawn' aspects do? You know what? If nothing else, they look interesting. Anything pulled from a monster that strong has to be potent, at the very least."

Since he already had an Ascendant Matrix set up, Joe pulled out a Unique-rank core and began pulling the new Special aspects out of his codpiece, where they ended up by default when he didn't have a specialized container. Soon he was holding a natural aspect jar with an indigo outer shell, though the interior flashed with a deep silver speckled with black lights.

"There we go, now I don't have to worry about using all of these up like the others I practically *wasted*."

Item created: Natural Aspect Jar of [Spawn]. Generates seven [Spawn] aspects per hour. 1,242/8420 aspects collected.

Slapping his hands together to get any remnant bug dust off himself, Joe turned to look at the clean up efforts going on. Thousands upon thousands of bugs still lived, a massive swarm still undulating in time with the movement of his bugzapper ritual. His first instinct was to immediately rush over and join in on the fun of squashing them, but he stayed back for one simple reason: a line in his quest that remained stubbornly blank.

Use 100 four-discipline Beginner ritual combat circles in live combat. (0/200)

"Well, Alchemy is out the window, as I have no way to put anything together without a cauldron." Joe pulled out his Ritual Combat Manual and a blank sheet of paper then began quickly going over the equations of his Beginner-rank ritual of Elemental Burst. "If I tweak the burn duration, reinforce these sigils... I'll need to adjust the syntax on that to make it work. Let's try-"

Happily, with his Magical Matrices skill in the middle of the Journeyman ranks, messing with Beginner and Novice-rank rituals was practically child's play. In under half an hour, he had managed to increase the damage output by nearly five percent and the duration by a tenth, all without increasing the cost of the ritual circle itself.

Something *clicked* in his mind, and Joe simply *knew* that using this variant of the ritual would qualify as using a two-discipline version. "There we go... now I just need to add in stabilizers, and it uses three of the core skills. Abyss, if I deal a little damage before activating the ritual, I can add in some blood and push it to four."

Finally ready to begin, Joe rushed into combat with an enemy that couldn't fight back. Perhaps not the most *honorable* way to complete his quest, but as he set out a long line of low-level stabilizers, and the battlefield began to resound with the repeated whining of small-scale rituals activating over and over... he couldn't find it in himself to care.

Creating Beginner-ranked rituals was incredibly swift, prac- tically only a thought standing between wanting the ritual to exist and activating it. As his quest conditions rapidly approached completion, Joe began using his Ritual Orbs to break limbs off the larger, elite version of the hypnotized bugs. Even as they screeched and turned to fight him, he would drip the ichor pouring from the wound on four or five rituals at a time, activating each of them in sequence to make sure they all had a chance to go off before the creature died.

Only as the sun finally dipped to the horizon, an entire day having been spent on this one battle, did the last of the bugs fall to the ground. A ragged cheer went up from the coven and the Poor Lifechoices as it was dropped, and Joe blinked several times, looking around and finding himself in a flame-scorched clearing reeking of cooked chitin and tacky with dried fluids.

Kirby trudged over, barely managing to rasp out, "All done. Can I pass out now?"

"I'll second that." Big_Mo started to sit on the filthy ground, only for Joe to dash to his side and pull him upright.

"No, we really shouldn't stay here." As the others looked at him with bleary eyes, Joe began pulling the group toward the now-far-distant tree line. "They had a Jester in their group.... who's to say they don't have more bad actors in their ranks? Fact is, if we want to keep what we've earned today, we need to get out of here and make camp somewhere safe."

No one could argue with that, so without another word, the four Ritualists slipped away from the area, entering the foliage of the Forest of Chlorophyll Chaos and vanishing into its depths in an instant, as its magic whisked them away.

CHAPTER THIRTY-FIVE

Trudging down a road that *finally* had landmarks he recognized, Joe took a deep breath and thought about what he wanted to say to his companions. Relentless fighting over the past week had taken a toll, clearly seen in how fatigue clung to them, but each would agree the excursion had been worth it.

One after another, they'd cleared the Novice-rank quest, thanks in no small part to having exhausted their prepared rituals against millions of hypnotized bugs. For his part, as the looming walls of Towny McTownface came into view, a rabid bear had made the mistake of crossing their path, and Joe was even able to complete the *next* part of the quest chain.

Quest complete: Mastering Ritual Combat II. Congratulations on proving your ability to coordinate multiple disciplines during live combat. By now, you must have started to get a feel for which path you plan to follow to its end, and the next quest in this line will reflect that.

Reward: 1) You have chosen to apply your reward to Alchemical Rituals, a surprise, to be sure. 2) You've gained a two-circle flourish along the cuffs of your Ritual Tower robes, denoting you as a Beginner combatant, embroidered in silver thread. Though almost entirely ornamental in design, your portion of the spoils increases by 1% from successful combat challenges on behalf of the Ritualist Tower.

Skill increases:

Alchemical Rituals (Apprentice IX → Student VII). Congratulations, as a student of Alchemical Rituals, you've shown a true desire to continue pushing the bounds of what is possible. You may now choose this skill in class quests which allow you to choose a focus.

Ritual Duplication (Apprentice 0 → Apprentice II).

During the multi-day journey back to town—which they'd only made to resupply and pick up their recently respawned coven members—Joe had placed shrines to Tatum to extend his fast travel network and pushed each of his Lore skills up to the Expert rank, thanks to some strategic use of his Knowledge skill.

Well, *almost* all of them.

For obvious reasons, his new Magical Syntax Lore was lagging behind at Journeyman three after he'd dropped two points into it. Still, considering it already acted like Ritual Circles' hidden mini-game, Joe was practically *vibrating* with anticipation over what the next rank might unlock.

Every skill he'd boosted to Expert had unlocked a shiny new profession-related perk, part of the reason Joe was pushing the others to rush back as quickly as possible. The excitement of testing them out for the first time made him need to *force* himself to stay with the rest of the group, instead of just getting there as fast as he could. The Ritualist, trying to take his mind off his agitation, pulled open the system notifications he had gained over the last few days and greedily sifted through the information again.

First was the Alchemy Methodology he'd earned, the 'Water Hyacinth Placement Methodology'. From what he understood, it would allow him to create Alchemy products extremely quickly, but only at the higher ranks of Alchemy.

Essentially, it would force him to place a single aspect to start with, then two, then four. Each placement would then double the number of aspects he would need to control and place simultaneously, testing his Intelligence, Dexterity, mana control, and knowledge of alchemy all at once. It was certain to be challenging, and he could only hope it would be at least as fun as Ritualistic Forging had turned out to be.

Architectural Lore had been a bit of a surprise when it hit Expert. Joe had been expecting something similar to the others but had failed to take into account that those had been *class* skills, and Architecture could be considered a general skill practically anyone could pick up. Still, it had been with great happiness that he'd earned a 'Load Lattice Legend', which promised to give him the ability to create entirely new blueprints for buildings based on a concept he was going for.

If he wanted barns, or if he wanted castles, Joe simply needed to declare it and work his way through a lattice that would appear before him. Correctly adjusting and optimizing the various pathways would generate a new blueprint he could use—actually, doing it incorrectly would *also* make a usable blueprint, and then the structure would have major issues, if he didn't figure it out before raising the structure.

The reward for Calculus and Number Theory had granted him 'Curvature Tuning', which barely made sense to him. Seeing as calculus, at its core, is all about rates of change, the mini-game purported to be all about understanding continuous flows as mana specifically shifted infinitesimally over a set space. He would apparently be presented with an incomplete equation, as well as a topographical map it represented, and need to quickly work it out. "I should really get something more specific to Magical Matrices... I wonder what *that* will offer at the Expert rank."

Lastly, Celestial-Arcane Interaction Lore had been, if possible, even more abstract. "Celestial Surfing...? When presented with a clear view of the stars, I can fall into a trance and literally surf between different celestial bodies that are shifting relative to each other. The closer I get to each celestial body, the more I will come in tune with conjunctions, oppositions, and trines. What is *that*? I understand converging mana streams and currents in conflict, but what's a 'trine'?

"Hey, the roads are getting a little crowded." Hannah's voice held a slight edge to it, and Joe blinked several times as he realized she'd been trying to smack him on the shoulder, only for his Exquisite Shell to simply allow him to filter out the sensation.

"Why would that be-?" Looking around, the Ritualist quickly found that she was correct—Towny McTownface was being absolutely *swarmed*. Long lines of people stretched several blocks down the road, and while they were moving along at a decent clip, joining that mass of humanity would cost them at least a couple hours. "Ah... none of this looks fun. We should— *ugh*! What is that *smell*?"

Without waiting for an answer, he quickly worked to redirect his Neutrality Aura to more carefully cover his nose as the thick and unfortunately *familiar* smell of unwashed adventurer hit them like a wall. "Right, we're here for a quick stop only, so let's get in and get *out*. Buy what you need for your rituals, ink, components, whatever it is, and put it on my tab. I'll go drop off our spoils and get it all converted to contribution points. Oh, also, I'll see what I owe you for your portion of the Matriarch we took down."

A chorus of grunts and nods were his only answer. Each of his companions looked absolutely worn down and raw from the near-endless fighting they'd been dragged into for the last week, but he was pleased to see that they were still moving with a sort of grim determination he had nothing but respect for. "Before I forget... good work out there. Hey, someone find Taka and Robert! We've got to make sure they get a fair share of the rewards. Last thing, uh, anyone want to just be carried by me over the walls? There's no way I'm waiting in line."

No one took him up on his exceptionally *generous* offer, deciding to enter the town slowly instead of being princess carried by the bald Ritualist as he jumped up and over the barrier. After a few awkward moments of waiting, he shook his head and threw his hands in the air. "Hey, your loss! I'll see you all when you *eventually* get in there."

As he began trotting down the road, a few grumbling complaints coming from the lined-up adventurers at his audacity, Joe started to fall back into his theory crafting and excitement—only for a loud, familiar voice to nearly knock him off his feet as it thundered across the open air like a trumpet.

"Oi! Baldy-boy, thought ye could sneak back inta town wi'oot sayin' hello, didja?"

Joe skid to a halt, flipping around and staring at the beaming Skald. "*Bard?* What are you doing here? I thought you and Alexis were off making a new life together!"

"Good ta see ya, too. But when the guild's callin' fer all hands on deck, an' they're payin' through the nose ta bring in every last soul they can get their grubby wee hands on, it's hard ta find a reason ta say no." Bard's smile dimmed, and he stepped out of line to walk with Joe. "But the real reason I'm here is I got a message from Poppy. He let us know ye were back in town, an' I had ta get down here an' warn ye 'fore things got too messy."

"Warn *me?*" Joe's left eye twitched as he thought about the various enemies he'd made on this world. "Don't worry, old friend. I'll cross that bridge when I get to it. I'm sure we're going to have people popping out of the woodwork to try and take the guild down as we-"

"The Jesters've been poppin' up all o'er the place these past few months. The Scholars've gone an' got themselves a new leader and a personal army under their banner." Bard was ticking off on his fingers as he spoke.

"A couple o' disgraced noble houses've been scoopin' up every merc the Wanderers didna manage ta snatch... but they only started that lark after they caught wind o' the public announcement sayin' you're puttin' a big upgrade in place. My class skills're screamin' bloody murder, Joe. Listen to me. What-ever's comin'? It's gonna be worth writin' a ballad over, and it's gonna push me up a few tiers. Heed me words, bud. Whatever ye *think* ye need ta do… do it *bigger*."

Though he felt a spark of indignation, Joe decided to hold his tongue and think over the facts. Slowly, he started putting together the pieces, thanks in no small part to Bard laying it out for him. "That Battle Scholar in Ardania, Lindon. He was talking about how he had 'smiling sponsors'. Do you think they're all working together?"

"I *know* they are, Joe." Bard pulled out a months-old parchment. "'Bout half a year back, there was a shady request posted. Some unknown lot lookin' inta how best ta control an uncontrollable monster. Didna take long 'fore the post vanished, nice an' quiet-like. I've been chasin' down scraps an' whispers ever since. An' lemme tell ya, Joe… everythin' I've found, every bone-deep instinct I've got, it's all tellin' me the same thing. They're plannin' ta unleash somethin' awful, and they're gonna do it right here."

"Uncontrollable?" Joe glanced over the request, leaning away from it in agitation as he read words such as 'peak power on Midgard' and 'only Master Beast Tamers and above need apply'. "Are you thinking it's going to be a World Boss, or…?"

The Skald shook his head, "Not that big, or the kingdom'd be breathin' down their necks already. Nah, I'm thinkin' we're lookin' at somethin' in the Master ta Grandmaster range. Still plenty o' kick, enough ta flatten a city if it's on the low end… or wipe a blasted country off the map, if'n I'm wrong and it's worse than I'm guessin'."

"All because I'm here, huh?" Joe closed his eyes, and when he opened them, his gaze was hard as he stared at his friend. "I guess it's a good thing I'm here before they let it loose in an attempt to lure me down."

"*There's* the silver lining." Bard chuckled as he relaxed slightly, head bowing in relief. "All I'm askin' ya ta do is treat it like the whole world's hangin' in the balance. Go hard right from the start. No holdin' back, no warm-up rounds ta test what they can take. Just hit 'em like they owe ya money."

Clapping his friend on the shoulder, Joe replied with a promise of violence in his words, "I absolutely will. Now, why don't you tell me everything you know, and I'll try not to get distracted by the thought of learning a Grandmaster curse so I can target every member of these people's lineage at once and rip it out by the roots."

"*Ha~ahh...*" Bard's initial laugh turned into a leery sigh, "Ye know, the worst part is? I'm not even sure ye *couldn't* pull it off. Here's what I've found..."

The Skald had put together an extremely comprehensive explanation to go along with his warning, and it painted a grim picture for what the Wanderers were going to face in the upcoming attempts at upgrading either the town to a City or the guild into a sect.

It was unlikely that they'd fight anything greater than a Unique-rank monster when upgrading to a City, it *was* still Midgard, but that was only assuming no outside intervention. Conversely, the sheer scarcity of cities meant it was possible that there were more resources available to throw against them as they were being founded, just like on Jotunheim.

Without breaking stride or warning Bard, Joe scooped his friend up and Omnivaulted to the top of the wall, waved at the nervous guard stationed there, then jumped again. They landed on the street and swiftly mingled with the crowd to ward off any hastily fired arrows.

Bard slammed a fist into the side of Joe's head, where it stopped cold. "Blast ye, Baldy! Give a man some warning before ya take him sailing in the air like that."

"Just figured you'd prefer to not lose your place in line." Joe could only be relieved that he had toggled off Haunting Shadows so he didn't need to worry about accidentally striking back at his friend. "Look, I've got some, *ehh*, decisions to make. I hate having to say goodbye already, but if you need me, look for me up at the Pathfinder's Hall."

They separated then, casually making plans to meet up for a coffee before Joe left Midgard again. As the Ritualist walked along the crowded streets, he intentionally chose to move with the slowly surging people instead of bounding along the rooftops.

The warning had settled heavily on his shoulders, and he needed to make a choice on how he would handle it. On the one hand, he'd explicitly told his coven that he would help boost their ranks and levels. They were meant to be his power base on this world, eventually feeding him with Journeymen or Experts on the next worlds.

Joe needed people he could mold into Masters so *he* could become a Grandmaster. It wasn't something he only *wanted* to do; his brief stay on Vanaheim had solidified this course of action as a *necessity*.

Conversely, this situation was absolutely his responsibility. Setting aside the fact that his presence had drawn out old enemies, he'd also been the one to earn the charter allowing them to upgrade in the first place. On top of that, even if he *hadn't* been the one to cause these issues, as the First Elder in waiting, he would've been duty-bound to ensure their defenses were ready. "Yikes. Three layers of 'this is my job'."

It was clear to him what needed to happen, and he could always take more time training people *after* this crisis had been averted.

Feeling a bit more relaxed now that he'd made his choice, Joe glanced around the town, which had the distinct feel of being a pressurized cauldron on the brink of bursting. Between the new arrivals getting separated and shouting for each other, the trinket salesmen shouting about their overpriced souvenirs, and the immense noise coming from the crafting district he'd finally come alongside, it was clear this town was barreling toward conflict, one way or another.

No longer needing the press of people to remain lost in his own thoughts, he launched himself upward, gasps and shouts of concern trailing him like the tail of a comet. From there, it was only a matter of seconds before he was landing on the street in front of the Pathfinder's Hall.

Happily, no one attempted to bar his entrance this time around, though one stubborn ticket taker chased him all the way to the door—only to screech to a halt when the Juggernaut stationed there turned its head and stared her down.

"Joe! You're back! Come, this is wonderful, truly marvelous!" Though the Pathfinder's Hall was full of tourists and people trying to plot their own path forward, Boris had lit up and rushed toward him practically as soon as the Ritualist had stepped into the building.

A frantic light was shining in the Scholar's eyes as he grabbed Joe's arm and pulled him along. "I feel like I'm on the cusp of a fascinating breakthrough—I just need... oh, I'm certain it's only a few more data points. The only trouble is, well, I need them from what most would consider *unsavory* classes. If I'm reading this right, the interplay between the normalized distribution should tend toward the central part of the bell curve, but it is those at the *outlier* endpoints that truly push the bounds of-"

Though he tried to listen patiently, Joe had absolutely no idea what the man was talking about, and as he waxed eloquent, it only became more apparent that Boris was all but writing a dissertation at this point. The Ritualist took a moment to inspect the room as he walked with the Scholar still chattering away, then distracted the man and adjusted their path to sneak into the basement area.

The entire time, the elderly man rambled on excitedly, likely not even noticing that he was being led around. Finally, Joe could only chuckle warmly and wave Boris away. "Sounds like you've been having a good time. Please, don't let me get in the way! With all of the people arriving each day, I'm sure you're going to find your missing data points coming sooner rather than later."

"You don't say?" Boris's eyes went wide. "But of course! When the central curve is gathered, the outliers will convene on them, whether to uplift them or prey upon them as they can! I need to be watching the class constellations, waiting for the moment-"

"Don't forget we're going to be upgrading the building in just a few weeks!" Joe shouted up the stairwell as Boris rushed off. "If you don't have what you need by then, you'll probably get it soon afterward!"

Going up the stairs at a far more sedate pace, Joe heard Big_Mo chatting with someone and tensed up as he prepared to give his coven the disappointing news that he needed to cut their training session short. As he approached the group, noting how deeply engaged in discussion they were, Joe was the one taken by surprise when they noticed him, immediately fell silent, and turned to him with firm expressions on their faces.

"How did you all get here so fast-"

"Joe, we've been talking." Hannah was the first to speak, cutting off Joe's words, but Taka couldn't hold himself back.

Speaking right over her, he spewed out his thoughts in a surprisingly concise manner. "At the end of the day, we're members of the Wanderer's Guild, and it's practically under attack right now."

Taka took a deep breath, looking as though he were about to break Joe's heart and feeling bad about it. "We have to stay here and set up defenses to help protect the guild. I know it's weeks out, but I don't know if we'll be able to get back in if we cut it too close. Plus, now I have so many new things to test, so many projects I want to put in place-"

"I'm tired of walking so much!" Kirby chipped in brightly. "I don't mind blowing up bugs and wild animals, but getting to them is annoying when my feet hurt all day long."

"I... want to do my own expedition, without the safety net." Robert half-raised his hand. "There was a lot going on, and I feel like I leaned on you a little too much."

"We know you have your heart set on power leveling us, but could you let us off the hook? At least until this is all over?" Big_Mo's question hung in the air, clearly showing that this had been the main point of their discussions.

For his part, Joe felt relief flooding him, though he managed to school his features into a mask of contemplation. After a moment, he decided they didn't need to know he'd already been planning on putting them off in favor of his other obligations. "Just want to clarify... you're all going to be taking this time to build up your skills and focusing on the areas you're thinking of specializing in, yes? No one's going to be falling into old habits, maybe making dolls for only a *few* hours a day?"

He let the silence hang just long enough for them to begin to shift uneasily, but before they could backpedal and make *him* have to be the one to cancel their trip, Joe allowed himself a nod. "Good. I'm looking forward to seeing what all of you can accomplish with so much time. I'll make sure to get you a hefty amount of contribution points you can spend on your own projects, but only if you're all absolutely certain. No slacking off. I expect to see real progress."

Each of them eagerly nodded along with him, relief palpable as they began talking amongst themselves for a few more minutes, only to slowly begin drifting away—no doubt as excited to practice their craft as Joe was.

Now freed from any immediate responsibilities, the Ritualist turned on his heel and strode deeper into the Pathfinder's Hall, mind already racing as he began working out exactly what he'd need to face whatever was coming for them.

"Without having a few Grandmasters around to share the strain, this is going to be tough. But, if I'm going to take Bard seriously and throw everything I can against whatever's coming, there's only one real option..."

"The only question is: which Master-rank ritual should I throw at them?"

CHAPTER THIRTY-SIX

While weeks of preparation might have seemed like plenty of time, creating a Master-rank ritual, even with a diagram handily provided by one of his books, was nowhere close to an easy task. First, if he went too fast and made mistakes, Joe wouldn't need to wait for a wave of *monsters* to wipe out the town; he'd probably do it all on his own. Second, as he only had a single Artifact-rank core, he had at *most* two attempts at making the ritual.

So, Joe did what any true practitioner of high-level skills did in a situation like this: he procrastinated.

Days began to slowly blend into one another as he set up stabilizers for his low-powered test rituals, his casual notes began to turn into piles of loose leaf paper as he carefully wrote out his thoughts on the sundry diagrams, and only then did he even decide which of the rituals he was going to be attempting to make. Surprising even himself, Joe didn't pull from his more extensive list of dangerous rituals he'd acquired long ago. Instead, he decided to keep on with the Ritual combat manual's offerings to ensure he got the double whammy of making something that would for sure count toward his ritualistic combat chain quest.

"Ritual of the Cataclysmic Tempest." He let out a sigh of satisfaction as he lay his book down and started getting ready for the next step. "As always, preparation is key. Actually, if I could make some Expert-rank stabilizers, I'm sure that'd go a long way toward easing my mind when I'm working on this. It's not going to be enough to guarantee success, sure, but…"

For the first time in days, he pulled himself out of his underground refuge, trying to blink away the diagram that kept popping up in his mind. It was a swirling stain on his thoughts: complexities, references, and interactions he'd been studying. Practically stumbling into the guild's smithy, Joe manifested his aspect hammer and walked up to an empty, cold anvil. "A little bit of movement should help me clear my head. Work up a little sweat, let all of the angst seep from my pores. Yeah…"

"Hey, you all right there, buddy? Ya seem a little out of it." To the smith's credit, he didn't immediately try to kick Joe out, instead trying to gently help him. "I can see you're a member of the guild, so you're entitled to use the place, but there's a standard hourly cost-"

"Not a problem," Joe mumbled at him, pulling out a Rare core and tossing it over. "If that doesn't cover it, just let me know."

"Er…" The smith looked down at the shining orb which had practically appeared in his hand. "It's not contribution points, but yeah, that should do it. Look, why don't I get your furnace going? A cold anvil's not gonna-"

Joe lifted his hammer, which immediately became wreathed in infernal flames, "Really, not a problem."

"Do you need to purchase any ores-" The smith fell silent as a cage of light appeared on the anvil, a blob of aspects forming in the center of it. "Right. I'm catching on. I'll just… be over here. If you need any help, or if you're feeling unwell, I'm here for you."

"That's rather kind of you," Joe managed to get out just before ritual circles appeared in the air above his blob of aspects.

The smith flinched away as the strange bald man struck with unerring speed and precision, just as the circles lined up, and a thunderous *clang* rolled through the shop—followed immediately by another, then another, so fast they seemed to overlap. Before the man's eyes, a pattern appeared where the blob had once been.

At the moment, it was still a flat, blank slate. But with every precise swing of Joe's hammer, a fresh millimeter of structure formed. The design rapidly took shape as a five-pointed star composed of joined pyramids, welded at their base to converge around a central octagonal gap.

"Huh... not exactly what I was expecting it to be, but... what do I know?" Joe murmured to himself as he started on the next one, rapidly building it out and creating another. "At least thirteen of these per ritual. Oh *no~oo*, I might as well make five sets just to be safe. *Heh.*"

Hours slipped by, and a growing stack of star-shaped constructs piled up beside the anvil Joe was relentlessly hammering. The smith hadn't moved an inch, eyes locked on the process and absorbing every detail. Each time his own skills resonated with Joe's work, the smith flinched involuntarily and gulped as he gained benefits just from observing.

Then, as Joe completed the sixtieth stabilizer, the star pulsed with light and transformed—morphing into a pentagonal prism. Indigo light flared as the shape stretched, becoming a sleek, tubular form with two common bases and a flawlessly uniform cross-section. A sound similar to a trumpet being blown in time with a cowbell ringing gently filled the area, a rare sign of the system itself upgrading a created item.

Only then did Joe pause in his work, staring down at the unintentional creation with a tish of annoyance on his face. "It's Expert-rank now, but it pulled aspects out of my storage to make it happen? I guess it's good to know I won't be able to get a free upgrade if I don't have the necessary materials on hand. Hey...wait a moment. Do these link together?"

Grabbing one of the Journeyman-rank stars, he slotted the

prism through its center, where it *clicked* into place halfway down the bar. "Ah. They're meant to work together. How is that going to work with the ritual circles? *Wait!* At the Expert rank, it's necessary that they're free floating around each other, so this sort of combination *does* make sense if I want to condense the overall size of the ritual."

"Mister… will you teach me?" Joe froze in place, having long since forgotten he wasn't alone. He turned to look at the smith, who was staring at him with burning desire in his eyes. "You're part of the guild, right? I can pay!"

"Uh…" Joe glanced at the anvil, then at the Rare core still unconsciously clutched in the smith's hands. "I'm not going to formally teach you, but you're welcome to watch? I already talk myself through what I'm doing, and I'm not so stingy that I would mind if you listen in. Just to warn you, I don't have a smithing skill. I am doing Ritualistic Forging. It's… pretty different from what you know."

"Close enough to get me two skill levels so far, just watching you, not to mention what you've done for my lore." The man leaned forward, licking his lips excitedly. "To think, I almost didn't take the shift tonight!"

"Right." Joe pulled on the stabilizers, a slight frown gracing his lips when they didn't separate from each other. "Abyss, they slot together permanently? Well, I guess I can't have just *one*; that'll be less stable than having *none*."

Having already decided that tonight was all about seeking refuge from intellectual overload by creating tangible items, Joe decided to go for broke—especially now that he had the excuse of helping out a fellow guild mate. "Between my Ritualistic Forging giving me a fifty-two percent chance to successfully create Expert items, and my Ritual Lore giving me a fifty percent boost to that, I have an automatic seventy-eight percent chance of being able to make these. If I'm *careful*, that goes up a little bit. There's still a good, let's say one in ten chance that whatever I'm making is going to explode. All that to say, you know, don't stand too close."

"I'm not too worried about the risk. What is the respawn room *for* if you never use it, am I right?" The casual attitude put a smile back on Joe's face, though the next words turned it into a rictus grin. "Before you get started, just for the lore of it, I gotta know, is the *singing* a necessary component?"

"That depends entirely on what I was *chanting*. Not singing." Joe slowly slid his gaze to the side until he could see the smith perfectly. Going by the carefully neutral expression on the man's face, perhaps it was better if he didn't know. "The words themselves don't matter so much, it's all about 'can I endlessly repeat them'. That's one of the 'ritual' parts of Ritualistic Forging."

"So, you don't plan those lyrics... in advance?" The man coughed into his fist, not meeting Joe's eyes. "You might want to think about it. I know a pretty good songwriter who can put something together for you at pretty much any tempo you want to keep."

"I might take you up on that." Joe relented after another moment of letting the smith sweat. "Now... let's make metal. I need seventeen of these pentagonal bars for one active project, and since I was making five sets of the last one-"

The night passed swiftly, even if the production of the stabilizers didn't go anywhere near as quickly as he'd hoped. Where Joe was able to rapidly create Journeyman-rank versions, the octagonal bars took fifty-two minutes *each* to become fully formed and solidify.

At the end of the second hour, another man came to trade out with the smith, only to be shooed away by the practically manic metal-maker. Perhaps it was the interruption, or simply Joe getting overconfident, but as the third bar started to solidify, heat poured off his hammer and consumed the new item— melting into a thick slag that fell onto the anvil and cut the oversized chunk of metal cleanly in half.

Then the flames erupting from the hammer wrapped around the entire pile of destruction and *slurped* both the failed project and the now-liquid anvil into... nowhere. Joe and the smith froze, locked eyes, and silently moved to the next workstation without acknowledging the horrifying scene. By the time sunlight was flooding into the space, Joe had only managed to create *five* stabilizers on purpose, leaving him with a total of six. "They're useless on their own, but... it's a good start."

Only then did he start to realize the truly monumental task he had taken on by deciding to push each of his class skills to the peak of Master rank. This was what people had been warning him about for a long time, and perhaps why they had given him such pitying looks on Vanaheim when he had so casually declared he'd eventually become the Class Sage.

If he'd been a standard craftsman, it was a task that would have taken centuries, perhaps an actual millennium to accomplish. Between sourcing his materials, handling the failures, and doing the actual work of creating the items? Well, it was no wonder the path of a craftsman trying to push into the Grandmaster ranks was one that his Dwarven friends had been walking for hundreds of years. "I love the unique advantages I have, but all they mean is that I can get the job done faster. It doesn't let me skip the actual work. Know what I mean?"

He turned to look at the smith, only to find that the man had long since passed out and was snoring on the floor in a small puddle of his saliva—which kept being cleaned away by Joe's Neutrality Aura, only to reappear after a few seconds. "Buddy... nasty. I bet your pillows have big brown water stains, don't they?"

Involuntarily shivering at the mental image, Joe mentally checked his own state and found that he was still fresh and ready to continue. Still, after making what essentially amounted to a half-dozen two hundred pound metal bars, he was ready for a new challenge.

Glancing around to make sure no one was waiting for his spot, Joe finally pulled out the blueprint he'd earned from 'Student Reductionist II'. "A ritualistic cauldron template. A Journeyman-rank reward, earned from a Student-rank quest, which was to complete an Expert-rank task. I suppose that the math on that one makes sense. Means and medians of effort and recompense, or something. Still… hundreds of tiny details, articulating edges, and moving parts. Too much fun. Let's do it."

The ritual cauldron was nothing like the traditional Alchemy cauldron he'd been using to date, which was essentially an oddly shaped pot with a lid. Instead, this one was an intricate framework of bands and rings, with a handle on either side that allowed the gyroscopic contraption to be settled onto a pole on either side and otherwise free floated. There was a perfectly circular cauldron at the core, which, when the rings were in motion, would be sealed simply by the motion of the bands covering it.

He got started, excitedly allowing his aspects to flow into the Ascendant Matrix and hammering away as the ritual circles locked into place. Although the item itself was of a lower grade than the stabilizers he'd been making, the sheer *complexity* of the design meant he needed to move far slower to properly align everything as it was put together.

Even then, he had only worked for ten minutes before he encountered an aberration—as his hammer came down to the upper right quadrant of the slowly forming cauldron, a secondary set of circles appeared on the opposite side, aligning for an instant, only to vanish as if they had never existed.

"What was *that*?" He'd almost lost himself in the minigame, allowing his mantra to guide the speed, and yet he had somehow *missed* one of the strikes he was supposed to be making. "How could I possibly miss a set of rings? It's only a *Journeyman* design!"

At that moment, he completed the core framework of the cauldron with a deafening **clang** as he swung nearly twice as hard as had been required previously. Even then, he barely managed to land his hammer as the lightning-fast rituals flashed past each other. The heavy cauldron formed out of the mass of aspects at that moment, boiling out slightly farther into a casual ring shape as Joe manipulated the glowing aspects with Mana Manipulation. "That's the big parts; now comes the *finesse*."

With his strength, he didn't need to throw a huge amount of power behind these swings, instead merely tapping with regularity as he formed the first band of the gyroscope. His hammer shrank down to nearly jeweler's tools size as he began working on the connection points between the cauldron and the innermost orbiting circle.

Then, just as he was completing a perfect tap, a second set of circles appeared on the opposite side again, only to vanish in a flash so quickly that he *almost* thought he was imagining them.

"You're lowering my perfect strike percentage!" Joe snarled as he let his left hand fall to his side, splitting his attention to form a secondary aspect hammer. Between the three tasks of chanting, swinging, and forming a new tool, he mistimed two of his next swings; they were only 'good' hits instead of 'perfect' ones. Still, he wasn't too worried, as the cauldron was coming together beautifully.

Even better, while he was working on the outermost ring, he saw another flash, and this time got his left hand into position and struck from both angles at the same time.

The aspects flashed with a brilliant, scintillating light, power sinking into the framework as the secondary set of ritual circles appeared again. Only as they became a regular offbeat did Joe realize he'd likely missed out on anywhere from a third to *half* of all potential strikes he could've been making. Still, he reminded himself it was better to learn on a low-ranked object such as this, rather than figure out he had been consistently failing while working on a high-power, high-risk project.

Piece by piece, he layered the structure together and finally tapped the last pin into place. He stepped back as the system went to work. Just then, he saw the flames around his hammers beginning to glow intensely… just as they had when his last project had failed and been consumed. "No! Come *on*, that took like three hours!"

The system didn't seem to care. Flames erupted from his hammer and wrapped around the newly-created cauldron. Newly-minted metal began to crack and bubble as the infernal flames washed over them… but instead of turning the project into slag, a hair-thin layer peeled away. What was left behind were harsh, geometric symbols glowing with red and purple lights before cooling into burned-on black.

Soon, the beautiful chrome exterior had been replaced with a soot-black onyx coloration which made the cauldron look as if it were about to fall into pieces at any moment. Just before the flames would have consumed the cauldron in its entirety, it unleashed a potent aura, and the flames were sucked into the open top. Then the central container twisted on its own, sealing the fire inside.

Item created: Infernal-touched Ritual Cauldron (Special. Upgradable.)

Primary effect: allows three-dimensional reagent placement within the sealed compartment.

Secondary effect: Infernal reinforced metal reduces risk of pill explosion by 14%.

Tertiary effect: Infernal purification. By paying 1% of the total mana and material cost of the previously created alchemical item, you may instantly purge all contaminants, residue, and imperfections from the interior of the cauldron.

Caution! Using the tertiary effect will engulf the cauldron in flames, rendering it unusable for 15 minutes while it uses the heat to self-repair and reset to optimal condition.

Upgrade conditions: successfully create 100 Journeyman-rank alchemical products using this cauldron. After doing so, paying 10 times the material and mana cost of the cauldron's initial creation will allow you to bring it up to the Unique rank.

Although he was absolutely thrilled at the success of the cauldron, Joe didn't allow himself to get *too* excited. "Good… I *hate* cleaning goo outta these things. Plus, this'll be usable all the way through the Expert ranks. I can't count on it being able to turn into an Artifact, but maybe after I upgrade it, there'll be that option?"

Another thought tickled at the back of his mind, and Joe realized that he'd just discovered perhaps the most important part of how his class skills supported each other. "If I can use forging to create the items required for performing alchemy, could I use alchemy in reverse? Make some kind of alchemically-treated forged items? What if I'd managed to enchant this cauldron as well... what extra benefits could it have? Maybe I can even increase my odds of successful infernal refinement if I can work out the math of the added effects using Magical Matrices!"

Shaking his head at the possibilities suddenly swirling through his mind, Joe let his hammers vanish into his storage devices and walked out of the smithy, leaving the smith still soundly sleeping on the stone surface.

"I've come so far, and it's obvious that I've barely even scratched the surface." Joe glanced up at the sun, assessed his mental state to see if he needed a nap or not, and began walking back to the Pathfinder's Hall. "Am I just going to put this new cauldron away? Absolutely *not*. Who needs sleep when I've got new toys?"

CHAPTER THIRTY-SEVEN

Joe finally allowed himself some time to rest later that day... or had it been two days since he'd been in the smithy? Blinking tired eyes, he decided it didn't matter that much. Still, before he could allow himself to sleep, the Ritualist pulled open his character sheet and looked at his skill increases—immediately deciding it had been worth all the effort.

Name: Joe 'Monarch of Mana' Class: Reductionist
Profession I: Arcanologist (Max)
Profession II: Ritualistic Alchemist (7 → 9/20)
Profession III: Grandmaster's Apprentice (15/25)
Profession IV: Ritualistic Metalworker (3 → 7/20)
Profession V: Ritualistic Numerologist Novitiate (1/5)
Profession VI: Arcane Enchanting Theorist (5/5) This can now be used as a prerequisite for __any__ enchanting-based profession!

*Character Level: **30** Exp: 465,000 Exp to next level: 31,000 (Locked.)*
Rituarchitect Level: 13 Exp: 87,450 Exp to next level: 3,550
Reductionist Level: 10 Exp: 72,615 Exp to next level: 5,385

Hit Points: 1,800/1,800
Mana: 5,610/7,310
Mana regen: 64.5/sec
Stamina: 312/1,524
Stamina regen: 6.46/sec

Characteristic: Capped Score (Raw score)

Strength (bound): 150 (278)
Dexterity: 150 (277)
Constitution (Broken): 138 (277)
Light Intelligence (bound): 150 (283)
Wisdom: 150 (270)
Dark Charisma: 150 (229)
Karmic Perception: 150 (280)
Luck: 150 (223)
Karmic Luck: 99 → 92

Skill increases:
Coalescence (Journeyman VII → Journeyman VIII)
Mana Manipulation (Journeyman VII → Journeyman VIII)
Mental Manipulation Resistance (Beginner I → Beginner V)
Teaching (Journeyman III → Journeyman VI)
Alchemical Rituals (Student VII → Journeyman 0)
Magical Matrices (Journeyman V→ Journeyman VI)
Ritualistic Forging (Expert II → Expert III)
Magical Syntax Lore (Journeyman III → Journeyman V)

As exciting as it was to see his skills suddenly jumping so quickly, he could only *partially* credit his own efforts. Certainly he'd been working hard, but he had also been doing it in the shadow of the Pathfinder's Hall, with its four times multiplier to skill gain. "I'm either going to have to snatch that and take it with me when I go to a more permanent base, or I'll need to make another one everywhere I set up shop. Eh, nah... that's a habit that'd get expensive pretty quick."

As tempting as it was to throw himself down the path of a pure crafter and stop worrying so much, the fact remained that a large-scale battle was imminent and looming ever closer. If he didn't start getting to work on his Master-rank ritual, he wouldn't be finishing it before the battle started, and he would certainly be far too busy *during* the conflict to work on it then.

Before he even realized he'd fallen asleep, he was being poked by a moist pseudopod. *Wakey wakey!*

"Ughhhrrrupmphh." Joe made an unflattering sound as his crusty eyes literally cracked open, taking in the ever cheerful coffee elemental dancing back and forth in front of him. "Mate? Mmmwha-time is it?"

Coffee time!

Sipping on the hot liquid did much to restore his mental clarity and general feelings of comfort as Joe peeled himself out of bed like a slice of deli ham being pulled from a pack. Sipping the last dregs of his coffee, the Ritualist looked around the small, cramped space he'd been sleeping in. "Why am I like this? Before I came back to Midgard, I can't even *remember* the last time I slept."

Then he remembered he'd been checking on his status before passing out and had practically ignored the broken Constitution tag. "No! Maybe I'm still being worn down by the limiter I'm wearing, even though my Constitution is lower than it needs to be? Okay... it's well past time we fix this."

He had spare Ritual Orbs, after all. Even though his hands were *itching* with the desire to jump back into work now that he was cognizant once more, it was far more important that he be able to work for *longer*, instead of having to be interrupted by the constant need to sleep.

Holding the orb up to eye level, he grabbed it with his mind and had it spin in place while he inspected its glossy, chrome surface. "How am I supposed to write out your enchantments now? It was hard enough when I just had to figure out how Constitution impacted me, now I have to think of the main effect, what Stoic Constitution means, and all the little extras you keep grabbing."

Yet, even before he got too deep into planning, he needed to create a binding agent. Pulling out his Ritual Alchemy cauldron, Joe grasped both handles and lifted it, holding the two hundred and fifty pound setup in a trap bar deadlift pose. Thin filaments of mana raced out from him, generating a perfect cube of Ascendant Matrix around the sealed central cauldron. "Mmm... probably don't *need* to do that, but it's best to keep the habit."

From there, a simple application of mana caused the outermost ring of the gyroscope to begin slowly spinning, sealing the open cauldron and swirling a thin metal casing around the interior. His fingers began to tingle as he shifted his grip, increasing the flow of mana and starting the syrup-like flow of aspects *out* of his storage and *into* the cauldron.

As with every recipe he would create from now on, Joe inserted a single Common-rank aspect to begin using his new Methodology. As he did so, the next rings of the gyroscope began to spin, causing the central area to begin zipping around, eventually reaching centrifuge-like speeds.

Ignoring the high-pitched whine coming from the rotating sphere, two more aspects were carefully placed in the contained chaos. Four more, then eight. Sweat dripped freely now, coating his skin and soaking his shirt, though chilling rapidly as the air in the chamber seemed to heat from the frenetic activity of the gyroscope. He spared a moment to lament on how he needed every drop of mana and therefore couldn't have his Neutrality Aura active... then there was no more room for intrusive thoughts.

Eight aspects became sixteen, thirty-two, sixty-four—Each round of placement was interrupted only by Joe mentally sealing each aspect in its position relative to the others, all to make sure that, the moment he relinquished control, they would blend together into a single, homogeneous whole.

One hundred twenty-eight, two hundred fifty-six... Joe

stopped counting each rung he climbed, only as he added two thousand forty-eight of the various-rank aspects in a final burst. Immediately, he retracted his mana, allowing the aspects to smear into each other, blend, and condense as the rotation slowed on its own over the next long seconds. He found himself heaving for air, dazed and off-balance from the sheer level of fine control he'd needed to maintain while splitting his attention into tiny threads of power.

The methodology was simple and slow to start, but the complexity and difficulty was the *definition* of exponential.

When the cauldron was finally spinning at a manageable level, Joe pulled on either side of the handles, instantly bringing the cauldron to a sudden stop and locking in place. Grabbing the metal cover, he flipped it over then covered the small opening with a vial and flipped the orb upside down. Though he had likely only needed an Uncommon version, since this was once again the third Characteristic he was binding, he'd made a Rare version—both for the practice as well as to smooth the process, since he had an upgraded Characteristic and wasn't certain how that might impact the binding process.

"That's all the alchemy I need to do for the next little while, so…" Joe stepped away from the enormous contraption, mentally reaching out and activating the infernal purification function. This had quickly become his favorite part of alchemy. Green flames exploded out of the cauldron, only to struggle against some invisible barrier as though desiring to consume the world, and he watched on, the flames reflecting in his eyes as they danced, writhed, and were eventually *slurped* back into the central cauldron—now glowing white-hot.

With the exciting part over, the Ritualist pulled out an inscription tool and activated Essence Cycle.

Closing his eyes, he delved into himself, trying to seek out an exact description of Stoic Constitution, what it meant to him, how it influenced the world around him, and where those lines blurred. Minutes, or maybe hours, slipped past before he finally opened his eyes. A mouthful of blood hit the ground as he spat, the price of draining his mana to nothing and forcing it to regenerate, all while his health quietly bled away beneath the pain.

Blinking at the now fully inscribed surface of the orb, he realized with satisfaction that he could fully recall the entire process from start to finish. "Good… that's getting easier. The last part is putting it all together."

He used Somatic Ritual Casting for the first time since his return to town, and in only a few minutes, his Ritual Orb had come into full alignment with his body. He felt a surge of wellness as his broken Characteristic was restored; the sensation went far deeper than a mere twelve points would account for. It was reassuring to know that taking the time to fix the issue had been worth it.

"Finally, after all that effort, I can get to work. Abyss, it feels like I've been breathing exclusively through a straw for the last two weeks." He threw open the room of his door, and with each step felt two percent better, until he was practically skipping along, leaving a trail of dust swirling in his wake as he rushed into the Grand Ritual Hall.

The moment he stepped into the hidden chamber, his eyes landed on the elaborate ritual diagram he'd been painstakingly carving out. The building had an impressive knack for reading his mind. "Hmm…I should talk to Boris about that. Maybe it's not quite reading my thoughts, but picking up on mental impressions. Come to think of it, maybe it's working off the same principle as my Ritual Orbs? Attuned to ambient thoughts and intent?"

Not wanting to go too far down that rabbit hole while he had important deadlines looming, Joe focused on what he knew for sure the Ritual Hall gave him: namely, the ability to create the exact ritual diagrams he needed and leave them in place semi-permanently, meaning that he could practice, practice, practice.

Pulling out his notes, he carefully arranged the documents he needed, then wiped the current floating diagrams away with a wave of his hand. The enormous circles burst into what looked like nothing more than glittering black dust, which settled to the floor and blended in perfectly.

With a surge of intent, the dust burst from the floor once more, quickly forming into the familiar diagrams, circles, and sigils. He went over every detail, every *inch* of the diagram as he made it, working to build mental pathways, muscle memory, and try *anything* he could to increase his chance of flawlessly completing the ritual when he made the real version. Minutes began passing like the grains of sand falling from an hourglass as Joe worked through the minute details of each concentric circle. As each became visibly distinct, he delighted in his perfect successes and visibly flinched with each realization of a flaw.

"Ritual of the Cataclysmic Tempest... I'm going to have to assume the name isn't just for show." The Ritualist heaved a deep sigh as he delicately wove the Expert-rank circle, carefully placing the base sigils and writing out equations. "The worst case isn't even having it fall apart while I'm making it. No, that dubious honor goes to the fact that if I activate it, and it back-fires, it's going to destroy... pretty much everything out to the horizon."

From what he understood of the Master-rank ritual, he would essentially be creating a short-lived sentient hurricane that was condensed into a specific area, based on parameters he set. Joe was rather leery about this, as the fact that the ritual would be 'somewhat sentient' added on the complexity of needing to make sure he didn't do something to upset it while it was active. If he did, it might ignore his directives out of sheer spite. "Never thought I would have to worry about making Charisma checks on my own creations..."

Though the thought made him internally chuckle, his face fell as he found a series of numbers and pictograms he'd accidentally created in a mirrored format when he copied them over. Letting out a sigh of defeat, he snapped his fingers and allowed the entire diagram to crumble away.

"Feces. Probably did that when I was trying to apply Magical Syntax Lore to the Apprentice-rank circle. Of course that's going to have an adverse reaction if I don't understand what the higher-rank circles need. I'll just end up simplifying an equation that needed to be in the long format in order to be read correctly at the higher... bah."

Luckily, he had more time and was able to treat the process like getting ready for running a marathon. It gave Joe the opportunity to get everything right, get himself in exactly the right headspace, and know for sure what he needed to get done. It was also *fantastic* training for his Lore skill, which had even gained a point without using his Knowledge spell for the first time in a long, long time.

While he was proud of himself for earning that level, it didn't stop him from activating Knowledge and dropping another two points into Magical Syntax Lore—as that skill was what was truly holding him back from being able to *improve* this ritual.

Skill increases:
Ritual Lore (Expert 0 → Expert I)
Magical Syntax Lore (Journeyman V → Journeyman VII)
Knowledge (Expert 0 → Expert I)

"Once I get Syntax and Magical Matrices high enough to be able to reduce the total impact it has on the ambient mana, I'm *totally* going to be using this ritual as an Expert-rank version." Joe allowed himself a moment to daydream, picturing himself using a focused hurricane to knock over a mountain range casually—and it *would* be casual usage if he could pull its rank down.

When it came to supplies, especially cores, well...Jotunheim had no end of Unique-rank creatures. A couple weeks there could set him up for a long time. Shaking off the excitement and ambition flowing through his head, Joe lifted his hand and started over, forming the Novice-rank circle and double checking his work.

The next days passed in a blur of focus, motion, and intense study. Magical Syntax Lore didn't give him anything new or interesting after reaching the Expert rank, so he had split the boost given by Knowledge between it and Ritual Lore, bringing both of them to Expert-rank six and Knowledge to Expert three. Even with his rapid advancements, he actually *didn't* spend every waking moment in the Grand Ritual Hall.

When he ventured out, Joe found that he wasn't the only one burning the candle at both ends in preparation. With the planned upgrade only a few days away, his coven had thrown themselves into their work with a fervor that bordered on self-destruction. Hundreds of combat rituals had been set up and distributed to the town's walls, bought and paid for by the guild to supplement their magical damage output.

At least twice a day, Joe would answer a question one of them had on a new ritual they were designing, and he was frankly quite shocked and impressed by their creativity.

Kirby, for one, had been working to combine the Ritual of Cloudstep with the Ritual of Marching Fishes and had succeeded in summoning a cloud of flying fish—but only once. It had taken a bit of fin-angling, but both of them had laughed when Joe realized that the specifications of the ritual made it try to resummon the *same exact* fish... who had already been caught and eaten by the swarms of hungry adventurers filling the walls. He'd been happy to help her figure out the necessary changes, and as payment, she had gifted him a couple copies of the Ritual of Cloudstep, likely knowing he hadn't had time to put any of them together for himself.

None of them complained even once about the grueling pace, even when their robes were soaked with sweat and pasty from chalk dust. Big_Mo, more often than not, treated Joe like a mystical shower, just coming to stand close by to get the blood off of him. For his part, Joe decided *against* asking how he came back looking as though he'd been bathing in blood each day.

Hopefully, that was an issue that would work itself out over time.

Even Robert finally made a reappearance, walking in one

day covered in cuts and bruises, clothing torn to shreds, but a happy smile on his face. According to him, he had managed to shave multiple seconds off his reaction time and consistently hunted monsters using only rituals. Even more impressive was the fact that he'd caught up to the others and completed his Novice-rank combat ritual quest line *without* the benefit of hundreds of stationary targets.

Lastly, Joe had been working on his other disciplines as well and had been going around the city installing mana stabilizers as permanently as he could. Since he had no earth manipulation skills, that usually meant punching a hole in the ground and wedging each stabilizer in place, then posting a sign that they were meant to be left alone...

...only for the sign to go away almost immediately, as it drew attention to the fact that the stabilizers *could* be moved— and therefore stolen.

An entire set of Student rank and below went missing before he had even left the area, so the next set was carefully placed in a very public area. As the ambient mana on Midgard was already extremely stable, almost no one understood what he was doing. Still, each stabilizer was rather eye-catching, especially once they'd been set up and were in effect. To his great relief, most people treated them like either sculptures or modern art installations.

Curious people poked and prodded at them, people took pictures beside them and posted questions on the primitive forums that had been springing up on their 'phones', but since they were all clearly part of a set, no one tried *too* hard to walk away with them. Frankly, Joe didn't really care what people did, so long as the stabilizers weren't damaged or moved.

After setting up a large ring of varying stabilizers that he could move to as needed, Joe created a more intensive version closer to the city: this time stabilizing up to the Journeyman rank. Finally, he set up *one* precious Expert-rank area directly adjacent to the Pathfinder's Hall. The second set at the Expert rank, and the last he'd been able to make with the limited amount of time he had, was already in place in the Grand Ritual Hall.

Finally, with every possible thing done that he could justify doing, Joe had to admit to himself that it was finally time.

"No more procrastinating. It's time to put together the ritual, or I'm going to have to request that the guild move the date for upgrades." A glance at the sea of people within the walls was enough to tell him *that* wasn't going to happen—the town was on the verge of *eating* itself at that point. Temperatures were high, and people were ready to fly into a duel over the smallest of slights.

He returned to the Grand Ritual Hall, where his coven was already gathered with eager expressions on their faces. Doing his best to prepare them, Joe made a dark promise. "This is going to *hurt*. It's going to take everything you have, and there's a good chance just putting the ritual together drains you dry. That's with *all* of you only being there to support me as much as you can."

Joe's slow, ominous words rang through the room, dimming the excitement slightly, but not extinguishing it. "But, I can promise you, on the other end of this... you'll be walking away with more knowledge, experience, and skill levels in rituals than anyone other than myself, until you get to Vanaheim. With that in mind..."

"...Shall we get to it?"

CHAPTER THIRTY-EIGHT

Joe stood in the exact center of the Grand Ritual Hall, preparing to put everything he had on the line. He glanced around at the five other members of this world's coven, feeling a pleasant tickling sensation in his mind as he realized they were filling each of the positions in the Beginner-rank circle.

Somehow, it felt fitting, as each one of them was essentially learning the foundational skills under him, a literal Master of Ritual Circles. He could only hope that, by the end of this, he could consider each of them a true apprentice.

The three Novice spots were filled by Mana Batteries, topped off and hopefully enough to refill his reserves as he worked with the incredibly mentally burdensome load of high-level aspects. The next layer was filled with seven people his coven members knew and trusted. With something this delicate, he didn't *want* to trust unknown entities, but he didn't have enough batteries to fill the open spaces. It was a frustrating fact that, when they decided to actually *activate* the ritual—not just set up the diagram—they would need a full contingent of people, or it could not become fully empowered and would certainly fail.

Everyone had eaten, rested as well as possible, and prepared themselves for the day. Even so, Joe could pick out a trickle of sweat beading down their foreheads, despite the cool, regulated air of the underground chamber. He understood better than most that they weren't reacting to heat, and there was no humidity to speak of. No... this was *anticipation*, the pressure to perform, the knowledge that, if they failed at any stage, they could only hope that the Grand Ritual Hall would survive *and* contain the damage they would otherwise wreak upon the town.

Big_Mo, Hannah, Robert, Kirby, and Taka each stood around him, and Joe truly felt bad about the harsh lesson they were going to learn today. Currently, they were filled with uninformed optimism: they were certain they could handle this, though it was sure to be difficult. He could only hope that, with his help, they would move through informed pessimism and directly into *informed* optimism once more, when they learned the true rigors of high-level ritual creation.

It was all too easy to hit the wall of difficulty they were speeding toward and think that simply shifting to something else would make life easier. The fact of the matter was, every class, every profession, had its own difficulties and trials. Shifting to another would only change what the pain points were; it wouldn't actually make life easier for them.

"As always, the first layer is going to be easy." Joe's voice echoed off the walls of the mostly empty room, and each of his people stood taller. "Remember, rituals are *designed* to allow people to share the burden. Focus on regulating the flow of mana from you to me, and don't worry about handling it—I can take care of that. Just keep it steady and do your best to stay conscious as long as possible."

Big_Mo scoffed at that. "As long as *possible*? You underestimate me, Joe! I'm going to be-"

"Ten silver says Big is the first to pass out!" Robert called immediately, his words quickly causing the others to devolve into a series of bets and rules for the bets, while Big_Mo sputtered indignantly.

Not wanting to be pulled into their tomfoolery, Joe allowed his fingers to begin dancing in the air, forming the first Novice ritual circle from the black dust of the Ritual Hall. Even though he *knew* it was perfectly designed, he quickly checked over it to act as a good mentor for his cohort. "This is familiar territory for all of us, a simple circle with a simple function. In terms of this ritual, all the Novice circle is doing is interfacing with the air around it, drawing it toward the center for use by the other layers."

"Question!" Kirby's hand shot into the air. "Is this essentially the same ritual we've all been working on, just at a higher level? Elemental Burst?"

"No." Joe pulled out his own ritual combat manual, flipping it to one of the back pages and tapping on the one he had selected. "Don't look too closely, as I understand that *you'll* let your eyes bleed before giving up on reading these, but this is called the Ritual of the Cataclysmic Tempest. It essentially creates a sentient hurricane that hunts and batters all targets within its scope."

"Then why is the Novice circle the exact same as Elemental Burst?" Taka's innocent question caused Joe to freeze and reassess the circle that he'd been designing over and over for days.

"It's…" The Ritualist's mind went blank as he realized they were correct. "Abyss, here I've been treating it as something entirely new. Only at the second circle is it different, as it functions to selectively inhibit the other elements. How did I not notice that?"

Hannah decided to throw him a lifeline. "I'd bet it's just an experience thing. When's the last time you really paid attention to a Novice circle? Also, we don't have time for you to go down the rabbit hole of seeing how this changes things, so just get going."

Joe froze again, actively in the process of pulling out his notes to see if any of his equations from the Ritual of Elemental Burst could be implemented in this Master-rank ritual, and quickly stuffed them back in his codpiece. Only a few seconds later, the secondary circle had appeared, empty spaces in the diagram surrounding each of the coven members. "Right! The Beginner circle is only slightly more intricate, adding in targeting, delay, and elemental exclusion."

He spoke the entire time he worked, feeling his teaching skill at work and slowly pulling at his mana reserves. That was fine, as the amount of mana he had during initial setup didn't really matter. He could take as many breaks as needed, all the way until he added the first aspect overlaying the design he was setting out currently—then it would be one of the *only* things that mattered. "Apprentice layer, this is more than just reinforcement and damage output. It's adding in target filters, protections for the caster, and an instant exponential increase in variables."

Pressing into the Student circle, which actually took a few minutes for him to put together, Joe began explaining the connections between each of the circles to this point, and how this one took those, altered, rearranged, and interpreted them.

If he had to describe the circle's function in one word, it would sound annoyingly corporate: 'synergy'. No longer was it just a one-to-one instruction. Now it was taking each of the previous circles and adding on a deep layer of complexity of meaning. "The last thing you should check when you're creating this portion of the diagram is here... there's a sub-portion which shows a recursion variant. If you can read the diagram you've made, and you get a different function at the output than the recursion, it means you have a parasitic pattern you need to unweave."

"If it's different, you need to start over?" Taka was following along perfectly, much to the apparent surprise of the others, though Joe understood it was because of the man's deep appreciation for the Magical Matrices part of rituals.

"No... it's kind of like a teacher's version of math problems." The bald man tilted his head to acknowledge the question. "The diagram is showing your work, and so long as you get the same *answer* as the recursion, everything should work out just fine."

"How have I never noticed that before?" Hannah murmured just loudly enough to be heard, prompting Joe to answer her, even if the question hadn't truly been directed at him.

"It's a lore thing, Hannah." Even as he explained, he never stopped working, knowing that, if he took time to pause each time they didn't know what was going on, he would be working on this for the next few years. Nodding at the volunteers on the outer edge to acknowledge their presence for the first time since starting, Joe pressed on with, "Rituals are fantastic because, technically, anyone can make them, even without the class. But if you want to understand the true depths of them, you need to do research. *So* much research."

Or have a spell given to you by a deity which allowed you to skip those steps, but he wasn't about to fess up to that. He continued designing the circles using the Grand Ritual Hall's functions, though he noticed more blank stares than understanding as he hit the Journeyman circle, and he stopped explaining entirely when he was working on the Expert version. He had turned to see Hannah staring at him with a rictus smile that was practically glowing, even as blood flowed from her ears, nose, and eyes. The less pain tolerant among the others had long since covered their ears.

"Isht's *beautiful*." Kirby's words were accompanied by a small slurry of sanguine spittle as she spoke. "These aren't just patterns, circles, whatever term you want to use. Look at that... at this point, it's a *concept*, and I can already tell that it's on its way toward being a neural network or something similar. No wonder magical items gain intelligence as they hit the higher tiers. In order to function, it has to understand *itself* at the very least."

"You and I are going to sit down after this is all over and have a long talk about your potential as a loremaster," Joe informed the swaying woman. "Before that, why don't you sit down? That'll work just as well as standing there all day."

Five hours later, five long hours of almost total silence, and the final circle had been completed. Joe had everyone leave their spaces and walk around the diagram with him, looking for anything that seemed out of place. Of course, he had them working on circles they could understand, while he started at the outermost ring and made his way in. Two hours of meticulous inspection later, and they were as confident as possible, ready to begin channeling aspects and mana to transform the framework he'd been designing into a fully realized ritual.

"Mate, they're looking a little peaked over there. How about a pick-me-up before we get started?"

After taking a nice, long break, each of them came back refreshed and ready to push onward. None of the members of the coven were so low in Characteristics that they needed to sleep every night, at least not when they weren't trekking through the wilderness and actively fighting for their lives. After the happy little elemental had waved its goodbyes and vanished, Joe took his position and waited for the others to do the same— much to the confusion of the volunteers.

"Aren't you *done* now?" the friend Taka had brought along was among the first to voice an objection. "That thing looks crazy, and we've been here for-"

"I *told* you this was an all-day thing!" Taka shot an embarrassed glance at Joe before explaining to his friend more elaborately, "That's all been the design work, now he has to overlay this design with his resources and such. Think of that like the scaffolding going up around a construction site. Now that it's in place, he can actually start work on the building itself."

"*Then* it's done?" came the impatient question.

"Still no, it'll just be ready to be activated." Taka let out a hesitant chuckle and shot his friend a smile filled with meaning. "Seriously, just wait a few moments, and you'll understand why it's all done in stages at this level."

"I've given all the information I can... now comes the

dangerous part." Seeing that there were plenty more questions, but they were being held for the moment, Joe sat down in a meditative position. Taking a deep breath, he reached toward his chest, grasping the limiter he'd been wearing since he came to Midgard. "I'll do my best to keep myself as still as possible, but I need my full mana pool if I want to make this work. Do your best to stay conscious and learn as much as possible. If the worst comes to pass... I'll see you at respawn."

"Excuse me? I thought you said this was *safe*-"

Pressing the release button, Joe had to restrain himself from letting out a groan of relief as the hypodermic needles extracted themselves from his skin. His joints were allowed to move freely once more, and the haze the limiter induced in his mind slowly faded over the next few seconds. Immediately, notifications began to pile up, and he allowed himself a moment to read over them as he once more got to be comfortable in his own skin.

Strength: 278 → 289
Dexterity: 277 → 288
Stoic Constitution: 277 → 291
Light Intelligence: 283 → 293
Ritualistic Wisdom: 270 → 280
Dark Charisma: 229 → 239
Karmic Perception: 280 → 292
Luck: 223 → 241
Karmic Luck: 92

Each of the increases had an explanation that came along with it, with most of his Characteristics gaining ten points directly, though Stoic Constitution gained more due to being set as the focus for his Artisan Body.

Luck obviously had the highest increase, but Joe could only assume that was because it had started far lower than the others, and the limiter was designed to help bring each of them into balance. Still, the numbers didn't make sense for a moment, until the haze fully dissipated from his thoughts, and he remembered how his mental Characteristics fed a portion of their numbers into the physical ones.

The Ritualist *almost* shook his head in disbelief, catching himself at the last moment but still sending a swirling breeze through the open space.

He deactivated each of his defenses and auras, allowing his mana to fully regenerate to its over-twelve-thousand maximum. In no time flat, he felt swollen, bloated by the sheer pressure of his unbound mana pushing outward on his skin. Every sense was back to full functionality. More than that, they were hyper-sharp. For a long moment, he felt like a nexus of power contained in an insufficient vessel—and he locked that mindset in, wanting nothing more than to capture it in his ritual.

So he began.

It took absolutely no effort for him to fill the Novice design he had created with aspects, guiding them along with a thread of mana and only a hint of intention. The Beginner circle was the same, though he heard a slight grunt of surprise from the members of his coven as their mana pools were suddenly pulled on.

As he began the Apprentice circle, silver aspects flowing from the aspect jars carefully arranged around himself, he noticed that each of his people were focused on regulating and modulating their own breathing, though they retained enough willpower to carefully watch what he was doing. Conversely, the volunteers twitched and groaned as they fed in their own mana, woefully unprepared for the amount of power they needed to channel.

Light blue aspects followed as he slipped into the Student-rank ritual. They fell into place with a gentle, yet firm tug on his mental reserves. At that point, he slowed down slightly, though of course never allowed himself to stop—as that would all but guarantee the ritual destabilizing and failing. The Journeyman circles didn't *require* Special aspects, and he certainly wasn't about to monkey with the design by testing a new formula without careful consideration. Instead, he substituted with indigo Unique aspects, deciding it was worth the extra invest-ment, since he had plenty to go around.

However, the heavy mental burden, while easy for Joe to handle, had unexpectedly increased significantly on the others. The shock of the sudden ramping up of intensity cleanly knocked out every volunteer *and* Kirby. Big_Mo could barely even get out a strained cheer at the fact that he'd won one of the first of several bets with the others.

Aspects and mana boiled through the prepared channels like warm syrup, slowly filling every nook and crevice of the design. This ring took roughly an hour to complete, and by the end, Hannah was breathlessly panting and visibly swaying. Taka was muttering a sequence of numbers under his breath to stay awake, while Robert and Big_Mo were staring each other down, each waiting for the other to fall so they could win their secondary bets.

Joe couldn't pay any attention to them any longer: shifting to the Expert circle proved to be an even more brutal transition than the last. It *required* Unique aspects, and the insertion point immediately branched three-dimensionally and quintupled the mental burden by doing so. Even he started feeling the strain, so by the time he'd placed the first sigil in its entirety, merely thirty minutes later, Taka and Hannah had both slowly crumpled to the ground.

The final two coven conscious members blinked at the same time, unable to lift their eyelids to see who had won their bet—yet Hannah rallied, forcing herself up for another moment and sent a final burst of mana as she laughed and passed out.

Leaving the weight of the ritual entirely on Joe.

Frankly… he was still having a pleasant time. Although the strain was high, it was always a truly *magical* experience to thread the movement-resistant aspects into place. Right on schedule, at the end of the fourth hour, the fifth circle settled into position, stable and ready to be connected to the last of them.

Joe's eyes flicked down, landing on the brilliant orange

aspect jar he finally got to tap into. It had reached nearly two-thirds of its capacity over the last week, and he'd been absolutely *itching* to create something with it.

Natural Artifact Aspect Jar (Artifact). Maximum capacity: 7,811/12,500

His mana swarmed into the jar, extracting the first Artifact-ranked aspect. Immediately, the air *crackled* with neon orange light.

The aspect actively pushed against him, no longer just a weight he needed to lift or a burden he needed to bear. It had its own presence—*it* wanted to be in control.

Gritting his teeth hard enough to make them creak, he wrapped the aspect in a sheath of mana, shoving it into position while simultaneously pulling on it to extract a long line of orange light. Visually, it was similar to a smith pulling wire out of a blob of molten metal. The ultra-thin line was perhaps a quarter the thickness of a hair but was nearly as inflexible as steel to his mental senses. Every line he drew out tested his resolve with immense pressure, probing against his Mana Manipulation and finding it *wanting*.

He heard echoes of the aspect with his Magical Synesthesia, scoffing at him for being so foolish to think that he could successfully work on *it*, an *Artifact*-ranked material, using only the Journeyman-tier tools he could bring to bear.

Even so, Joe held his ground, having done this before—even if it *had* been with the help of people far more powerful than himself. As he led the aspect through the diagram, he could feel it pushing against the geometry of its cage, probing for weak spots it could burst through and make its escape. Strangely enough, as the magic whispered threats at him, he *learned* from it: the aspects chuckled at his efforts, pointing at his failure to use a blank sigil location for a token or an alchemical input.

It *lunged* toward a minuscule opening, gibbering gleefully at the fact that there was no forged needle injecting tranquility through the hole. But, more than anything, it howled with laughter at how much of itself Joe needed to use—mocking his failure to reduce his consumption by improving the formulae as its weight ramped upward astronomically.

There were odd side whispers as well, conversationally hinting at *other* things he could have added into the mix that he'd never even considered. Still, as he focused on those, they clammed up, refusing to enlighten him with knowledge he did not yet possess.

As much as Joe wanted to simply sit and meditate on what the aspects were telling him, he could only continuously plod forward, a draft horse dragging an oversized burden to its final destination. His mana dropped continuously, topping out at nearly a hundred and fifty points per second, outpacing his regeneration by a *long* shot. His hands began to tremble, the non-limited tremors shaking the stone floor of the building.

His vision narrowed, and Joe began hyperventilating ever so slightly, causing the limp bodies of his coven members to flop back and forth with the wind generated by each inhale and exhale.

At the two-thirds mark of completing the Master-rank circle, Joe coughed violently, blood splattering across the ground as his mana pool ran dry. He reached for his Mana Batteries, only to realize they had *long* since run out of power. His health rapidly began ticking down, substituting his vital essence for a few more drops of energy to feed the ritual. The ritual hovered on the edge of collapse, and the aspects went still, like a cat preparing to end the game by springing at a mouse.

Joe scrambled internally even as his heart clenched up, blood pouring from his lips as his Stamina was consumed whole cloth. Just before he gave in to despair, his eyes went wide as he remembered a benefit he had never had to use, as there had before never been a time where he needed more power than he was able to generate.

"*Monarch of Mana!*" the Ritualist gasped out, causing the active portion of his title to come into effect. The moment the words left his lips, the world obeyed. Ambient mana folded inward like a collapsing star, funneled into him in a rush that threatened to tear him apart. His mana pool surged from bone-dry to *brimming* with power just waiting to be fed into the ritual. "Ohh... that's the good stuff."

The Artifact-ranked aspects had been lulled into a false sense of security, assured in their impending, explosive escape. Joe pulled deeply on the aspect jar, flooding the ritual with aspects that almost seemed too surprised to put up as much resistance as they usually did. They caught on quickly, and for the next few hours, Joe struggled immensely, the battle coming to a head as twenty-three threads of mana appeared in the final sigil simultaneously, weaving together and being pulled into a larger strand.

Though this was the final stretch, when the aspects formed into a thick bar of power, they had more capability to resist. Joe *snarled* in annoyance as he found himself trapped in an exhausting mental tug-of-war with the orange energy.

His mana approached empty once more, and this time, there would be no sudden refill he could take advantage of. In a final, desperate attempt, Joe focused all of his willpower on *yanking* the aspects into position...

...and they clicked into place.

The final few whispers they let out sounded just as surprised as the Ritualist himself. In a fury at being *molded*, the aspects trapped in the ritual circle shimmered, managing one last attempt at breaking free.

His Ritual Magic, Ritual Circles, and Ritual Lore skills all came into effect, and the odds of successful completion shot upward—only to be weighed against the stability of the area, the density of power he had packed in, and a myriad of checks and balances he was *certain* were happening behind the scenes.

Then, finally, the ritual settled, the orange glow fading away as the aspects reconstituted themselves in such a way as to perfectly generate the Master-rank ritual.

Joe exhaled slowly, slowly blinking his eyes open and watching the thin veil of steam rising from his entire body. Reaching a trembling hand up, he felt his forehead, already cooling, but definitely having gone far beyond the temperature a healthy human should have. Giving himself a few moments to recover, he reactivated Neutrality Aura, and his sopping wet robes quickly began to dry. The humidity was recaptured from the open space around him, purified, and injected into his body, swiftly rehydrating his effort-desiccated body.

Finally, when he felt that he'd returned to normal, Joe ever so slowly reached up to his chest and reactivated his limiter. His joints constricted, pinpricks of pain appeared all over his body, and a slight haze of confusion settled over his mind.

At the same time, Joe let out a deep sigh of relief. "We did it. No more excuses, no more delays. It's time to upgrade the town, the guild, and... I told you I'd be back in time for the wedding, Mom. I'm gonna make it."

CHAPTER THIRTY-NINE

"-And so today, we don't just build our future, we secure it! We create a true *legacy*!" As the bureaucrat in a tailored suit finished his speech, he threw his hands into the air and beamed around at the jostling crowd. Completely unexpectedly—at least to Joe —they responded in kind, raising a cheer that shook souvenirs off of shelves and rattled windows. "Now, if our First Elder-in-waiting would do us the honor of initiating the upgrade... we can finish this up, get paid, and everyone can go home!"

That earned him a round of laughter that left Joe absolutely shocked to his core. In a normal voice, which he knew wouldn't be heard by anyone in the crowd, the Ritualist spoke to the man he saw as nothing more than a glorified hedge fund manager, "Do you secretly have a maxed out Charisma score or something?"

"*Absolutely* I do," came the deadpan response as the bureaucrat waved at the building, the smile never leaving his face as he nodded along excitedly as though Joe had just promised him the world. "I've never left Midgard, so I'm actually able to have it all the way up to two hundred points, so long as I keep the others at the Mortal Limit."

"Impressive, and I admit I'm even a bit jealous." Joe turned to look at the crowd one last time. The people were surging with excitement and energy as banners flapped overhead, musicians played cheerful tunes, and various food stalls did a brisk business. He could only be impressed by the fact that no one else seemed to notice how every last one of the temporary shops had a subtle mark on them which showed them to be owned and operated by the guild itself. "I've got to give it to you... there's a level of attention to detail here that I admire."

Joe swirled dramatically to face the Pathfinder's Hall, a resplendent white cloak fluttering out as he did so, briefly revealing the Ritual Tower robes he wore underneath to the onlookers. Even though he knew that the platform he was standing on had been put together that day, it blended in so seamlessly that, if he didn't know better, he would have sworn it belonged there.

As he lifted his hand, the crowd started quieting; this was no small feat when they stretched across every open space of the town, filled every window, and violated at least three fire safety regulations by using every last *inch* of rooftop space to see what was happening.

He didn't technically *need* to touch the building, as he could directly interface with it mentally, but Joe wasn't above a bit of showmanship of his own. Palming his inscription tool, he generated a Novice-rank Ritual of Glimmering, flipping a variable and activating it just as he touched the wall to cause a brilliant orange light to blaze out of an intricate design.

While the people 'oohed' and 'aahhed', he was quickly making his way through system notifications.

You are initiating an upgrade for the Pathfinder's Hall (Grand Ritual Hall). As the initial construction of this building required five times the actual resource cost in order to build, the upgrade will merely require four times the initial investment of Artifact-rank material and lower to upgrade the structure into a Legendary version. Please provide 80 tons of builder's grade steel, 20 tons of... of... recalculating.

Please provide aspects in the following quantity:

Damaged: 204,007
Common: 126,784
Uncommon: 54,599
Rare: 23,036
Unique: 8,225
Artifact: 5,725

The numbers were absolutely eye-wateringly painful. Joe gasped at the sheer number of Unique rank necessary but felt as though he were going to swoon over the Artifact needed. "Are you *kidding* me? The ritual took less than five hundred Artifact aspects, and this is going to take ten *times* that many? Abyss, I don't even have enough Unique-"

Joe's face went blank as he recalled that he could damage an aspect, causing it to burst into a huge number of its lower-ranked variants. Taking a deep breath, he pulled out and intentionally destroyed a single Artifact aspect, creating a firework effect that drew great appreciation from the people around him. Their excitement was cold comfort.

If he hadn't had a way to regain the wasted aspects fairly easily, Joe would have called the entire process off, no matter *how* many people had been hired for the day.

Even so, he had accomplished his goal. Destroying that one aspect had given him every bit of the Damaged, Common, and Uncommon requirements, but had only fulfilled an eighth of the Unique rank. Happily, between what he had stored and what the Artifact-rank aspects were worth, he only needed an additional three thousand in total. Still, with each bursting aspect, he felt himself squirm in frustration.

"So much power *wasted*."

Initial cost accepted. Please provide two Artifact-rank cores.

Staring at the request blankly, Joe slowly shook his head and prepared to offer his condolences to the leadership. Even if he wanted to, this wasn't something he could fulfill at the moment. "Why only two? Oh! Right, my fifty percent ritual requirement when building this place. Building it only used half the power of an Artifact rank core..."

Cores not provided. The upgrade will proceed, but the structure will run out of power to function if the necessary cores are not provided within 7 days of successful upgrade, and collapse. You may choose to cancel the upgrade, but doing so will forfeit the investment of aspects. Proceed?

"Yes." Joe grumbled at the screen, wondering where he was going to get ahold of two such cores in the next week. Yet, before he could start thinking of how to leverage his guild contacts, notifications began to roll in one after another.

Construction halted. The required settlement level is too low to proceed. The permission of the sovereigns of Ardania is required in order to upgrade the current settlement level from 'Town', to the necessary 'City' tier. Or, you can force the upgrade and initiate a war for control of the territory.

Joe immediately produced the royal mandate, holding it in the air where the electrum-embossed golden certificate caught the sunlight. The sight of the mandate caused the crowd to go wild once again.

Mandate confirmed. Proxy permission granted via written documentation of King Henry and Queen Marie. Initiating Town Hall upgrade. Initiating Pathfinder's Hall upgrade...

Process halted.

"Oh, for-" Joe clicked his fingers, creating and activating six Ritual Circles of Glimmering around the first, making it appear as though everything was fine and proceeding normally. He shifted his feet back and forth quickly, generating a slight breeze that caused his cloak to flutter out behind him, all while dealing with the system messages as quickly as possible.

The current controlling faction in the town 'The Wanderer's Guild' is too low in rank to be in control of a City. In order to proceed, the Noble Guild must either be in the direct control of a Ranking Noble of Ardania (Duke or greater), or sit as a sovereign-equivalent power by becoming a Sect.

The current owner *of the guild, Aten, is not a Ranking Nobleman. Would you like to use your mandate from the crown to combine both upgrade attempts and take a branching path forward for your guild and settlement? Doing so will initiate the upgrade of your guild into a Sect, and the Town will upgrade into a 'Sect Territory' instead of a City.*

This will have far-reaching ramifications, including new responsibili-

ties, requirements for entry, and pro bono work from your Sect to the kingdom to maintain a positive reputation. Failure to maintain a positive reputation will be seen as a direct challenge to their authority and pit your forces against theirs for control of the territory.

Proceed?

"I'm going to be off-world, so it's not my problem." Joe firmly pressed the 'yes' button in his mind, then waited as the system went quiet for a long few moments.

Then the town trembled.

A beacon of light descended from the sky, bathing the Town Hall in scintillating light, as though the bifrost had found a new home. Even from a distance, Joe could hear the creaking of floorboards as they were strained beyond their capabilities, tiles exploded into shards and reformed into a thick masonry, and the structure as a whole began to elongate and stretch upward —clearly on its way toward becoming a small skyscraper.

But Joe was far more concerned with the Pathfinder's Hall he was touching, where immense cracks had formed along its entire egg-shaped dome.

Brilliant light poured from the cracks, fighting with the sun to illuminate the area. What *looked* like damage spread quickly, and soon the entire structure was shimmering as the light intensified and faded, dimming and pulsing in time like a heartbeat. Just as he thought it would burst and reveal what lay below, the upgrade stopped, and yet another notification appeared.

Going by the murmurs of interest rising behind him, Joe wasn't the only one who'd gotten this particular notice.

Area notice! The current Town, Towny McTownface, is about to undergo an upgrade trial.

Area notice! The Guild controlling this Town is attempting to upgrade. If you do not want to be caught in the crossfire, it is recommended that every non-affiliated person leave the area immediately.

Double upgrade attempt registered. The parameters for the upgrade evaluation will now be determined. Calculating…

Guild size: Large+.

Guild rank: Noble Guild.

Average level: 21.
Average level of Guild members on-world: 14.
Zone: Midgard.
Local Zone difficulty: Low.
Scaling base modifiers based on variables-

At that moment, things went very, *very* wrong.

A snarling, cough-like whisper Joe had been hearing suddenly became far louder. At first, he had chalked it up to someone in the crowd having a bad day, but as his ears twitched, he realized he wasn't hearing a sound—he was hearing the whispers of magic.

Going by the tone and sheer madness in the voice, whatever was coming wasn't pleasant. He flung himself around, eyes searching the crowd and zeroing in on a nondescript man standing almost directly under the platform and looking up at him with a bland expression.

He was dressed in plain clothes. There wasn't an insignia to show his affiliation, no aura of power or bloodlust to give him away. There wasn't even anger in his eyes when he lifted a stone jar with both hands and twisted the top and base in opposite directions.

A foul, wet *hiss* split the air—corrosive, gleeful, and reeking of malice.

Tiny dots of darkness squealed as they fled the container, like steam escaping a pressure cooker. They left streaks of filth in the air as they homed in on… the golden mandate?

Joe threw himself out of the way, but the energy moved faster, not at all put off by his attempts at fleeing. They homed in on the golden plate, rapidly soiling its surface and creeping toward his hands. The Ritualist tossed the document back at the platform to keep the foulness off of himself, and it spun through the air only to slam point-first into the wooden platform.

It stuck there, vibrating like a shuriken that had sunk into its target.

Modifier added: Crab bucket curse.
You might try to escape, but you'll always be pulled down to our level.

Trial difficulty increased to maximum allowable tier.

Trial mode changed: Monster Waves → Singular entity (Premeditated).

Objective: Defeat the (System-Weakened) Legendary monster which will be released at the outskirts of the territory controlled by this Town before it destroys your Town Hall. No additional enemy types will be generated.

Reward: Sect ascension, literal and figurative. Sect Territory designation. Legendary upgrade for the Pathfinder's Hall.

Failure: blacklisting of the Wanderer's Guild on Midgard. Total destruction and seizing of all guild assets should the kingdom survive the rampaging monster.

The curse will stay in effect until the singular entity is slain.

Joe barely noticed as the man who released the curse was cut down by the guards—not even bothering to defend himself as his lifeblood was sprayed across the cobblestones.

The damage had already been done. The curse released. The golden mandate was surrounded by a thick, *buzzing* miasma of dark energy, practically goading people into trying to pick it up.

In the next moment, the Ritualist expected people to start realizing that a Legendary monster was on its way and run for their lives. He wouldn't blame them—none of them had signed up to fight something like that. But… once again the system intervened.

You have been marked!

Attempting to leave the bounds of the trial will result in the automatic application of the [Crab Bucket Curse] at a personal level to each person attempting escape. Curse effects: skill gain rate -400%. Duration: Indefinite.

All teleportation-style skills or effects are ineffective for all parties when attempting to leave the designated trial area. The spawn point for everyone in the area of effect has been set to: Pathfinder's Hall, temple. Respawn speed: instant.

Even in death, there is no escape.

Trial initiates in: 29:59…

"They've killed us all!" came the furious call from somewhere deep in the crowd. "This was all a setup! It's the Red Mist all over again!"

Weapons were drawn all over town, as each person looked at each other with deep distrust. Joe glanced at the bureaucrats on the podium, waiting to hear their take on the situation, only to notice that they were huddled together, whimpering in fear. "*Celestials'* sake, they were going to teleport out of here and wait for the results, weren't they?"

Jumping back up onto the platform, he tried not to shy away from the dark miasma of the curse as it stretched ever so slightly toward him, as if trying to lure him into moving closer by pretending it wouldn't strike.

Filling his lungs with a deep inhale, Joe put all of his effort into shouting over the immense hubbub—even considering taking off his limiter, if he needed to do so.

"We *prepare!*" His words rolled across the space, and the panicking crowd instantly turned toward him, hope warring with fear on their faces. "We know what's coming! It's a Legendary monster. Sure there's a few extra issues we weren't expecting, but it's going to be weakened by the system! You know what *that* means?"

He looked around, waiting a few long moments to build up their curiosity. "It means that it won't be all that much stronger than an Artifact-rank creature! I led a team to support another guild that slew one of those mere weeks ago! Think about it. Even if it's weakened, it's still a *Legendary* monster! Legendary! What sort of titles might you earn? Rewards? Think of what it'll be worth in terms of crafting resources… and all of that *before* you're paid for doing your job!"

With only a few words, the tide of emotions started to turn in his favor, and Joe felt his Dark Charisma humming along at full strength as he incited them further. "In less than thirty minutes, we're going to be fighting for our lives. *Sure* there's a curse on the area now, but whoever just did that made a serious mistake. When some of us are cut down—and believe me when

I say not everyone is going to survive this—we'll come back instantly! Throw ourselves against the monster again! An endless tide of fighters cutting it down means we *will* eventually win!"

"It means none of us are going to miss out! We'll be here and ready to get what we deserve!" The Ritualist could practically see the moment fear turned to excitement and greed, so he decided not to push it any further. "Get out there, get ready, fight like your life depends on it… and grab all the loot you can hold!"

CHAPTER FORTY

Standing on top of the outer wall of Towny McTownface, Joe tried to keep his face stern and serene. There was no point in letting every random person know how he was internally quailing at that moment. "This is the problem with leaving enemies alive. They pop up at the most *inopportune* moments."

The town was alive with excitement behind him, as hundreds of guild members, mercenaries, and perhaps a few saboteurs prepared for the upcoming fight. Joe checked the timer once again, noting how it was seeming to speed up as the last minutes ticked away, though he was certain that was just his frenetic focus causing it to seem as such. "Legendary monster... it took Jake the Alchemist intervening to bring down the last one. How's something like *that* allowed on Midgard, weakened or not?"

He considered what might be coming after them but kept drawing a blank at where they would find a monster of that caliber there. Even the Planthopper Matriarch had only been an Artifact monster—comparable to a Master-rank human. The fact that this low-level world even had stronger monsters was almost a surprise, even knowing that it must have at least one World Boss tucked away in some hidden corner. "Only a minute and a half to go-"

Caution! High levels of ambient mana instability detected. Further use of Master-rank or above abilities will increase instability.

Joe perked up, immediately scanning the horizon for a sign of a monster's early arrival, but upon finding nothing, he spun around and regarded the town. Unlike with the curse, there didn't seem to be a malicious source—instead, his eyes were drawn to the Pathfinder's Hall in the central portion of the town, which had paused in its upgrade and was visually distorted by the haze of energy rampaging around it. As soon as he recognized the actual issue, Joe received another notification.

Complete the Pathfinder's Hall upgrade to stabilize the local ambient mana fields by one rank!

"Abyss, of course it chooses this moment to make things harder than they need to be." The Ritualist let out a sigh of frustration. "Sure would love to have some of the stronger guild members here. Heh, Aten could probably slice whatever's coming directly in half if he were able to use his 'Might of the Guild' ability. Sure, using it would turn half the continent into a crater, but sometimes holding the button to a doomsday weapon is what you need to feel safe at night."

The guild leader had to have been at least approaching Joe in overall stats and was fully specialized into a combat role. If he were able to boost himself even further by drawing on the collective characteristics of the guild, he could probably fight Grandmaster *Havoc* casually—let alone some random monster.

Joe clicked his tongue as he remembered what the town's leadership had shown him when he informed them that the buildings were ready for an upgrade: a memo. Aten had sent his best wishes and an explanation for why most of the power-houses of the guild would be unable to attend.

Simply put, most of them didn't have any access to limiters. Even if they *did*, they had gotten used to combat on the higher worlds and wouldn't be anywhere near as effective back there.

The next most common reason was the sheer number of

people still lost on Jotunheim. Even if they'd been traveling for the last six months, they might not even be on the same *continent* as the bifrost. The people from their guild who had only recently ascended were caught up in trying to navigate the Elven theocracy, and getting permission to leave that world now required certain guarantees Aten wasn't willing to authorize them to make.

In other words, Joe had to make the best of the situation and hope all of their preparation would be enough.

As the final seconds ticked away, the wind picked up, warm and sour with the flavor of blood. The Ritualist waited as the countdown struck zero, bracing himself for the collapsing of the ambient mana in a certain direction, which would tell him where the system had spawned their monster. Perhaps it would burst out of the ground, appear out of nothing, or announce its presence with thunder and lightning as the skies howled about the first Legendary monster walking upon the world's surface.

Instead, reality folded in on itself in an ominous twist, then exploded outward as a vast spell circle.

Joe knew enough about rituals to know that this was something different: an enchantment, item, or perhaps just a massively powerful wizard casting a gate spell. The arcane geometry burned itself into the air itself, perfectly perpendicular to the ground and hundreds of meters in diameter. Thousands of sigils spinning around the circle popped one after another, a domino effect that increased in speed until the final one blackened and turned into dust. Then all of it was *sucked* to the center of the circle.

Space began to stretch, looking for all the world as though Joe were staring at the tunnel created by a pair of mirrors placed in front of each other.

"Celestial feces... *that's* what it meant by premeditated." The Ritualist leaned forward, gripping the stone parapet hard enough to begin crushing it. "The system isn't spawning a monster just for us. Someone's opening a door and bringing it here. The cost... no, the restrictions must've been lifted an insane amount, since we were supposed to be having a trial. Whatever's coming... someone's specifically chosen it to counter whatever we can throw at them."

The immense white lines of magic began sparking, shifting to blue, silver, red... then the land around the spell circle exploded into flames. Trees were reduced to ash in that heartbeat as the top layer of fertile soil baked into a solid block for what must have been half a square mile. Smoke belatedly erupted into the air, catching on to the fact that there had been a fire several seconds after it had already consumed everything in range.

"Must've been a countermeasure in place in case someone raced into that space to deface the circular trace before they could establish the spell's place." Joe murmured in frustrated acknowledgment at the creativity of whatever spellcaster was facilitating the situation. "I wonder how they worked that feature in—what is *that*?"

Something shifted behind the coiling curtain of smoke, not moving so much as *uncoiling*.

A thunderous detonation rolled over the area as a mountain of flesh landed on freshly solidified soil. The smoke dissipated in the next second, blasted away as a tube of knotted, fused body finally found it had enough room to stretch out. With his recent exposure to bug monsters, Joe's mind immediately went to some kind of gargantuan centipede, but the truth was... just so much worse.

It didn't have legs. Instead, each of the myriad protrusions was an enormous arm, similar to the next only in that it was immensely muscular, with tendons, veins, and various shades of skin bulging out. What Joe could only *hope* was its head suddenly swung toward them, and the front of the creature peeled back to reveal a horrible mouth which yawned open to show layers and layers of not just teeth but *mouths* tucked behind circular rows of jagged teeth spiraling inward toward nothing.

As the main portion of its maw opened wide, each of the smaller mouths did the same, and an instant later, its scream of excitement washed over the walls, nearly knocking people from their positions from the distant shockwave alone.

"*UUGHHH!*" It was a man's deep, grunting bellow—like a barrel-chested powerlifter setting a personal record and shouting his triumph. Joe's head swam, not from the sounds or some extra effect. No, it was because he *recognized* the sound… and that fact absolutely terrified him.

"Gameover?" The word came out as little more than a whisper of disbelief. "It can't be… I buried you! There's no way it could've dug itself out, not to mention how different it looks. No. I must be wrong. I *have* to… *please* be wrong."

Joe's eyes shifted to the enormous gate still in place behind the monster. If it were possible, his jaw dropped further. *People* were marching out through the portal, tens, dozens… *hundreds.* "The system said it wouldn't spawn any extra enemies! What is *happening* right now?"

The first clear group of them, hundreds of warriors in armor that had been recently polished, but couldn't hide the signs of repair and constant use, held banners proudly. Ornate, elegant things which had been marred with a violently slashed 'X' across their surface.

Fallen noble houses.

Then came a large contingent of what Joe initially thought of as paladins. They were clearly a cut above even the elites of the noble houses, each of them wearing perfectly matching armor with winged helmets and wielding enormous hammers, axes, or maces. Focusing on them, the Ritualist was able to pick out a single incongruity which gave away their true identity: every one of the faces showing in the open-faced helmets was sporting thick, square-rimmed spectacles.

Joe slammed his fist on to the stone in front of him, sending a chunk of it flying. "Bard was right. The Scholars are behind this, or at least the Battle Scholars. I *knew* I should've gone back and taken Lindon down."

The last distinct group arrived at that moment, tumbling out of the portal and springing off their hands to join the others. They danced, cartwheeling along while trailing scarves, their masked faces painted with cheerful grins.

The Jesters didn't try to hide their true nature. Long, wickedly pointed knives were held in every last one of their grasps. All of their acrobatics came together at that moment to bring them together alongside the Legendary monster, the bells stitched into their clothing and hats ringing out, audible even from that distance.

They shifted into a strange pattern, each of the painted people striking an odd pose. Immediately, Joe sensed a shift in the mana and quickly activated Essence Cycle. Power was flowing through the gate, washing over the Jesters and being altered in a familiar manner—this was exactly what it looked like when Socar created a permanent formation by altering the terrain itself, yet somehow these... *people*... were able to do so with just their bodies.

A gentle whisper reached his ears as he focused on the magic barely able to cross the distance and give him a hint of what was happening.

Calm. Patience. A promise of hunger satiated. They cannot run. They cannot hide. All will be food.

"Emotional control formation?" Joe grimaced at the memory of how the Jesters worked. "But how is that *enough*? That thing should be attacking anything that comes near it, including them!"

"Aggression and emotional state have reached acceptable parameters! Sixty-four percent chance the beast will follow orders for the next three minutes. Move, *now*!" The leading Battle Scholar did nothing to try and hide his intent from the defenders of the town, his enhanced voice echoing across the walls. "Beast Master! Begin the slaughter!"

The huge, gaping maw of the beast dipped slightly, and now that Joe was focusing on smaller details, he noticed a blip along the back of its head that he'd initially mistaken as a blister of some sort. Now that it was moving, the Ritualist saw that it was actually a man sitting inside a cage—just like what divers would use to watch sharks swim around them. The tiny metal structure had thick cables stretching out, ending in enormous bolts that were driven directly into the monster's flesh.

"All group casters, focus fire on that monster!" Finally, the guild was reacting. Moments later, an enormous bolt of flame launched into the air, spiraling and hissing like a firework as it tracked toward the summoned beast. As it closed in, what had looked like a semi-truck of plasma up close appeared as nothing more than a pinprick of light as a grotesque hand shot forward and *caught* it.

The flame was squeezed, and while the limb certainly took damage, charring and smoking, it was clear the damaged flesh was already healing.

"Keep it up!" came the calm command. "I want four of those every second! Archers, prepare your longest range attacks! Engineers, get those trebuchets and ballistae primed!"

The creature took a step forward, perfectly in synchronization with the Jesters who danced forward, maintaining or shifting their poses depending on the energy flowing around them. It was then that Joe's fear was confirmed: as the beast took a step onto the guild's official territory, a notification popped up to warn them about what was coming.

Area alert! The Legendary (System Weakened) Monster 'Gameover' has intruded upon the territory of the Wanderer's Guild! This sliver of the Burning Mind is an apex predator. It is not a beast meant to be fought; it is a disaster you can only hope to survive.

Prepare accordingly.

Joe was simultaneously happy and deeply concerned that the system didn't warn everyone of the true danger of fighting Gameover. Getting eaten meant *deletion*, no respawns allowed. If that had been clearly stated, Joe knew that not one person, highly-paid mercenary or otherwise, would have remained in the area. Every last one of them would've immediately scattered to the winds, curse or no.

On the other hand, *not* giving that information seemed... harsh.

The next salvos landed, most of the magic detonating along the hard-to-miss body of the Legendary monster. Each of the spells which were ever so slightly off target still landed amidst the enemy, sending people scattering or forcing them to start burning through their mana and defensive items.

The attacking legions let out a roar and charged, quickly outstripping the monster, which was moving as if in a trance, hypnotized by whatever the Jesters and Beastmaster were doing to it.

Joe could only thank his lucky stars that they hadn't simply unleashed the creature and were instead guiding it directly toward the central gate. Realistically, he wasn't sure why they *hadn't* just let it rampage—but he could only assume that getting it under control in the first place was not an easy task.

"Perhaps, if they relinquished control even for a short while, they wouldn't be able to get it back? Let's see if I can make that happen while it's still far enough away that it eats *their* people instead of mine," Joe darkly intoned, turning and Omnivaulting toward the center of town, even as the attacking groups reached the midway point to the walls.

Though he was certain his rapid repositioning would cause some concern among the ranks, he couldn't worry about that right now. Just as Bard had warned him, if Joe didn't throw everything he could at this threat from the start, there was no way they'd be able to win.

"Twelve and a half thousand mana for the initial activation of the ritual," Joe muttered frantically to himself as he started calculating out his power requirement needs. "I can use myself, three people at the Novice circle, five at the Beginner... I need seventy-five total people, other than myself. Just need to find some people with hefty mana pools-"

As Joe was falling with style across the town, his eyes landed on what he hoped was the solution to his problem: what looked like an entire battalion of mages, or at least people in robes, were trying to push through the heavily populated streets to get in range of the conflict. He swooped down, tucking and rolling, only to land on his feet in front of the apparent leader of the group. "Hi there! Are you trying to find a way to bring all of your magical power to bear?"

"Out of the way. We were hired for a job, and I don't care how many people plan to stand around and wait until the fight comes to them, *we* are-"

"I like *you*." Joe nodded approvingly at the man's attitude. "What's your name?"

"I am Conrad Stevens, Expert Accursed Summoner." The Mage stood tall, glaring down at Joe, but frowning as if he recognized the man he was speaking to.

"And he's just *awesome*," one of the Accursed Summoner's companions gushed as he stepped forward and slapped Conrad on the shoulder. "He's got some of the coolest spells you'll ever see in your life!"

"You want to see this monster attacking the town get *tapped*?" another spoke up, practically *oozing* hype man energy. "Conrad here can summon an entire squad of bros to help beat that thing down."

"Bros?" Joe blinked at the term he hadn't heard from a human mouth in... a long time. "Oh, you are just going to absolutely *love* Jotunheim. Look, I'm the highest ranking member of the guild on this world. Actually, highest ranking on *any* of the worlds, besides wherever Aten himself is at the moment. Now please believe me when I say your talents would be far better served helping me *right now*."

"Oh snap, that's *Joe*! The Red Mist guy!"

Concern flashed in their eyes, though Conrad simply crossed his arms and raised an eyebrow. "You've got something legends like that are made of to throw at this monster? I admit I don't know exactly how difficult it's going to be to fight it, but the world wouldn't give us a trial we can't face."

Even before Conrad finished speaking, Joe was looking at him with a soft expression, like a parent seeing their child declare they'd be an astronaut. "That's so... *nice* that you think that."

The Ritualist lifted his hands and waved them in a shooing motion. "All right, back the way you came! You guys want to see a hidden chamber? Who am I kidding? Everyone loves secret rooms, that goes double for magical types!"

CHAPTER FORTY-ONE

If he'd been expecting the tension to lessen after going underground, Joe would've been sorely disappointed. Instead, Conrad and his battalion of Mages looked around the area, somewhat dazed at the strange, new location that had been under their feet dozens of times without them knowing about it. Now that they were in what felt like a secure location—though it was anything *but* with a Legendary monster on the rampage —they had no outlet for their adrenaline.

Trying to control his twitching fingers, Joe started directing the ambling people into position, barking at them to stand away from the completed ritual floating in the air, and not to adjust the positions of the metal contraptions scattered around seemingly at random. "I don't care if you stand, sit, lay, meditate, or pray! Once I tell you you're in the right spot, *don't* move out of it!"

Conrad was placed in the Novice circle, directly adjacent to Joe so he could help direct the people he'd brought with him. "What are we supposed to be doing, anyway?"

"Large-scale magical effect. I need all of you to channel

mana with me so we can get it going," Joe distractedly informed him as he pulled out his inscription tool and carefully began adjusting the coordinates for the effects of the ritual to manifest. "The hard work is already done; we just need to get it spinning up."

"Tell me straight, man." Joe blinked as Conrad shifted ever so slightly, his facial features adjusting, his clothes fitting slightly less perfectly. "Are we going to be putting ourselves at long-term risk? I don't need any of my people exiled-"

"It's not the Red Mist we're going to be using here." Joe shook his head, though his eyes remained locked on Conrad's face. "Are you wearing an illusion, or something?"

"No!" came a forced-cheerful shout. "Our boss is just a bit of a shape shifter! It's a pretty awesome effect of his class. You should see what he can do in each different form. Pretty awesome all the way up *and* all the way down."

Just like that, Conrad was back to his original self, a bright smile gracing his face. "Thanks, buddy! As for you... yeah, we'll help. Clearly, you've been putting this together for a while, and it's not like you set this up in secret. Something this big had to have been funded by the guild as a whole, right?"

"...Sure." Joe frowned slightly. "Yeah, that would make sense, wouldn't it? Instead of using all of my own resources-"

"I've got the stream going!" One of the Mages held up a thickly enchanted crystal. "We're live, but whoever's streaming is obviously doing so illegally. Look at that, they keep dropping their recording orb into their pocket whenever someone comes near 'em. As if the guild has nothing better to do right now than hunt down influencers. Hang on, I'll turn the sound up."

"-Please don't forget to subscribe, since this might be my last-ever video!" A new voice suddenly rang out through the room, and even though Joe tried to ignore it and adjust the coordinates of the ritual, he still found himself pulled in as the person on the other side detailed what was happening out in the town. "They brought in some serious artillery, but whoever's trying to breach those walls came prepared. Look at those phalanx-"

The sound was muffled suddenly, earning a few chuckles from the people who were straining to see what was going on, though luckily remained in the positions they'd been assigned. "-About that, the Wanderer's Guild has put a gag order on anyone recording the events, except for them. But we aren't going to let them get away with writing history however they want it to look! Anyway, the phalanx has been used since ancient times, but the interlocking shield pattern combined with the enchantment creates a bubble shield that's blocking even close-range artillery blasts-"

The running commentary focused on what Joe considered extremely odd and inane facts, instead of simply giving a breakdown of what was happening across the battlefield. He was happy to tune out, until a few minutes later, another phrase caught his ear.

"I don't know how they're doing it, but clearly they have some of the best coordinated Elemental Mages I've ever *seen* in this guild. Fire, wind, and stone shards are blasting out at almost *exactly* once every second. Consistent output, even if it looks like the damage is low. Maybe they're working on building up an elite synchronized Mage corps, but haven't had time to get their levels up yet?"

"Sounds like the rituals are getting used." Joe could only hope that his coven members were getting credit for their rituals being activated during combat.

"-Seriously, perfect coordination. No idea how they're doing that. I'd get closer, but... *look* at that thing! In case you're getting too excited, no, those *aren't* tentacles. Those are arms." Joe wasn't certain if the commentator paused for effect or to hide what he was doing again. "Watch how it moves! It doesn't walk, it's basically grabbing the ground and throwing itself forward each time it's... I want to say *allowed* to move forward? Here's a question for the listeners—if we have fingertips but not toe tips, why can we tiptoe but not finger-tip? First person to get me a good answer to that wins this week's-"

An explosion rattled the room they were in, and Joe glanced upward to make sure they weren't in danger of having the ceiling collapse on them. Seeing that not even dust was falling from above, he finished his calculations and stepped back slowly. The room was dead silent, though in the next instant, the influencer proved he hadn't been 'tapped'.

"Did you see that? I swear, it missed me by three feet at most!" The man laughed nervously. "Looked like a catapult tossed a rock, only for the War Mages to super-accelerate it! Just before it hit those Paladin-looking invaders, one of them somehow caught it with the flat of their hammer, swung it around, and sent it back! It's obvious we're not dealing with neophytes, these are battle-hardened-"

"I *hate* it when other people are good at using physics against me," Joe half-heartedly growled as he got into position. "Everyone get ready! We're going to activate this as soon as that big bad gets right in front of the gate. Also… whoever's got that stream going, keep it up."

A few familiar figures burst into the room, Joe's coven coming at a run. Hannah looked absolutely panicked, but when she saw that the ritual wasn't yet going, it appeared like she was so relieved she could faint on the spot.

"*Don't start!*" Frowning at the demand, but not about to ignore someone who looked like they had a good reason for what they were saying, Joe simply made a rapid hand gesture to get her to spill the information. Hannah sucked in a breath, coughed hard, then managed to croak out, "That thing is *Gameover*… isn't it?"

"Yeah, so you'd think you would want me to get to blasting as quick as possible." Joe lifted his hands, his eyes going wide as he had to physically restrain himself from activating the ritual.

"You can target it directly!" she shouted, voice overly loud from excitement and not the expected panic. "We still have its blood!"

"-Look at how it took that spell to the face like a champ! That's the first time I've seen *any* damage stick, nice shot!" the livestream announcer bellowed into his microphone-analog. "Look at those Jesters panic! They know it's hurt—oh. Oh, no."

"What's happening?" one of Conrad's people called, only for the person holding the crystal to shake his head.

"Look friends, I have no idea what's going through their heads... they're throwing their allies at the monster. It's... it's eating them!"

Just then, the system decided to drop the bomb Joe had been fearing since the start of the conflict.

Area alert! The Legendary monster, Gameover, has just demonstrated a unique effect. This monster possesses an evolving threat level, and anyone consumed by this entity will strengthen it and potentially grant the monster devastating new abilities. If you are killed by the creature by being eaten, you will no longer be able to respawn.

Prepare accordingly.

"They're *running*!" the announcer shouted in a panic. "For anyone not nearby, we just got told that this thing *deletes* you if it eats you! You're not tapped, you're... I don't even know what to call it! Looks like a full quarter of the mercenaries on the wall are trying to skip town. Curse or not, I think it's a good idea! Abyss, right, for those of you just joining, at the start of this, we were warned of a curse-"

Though a few seconds had passed since Hannah's declaration, Joe was still trying to process it along with all the new information. "What do you *mean* we have its blood? Didn't you use all of it back when it twisted your ritual?"

"No. Not all of it." Hannah rushed to the back wall, where Joe had once upon a time set up a small storage area. Brushing away a layer of ash and dust she'd used to camouflage it, Hannah quickly peeled back a section of what looked like the wall, revealing an angrily-glowing jar. "There was some left over. It's... *highly* mutagenic, so there was no way for us to dispose of it safely. It's just been in there for the last couple years, mocking us with its continued existence."

"Give it here… I think I'll be able to control it and force it to stay where I want it to go." Hannah came over and ever so carefully placed the jar—with less than an eighth of an inch of crusty, dried blood at the bottom—into his hands.

Knowing that the material was likely hiding its true danger, Joe pulled a taglock out of his ring and carefully dipped the super-sharp needle into the sludge. Immediately, the blood collapsed around the device, attempting to suck it into its depths, such as they were. Joe firmly pulled back, snapping the slurping tendrils and using his Mana Manipulation to condense what remained into a tiny bead of blood at the tip of his needle.

It fought against him, but when compared to the power and mental strength needed to wrangle Artifact aspects, Gameover's blood might as well have been contained in a spherical force-field. His control held firm, and he carefully returned the jar to Hannah, who swiftly covered and sealed it once more. Speaking in a slow, calm voice, Joe turned and inserted the needle into the blood enchantment targeting slot. "Go put that away, then I need all of you on the Beginner circle. Let's get you all some skill levels."

He tried not to be annoyed at the fact that he'd *already* input the activation coordinates, as altering a prepared ritual was always a dangerous proposition. Still, as he hadn't turned them into radioactive mist, he could only chalk it up as a good way to get some practical experience. "Everyone, prepare yourselves! This is going to suck… the mana right out of you."

As the ritual got its first taste of mana, a deep, unrelenting hunger for *more* made itself known. The entire ritual chamber groaned as the enormous circles *contracted* slightly, yanking everyone closer to the epicenter of the diagram being imbued. "If anyone is feeling a pull on their mana pool, just remember to keep it flowing steadily. The outermost ring needs about twelve thousand five hundred points of mana-"

"How much of this could you power on your own?" Kirby's question caught Joe off guard, but it was innocuous enough that he was able to focus on channeling into the ritual.

"Uhh, about half of the outer circle safely, for this world."
Joe replied after a lightning-quick calculation. "Then there's still
the other six circles, so... in total, we're looking at anywhere
from thirty-seven to forty thousand mana in total. I can't do *that*
on my own!"

A sudden air pressure shift rippled through the room,
tossing piles of neatly stacked notes, books, and shattering
various alchemy equipment that had been left out and about.
Joe sent a sharp look at Hannah, who shook her head—the
excess blood had been safely secured.

Trying to get his heart out of his bowels now that he was
certain there wasn't a random Eldritch essence being added to
the mix, Joe held himself firm as the ripple turned into a
breeze, then air was being *sucked* into the center of the ritual
like a tornado passing through a pipeline.

Joe's robes were snapping against his body, and he strained
against the pressure, though the now-active ritual would hold
him in place. As he watched several people get bodily shaken
and back and forth, he amended his thought. Technically, the
ritual would only hold him within the bounds of his assigned
space.

Big_Mo let loose a wild laugh. "It's like the Pathfinder's Hall
is taking in a deep breath! Maybe this'll make it finish its
upgrade faster!"

"Just be happy we're allowed in the underground space
while the upgrade is happening." Taka's offhand comment
made Joe's eyes go wide—he hadn't even considered they
might've been locked out of the building as it shifted. It *had*
happened before.

"Steady!" Joe roared over the howling wind. "We're going to
be just fine! There's plenty of us, and we've all got mana to
spare."

At that moment, one of Conrad's people jerked in place,
blood splashing into the air before he vanished—instantly sent
to respawn. As people began to react with panic, Joe scanned

the room, gritting his teeth in frustration as he saw random weapons and other items blowing into the room, having been pulled in from the outside. "There's no enemies! It's just the wind making things fly at high speed! Defensive measures!"

Splitting his focus, Joe started ordering the stairway to close up, and the wind shifted to a high-pitched shrieking as it sealed... almost instantly turning the chamber into an airless vacuum as the last of the air was pulled into the ritual. Eyes bulging, he dropped the stairwell once more, and the structure was vibrated into rubble by the rapidly moving wind. Joe clenched his teeth as the stair-shaped chunks of stone were flung across the room, crushing a few unfortunate people in their path.

The howl of the wind was no longer just noise—it was a force ripping at robes, rattling teeth, pressing against lungs so hard that every breath was a fight. Joe could feel it deep in his bones, a relentless pull that wanted to suck the life out of everyone in the room. His legs were locked, feet braced wide, and *still* he slid an inch across the polished floor as another gust tore through the chamber.

Joe tried to shout encouragement, but his voice barely reached his own ears. All around him, Conrad's Mages did their best to survive the fallout of Joe's mistake as the air pressure fluctuated wildly, sucking the breath from their lungs. Their teeth clenched, skin was slick with sweat, faces pinched and paling as they split their attention between trying to push mana into the ritual and pull air into their lungs.

A woman in the Expert ring stumbled, jerking as the rushing wind slammed her sideways. Before the circle could spin her out of the danger zone, there was a sharp *crack* and the woman vanished, her body shunted to the respawn point. Joe's heart lurched. "Abyss, I didn't even see what hit her!"

"Another down!" Conrad called just as two more Mages slumped, their eyes rolling back as they crumpled to the floor. One popped out of existence; the other lay twitching, unconscious, but still unknowingly donating the last dregs of his mana.

Joe gritted his teeth, forcing his own mana outward and pulling more from his reserves as the flow from his helpers rapidly shrank in volume. His body trembled under the strain—his shoulders locked like iron, his fingers numb from the chill of what felt like upper-atmosphere wind.

"Come on... come *on*! Just a little more-" Joe flinched as a stone struck him in the back, only to be held in place by the gale. Sounds seemingly impossibly reached him, and Joe realized it wasn't *just* a stone—it was the viewing crystal.

The announcer's voice raggedly reached his ears, only possible due to Joe's incredible senses. "-this is bad, this is *so* bad! They're running! The mercs are fleeing, dropping gear—no! The monster's after them! I can't—*gah*—okay, okay, it's gaining on them. Maybe they'll make it... the attackers are panicking! That *thing* is eating anyone in its way. Y'all, I'm getting outta here. I'll leave this where you can watch, but I'm just gonna take the curse and-"

The voice vanished as Joe was spun by the ritual, and the crystal flew off to slam against the wall.

"Thank... the celestials... we didn't use the directional version." Joe's vision tunneled as all his mental strength went toward pumping the combined mana channeling into him into the activation of the ritual. His blood burned like liquid fire, and people kept collapsing around him.

Big_Mo was on his knees, teeth bared in a grimace, biceps bulging as he pushed out every last drop into the circle. Kirby was swaying like a reed in a storm, watching everything that happened with utter delight, even as fragments of rock tore furrows through her skin. Hannah was dazed but not gone, still barely clinging to the lines, a flicker of mana pulsing weakly from her fingertips. Taka was pale as a corpse, his lips moving silently as he mouthed numbers under his breath, counting something only he understood.

Joe pushed harder.

The chamber shook again as another explosion sounded out from the surface; not a sharp sound, but a low, threatening rumble, as if the walls protecting the city were being torn from their foundations. At that moment, a blinding pulse of light raced along the circles, flaring outward like a supernova contained in a single room.

For one terrifying heartbeat, Joe thought it was a failure. The world froze, and it took a few breathless moments before he realized the *world* hadn't frozen... the wind had just died down.

Papers fluttered to the floor. Broken glass *crunched* under the shifting feet of those who remained awake and able to move under their own power.

Joe staggered away from the primed ritual, which had condensed into a beachball-sized orb of storm contained within a sheath of rippling ritual rings. Around him, bodies were slumped against the walls, some unconscious, some groaning in pain. Big_Mo started laughing softly, even as he hit the ground. "Made it! You owe me ten silver, Robert."

Joe's fingers twitched. One thought, one pulse of will, and the storm would be unleashed. He held back his instinctual activation of the ritual only thanks to the sudden resumption of noise: static. Distant shouts of alarm were coming through the cracked viewing crystal at the base of the wall, at least until it let out an alarming *pop* and shattered fully.

"That was the coolest thing I've ever done, Joe." Kirby's voice was thin, confused, cracked raw from strain. "Uhhh... why aren't you-"

"We all need to evacuate," he told her while reactivating Neutrality Aura and started to heal those around him at the same moment. "If being next to it while *prepping* the weapon killed a bunch of them, who knows what'll happen when it's let loose?

Joe exhaled, his breath shaky. His eyes lifted from the ritual, turned toward the ruined stairwell and the battered streets beyond. "Get them out of here, and I'll get eyes on the target."

"Wait. *Wait*! I'm coming with you!" Hannah hollered as Joe

ran off without another word, rushing toward the mostly demolished exit.

Everyone scrambled to rise—staggering, leaning on each other, evacuating the unconscious, or limping after him as the Ritualist vaulted over a heap of rubble and vanished into the stairwell.

CHAPTER FORTY-TWO

One of the explosions and crashes that had shaken the Pathfinder's Hall revealed itself as Joe took to the rooftops—three sections of the eastern wall had collapsed, all the way from the main gatehouse to nearly halfway to its sharp northern shift. The Ritualist felt his stomach sink as he witnessed his people getting cut down like chaff, only their sheer number advantage in the gap letting them maintain any semblance of success.

The guild was fighting tooth and nail, pushed to their absolute limits by the overwhelming forces arrayed against them, as the fallen noble houses had brought an army easily on par with the Wanderers on this world, and they had far more training as a cohesive force. The attackers pushed forward as a unit, protected each other, and slowly but surely cut their way through the panicked defenders.

Whenever some brave combatant rallied those around them, Jesters appeared right behind them, knives creating their own unique flesh-sheath for a moment in that key figure before the assassins vanished in a puff of smoke and laughter. This caused the lines to collapse faster, as no one could take charge without fear of being struck down and sent to respawn in the next instant.

Every trebuchet, every ballista launching what was intended to be a deadly payload was neatly turned aside by the Battle Scholars, who intercepted and twisted their trajectory and angle as if the laws of motion themselves bent to their will.

Joe ground his teeth as one of them—recognizable as Lincon even from that distance—was tossed in the air by a trio of companions, almost impossibly caught a boulder with a spike of his weapon, then tossed it into the wall. Another huge chunk of masonry exploded into rubble, and a dozen men fell as their firm footing failed.

Only one thing kept the guild from having been routed already: the instant, endless respawn they'd been cursed with.

As soon as they were felled, they would be running from the temple, an endless stream of grim-faced men and women rushing to reinforce their friends. Already, many of them had lost at least one level, which would undoubtedly make it easier for them to be killed once more. When that last puzzle piece fell in place, Joe finally recognized the ploy of their attackers for what it truly was.

"Abyss... they're gonna grind us down until we're at our weakest, let us have some hope of defeating them. Then, when we can't do a thing to stop them, or when they get bored, we'll get eaten. They want us to die over and over, lose all hope, then vanish forever." Joe scanned the field of enemies surrounding the town, his eyes finally coming to rest on Gameover. "Someone's recording this for them, I'm sure of it. They'll offer this as a warning to whoever goes against them... unless I can get rid of the linchpin of their plan. Celestials, I hope this works."

Across the battlefield, the massive, writhing shape of Gameover lurched—turning back toward the town now that he had finished chasing and devouring a pack of mercenaries who'd broken ranks and fled into the countryside. Joe watched, heart pounding, as the Legendary monster seemed to lock onto him from across the distance, let out a deep, hungry grunt of excitement, then thundered toward the gap in the wall like a nightmare come to life.

Just as suddenly, the creature slowed, its monstrous arms dragged through the dirt, grabbing trees and shoving them into its mouths to satiate the endless hunger filling it. The Jesters had reappeared around the great beast, leaping and flipping through the destruction like streaky, watercolor rainbows. They danced into a pattern the Ritualist was becoming far too familiar with, and each twisted motion caused Gameover to jerk and fight... until it finally shifted away from the gap and toward the main gate of the town.

They had reclaimed control.

"It's gotta be an intimidation tactic, right?" Joe muttered his confusion as he lifted a small, metal key. "Or is there a deeper reason they'd target the gate?

"Hey!" A jubilant shout came from below, as Taka saw the object Joe was clutching. "Is that what I think it is? You used my key?"

"You know it. Gotta tell you, this was a brilliant piece of work. Even if I had to hand this off, one of you could finish it," Joe rumbled as he lifted the Remote Access Key, pointing it at the monster in the distance and twisting it. "The target is at a good distance, and I can only hope the others in the secret room listened to me and evacuated. Nothing to do now but..."

His next words were cut off by a howl of wind, nearly jerking him off his feet an explosive roar of wind rushed to the Pathfinder's Hall once more. Joe instinctively dropped into a low crouch as he risked a glance backward, but then his attention was quickly, *utterly* consumed by the ritual circle that had just appeared in the sky above Gameover.

The Ritualist's eyes watered against the savage glare it was casting: a pale yellow light suffusing the world as the Artifact-orange coloration of the Master-rank ritual was washed out by sunlight. A faint *click* echoed through the oddly still-perfect streets of Towny McTownface—the sound delicate, like the front door to a home unlocking.

Then the sky shattered.

Above the town, clouds erupted violently from previously empty skies, staining the blue expanses as though millions of gallons of oil had been dumped into the open air: a boiling, convulsing mass of black, slate, and sickly green shot through with veins of lavender lightning that throbbed like corrupted arteries. The clouds spread outward, spiraling in unsettling fractal patterns.

Under a sky now a cross between eerie grayscale and a pulsing, brilliant orange, Joe's skin prickled, the fine hairs on his arms rising as a pressure heavier than mountains pushed down; seeming to *just* miss landing on him and turning the entire settlement into a pancake.

Raaaaa~ge!

His breath caught in his throat as the first scream of the wind sliced through the city, sounding almost like words as it sheared through the sky. Then again, it very well *may* have been the storm coming alive, announcing to the world that it was contained, bottled into one location, and it would *not* be submitting to its new reality.

Threads of mana as thick as the anchor chain of an aircraft carrier lanced from the ritual's glowing circle, stitching reality itself together into an impenetrable dome to contain what had been summoned onto Midgard. The Ritualist watched as they clattered into place one by one, feeling the aura of the storm's fury ripple outward in waves as it gained more and more awareness.

One thing was clear beyond measure: the storm *hated* the hamster ball it had been forced to flow into, and it would do *anything* to be released.

The air pressure plummeted in an instant, and Joe clapped his hands over his ears as the atmosphere inverted, a vacuum surge drawing every loose scrap of air toward the ritual's heart. His ears popped painfully, his skull throbbing as dozens of people were sucked into the air, only to be tossed to the ground like discarded toys.

Glass exploded in a deafening cascade from windows across the town as the shockwave passed. Dust and debris whipped into the sky, spiraling in unnatural currents that defied gravity and common sense. Whole roofs were yanked from their beams like paper hats—though Joe noticed with a fraction of his attention and smugness that none of the buildings *he* had made were damaged in the slightest.

At the heart of the maelstrom, Gameover had it far worse than any of those merely caught by the odd eddy of power. Its body thrashed as winds the strength of hurricanes slammed into it from all sides, churning it like a blender formed of pure pressure.

Its massive arms clawed at the earth, trying to anchor itself in place to stand firm, but the ground itself betrayed it, liquefied into aerated soil as the gale tore at the surface. Loose skin, ragged sinew, entire limbs, all of it began ripping away. They flayed the monster piece by piece as debris found a new home, lodged in the monster's body, only to be ripped out, spun through the enclosed space, and lancing into Gameover from a new angle.

Joe's eyes watered as he looked on, forcing himself to watch, to *learn*, from every moment of this. Since he knew what was *supposed* to happen—thanks to adding a blood-bound targeting mechanism—he was able to capture the moment space itself buckled inward, distorting in mesmerizing ripples as though reality were being folded by the colossal, unseen hands. The edges of the ritual pulsed and bent inward, cocooning the monstrous storm and sealing it into a pocket dimension to shield the outside world.

Katabatic winds joined into the maelstrom in the next instant, bringing a frigid wall of air that crystallized all moisture instantly, and reduced the Beastmaster sitting on Gameover's head to a red smear as every cell in his body burst at the same time.

Frigid air from the upper atmosphere came crashing down with a violence that eclipsed every memory Joe had of terrible thunderstorms or even what he'd seen happen naturally on Jotunheim. A wall of dense, compressed, frozen *nitrogen* poured into the rituals' contained space, suffusing and altering the already-raging cyclone. Where hot and cold collided, the storm thickened and solidified, gaining *mass* and turning into a physical presence capable of crushing stone, bone, and metal.

Gameover arched back, its many mouths shrieking in every direction, its body outlined by the twisting spiral of the storm around it. The winds hit hard enough to crack bone, crush metal, gouge stone. Every gust battered the Legendary monster, pinning it, slicing at it, stripping away layers of the abomination's flesh like an onion being peeled by a professional chef.

The Ritualist shook his head, trembling involuntarily as he realized that without Hannah, he would have simply unleashed this storm into the world uncontained, giving it only a direction and point of origin. It could have obliterated the countryside, erased the town, and scoured the world clean for an unknown distance.

But the perimeter of the ritual held, coaxing the wind to turn its anger on the beast it had been brought to destroy, instructing it that *perhaps* it would find release after it had fulfilled its task. Joe could feel the strain—like holding a rabid beast on a short leash, hoping it would destroy his enemy and be satisfied, only to then fade away.

The mana pressing down from the sky started to warp the air, bending it into distorted mirages. Reality flickered, suddenly unstable as the dense air turned fully opaque, hiding the monster behind a wall of frosted, roiling clouds unnaturally held at ground level. Storm winds howled, rising to a pitch so high it ceased to be sound and became vibration, shuddering through the bones of every living creature in the city.

The pressure made ears pop, made the sky pulse, made dust lift from the ground for miles in all directions. Joe slowly shook his head, weak in the knees at having created this weapon without knowing *exactly* what it would do. "If anyone ever asked if I enjoyed my first taste of controlling the ultimate elemental burst, I'll only be able to honestly say that I only *weathered* the storm."

A cold tingle, a sixth sense that Something was going terribly wrong finally gave Joe the impetus he needed to tear his eyes away from the globe of destruction now sitting in the middle of the no man's land like the world's largest marble.

From three separate points on the ruined field, the enemy forces were moving into a new position with practiced precision —smooth, deliberate, and coordinated in a way that could only mean one thing: they had been ready for this.

The warriors attacking the walls of Towny McTownface fell back, retreating even before the storm had reached its peak. A knot of fallen nobles stood in the center of their formation. Golden, gem-encrusted relics were held high, trembling in the hands of their bearers... perhaps family heirlooms, passed down through generations, filled with history and significance? The ranks of warriors closed in around them in a tightly packed wedge, banners flying high and proudly to show that they were *regrouping*.

Not retreating, merely moving into the next phase of their battle order.

To the east of them, the Jesters—blood-painted and laughing—were dancing in synchronized steps. They spun, flipped, and moved, each motion calculated acrobatic perfection, each flourish of the hand drawing looping sigils in the air as black diamonds appeared in their palms. One by one, they crushed the altered components and scattered the black dust into clouds that remained in the air, the unnatural stillness clear with the raging atmosphere causing chaos all around them.

To the west, the Battle Scholars formed up, the final piece needed to create an equilateral triangle with the orb of raging wind in the center. Silent, severe, clad in shining armor and hefting oversized weapons, they moved together in perfect synchronization like a mastercrafted clock. Tools were retrieved from bags or belts; weighted implements such as rods and pendulums or stacks of paper were revealed as talismans in the next moments.

What looked like nothing more than confetti at that distance burst out from them like a paper blizzard, wrapping out in one direction to connect with the black dust of the Jesters on one side and the golden threads of light on the other. Light and darkness stretched across the space between the fallen houses and the assassins, until a single, unbroken triangle formed of magic and precious components, guided by formations and exacting equations, was formed around the storm Joe had brought to bear against the Legendary monster.

It was only then that Joe started to realize he may have lost. While he had called down the sky itself to attack on their behalf, and it was truly breathtaking, terrible, and magnificent... it was also... *expected*. Perhaps not the storm itself, but the *ritual* Joe used to bring it into being.

If one thing was clear about the situation, it was that his enemies had come specifically prepared to counter the Ritualist.

Unable to process the situation, Joe instead almost unconsciously tapped into Essence Cycle, the golden eye etched on his forehead flaring with light as he began watching what his enemies were doing through a separate layer of reality. To his great annoyance, they *weren't* casting a spell.

They had formed a ritual and were using it to counter his.

It was certainly a primitive one, but that made it no less potent—fueled as it was with great sacrifices and empowered by the mana pools of hundreds of people. As soon as he recognized it for what it was, Joe attempted to reach out and tap into their control, hoping to subvert, destroy, or disrupt their creation.

But once again, his Mana Manipulation failed him. He simply couldn't stretch his mana across the distance to act against them, and exposing himself by rushing out to get close would have only ended in his death. All he *could* do was watch as the prepared counter-ritual tightened around his own, far more powerful version.

It wound around his Master-rank ritual like a strangling vine attaching itself to an ancient oak tree and began to dig into it, *squeezing* the life and power out of the ritual containing the storm.

Ding!

Congratulations! By careful study of a convergence of power, you have learned the basic ritual design 'Ritual of the Refusal of Three'. This is an Expert-ranked ritual, requiring three set boundaries which fully contain the magical effect the ritual is targeting. The owner of the ritual may target any channeled or instant effect of magic within the bounds, fully countering and cancelling the intended effect.

If the effect is a higher rank than the ritual, it will take additional time and resources to negate and may not be fully successful.

Joe's heart pounded as he read over the notification. "May not be *fully* successful? In other words, it might just disrupt the ritual and release the storm?"

Just then, he watched the first crack ripple through his Master-rank ritual, sealing in the same instant. Still, with even that momentary disruption, the storm screamed in defiance, lashing out with hurricane-force winds as it tried to break free of its cage—joining in on the siege and speeding it along.

Space warped as the converging triangle reached the ritual circle rotating in the sky, spinning contrary to the Master-ranked circle and grinding against it like the brakes on a freight train trying to slow a thousand fully laden cars in time to prevent a collision.

"Joe!" Hannah grabbed his shoulder and shook him, having climbed to the roof to get a better look at what was going on. "What's happening?"

"They're..." He coughed, tasting iron and realizing he'd been clenching his teeth so hard that his gums were bleeding. "They're countering my ritual."

A ripple shuddered through the air, a shockwave visible to the naked eye.

The nobles braced, blood pouring from their noses as their mana reserves drained dry, their heirlooms dissipated and long-since destroyed to the last speck of precious gemstone. Jesters continued their endless acrobatic dance, looking as though they were about to collapse. Conversely, the Scholars stood stoic and grim, having clearly accounted for their expenditure and ensuring they had extra material and mana to spare.

Crack.

Joe's storm flickered. The vast circle of over Gameover shuddered, destabilizing, skipping like a broken record as it fell out of the sky, catching itself only when it was perpendicular to the ground, its base nearly touching the scorched, wind-swept clay-layer.

The winds faltered as the sky hiccupped. The layered containment of space warped, warbled, and began to unravel. Gameover lunged forward, its head bursting through the opaque cloud layer and directly through the ritual circle, for a long second wearing the circle like a fashionable choker neck-lace. Endless numbers of arms lashed out, closed fists impacting the ritual and adding to the damage of the whirling triangle grinding against it.

With one final, echoing *crack*, the ritual burst apart into flaming torrents of rapidly expended mana and aspects, lighting up the sky with blazing plasma as the atmosphere ignited. The storm *howled* in glee as its controlling, guiding hand vanished, and the ritual disintegrated in a blinding pulse, collapsing against the ground and igniting a shaped mana detonation that sent debris, dust, and bodies rocketing skyward.

Joe staggered back, eyes wide and searching as the sun above vanished behind a wall of rubble. The ground and sky reversed, millions of tons of debris ripped out of the cratered planet and tossed into the air to become the plaything of the unleashed sentient storm.

Another sound emerged on the heels of the storm's gusts: a grunt of endless hunger.

The Legendary monster, torn to shreds, flayed, battered and broken in thousands of places along its gargantuan body... was now free to feast.

"It wasn't an intimidation tactic! Ah, they got me good." Joe was almost laughing as the truth blazoned clearly in his mind. "They didn't care about making us afraid,\ or grinding us down or making Gameover hit the front gate. None of that mattered. They were just waiting for me to show my trump card in an open enough space that they knew they could move against it."

Joe turned to Hannah, who was looking at him with great concern as he limply waved into the dark distance. "I've become too predictable. They countered me perfectly... and now I can't do a *thing* to stop them."

CHAPTER FORTY-THREE

The unnatural darkness settled heavily, sunlight trying and failing to regain its prime position. It felt fitting to Joe, seeing as he was collapsed to his knees on the rooftop, arms hanging listlessly at his side as he waited for his turn to be devoured. At that moment, he didn't feel fear or even anger. He was numb—imbued only with the knowledge that he had *failed*.

He heaved a deep sigh, only managing a lungful of clean air thanks to his still-active Neutrality Aura. When his shoulders started to shake, Joe blankly thought that he had started laughing, until a thin stream of sunlight dappled the world around him for a moment, revealing Hannah's determined expression that *almost* managed to hide her wide, fearful eyes.

"Get *up*! There's gotta be something you can do!" Her words were almost drowned out in the soft, constant white noise of the wind howling behind them and sand pouring out of the sky and settling back on the ground, just barely louder than a heavy rain would sound. "Something *we* can do! I don't care if we have to go back there and figure out how to unleash some kind of twisted magic again, I don't care if it's *me* that gets exiled this time. We need to find a way to *survive* this!"

"Something about ends not justifying the means," Joe murmured half-heartedly, reaching up and gently pulling her hands off his shoulders. "Fake platitude, then I'll come up with a solution that works based on the attempt at letting you down gently."

"What are you saying?" Hannah clearly had no idea what he was rambling on about. "Snap out of it, Joe!"

"I just don't know what you expect of me." The bald man heaved himself to his feet, deciding that he should at least put up as much of a token resistance as possible. "I don't have a solution to this. I've got nothing. Pretty much all of my effort had been put into *that* ritual. I suppose we could go and try to put something else together, but anything less than Master rank is just going to be an annoyance to a Legendary monster like Gameover."

UUGHHHHHH!

"See? He agrees." Joe chuckled as he moved forward, striding toward the edge of the roof as though caught in a dream. "Can't be far off now."

At the edge of town, limbs shot forward like spears, dozens of arms coated in knotted tendons and rippling muscles moving so fast they displaced the falling rubble, forcibly creating a clear space and allowing visibility. The lamprey-like face began to slowly snake up above the gate, the limbs clutching onto screaming defenders hauling people into the waiting jaws.

"Kill them!" The call went out barely in time, released by an Archer at the same moment he expertly placed an arrow in the first victim's heart. With a dawning realization, the others began targeting the people clutched by the monster, trying to make sure they weren't going to be permanently removed from the world. A quick death, followed by a respawn? Unfortunate, but far preferable to the alternative.

Yet the monster didn't seem at all concerned, simply remaining in place as it grabbed more and more of the defenders from their positions. With each bite, its body rippled, blood and flesh knitting back together, visibly refilling areas where chunks had been torn out. Finally, the defenders were too slow to save someone, and Gameover shivered in delight as it mutated, long black claws ripping from the fingertips on its many hands.

It shifted from closed-fist grabbing to treating its digits like toothpicks, skewering people like mini sausages and popping them into its mouth like hors d'oeuvres.

"Come on, Joe! You're not just a Ritualist, you are *the* Ritualist! You don't *get* to run out of plans. You don't *get* to give up." At this point, Hannah was practically shouting in his ear, so he leaned away, shooting her a complicated glance as she continued to rant at him. "Your snarky little comment just now? Yeah. Do that. Figure something out."

"There *is* nothing else." Joe blinked a few times, definitely only cleaning dust out of his eyes. "I gave it everything I had, and it *still* wasn't enough. I'm one guy, and that's three major organizations putting centuries of accumulated wealth and knowledge into play against me."

"You bottled up a storm and *threw* it at them." Hannah's incredulous words cut him deeply. "They only stopped you *once*. How many more times do you think they can do that?"

"They don't *need* to stop me again." He looked at her directly and realized she was cupping a hand to her ear, clearly having not heard him over the wind. "I said they don't need to stop me again! I only had the one ritual. *One* chance to hurt that thing enough that the rest of us could work together to bring it down, and it's clear that I put my only egg in the wrong basket!"

"What? I can't hear your self-deprecation over-"

"The wind, *yeah*, I *know*." Joe froze, wide-eyed as he held up his hand, covering Hannah's mouth and earning a death glare at the same time. "No. *Wait*! The wind... why are we still hearing the wind?"

Looking at Gameover, his initial hope was dashed. While the majority of the ritual he'd unleashed had been destroyed, there was a chance the storm would retain sentience and continue its existence after being unleashed. But if that were the case, at the very least, it wasn't going after the fleshy abomination. Then, following his ears, he looked back at the Grand Ritual Hall...

... just as the sound of the wind stopped entirely.

Joe's thoughts still felt sluggish, and he felt properly thick as he voiced his thoughts in the sudden calm. "What was that all about?"

"It's been doing that since you turned that key." Hannah impatiently reached out and shoved Joe's chest, only to stumble away as though she had tried pushing over a mountain. To her, thanks to the disparity in their Characteristics, he may as well have been one. "Focus on the problem at hand!"

"I *am*." Joe's eyes were glued to the Pathfinder's Hall that he could only catch intermittent glimpses of as the fallout continued raining down around them. "If the wind had been being sucked back into the building ever since we activated the ritual... I had just chalked it up to a side effect."

"So what?"

"So..." Joe turned his wide eyes to look into her narrowed ones. "What if it *wasn't* a side effect? What if it was absorbing the wind?"

"*What* was absorbing the wind?" Hannah didn't receive an answer, so she prodded Joe once more. "The building?"

The answer she expected didn't come, as the Ritualist was staring into the distance with a now-sharp gaze. It was still nearly impossible to see through the swirling rain of sediment, but as Gameover slapped a hefty arm into the gate, bursting through it on the first strike, the monster cleared the air for a bare moment—just long enough for Joe to get a clear view of the area.

"It *did*."

For just a heartbeat, he'd been able to see a *new* circle spinning into existence just in front of the shattered gate. It was as black as midnight, only able to be seen against the backdrop of darkness by being utterly impenetrable to the light. It wasn't yet fully formed, instead blooming into existence with ghostly precision.

"It shouldn't be..." Joe licked his dry lips, hoping against hope that he was right.

"Tell me what's happening!" Hannah demanded, looking for all the world as though she were about to wrap her delicate hands around his neck and start squeezing if he didn't speak.

"There!" His hand darted out, but the fraction of a second had been too small of a time for her to follow to where he was pointing. "It's a duplicate. A replica ritual thrown off by Haunting Shadows. I can't intentionally duplicate rituals at that rank yet, but there's a one in four chance that Haunting Shadows *can*. If it works, it'll only be half as effective, but it'll still be at the Master rank. If nothing else... it might buy us some time."

A horrendous ripping sound of splintering wood and tortured metal rang through the town as Gameover extended its myriad of arms *through* the city gate and pulled in all directions, destroying the barrier as surely as if it had been struck by a meteor. The creature let out a rhythmic grunt, the most hungry, sinister laugh Joe had ever had the misfortune of hearing.

The monster pounded the ground with its fists as it slowly began to squeeze itself through the space, savoring the scent of fear washing up off of its waiting prey.

Then the circle completed itself, pulsed once, and activated.

It didn't burst outward like an explosion, nor did it fold space and wrap around the monster like the original had. No, this one had all the same, original properties as the ritual Joe had created *before* adding Gameover's blood to the targeting matrix. The wind that had been siphoned to create the storm was released as a single, focus, honed *beam* of katabatic compression dozens of meters wide.

It roared through the dust-choked battlefield with a shriek that drowned out even the monster's guttural bellow of pained confusion. Gameover didn't have a chance to brace; the moment the contained storm struck it, the creature's rubbery flesh shredded like wet tissue paper in a tornado. Over one and a half seconds, a deep, gaping channel was cut through its midsection, nearly perfectly severing a third of its lower body away.

Only a relatively thin section kept it connected to the main body up near where Gameover's head was poking through the gate, forced to the ground by the immense pressure. Dozens of arms were sheared off, and Gameover let out a sick gurgle as its sinewy hide was torn apart, a sharp deviation from laughing off magical artillery only a moment prior.

But that was only where the storm began. It certainly wasn't about to *stop* with monster flesh. Like a tornado moving perfectly parallel to the ground, the newly awakened storm gathered and pulled a huge swath of debris along with it as it punched through the beast and roared through the clogged air... all but vaporizing the forces of the fallen noble houses as it passed into their ranks.

Knights and their commanders—mages and archers, shield walls or militia, the orderly rows and phalanxes were caught flat-footed by the magical, razor-edged windstorm—all were sheared through like a scythe through dry wheat. Plate armor was pulled apart, hundreds of pounds of metal turned to needles—the largest chunk that remained of any of them.

The attackers stared open-mouthed as the majority of their forces were wiped away in an instant as the storm continued onward, digging a massive channel into the distance, sending trees and ground flying, even as the vast majority of the dirt that had been suspended in midair was sucked along with it. Just like that, the local topsoil was spread over dozens of miles.

Joe watched with narrowed eyes as the masked Jesters immediately shifted their plans and abandoned their allies, darting to the side of the conflict and circling wide around the town. He tracked them as far as he could, sadly not able to see them after they vanished into the dust cloud cover. They weren't *fleeing*, this much he was sure of. Right now was going to be their best chance to be rid of him forever, and they both knew it.

But the real surprise? That was the reaction of the Battle Scholars. The previously stoic, hammer-wielding elite Scholars had maintained perfect control of the situation until now. They'd been calculated, professional, all but unflappable.

Not anymore.

As their allies were shredded, the noble army erased in an instant, the Jesters dispersing to start taking out individual targets, the Scholars just... *snapped*.

Their detached poise vanished as they began to rage. They tossed their weapons to the ground, calm expressions shifting into twisted snarls as they began bickering amongst themselves, pointing at each other and hurling accusations. In a word, they straight up threw a *tantrum*.

"Heh... I guess setting up this situation, controlling a Legendary monster, and dumping resources into a counter-ritual wasn't cheap. Maybe those nobles were supposed to pay them *after* this was all over? Guess *that's* not going to happen."

Even as the attackers splintered along faction lines, the wind continued to rage, still centered on Gameover and slowly forcing it back and away from the gate. Still, even as the wind cut the beast in twain, it somehow only revealed that the monster was even more horrifying than it had initially seemed.

There didn't appear to be any organs to spill out. Instead of showing intestines, lungs, or anything that could be found in any normal creature... as layers of twitching muscle pulled apart, the lacerations manifested additional mouths. Flowing blood collected across the surface of the open wounds only for a moment, then tiny arms began sprouting next to the mouths like mandibles on an ant.

"*UUugh.*" This time, the deep grunt was one of effort. At the same time, dozens of hands dropped to the ground and clawed into the windswept surface, and the Legendary monster pulled itself forward fractionally, fighting against the wind the entire time.

Joe's mouth went dry. "It's not just *enduring* the attack, it's pushing through it. If we wait any longer, it's going to break free. Hannah... stay back. Stay safe."

Joe ran to the edge of the unsteady building he was on, shoving off with all his might and roaring at the top of his voice as he reached the apex of his Omnivault. "This is our only chance! Cut that thing to pieces, this is our last resort!"

"Cha~arge!"

CHAPTER FORTY-FOUR

The echo of Joe's command to charge bounced back to him *twice* before people started to realize he was actually being serious. In their eyes, nothing much had changed. Sure, the monster was being pushed back ever so slightly, and it was using its hands to move incrementally forward instead of gobbling down their friends, but the pressure on them wasn't going to let up anytime soon.

Then, a young Archer with high perception shouted with surprise through the lull, voice cracking with disbelief, "They're... they're *gone*! That blast hit the army, and it squashed them like a bug on a windshield!"

Sunshine shone down on them once more as the debris was funneled away, revealing only a fraction of the forces that had been arrayed against them. A bloodied swordsman transformed his relief into renewed purpose, weapon held high as he rushed to the edge of the wall. "We can do this! *Charge!*"

The call was taken up across the entirety of Towny McTownface, and the fear and frustration the defenders felt rapidly transformed into excitement and deadly purpose as they found a release for their bottled emotions. Yet, even as wave after wave of guild members and mercenaries thundered forward, lifting their blades against the pinned-in-place monster, a susurration of confusion and frustration rose from the ranks of the Mages.

"I can't cast!"

"What's happening to my magic?"

"Healing is broken, just finish them off and have 'em respawn!"

Even Joe could feel how chaotic the ambient mana had become, what with the equivalent of three Master-rank effects causing the air to begin rumbling, the ground to shiver, and the weather to alter in the blink of an eye.

Sunshine became rain, became snow, all melting into steam as it hit the ground. Between the interrupted upgrade of the Pathfinder's hall, his shattered ritual circle, and the Master-rank replica of the same being created by his Haunting Shadows, he could only help by pausing for a moment to add his voice to the mix.

"If your spells are under Journeyman rank, don't even waste your time! Either switch to a weapon, or get out of the way!" The Ritualist could only grimace as perhaps an eighth of the group managed to put together a spell, casting it ineffectively against the side of the abomination fighting to devour them all. Then he was away, his Ritual Orbs orbiting his head as he closed in on Gameover.

"Don't let it eat you while you're still alive!" a hulking Warrior shouted as he brought his blade down to bite deeply into a cabin-sized fist. "But if you're going down a gullet, do your best to make it choke!"

Shields were raised ineffectually against flailing limbs, weapons were flashing back and forth, chopping out chunks of flesh, which regenerated in the next moment. No one wanted to stand too close to anyone else, knowing a single fist could take out entire groups at a time. Joe watched as they closed in, danced away, attacking monsters and allies alike as needed.

It was a final, desperate gamble, but he could only see grim determination on their faces. The fear of true death had lost its hold on them long ago, dozens upon dozens of respawns not only over the course of their life since coming to this world, but in just the last few hours for many of them. At this point, the loss of levels was worth it if they could inflict a wound that wouldn't heal on the beast.

Still, a Legendary monster wasn't something easily defeated. Gameover's countless fists slammed into the ground, sending geysers of dirt, stone, and felled humans into the air, corpses being flung around like discarded dolls. But almost every defender that fell showed up within the next few minutes, once more charging weapon-first at the gargantuan creature.

Truly...? It didn't seem to mind.

The monster responded to their valiant efforts by managing to spear three defenders at once, skewering them like olives on a toothpick and tossing them toward its main mouth, teeth clacking and grinding against each other in preparation of a treat. Nearby allies desperately lurched forward, blades, clubs, and arrows rushing up to meet their friends and grant them a merciful, *temporary* death. Each weapon that struck true denied the beast additional stolen strength, though they could do nothing to stop its endless regeneration.

Joe sent his orbs sailing at the creature at an angle, making sure that they would either pierce all the way through the flesh or bounce off of it—he wasn't ready to risk losing any of his gear this early in close range combat. He jumped, twisted, and distracted, sending Dark Chain Lightning to bounce between its body and its limbs, much to his delight. Yet, as one of the few spellcasters able to *use* his magic, let alone inflict any form of serious damage, he quickly gained more attention from the creature than he was happy to have.

Gameover didn't appear to have any eyes, yet its head lashed around to track Joe perfectly, a few of its larger arms lifting high and swinging down with all the force of an avalanche focused into a single point. The Ritualist spun and shoved off the ground, barely ahead of the wave of earth and stone that raced after him from the point of impact. Even before he landed, another arm was coming down, following his path perfectly.

Joe pushed back and away, hoping to throw the monster off, but instead found himself trapped between the two arms as a third whistled toward him from on high. Bracing himself, he prepared to take the hit, only for a single man to surge forward, leaping into the air and directly grasping the fist as it came down.

Taking the chance for what it was, Joe leapt away, barely escaping the other arms before they clapped together and released a concussive shockwave. Glancing over his shoulder, he was startled to see that the man who had saved him was still holding on to the fist, caught in a tug of war as the monster attempted to yank its limb free. The barrel-chested Barbarian clad in a too-tight leather vest and Daisy Duke short-shorts wasn't someone he'd yet met, but Joe made a mental note to thank him when he got the chance.

"Should have stayed in your own *lane*, worm!" The man was bellowing dramatically as he yanked back and forth on the grotesquely muscular arm. Another hand grabbed at him, and Joe winced as it closed in, expecting the man to be crushed instantly.

Instead, to his astonishment and bewilderment, the Barbarian dug his feet into the dirt and braced himself, flexing hard enough that veins popped out across his body, his lats swelling as he twisted his torso and seemingly impossibly *ripped* the arm out of its socket, barely managing to escape the razor-tipped claws of the second hand swiping at him.

The torn-off limb was grabbed and pulled to Gameover's mouth, gobbled up just as happily as any other wayward biological material.

"That's what's *up*! No one crosses the Double White Line!" The huge man struck a pose, flexing 'intimidatingly' at the eyeless monster as Joe's jaw dropped.

"Did that guy just arm wrestle a Legendary monster… and

win?" He hit the ground with his left foot, swirling his right out and around him in a half circle to bleed off his momentum. "Seriously, who was that?"

"That's a freelance mercenary, goes by 'Double White Line'." Joe glanced at the familiar voice, startled beyond belief to see Mr. Johnson, the bureaucrat in charge of the town, casually strolling toward the melee. "Frankly, it appears that, when we hired him, we may have low-balled him a bit. I wasn't expecting his particular blend of combat to be quite as… effective as it's turning out to be."

"Why are you out here?" Joe blurted out the question, cursing internally at how he kept letting his mouth run away with his good sense. "That is… I don't think this is a safe location for someone like yourself."

"Yes, well." Mr. Johnson held up an oversized briefcase. "We've decided to take a more active role in this battle, now that a good chunk of our investment expenses will be covered. You see, everyone was informed they would be paid for their services based on their contribution, weighted by their level. Since the vast majority of those assisting with combat today have lost several levels at the minimum, and our Guild members are paid exclusively with contribution points, our total necessary payout will have dropped significantly."

"Not to mention those who will fail to collect either from having fled combat or being eaten," another voice chimed in, and Mr. Johnson nodded at a man who could've been his twin, had their facial features been *slightly* more similar.

"An astute point, Mr. Banks." Before Joe could grab them by their collars and feed them directly to the monster out of sheer desire to make the world a better place, Mr. Johnson lifted his oversized suitcase and began undoing the latches. "Anyway, I've been authorized to empty the majority of our on-world coffers in an attempt to ensure our survival."

"Pretty sure that thing has no interest in taking a bribe," Joe stated in a scathing tone, only to be absolutely ignored as the two bureaucrats grabbed a handle on either side of the brief-case and pulled to hold it tight between them.

"Mr. Banks, your authorization for accessing the treasury?" Mr. Johnson inserted a key on his side of the case.

"Authorization granted, Mr. Johnson." A second key was fitted on the other side. "Time to solve this problem like we used to in the old days..."

"Throw money at it." As the words left Mr. Johnson's mouth, the case popped open, and coins of all denominations, silver, copper, gold, and even a *platinum* or two launched out of the open case, glowing like shooting stars as they crossed the distance and sank into the rubbery flesh of the monster. "Mr. Joe... currently we're paying a premium price to create an effect known as 'shred' damage. It's not going to halt its regener-ation, but it'll force it to expend double the resources for it to recover. Do with this what you will."

Joe glanced at the monster again, just in time to see 'Double White Line' uppercut a fist coming down at him, causing a shock wave to ripple out and stop the fist dead, even as the Barbarian was driven a few inches into the dirt. "Yeah... between the mercenaries you hired and what you're doing, we might actually be able to make this work."

Running toward the gargantuan worm, Joe passed a group of men who looked extremely similar. Doing a double take, he realized they actually were all the exact same person—and he recognized them. "Conrad?"

"You know it!" all of the men shouted in unison. "Time for some foolhardy bro-vado! Can't let that guy show us up."

"Did you get everyone out before the ritual went live?" For some reason, Joe's question caused the man to grimace. "Oh. Well, at least it makes sense why you're out here on your own."

"I'm not on my own, I've got myself!" The squad of the same man high-fived himself, and Joe decided he needed to be done with the conversation before he got a headache.

Launching himself upward, he sent out a stream of black lightning, noting with a deep, grim pleasure that the flesh where his spell struck remained charred and weeping. Swirling his hands, Joe spun up a half-dozen ritual circles at the Apprentice rank, activating them as he fell through the air, leaving a trail of glowing circles dropping bolts of wind and oddly enough, shards of stone from above to impact the top of the monster.

As he was coming down, readying himself to start dodging grasping hands, the Ritualist instead found himself flying away backward as an explosion of confetti appeared in front of him, followed by a heavy hammer blow to his chest.

Joe spun through the air without a bit of control, the first time he'd been so helpless in the air since he had first achieved Aerial Acrobatics as a skill. Hitting the ground hard, he bounced and skid, adding to the light haze of dust in the air as he pushed himself heavily off the ground.

Taking a deep breath, he barely had half a moment to regain his footing before finding himself surrounded on all sides by a ring of dancing Jesters. Their painted masks smiled at him, even as their long daggers caught the intermittent sunlight and twinkled ominously at him. The Battle Scholar dropped from the sky, slamming his fist into the ground and shoving himself upright into an aggressive combat position.

"Oh look, those bridges I said I'd cross when I came to 'em." Joe lifted his hands, ritual orbs zipping around his body as he prepared to fight both the scholar and the jesters at the same time. "Lindon, you and your clown show *really* know how to show up at the worst possible moment."

An inscription tool appeared in each of the Ritualist's hands, and he snapped a trio of ritual diagrams into the air around him in an instant, duplicating them with a swipe of his hand and activating all six close at enough to the same time that it looked simultaneous.

Stone and compressed air ripped out and away from him, interrupting the Jesters and causing the tingle of magic that had been building up around him to dissipate. Two of them hissed in pain as fragments embedded themselves in their limbs, but the majority of them simply shifted their movement pattern, accounting for targeted magic and easily avoiding the next attacks.

The familiar buzz of mana being structured returned, though it was growing at a far slower pace now that they couldn't perfectly perform their routine. Lindon started circling Joe as well, though it was slower, more calculating. "You're an outlier, Joe. Where you go, chaos follows. It's no wonder that an *Occultist* such as yourself-"

"If a single person showing up causes an entire world to start falling apart, maybe things had been on their way there long before I ever got there." Flicking the air, Joe sent a burst of stone shards rocketing at the Scholar, who batted them away contemptuously. "Besides, I'm *not* an Occultist anymore. You know what? Here you are, blaming *me* for causing chaos, yet who was it that figured out how to put that monster into play? It certainly wasn't *me*. Last time I saw Gameover, I was burying it in a hole so deep I thought it would never see the light of day again."

"Just like *us*, yes?" This voice belonged to one of the Jesters, who each sounded identical... or at least we're supposed to. Yet, for some reason, Joe immediately recognized this man as the one who had bought a Creeping Death Squirrel from him so long ago, in return for his best liquid friend, Mate. "You left us with a misfiring transportation enchantment, which you bathed in acid and left to detonate. Our arena was razed, and our businesses and business partners were all but destroyed."

"Yet here you are." Joe began cautiously turning as well, trying to keep both of his enemies in view as they circled around him. "Not just surviving but causing problems all over again. How *did* you get out of there?"

"We enlisted the help of a society of mole people to dig us out-"

"Really?"

"*No*, you fool!" The Jester darted forward, blade flashing as he aimed for Joe's neck.

The Ritualist ducked the wild swipe, pivoting on a foot and

lashing out with a kick that the Jester blocked with both his arms—nothing less than a terrible idea. Even without a particular skill for kicking or any kind of hand-to-hand combat, Joe still had immense Characteristics. That simple kick sent the Jester flying, though he managed a far more agile and acrobatic landing than the Ritualist had managed.

As soon as Joe was off balance, Lindon stepped in with a heavy haymaker—the blow displacing air as the bald man jumped back and away. Following up with an Omnivault that sent him up and out of the encirclement, the Ritualist grimaced as the Jesters moved along with him.

Immediately, the tingling magic ramped up, and Joe was forced to jump away yet again, this time generating Rituals of Elemental Burst to disrupt their formations. Since they tried to continue with their previous pattern of merely dodging around the attacks, Joe stacked six of the rituals next to each other, two columns, three rows, creating an impassable wall of stone and wind.

Or, at least he *thought* it would be impassable. Seeing that they couldn't avoid the damage, they simply took the hits, moving faster through that space to minimize their injury. Grunting in displeasure, Joe pointed at one of them with his right index finger, his thumb straight upward, then dropped it as though firing a gun and blasting the Jesters with a stream of Dark Chain Lightning.

Black electricity jumped between them in a wide loop, ending *behind* Joe. While they faltered for a moment, they resumed moving, now frantically. "Can't take too many more of those, huh? *Good to know!*"

Using his other hand, as both had their own individual cooldown for the spell, Joe tried to zap them again, but Lindon appeared out of a shower of paper and caught the spell with a flying pen attached to a chain. The magical lightning trailed along the chain as Lindon tossed the other end to the ground like a dart, causing the spell to fizzle out as it ineffectually sank into the earth.

"Well, that was neat; how many times can you do it?" Joe swung his arm to the right, launching another spell as soon as it came off cooldown. This time it landed true, and the ring of Jesters near-simultaneously groaned in pain.

Yet the Ritualist couldn't celebrate too early, as a dagger appeared in front of him, held by an outstretched hand, then yanked backward, driving into his stomach as the Jester appeared behind him, holding him close and pulling the dagger as hard as he could.

The tip of the blade *screamed* as it grated against Joe's Exquisite Shell, and the bald man thrashed back and forth, trying to escape the combination grapple-and-stab. But no matter how he moved, the Jester mirrored his movements, putting his full effort into penetrating Joe's shell. Finally, he was successful, and the magical defense shattered into sparkling motes of light…

…allowing the blade to punch through Joe's gut.

As his health began plummeting, the Ritualist directed one of his orbs around himself, *cracking* it into the side of the Jester's head and shattering a portion of his mask. His assailant flailed away, leaving the dagger behind, twisted at a sharp angle from where it had entered. Gritting his teeth, Joe yanked it out but kept a firm grip on the long blade.

"*Abyss*, that hurts! That's… not cool. I didn't need a second belly button." The Ritualist glanced down, watching as his Neutrality Aura began working to seal the damage. Half-vomiting a mouthful of blood, he wiped at his mouth and allowed a dangerous smirk to tug at his lips.

"But I guess there's nothing wrong with having a naval reserve."

CHAPTER FORTY-FIVE

"Making jokes at a time like this, when your life hangs in the balance, is the mark of an *unwell* mind." Lindon stepped forward and threw punches in a rapid one-two motion. "You need to be put down... for the good of the world!"

"Humor's the only way I know how to bleed gracefully." Joe pressed a Lay on Hands into his gut, washing away the wound with a splash of water. He took a deep breath now that pain wasn't restricting him, ducking and weaving under the assault. "Good to know getting stabbed *never* gets more fun."

As he went low, Joe set his Ritual Orb of Intelligence to spinning, launching it up as he pushed back—fully intent on driving the weapon through the Battle Scholar so *he* could get a taste of perforated bowels. Instead, his opponent neatly side-stepped, somehow able to near-perfectly predict the trajectory of the weapon.

"I was chosen to hunt you down, as I am not someone you can defeat." Lindon spoke as coldly and methodically as he had ever done with Joe. "Your weapons rely on physics outside of your control, and angles are where I excel."

"I excel on spreadsheets." Joe slapped at a fist, pushing it out of the way just before it would have crunched into his nose. He followed up with a lightning bolt to the face, which the Scholar avoided… which was perfect, as he was never the target. Once more, Dark Chain Lightning circled the Jesters working to create a magical effect, and this time, they didn't recover anywhere near as quickly.

As they frantically resumed their dance, it became clear they were on their last legs, but it was just as obvious that whatever they were doing had almost been completed.

Another dagger snaked in from the side, but this time Joe Omnivaulted *toward* the Assassin, slamming his shoulder into the Jester's torso and sending both of them sprawling. As they both rolled, Joe released a point-blank Dark Chain Lightning into the nominal leader of the Zoo's Assassins, which bounced up and into those circling them.

One after another, the dancing Assassins dropped, bodies bursting like sausages left in the microwave for too long. Joe took a deep, ragged breath as he got back to his feet, nodding at the seething Jester—specifically at his ribs, where he had planted the dagger. "Thought I'd give that back to you since you were so kind to loan it to me. I tried to stick it where you stabbed me, but I guess I'm just not as good at navel gazing as you are."

A fist landed on the back of his head, and Joe stumbled forward, too dazed to react as Lindon followed up the strike with another tossed pen. It sank into the meaty portion of his trapezius muscle, and the Ritualist gasped in agony as the tip opened up, three hooks popping into the meat to ensure he couldn't simply yank it out. The back of the pen had a thin chain extending from it, which The Battle Scholar yanked on to pull Joe close.

Then another strike hit Joe in the cheekbone, breaking it as the enchanted gauntlet the man was wearing flattened the side of the Ritualist's face. Immediately, Joe's left eye swelled shut, and he tasted copper and iron as his mouth filled with blood. Two more points of agony flared as the Jester rushed forward and brutally slashed the Achilles tendon on each leg, dropping the Ritualist to the ground as he was unable to hold himself upright any longer.

Almost instinctively, Dark Chain Lightning flashed from his finger... only to wrap around and sink into the chain connecting his shoulder to the Scholar. Both of them grunted in pain, but Joe noticed with great alarm that his health didn't drop any further.

"Life tether is set," Lindon stated around clenched teeth. "If he tries to cast again, cut his hands off."

"Let's get him to the beast; I'm holding the formation steady." The Jester pulled on Joe's robe, lifting him half off the ground, then surprised him by slamming the pommel of his dagger into his nose with a half-twist. The world went dark and red for a moment as agony flared, then he hit the ground again as Lindon shoved the Jester away.

"*I'm* taking his health damage; knock that off! You're just breaking him for petty vengeance. Do it again, and our alliance is over." Lindon snarled viciously, the first time Joe had heard him speak in such a tone. "It's *over*. All we need to do is feed him to the creature, and we've succeeded in our goal. Don't let your overabundant emotions control you in the eleventh hour! Now, give me the health potions you brought for yourself; I have no intention of dying for the sake of this mission."

Joe struggled weakly, the taste of dust and blood coating his tongue as he was dragged like a rag doll across the churned battlefield. He wasn't even given the courtesy of being pulled by a limb, instead Lindon had wrapped his end of the chain around his own wrist and was pulling him along by the tiny harpoon lodged deep in the Ritualist's muscle.

The Jester remained where Joe could see him at all times, weaving erratically back and forth like a snake as he obviously struggled to hold himself back from sinking his knives into Joe's unprotected body.

The Ritualist reached out to grab at a protruding root, all that remained of whatever tree had been growing there, only for the Assassin to see his opportunity and chop down with a brutal overhead strike, removing Joe's hand at the wrist. Lindon howled with pain as the health damage was transferred to him, yet the Ritualist was the one left staring at his new stump in horror.

"*What did I say?*" Lindon roared at the Jester, who was merrily laughing and bouncing back and forth in place at the expression of dread etched on Joe's face. "This alliance-"

"Don't be too hasty!" the Jester cut him off with a sing-song tone. "I'm the last linchpin of the formation; get rid of me, and it's only *you and him* they'll see!"

Through the pain and swelling, a strange lucidity clung to Joe—the throbbing injuries in his skull, ankles, and arm oddly distant. He was able to think clearly, even though he should have been delirious from the concussion and blood loss. Yet it was only at the Jester's words that he realized how strange it was that no one had been coming to his aid.

He was being pulled into the thick of the fighting, his guild members lurching around as enormous arms came down, and teeth dozens of feet long gnashed not anywhere *close* to being far enough away. Even so, they passed through all of it as though they were ghosts, the determined eyes of the combatants sliding over them. To his dismay, though they were being constantly reinforced, it was clear fewer people were on the battlefield. Despite their best efforts, large masses of people must have been mercilessly shoved into the endlessly hungry *cavern* of a mouth Gameover sported.

Mustering his strength, Joe used his other hand to zap the Jester with a bolt of lightning, which bounced back to Lindon, then himself once more. All three of them grunted in pain, though before Joe could act on their momentary distraction, he felt a savage bite of pain as the blade flashed out once more, his other hand removed at the wrist.

"Hard to cast without *feen~gers*." The Jester drew out the word unnaturally, taunting him in a half-mad display. A manic smile showed through the mask where it had been broken earlier. "I may not be able to have the satisfaction of killing you myself, but I can butcher you down to manageable bites!"

"Try it again, and I'm wrapping the chain around *your* wrist." Lindon stepped forward and planted an open palm on the Jester's face, shoving him away from Joe. "We are all but *done!*"

The Scholar stumbled forward as a ritual orb *thunked* off the back of his head, and he whirled around to glare at Joe, just in time to avoid a far more deadly swipe from the Ritual Orb of Strength. The Jester jumped forward, grabbing the robes wrapped around Joe's knees, and hoisted him in the air.

Between the two of them, they hauled Joe across the last bit of distance, even as the Ritual Orbs Joe was controlling with his mind ricocheted violently off their heads, armor, bouncing between limbs as the Ritualist tossed everything he could at them.

His Ritual Orbs whirled through the air, a chaotic swarm of minor strikes. Most of the weapons were too low in rank to faze the two elites; their defenses barely registered the impacts. Only one gave them pause: the Ritual Orb of Intelligence. That one they respected, as its penetrating power cut deeper than they cared to risk. Each time it zipped past, both men tensed and expertly avoided the blow.

From the corner of his good eye, Joe saw dozens of people fighting. But the small sliver of attention he could spare latched onto Conrad as he, for some bizarre reason, was no longer fighting the monster. Instead, his clones had vanished, and he was frantically grappling with an oversized pheasant as it flapped its wings and pecked at him. The last Joe saw of the Accursed Summoner was the bird jumping at him with its talons lashing out while feathers scattered everywhere.

Now, all too close to the Legendary monster, Joe found himself being dragged through thick, sludgy mud. The churned earth had mixed with the endless fount of blood pouring out of the abomination, the caustic, mutating properties having an aberrant effect on what little life remained. Small bugs had tiny arms growing out of them, crushed weeds were tipped with deadly points, dripping poison or staring at him through unnatural eyes that had grown on their stalks.

A fresh shower of blood washed over the trio as Double White Line, bulging with muscles nearly as grotesque as the monster he was fighting against, succeeded in another all or nothing arm wrestling match.

"Feel free to *tap* out whenever you are ready to give up!" Double White Line howled at the sky as he hoisted the limb in the air, swinging it around to punch Gameover with its own limp fist. "I'll try to end you painlessly!"

"Celestial *feces*, they're actually going to slay this beast!" Lindon's voice was filled with incredulity. "We must hurry!"

"Should I go... intervene?" The Jester scraped his blades across each other suggestively. "Wouldn't want them to make all of our work be for naught!"

"No, of course not," Linden snapped at his contemporary. "Why must I be the only one who *thinks* through the possible consequences? All of our control methods have been spent, our Beast Master slain, and our resources and investors are gone. Let the creature devour him, then die immediately after. It solves two of our problems at once."

"Why snap two necks with two motions, when snapping two necks with one motion will do?" The Jester bobbed his head in agreement, then uncorked a bottle and upended its foul contents on Joe, seeming to delight in trying to practically drown him as the Ritualist coughed and sputtered, shaking his head back and forth to try and avoid the flow. "Well, any moment now, the blood essence will attract its notice. I suggest we cut and run."

A sudden rush of putrid air swept over them as Gameover's bulbous head lifted into the air suddenly then swung to face them. Crazed laughter spilled through the gap in the mask. "Effective, isn't it? A sentient storm actively blowing all scents away, tiny irritants chopping into its flesh, yet a *whiff* of its favorite snack gathers its attention."

"I can't untether him just yet; you've done too much damage," Lindon declared after a moment of hesitation. "He'll die as soon as the chain is retracted."

"Sucks to be you!" Acting with sadistic glee, the masked Assassin drove both of his daggers down, piercing through Joe's knees and pinning him in place. "*Buh*-bye now!"

"Foul *caricature* of a-" Lindon shouted after the Jester as the Assassin ran away, slipping into the mass of combatants and vanishing in an instant. "Had I not already planned for him to cut and run, I would be *quite* upset."

"Yowu cooullled juzzt-" Joe tried to bargain with the Scholar, only for the man to glance at him uncomprehendingly and uncaringly.

"Save your words." Lindon shook his head gravely. "Your life's tenure is officially revoked, and I am merely adjudicating and observing the outcome."

The Scholar stepped back, then farther away as Gameover's enormous head swung into position above the pinned Ritualist and sucked in a long breath, seeming to savor the scent of whatever disgusting mixture had been liberally poured over him. Joe's mind raced as he tried to think of any way out of this, any possible escape from this terrible fate.

A long tongue flicked out of Gameover's mouth, and he noted with a surprising lack of interest that it was tipped with yet another knotted fist. A pair of arms dropped out of the sky, landing on either side of Joe, half a dozen feet away but still close enough to send him bouncing into the air. The blades pinning him in place were torn out of the ground by the concussive force.

The monster leaned on one of his arms, the other lifting off the ground slightly and almost gently swinging over to Joe. They closed around and pinched the man off the ground, then up, and up...

As the mouth got closer, and he passed the first set of over-sized teeth, a conversation Joe had recently had played through his mind: Hannah shouting at him, defying him by declaring that sometimes the ends justified the means, that she was willing to be considered a villain if it meant surviving to live the life she wanted to live.

"Not gonna… go out like this!" Lifting his stumpy right arm, Joe decided to simply accept whatever consequences he was about to earn for himself. He inexpertly slammed the limb into his chest, pressing the button over his sternum and removing his limiter.

Immediately, his mind began clearing further. His stamina pool deepened, renewing his energy, and his mana pool flared as ambient energy rushed into him. "Lay on Hands!"

Nothing happened, and Joe felt an instant of panic as he realized he might actually *need* hands to cast that particular spell. Gritting his teeth, he circulated his mana and forced it into the long-since-familiar pattern, then unleashed the budding spell.

"Lay on *Stumps!*"

Water burst from the end of his wrists, stopping and collecting as a pair of watery hands that rapidly shifted into bone, cartilage, tendons, and finally skin. Immediately reaching down with his thankfully working fingers, he yanked the Assassin's blades out of his knees and slammed them into the fingers holding him in place.

The digits shivered slightly in surprised pain, then tried to toss him in. But Joe managed to force the blades deeper, maintaining his grip on the handles, thanks to his massively inflated Strength. His leg wounds were closing fast, sealing over even as he writhed. No longer bound by the Mortal limit, his every movement sent shockwaves tearing through the confined space, rebounding violently off the inside of the monster's body.

Unable to release its treat, Gameover pulled its fingers out and tried to squash him on the ground, but the Ritualist managed to get his feet under him and braced, matching the monster's force and enduring its immense strength as it tried to turn him into a Joe-flavored pancake.

Wanting its snack, yet unable to either let go of or crush it,

Gameover reversed course and pulled the bald man back into its endless row of recursive mouths. As they got past the first set, the enormous teeth slammed down. The monster bit directly through its own fingers and left Joe flailing in place as hundreds of mouths snapped at him, small arms forming and bursting through the surface of its gums to reach for him.

"Whatever it takes to survive," Joe whispered hoarsely, feeling the sharp burn of pain as the chain in his shoulder was pulled tight. "He has to know I'm not taking damage yet... which means he's still connected!"

Bitter resignation flowed through him as he raised his new hands and prepared himself to turn the world against him. Already, the system was screaming warnings at him, vivid red text filling his vision.

Alert! Alert! You have disabled your personal limiter. Continued actions may mark you as an enemy of Midgard. The countdown to being considered as a Raid Boss has begun.

"Yeah... if you didn't like that, you're *really* not going to like this." Joe stumbled as Gameover's fist-tipped tongue punched him in the face, sending him reeling back toward a waiting set of grinding teeth. Letting loose a primal, some might say *unhinged* roar, Joe pulled out the only thing he had in his inventory that might be able to deal serious damage to the creature trying to swallow him.

Raw Legendary aspects.

As soon as the flaming motes of energy were out of his storage, the system absolutely *lost it* at him. Joe knew what it was going to tell him, that he couldn't use aspects in this way, that by even *attempting* to do so, *he* would be the one to take the damage instead.

Exactly as intended.

Immediately, Joe felt a wave of all-consuming agony as every part of his body was suffused with fire, dealing *true damage* throughout his system. But instead of stopping, he pulled out more, the intense orange glow of the aspects lighting up the mouth and revealing the entirety of the horror waiting for him.

Uncaring of the damage, the mouths bit at him, the arms grabbed, and slowly, ever so slowly, the monster lit itself on fire.

Long past the point where he should have been destroyed, Joe continued releasing aspects, sprinkling them across the ground where the mouths happily bit into and swallowed whatever energy source it could find. "That's right! Eat it up, you disgusting worm... did you know that a gram of uranium has twenty billion calories? Doesn't mean I could eat it and never be hungry again. I'd just be full for the *rest of my life!*"

Even as he burned, Joe realized he was dying too slowly. Somehow, Lindon was managing to keep himself alive through the immense damage Joe was certain he was doing to both of them, and Gameover wasn't being cut down fast enough that Joe couldn't guarantee he would either die of the natural causes of violence *or* escape from the boss monster. "What *else?*"

The Ritualist roared in pain and frustration as a chunk of his leg was ripped off and sucked down by a small mouth he hadn't noticed, one he was certain had *just* manifested so it could bite at him. "What else have I been warned against?"

A thought appeared in his head, so clear that he was certain it had been inserted there by an outside source. Without thinking, Joe activated the ritual that suffused his body, which had been placed there by the system upon his specialization. As the Ritual of Reduction spun up, and the biological ritual he was filled with made itself known as dense black lines glowing under his skin, the Ritualist looked inward and activated Essence Cycle...

...peering into the depths of his body and reading as much of the Sage-ranked ritual he was meant to never so much as glance at.

Five seconds. His arms were gone.

Eight seconds. His legs had been removed all the way to the pelvis.

Ten seconds. If Joe had been able to look away, he would have seen a mouth beginning to close around his neck, the teeth almost breaking the skin.

Eleven-

-Joe's refilled mana pool, able to contain enough power that he had earned a *title* for it, ruptured at that moment. Over twelve thousand points of mana burst out of him as a sphere of raw, unfiltered power. His body disintegrated, starting in his solar plexus and eating away his flesh, bursting outward so violently in the contained space of Gameover's closed mouth that he forced the mutated flesh out and away. The power finally even tossed the Legendary monster's jaws wide open then broke them, its lower left mandible ripping off fully as its attempts at containment failed.

Finally, *finally*, Joe watched entirely with his mana sense, his eyes having long since burned away, as the chain keeping him tethered to Lindon did its job and killed both of them at the same time.

CHAPTER FORTY-SIX

Joe blinked, surprised he had eyelids at all, and glanced around the familiar room, which was absolutely bursting with people doing their very best to get outside.

"I'm in the temple of the Pathfinder's Hall?" Very carefully, Joe reached into his inventory and found his limiter, snapping it back in place and letting out a sigh of relief as the needles bit into his skin, dropping his senses down to a more reasonable mortal level, binding his limbs, and generally weakening him.

Immediately, the notifications from the system stopped flashing *as* angrily, though he was certain there were going to be severe consequences for his actions. "I did it…? I lived?"

As Joe's reaction time came more in line with the rest of the world, a shout ringing through the area perked up his ears and made him get moving. "Stop standing around and get going! Fight's not over yet!"

Slapping Tatum's altar as he passed, Joe winced in concern as yet another notification began blinking in the corner of his vision. "It'll be a bit, buddy! Still got work to do."

Joining the surging crowd, he pressed forward, trying to get through the bottleneck that was the doorway. Precious seconds passed as he propelled himself forward, debating on the wisdom of simply Omnivaulting over the crowd and trying to slip through. Just as he managed to burst through the entrance, he staggered to a halt as a deafening wall of sound reached him: warriors, mages, guild members, and mercenaries alike shouting in triumph and pumping their fists or weapons into the sky.

On the heels of the wave of noise, yet another notification popped into the queue. Happily, this one simply appeared in front of him, not requiring him to open his status and deal with the deluge that was certainly waiting for him.

Congratulations! The Legendary monster, Gameover, has been defeated!

Even more notifications began piling in on top of that, yet Joe kept moving, ignoring them even as his jaw clenched.

Burble! Mate joined in on the cheering, though Joe wasn't entirely certain if the elemental understood what was going on. Reaching down, he swirled his hand over the top of the cup, enjoying the steam that rolled onto his skin. **Hmm? Burble?**

"No, I'm happy it's over. It's just, if I'm being honest with myself..." Joe exhaled slowly, then bounded to the top of the building and began rushing toward the edge of town. "I'm somewhere between relief and irritation? I feel like I deserved to strike the final blow, but it didn't happen for at least five minutes after I died. I'm happy people aren't being eaten, so there's that."

Launching himself in the air, he spun in place and took a look at the extremely damaged town. Nearly half the wall surrounding the place had collapsed, there wasn't a *single* souvenir shop that had even survived the priming of his Master-rank ritual—perhaps not a *terrible* loss—and almost everything had at least minor damage from debris falling on it. Still, even with all there was to see, it was the Town Hall shining like a beacon that caught his attention.

Congratulations on passing the trial! The Town of Towny McTown-face is upgrading into a Sect Territory! As this is a momentous occasion, according to the guild charter, every member has been given the option to suggest and vote on a new name for the burgeoning Sect Territory.

Congratulations! The Noble Wanderer's Guild has passed its trial and has created its initial foundation on Midgard.

The Guild has become a Sect! All Elders of the Sect, as well as the Sect leader, have one year to determine the core mission of the Sect, or it will revert to 'Guild' status. The core mission will determine who is allowed to join the Sect in the future, as well as the requirements for doing so.

There must be a clear path for progression for all members, or the outliers must be removed.

Additional notifications appeared yet again, though these ones were automatically added to the list he needed to read over. Frankly, Joe was starting to feel nervous about how long he would need to spend staring glassy-eyed into the distance when he opened them... and so decided to keep putting it off for now. "Got to get out there and claim some of that Legendary monster. Burned through a whole lot of my Legendary aspects, and I'd rather directly refill-"

As he landed atop the remnants of the gatehouse, then launched himself forward once more, he found himself stunned into silence as he took in the beautiful day and how it clashed against the utter chaos of the battlefield.

First came the sensations, ambient mana whipping around him, collecting on his skin, trying to push him into the ground or crush him like a soda can. It was a violent tempest, nearly overwhelming, but terrifyingly familiar—this was exactly how he had felt on Alfenheim when he first arrived. The mana was potent, and condensing ever so slightly more densely each second. Everywhere he looked, weaker members of the guild— no, the *sect*—were struggling even to breathe.

Even worse was that Gameover was still twisting and writhing, arms lifting and slapping down, teeth gnashing, and in general looking as though it was very much still alive. Joe sucked in a sharp breath, preparing himself to fight, only to notice with great irritation that only three of his Ritual Orbs were still on his person—those bound to his Characteristics and therefore designed to be auto-returning. Before he could launch his initial attack, there was a tremendous...

Squelch.

The mammoth body of the monster contracted sharply, the arms going rigid, many teeth clenching so hard that they broke. After a moment, the sound repeated itself, and the body shifted, condensing even further, and the process began to rapidly speed up. The third time, the body jerked inward, then a horrendous sucking sound filled the area.

"Ugh, it sounds like someone's drinking jello through a straw."

Joe wasn't certain who said that, but as soon as the words entered his ears, he couldn't hear whatever was happening as anything else.

Gameover's skin ripped in dozens of massive lacerations, blood fountaining into the air as its flesh was *crushed* inward once more. It began shifting along the ground, slowly rotating in place and collapsing inward further and further. Joe watched in horrified amazement as huge chunks of the Beast were sloughed off, a lake of highly mutagenic blood pumped out into the surroundings, and the main portion of the body collapsed inward... ending with an enormous *clang*.

In the next moment, Joe landed next to the massive cauldron that had just hit the ground, surreptitiously scooping up the brilliant orange core that had landed next to it and storing it away in his codpiece.

"*Mister* Joe!" A familiar voice rang out as Mr. Johnson rushed over, Mr. Banks huffing and puffing along beside him. "I'll have you know that any spoils of war are the guild's by right, and whatever this *thing* is needs to be brought to the treasury this *instant* so it can be properly appraised."

Instead of denying them, Joe instead deflected by raising an eyebrow and looking at them curiously. "How is it that the two of you are able to function so well right now? Aren't you slowly being crushed by the chaotic mana?"

"I'll have you know we are the strongest members of the guild still on Midgard... besides yourself, of course." Mr. Banks puffed himself up, putting on a good show of being upset.

"Why, the sheer amount of coin I've spent on safaris and expeditions into tombs, or raiding sacred caches to make sure I reached the Characteristic cap *alone* would have beggared a lesser man!"

"How nice for you." Joe tried not to feel too nauseated at those words, instead turning back to the enormous cauldron, just barely shorter than he was, and cautiously reached out to place a single finger against it. "Anyway, I'm going to go ahead and figure out a way to hide this thing from everyone. Forever."

Item found? Cauldron of Avarice. This... item... is indestructible.

It cannot be removed from Midgard for any reason, by any method.

What goes in can never come out.

When it has absorbed one billion points of mana, the Unique monster 'Gameover' will be randomly respawned somewhere on Midgard, with this Item acting as a secondary core. Caution, this cauldron automatically collects ambient mana.

The item description was enough for him to want to keep it away from most people, but the next section was what made him sure it needed to be hidden even from his own sect.

Rewards can be obtained from the Cauldron of Avarice by supplying it with mana or mana-drenched items. Reward table for mana donated:

1: Blessing of the Burning Mind.

100: Random Uncommon Trinket

1,000: Random Apprentice-rank ingredients or crafting materials.

10,000: Rare class-specific Enchanted item. This can be a weapon, armor, or utility.

100,000: Random Unique-rank item guaranteed to be useful to the recipient.

The reward table continued increasing by a factor of ten, but it was the final reward that made even Joe falter and need to remind himself that this situation would repeat itself, should he help the process along. Not to mention, the next time he might not be around to help put the creature in the ground.

100,000,000: Mythic-ranked Core.

All rewards are able to be earned multiple times.

"Even if I wanted to go after that Mythic core, that'd mean

I gain one hundred million stacks of the 'blessing' of the Burning Mind." Joe shivered at the thought, remembering the cult leader who had infected so many people and wondering if perhaps this was how he had gained his bizarre, hypnotic power in the first place.

"What do you mean you're *taking* it?" Mr. Banks huffed self-righteously. "This belongs to the guild! On whose *authority-*"

"You're speaking to the First Elder of the sect." Mr. Johnson showed a surprising amount of awareness as he elbowed his peer in the gut, sending the man an intense stare to get him to back down. "Show proper deference. Besides, I'm sure he'll properly compensate us for the loss."

"I sure *won't*," Joe countered immediately, refusing to be bound to pay them for this even implicitly. "This item is cursed. Terribly, *terribly* cursed. I'm going to go figure out how to design a room that doesn't allow any ambient mana in, then seal this thing behind as many layers of defenses as I possibly can. Now, excuse me... I have to find something."

Joe tried to store the cauldron away, but for the first time ever, was unable to move a mobile item into his spatial storage. Frowning in thought, he turned away and began searching the battlefield, specifically looking for where he had managed to detonate Lindon like a particularly stubborn kernel of popcorn.

The spot wasn't hard to find: the area was still burning under the effects of Legendary aspects. As soon as he was convinced the Scholar had truly fallen in battle, Joe set up an Ascendant Matrix and began pulling the heavily degraded flames into his storage.

As he was reducing everything in the cage, soon he started getting random bursts of various-rarity aspects as the remnants of Lindon's body and armor were absorbed. Then, with a terrifying *pop*, some form of storage device was destroyed, and a surge of mana exploded outward, barely missing Joe as it shot into the air.

"Whoops." The Ritualist glanced at where a huge pile of treasure had appeared, only to start vanishing almost immediately. "Well, that stuff probably had protections in place anyway. Better to be safe."

Soon, all that remained of the pile were the things that *couldn't* be reduced—cores. Hoping he was right, Joe collapsed the matrix and walked over, scooping up all that remained of the assault group's resources. "*Yes!*"

The most impressive bounty was *four* Artifact-ranked cores, likely the majority of the war chest the three groups had managed to collect. With his prizes in place, Joe immediately got to work on reducing the multiple tons of shredded monster meat scattered across the battlefield, knowing better than to leave it alone and let someone use it for a nefarious purpose or have it turn something already dangerous into a deadly threat.

When the majority of the toxic mess had been cleaned up, with the rest being gathered using hazmat protocols, he moved to the next most important task: fixing the mana on the world that he *may* have irreparably broken.

Joe shifted the massive cauldron, getting a good grip, and began the slow march toward the half-complete Pathfinder's Hall. With the mass of metal grinding against his arms, and the weight of purpose grounding his steps, he finally let himself breathe. Ready to face the music, he opened the notifications that had been pressing against his mind like impatient whispers.

Warning! Power usage outside the bounds of the Mortal Limit has been detected. You are not wearing an approved power limiter, and your current output far exceeds the accepted zone threshold for Midgard. Due to the scale and intensity of your activity, even after repeated warnings, you have been flagged as a Raid Boss. Should you die while this flag is in place, you will lose experience equivalent to the formation of an Artifact-rank core as a reward to the person who slays you. -25 Karmic Luck.

Please refrain from additional high-tier output, or you risk triggering a World Boss class raid against you.

System notification: retraction. Classification adjustment in effect. After further analysis, your actions are now classified as sanctioned combat activity, as all excess damage is currently being absorbed and contained in its entirety within a Legendary-ranked prepared space. Thank you for carefully exercising within a stability-positive… place.

Raid Boss flag removed.

"Hey! Give me back my Karmic Luck if you're going to retract the rest of the punishment!" The system showed no indication of hearing him, merely bringing up the next notification in the queue.

Caution! Direct contact with aspects has dangerous consequences! Pulling aspects into the open air without proper preparation will result in the at fault party interacting with the aspect to become immolated!

You have removed Legendary-rank aspects from an Aspect Jar! -25 Karmic Luck.

You are on fire! You are taking flame-based True Damage.

Lindon of the Tri-Fold Path is taking your health damage.

Caution! You are attempting to see into the inner workings of Sage-ranked spellwork! Calculating… Intelligence threshold far too low!

You have intentionally ruptured your mana pool! Self-destruction is taboo. -25 Karmic Luck.

Title updated: Monarch of Mana. A monarch is the final person to die in their domain. If you are dead, everyone else who matters has been dead for days.

Effect added: Upon dying for any reason, you will detonate your mana pool, dealing damage per point of remaining mana in a sphere around you. Damage and range of effect are dependent on current total mana.

You have directly contributed to the destabilization of the zone 'Midgard'. If actions are not taken to restabilize the area within 12 hours, the changes will become permanent. The world will know exactly who has caused the instability, as well as the circumstances which made it happen. -50 Karmic Luck.

You have died. Experience lost: 10,500. You are now level 29!

You have contributed greatly to the death of a Legendary monster! Experience gained: 10,500. (12,500 originally, capped by the threshold of level 30. 250,000*contribution, which was calculated at 5% of the monster's total non-regenerated health.)

You are now level 30! Congratulations on your happy return to the level cap.

A mass curse has been broken: Crab Bucket curse. You are now free to leave the territory of the Wanderer's Sect without any ill effect.

The final notification was the most important to Joe, an offer from Tatum that he wasn't sure he should take or not.

Joe, as your people are about to defeat Gameover, I need to tell you that there might be a way to save those people who were eaten. It's risky, but if you want to know more, bring the cauldron to the temple. The sooner you make this happen, the more likely it is to succeed.

"First things first." The Ritualist pushed the notifications and information on his updated skills to the side with a groan. Looking up at the enormous, cracked, glowing egg-like dome that was the Pathfinder's Hall trapped in a failed upgrade cycle.

Pulling out two of his four newly acquired Artifact-rank cores, he pressed them into the side of the building, where they vanished as though he had instead chosen to absorb them for experience points.

The change was immediate.

Above the Pathfinder's Hall, the bright blue sky shifted, darkening in color not from clouds, but from an immense compression of mana. Joe watched, uncertain whether the stars twinkling in broad daylight were real or some side effect of his exhaustion. He could have sworn that he was staring through a hole in the sky, one that looked out into the black silence of space. Then the shell of the egg-shaped structure began to condense, dragging his attention back to the surface.

It was only after a long moment that he realized the Hall wasn't collapsing, breaking, nor simply *hatching* into a new form.

Huge plates of stone and metal swung inward, a soft grinding sound compared to the jarring slams that Joe associated with a building being torn down. Excess fragments dissolved into shining light and were pulled deeper into the still glowing dome hiding what was happening within. Spell circles and sigils appeared midair, fading in and out of visibility as the system wrote new laws into the space.

The rest of the upgrade happened in a rush, with the

building seeming to implode in on itself, leaving behind... a ruin?

Joe shook his head, reorienting his perspective as he looked at the singular, monumental archway which stood in place where the immense Pathfinder's Hall had once stood. The temple built into the overall design had condensed, now looking to be nothing more than a small addition built on the left hand side of the archway—though he understood it had also likely been altered in some way as well.

Dozens of people suddenly appeared out of nowhere, falling to the ground with startled exclamations, and Joe hurried to help Boris to his feet as the old man looked at him. "Joe? What in the world just happened? I was in the hall with all of the other non-combatants, then the building just... threw us out! What kind of hospitality is this?"

Before answering, the Ritualist let loose a breath of relief as the ambient mana of the world stopped trembling quite as violently. Checking his warnings, he found that the 'Master-rank usage meter' had dropped from five to four—meaning the world would now be able to recover on its own, given enough time, even if he didn't lift another finger to help.

A wide smile on his face, Joe simply raised an eyebrow and gestured at the archway, feeling a moment of smug satisfaction. The Scholar's jaw dropped as he studied the polished black marble embossed with thousands of class emblems, celestial bodies, and constellations that shifted across its surface moment by moment.

"We won, and the upgrade is complete. Boris, meet the newest Legendary building on Midgard. Something tells me the two of you are going to be spending a lot of time together."

CHAPTER FORTY-SEVEN

Grand Pathfinder's Hall. (Grand Ritual Hall) (Legendary) accessible benefits.

1. *Ritual stability increased by 100% per tier under Legendary. The Grand Ritual Hall is Now considered a Separate pocket dimension, able to contain damage to the peak of the Grandmaster output.*
2. *All rituals Legendary-tier or below may be created using materials one rank lower than required. The resulting ritual will be considered one rank lower than its design suggests.*
3. *At the owner's discretion, any visitor can change their current Class to another Class along with all core Class Skills to another registered by the 'Grand Pathfinder's Hall', with a 10% experience and skill level loss. All energy from skill level losses will be absorbed by the hall for alternative usage.*
4. *Access not granted.*
5. *Access not granted.*

"If people liked coming here before, they're going to go *nuts* for it now." Joe murmured with a soft shake of his head. "Want to go check it out, Boris?"

"Oh… oh, yes." The Scholar licked his lips then glanced sidelong at his current companion. "Are you going to allow me to retain my rights to remain here? I will do my utmost to ensure it's treated with the respective deserves, and-"

"Nothing has changed between us yet, Boris." Joe led the way, stepping through the arch… and the world vanished.

He hovered in a vast void, not at all lit as it was dark with stars and nebula, and crisscrossed with shifting patterns leading to what appeared to be an endless array of class emblems. There was no ceiling, no walls, no one else… just Joe.

And Joe. And another Joe? In fact, a different version of himself appeared on each of the class emblems. Some carried enormous weapons, wore a variety of suits of armor, just floated along with the wind whipping around them, or were surrounded by a vast assortment of purring monsters. It was clear that each of them represented a possible path he could swap over to, but the building read his intention, and each of them vanished in an instant.

He was a Ritualist, and a Ritualist he would stay.

"I know people were rushing to get in here. Does that mean this is all instanced now?" Glancing around, the void shifted, and he was able to see hundreds of other people arriving and looking around in awe, as he had just done. At the same time, he instinctively knew they couldn't see him in return, as this was a privilege granted to him as the owner and creator of the place. "Interesting… now how do I get to-"

The void vanished, replaced by the Grand Ritual Hall. No longer was it tucked away in some hidden basement. Now he had all the space to work with that he could ever hope for. Another flash of intent, and all of the restricted materials or anything that had been stored in the building was safely tucked away in this room, which he knew only he could enter, if he wished to keep it that way.

Luckily for everyone else, he didn't.

"Allow groups of people to enter together if they want to, grant access to the Ritual Hall to each of the members of my coven, and… otherwise, just listen to Boris. He knows the best way to make sure everyone treats you correctly."

The space around him hummed pleasantly, the building's sleepy, burgeoning awareness obviously pleased that he was speaking to it like a person.

"Can I get to the temp-" Joe found himself standing in front of Tatum's temple. Already, the enormous Cauldron of Avarice was on the altar, looming over him in a way that felt distinctly threatening.

Taking a deep breath, he placed one hand on the cauldron and another on the surface of the altar. "You said we might be able to save the people Gameover ate. What does that look like, Tatum?"

The deity appeared next to him, instead of pulling Joe to his own space around for once. Idly, Joe wondered if this had to do with the description of the cauldron, which stated that it couldn't be removed from Midgard for any reason. Tatum studied him quietly, his expression solemn yet determined.

"As I said, there's a possibility we can get those people back." Tatum's voice softened, his tone carefully chosen to persuade rather than push. "Look, Joe. I'm only telling you this because I knew you would want to know. You're someone who tries to fix things, even when it's hard. But this is risky. Very risky. Still, it's their only shot at respawning, rather than facing permanent death."

Joe withdrew his hand from the altar, folding his arms tightly against his chest. For a disconcerting moment, he saw the nubs of his arms, the ends still bleeding and destroyed from being gnawed on by the Legendary monster. He exhaled slowly, avoiding the deity's gaze as he rubbed his hands together just to feel their warmth and solidity. "I guess… I mean, what else can I really say? You're right. Tell me what needs to happen next."

"Since you are standing in the most potent temple of mine on the planet, wielding the most potent spell I can offer you, *and* you're My Chosen Legend..." Tatum's words dangled in the air for a long moment, more ceremony than information. "I can tap into your spell, amplifying it beyond your limits. If you cast your Mass Resurrection Aura with my help, I might be able to pull their akashic records from the depths of the cauldron. Again, it is risky. With a cursed... item... of this caliber, you could lose everything from your characteristics to your class. I'm talking about *everything* you've worked to gain."

"If I don't agree... they're gone? Permanently? No chance that somewhere down the road we might find a different way to take care of this?" Joe exhaled slowly, torn between potentially starting over from scratch and getting on board with the deity's plan. For a brief instant, his gaze flicked toward the temple's exit. But he reluctantly turned his gaze back, extending a hesitant hand toward his deity. "The faster we do this, the better chance we have of making it work, right? Better one person having to start over than hundreds of people being gone forever."

Tatum met his doubt steadily, his shadowed eyes patient yet unyielding. "There are no certainties, Joe. But you're the hero they need. You know it, I know it, and I think you knew you couldn't walk away from this as soon as you learned there was a chance to bring them back. Make no mistake; you're their only hope."

The cauldron seemed to recoil away from Joe as he reached for it once more, light itself fading away as the clearly somewhat intelligent item drank in the light around it, as though it could hide from his gaze. As his palm rested against its surface, the Ritualist could feel it shift and wiggle slightly, as though it had a heartbeat that was rapidly pulsing—the entire item felt disturbingly fleshy, though his eyes promised him he was touching metal.

Tatum rested a hand on it as well, forced to remain half-substantial on this low-powered world. "Here goes... nothing? Everything?"

"Stop being dramatic and get to work," Joe firmly ordered

the deity, earning himself a coy half-smile from the immensely powerful entity. Feeling an intense wave of energy flow into him from the deity's touch, the Ritualist steadied himself and, with one last deep breath, began casting the spell.

The resurrection aura ignited, far more powerful and potent than he had ever been able to manage on his own. Lavender light, tinged with celestial gold erupted outward in a perfect sphere, crawling away from him, only to be firmly grasped and directed into the opening of the cauldron.

Immediately, Joe was forced to grit his teeth as an immense suctioning force grabbed onto the deity-made tendril and *pulled*.

Crackling static discharge spat along the rim of the cauldron, and Joe realized his aura was fully active—his mana pool sputtered to empty, now entirely reliant on being supplemented by the divine energy Tatum was channeling through him. The soft, warm light which promised instant rebirth thickened into something heavier, a *demand* that the dead would be pulled back.

The Ritualist could feel how the tendril he was extending shifted, folding inward as it grew smaller appendages, creating a gold and lavender hand that seemed to be scraping the inside of the bottomless pit that was the cauldron.

Tatum started murmuring words of encouragement as he pushed the skill far past its bounds, the Student-rank spell quickly shifting to what a Journeyman could do, an Expert... a Master. Then things got *strange*, the world going wavy as it became more powerful than Joe had ever personally experienced—punching through the barrier as a Grandmaster spell and *still* increasing in potency as the deity whispered, "Just have to make this stronger than the pull to the abyss-!"

Joe couldn't even manage to nod. Understanding? Agreement? None of that mattered. All he could do was try to breathe as the raw, surging energy flooded into him like a dam breaking and emptying into his body. Every instinct *screamed* at him to seize control of the power, to shape it, to do *something*.

But he knew. He knew that, the moment he tried to direct it, to impose his will, he'd be brutally shredded from the inside out.

So he didn't. He just braced himself, clenching his teeth and mentally anchoring himself as deeply as he could. "Be a conduit... I'm not channeling, I'm just going with the flow."

"There!" Tatum's voice rang with uncharacteristic excitement, but the words barely registered. "They'll have lost a lot of experience, but even the earliest ones eaten haven't been fully eroded!"

As the voice echoed back and forth in his mind, Joe wasn't sure if he was hearing correctly or hallucinating. Then came another pulse of wild, unfamiliar energy as Tatum cried out again, "The boundary is thinner here! The world remembers them. The system wants them back!"

The power of the spell somehow ramped up yet *again*, and Joe, looking at his own hands, realized he had seen immense, coiling concepts such as this in only one other place—the Sage-rank Ritual of Reduction built into his very being. He held *very* still as Tatum did whatever it was he was doing... only to hear a slight *hiss* of concern as the deity sucked in a sharp breath.

"Don't worry, I'm just trying to pull them out, and the cauldron is fighting back. It's like fishing in boiling acid with an open hand; it nibbles on you while you're swishing back and forth." Tatum grunted and shifted, and Joe felt the 'hand' of power began to twist, becoming strings that pulled in multiple directions with independent, gyroscopic rotations that formed overlapping intersections-

The Ritualist felt himself vomiting but had no way to control himself as the foreign concepts acted like motion sickness on his brain, beginning to break him down from the inside out. Tatum calmly instructed, "Hold on, just a *little* bit longer. I'm about to pull the first of them out."

Just as he finished speaking a man appeared in the temple, instantly collapsing to the floor as his eyes rolled up in his head.

The cauldron didn't *appreciate* losing its food and began to fight back in earnest.

Joe felt the wind rush out of his lungs as Tatum's power clamped down on him like a vice, forcing his mana channels into the correct alignment and holding them steady and open as power poured through the human—someone with a body not designed to contain or even *withstand* the briefest touch of such potent energies. Though the divine mana was utterly pure, as steady as the depths of the ocean, it wasn't *Joe's*.

He began to spasm as the Mass Resurrection Aura flared more powerfully—beyond what even the most potent of Skill Sages could accomplish—and Joe's arms began to shake violently as his muscles began contracting, even though Tatum was doing his best to keep everything in alignment.

"I've almost got the next one! It'll go faster, now that I've got the process down." The divine-infused spell pulsed again, alongside a supportive squeeze from Tatum meant to help him stabilize his mentality—but in his excitement, the deity used too much strength.

Joe's collarbone snapped under the pressure, and the distraction resulted in him attempting to automatically regulate his pain, which sent him reeling mentally as he attempted to flare his mana... but he didn't have any. Instead, he brushed against the delicate, powerful working that was flowing through him.

The resulting loss of control caused the entire Spell to shatter, from the point where Tatum had amplified it all the way to where it was embedded in his soul.

Joe didn't scream. He could barely even *think* as power flooded through his body, bouncing back and forth and causing havoc within him. Steady, divine power turned acidic, and corrosive as mana arced through him.

The rampaging energies lasted only a heartbeat before Tatum managed to decouple his power, pulling every last drop of it out of the vessel that was his champion... but the damage had already been done.

Even through the soul-searing agony, none of them missed the rumble of contentment—somewhere between a laugh and the wamble of a starving stomach—which escaped from the depths of the cauldron.

The Ritualist's body spasmed violently on the floor, his muscles seizing as unpredictable waves of agony rolled through him at odd angles. He was used to pain; abyss, he had been mostly *eaten* only a few hours previously. But this was different— it was deeper, *pervasive* in a way that Joe knew a simple respawn wouldn't fix.

"Stop moving!" Tatum's voice cut through the instant delirium. "Give me a chance to pull the shards out!"

Joe tried to answer, but whatever words he would have spoken only came out as a gargle of blood and shredded tongue. He could feel his muscles popping, his bones starting to break under the stress as his ligaments tore. Tatum was kneeling behind him, hands pressed to his chest and forehead with an *extremely* concerned expression on his face. Lavender and gold threaded through Joe as if the deity were sewing him up with magic. Power passed through in the blink of an eye, somehow still remaining careful and hesitant.

The Ritualist felt like there were cracks inside of him that had been closed, ruptures that had been mended as well as anyone could hope for, but when he found a void... both he and Tatum grimaced at the gaping wound. Still, the Ritualist was able to relax his physical body, and a moment later, dark water washed over him as Tatum healed the stress damage and tears. "What... just happened?"

"The worst outcome... somehow." Joe slowly turned his eyes to Tatum, who was speaking as if he were only *confused* as to how this had come to pass. "But it *shouldn't* have been this bad. A debuff at most, how is it possible that the skill itself shattered? Especially when I was personally containing it? Not just that, it exploded *inward*. No... your Karmic Luck was *negative*? *How!*"

Joe tried to speak, only for Tatum to stop him. "No, never mind that for now. Fragments of the Mass Resurrection Aura are embedded in your soul—splinters too small for me to grasp, as I was automatically locked out of that space, since the damage done to you is technically my fault."

Tatum's voice was edged with guilt, but he didn't hold back from delivering the harsh truth. "I'm so sorry, Joe. I… I *knew* this could go wrong, but I couldn't stop myself. Even now, millennia later, I still can't forgive—*urk*, that is, I can't forgive the person who created this cauldron. Now my vendetta has possibly ruined you. I did what I could, but… now only *you* can fix the rest of it."

"But it *is* fixable?" Joe's head dropped to the ground, the cool stone pleasant against his feverish skin. "That's all I needed to hear. No, actually, it's not. *How* do I fix it?"

"You'll need to go into yourself and pull each and every fragment out—delicately—then surround them with your mana and crush them into powder." Once again, Tatum's voice turned hesitant. "The upside to this is that you'll be able to feed that essence back into your other skills to reinforce them. You might be able to get a full-on upgrade to a few of them if you focus your efforts."

"An upside implies an additional downside." Joe closed his eyes as he said the words, "What aren't you telling me?"

"Your mana pathways, your meridians, your energetic capillaries, however you want to call them… almost all of them burst." Tatum's words felt hollow as he spoke. "If you try to use your spells right now, empower rituals, any of that, you'll need to individually grasp chunks of mana and form the spell diagram manually. Otherwise, your mana will just spread through your flesh like ink spilled on paper. Messy, hard to clean up, painful, and utterly wasted. You need to rebuild your entire mana system from scratch, because right now the entirety of your magical circulatory system has no guidance at all. It's utterly *unmapped*."

Joe lay where he was for a long few minutes, thinking through his options. Finally, his eyes landed on his Mana Manipulation skill—still stuck at Journeyman level eight. "I'm guessing a Journeyman in Mana Manipulation doesn't have what they need to remap their meridians?"

"Sorry to have to kill off that hopeful tone, but… not even

close." When Joe opened his eyes, he saw that Tatum was almost entirely transparent, fading away even as they spoke. "You need to start there. Work on this for however long it takes... but please know I won't abandon you. Please forgive my... no, I don't deserve to ask that of you right now. You should have someone bring you to the bifrost right away, and-"

"In a week or so." Joe's eyes slowly closed in a long blink as his mouth set in a firm line. "There's only one thing that's been keeping me on this world this long, and I'm not about to miss out on it now."

"What could possibly be more important than fixing this... mess?" Tatum's ghostly form waved to indicate the entirety of Joe's limp body.

Instead of answering, the Ritualist shifted his head painfully to look over at the man they had pulled out of the cauldron, who was starting to sit up, groaning softly in pain. "Hey. We saved one, right? He's going to be okay, right, Tatum?"

"Uhh... probably...?"

That wasn't Joe's favorite answer, so he called over, "Hey! You okay? Do you remember anything that happened to you?"

Blinking rapidly, the pale man looked over and looked at Joe uncomprehendingly. The Ritualist tried again. "Where are you from? What's your class? Nothing? Do you at least remember your name?"

"Ed." The man finally managed to spit out, slumping over and groaning as he massaged his temples.

"Fantastic." Joe looked upward again, devolving into disbelieving laughter when he noticed that Tatum was nowhere to be seen. "Blew out my mana, destroyed a skill, I can barely move... and all we managed to do was un-tapp Ed."

EPILOGUE

A hidden chamber on Vanaheim, almost always left empty and desolate, was now filled with Grandmasters standing stiffly in clusters. Their doubting tones were clear to the Sages in attendance, even if they *did* manage to hide the actual content of their conversations via various means. Finally, enough people had arrived that the Sage of Swords, Eldrin, was able to break the silence, his words cutting through the tension like a blade.

"Enough of this backbiting and gossip mongering! We will speak plainly, or I will find better things to do with my time." He glanced around sharply, all but radiating controlled impatience. "Someone give me a clear report! What has the expedition to Jotunheim discovered thus far?"

"Sage Eldrin," a Grandmaster of the Stormbinder Tower, her rank clearly distinguished by the vivid carnelian lightning embroidered into her robes, stepped forward and spoke with a bell-like voice. "The expedition is not going according to expectations and certainly nowhere near aligning with our ambition."

"I nearly started a war getting you this opportunity; please tell me the tower I chose to raise a Sage in is not about to fail to a group of shield-bearing *damage soakers*!" If he had been trying to be subtle about his warning, the way Eldrin's voice nearly rose to a shout was enough to force the others back and steady themselves against the sword aura that made it feel like they each had a blade against their throat.

The Grandmaster continued speaking as though she hadn't been interrupted, "Jotunheim has provided immense resources already, tons of raw metals, plants rich in mana, an unprecedented supply of monsters to refine our martial and magical skills against-"

"Yet I see no Mythic core glowing in your hands, ready to be absorbed by the finest among you," the Sage impatiently prompted. "Is it just too strong for you? Should you be attempting a raid on a *lesser* world than even Jotunheim?"

For the first time, the Grandmaster hesitated, albeit briefly, her eyes darting to her peers for support. "Of course not, Sage. That would only stifle our combat power unnecessarily. The true issue is that, despite thorough searching and advanced scrying methods, we've as of yet... failed to even *locate* the World Boss. The sheer immensity of Jotunheim defies words-"

"It's a Titan made of ice and snow. As large as a mountain range!" Eldrin's voice held a dangerous edge. "How could it be possible that you can't find it? Do you not have talismans and scrolls you can use to seek it out? Ample resources you can put to use hiring whoever you need? Did you expect someone to hand you a convenient map with its location *marked* for you?"

Though she flinched, the Grandmaster stood her ground. "It will happen, Sage Eldrin. It's just that the difficulty is far greater than we imagined. Without proper infrastructure, the rampant mana disrupts detection spells. Mundane scouting techniques are hindered by the extreme terrain. As we speak, the entire planet is going through an environmental shift—the first in recorded history. The planet is well known to be locked in an eternal winter and yet is now somehow experiencing its first springtime. The World Boss is moving around, yet we can't even guarantee that the traces we found of it were from... well, *it*, since the world is being reshaped beneath our feet!"

This revelation caused the guests in the hidden chamber to begin murmuring uneasily. The Sage of Illusions, Rothric, joined the conversation thoughtfully. "A planetary thaw? Everywhere you went, you say? Fascinating… I wonder what could be happening that every last frozen section of the planet is heating up all at once."

"Perhaps it is the fault of the World Boss itself?" the Grandmaster hesitantly offered. "After all, our historical records indicate that it *is* the cause of the previous endless winter. Could it be that someone has already slain it and is simply holding onto its Mythic core to keep it from respawning?"

"By your own logic," Eldrin scathingly retorted, "that's impossible, as you've mentioned that you have been able to detect it for short periods of time before your spells are disrupted. Or was that something you said simply to *appease* your benefactors?"

"Sheathe your temper, Eldrin." Rothric calmly stepped in, placing a gentle hand on his fellow Sage's shoulder and examining the quaking Grandmaster. "As we know, this Mythic core is critical to the future of our own world. Your future, our future, and everyone allied with us or not, even if they don't understand. If conventional methods have failed, perhaps it is time to employ *unconventional* means?"

"I… I don't understand," the Grandmaster who had taken on the burden of the Sage's undivided attention finally began to falter, sweat beading on her forehead.

"Do whatever it takes," Rothric instructed flatly. "Pay *any* price to win. Broker deals with someone who has means beyond your own. Approach the locals for more than just temporary housing. Hire a guide who has been traveling about the world. Consult with a fortune teller, for all I care! Just. Get. *Results.*"

Eldrin's voice filled the chamber once more, slightly softened, though a core of steel remained. "Understand me clearly. The first Sage elevated from these expeditions decides which way the balance of power tips. We cannot afford hesitation. I second Rothric's decision. Any price they demand is a price worth paying. For the power to influence the future of this world? For a chance to ascend once more? No cost is too high."

————

"-You may kiss the bride!"

The crowd erupted into joyous applause, cheers echoing through the sunlit plaza of Towny McTownface, the war-torn streets cleaned up, emptied for everyone except sect members and invited guests, then transformed into a renaissance festival wonderland for Brenda and Blas's wedding.

Streams of vibrant ribbons and lanterns fluttered in the warm breeze, casting dancing patterns across the cobblestone streets and brightly colored tents that had been erected everywhere to hide the damage that couldn't be fixed. Music burst forth from a cluster of musicians tucked beneath a nearby pavilion, their melodies buoyant and celebratory.

Joe watched with complicated emotions filling him as the captain of Ardania's City Guard stepped in and planted his lips on Brenda's. The Ritualist looked away, slightly uncomfortable with how close he was standing to the extended, *still* going, okay-thank-goodness-finally-ended kiss. Happily, it was one of the only complaints he had that day, and it was his duty as the best man to stand close beside them and witness their marriage.

As they stood upright, and Joe was able to take in the absolute adoration his mother was beaming at her new husband, a genuine smile brightened his face, despite the intermittent spasms of pain he did his best to carefully conceal beneath his composed exterior. Yet within, the mana pathways ruptured by his destroyed skill crackled unpredictably, sending sudden jolts that threatened to shatter his careful composure.

The Ritualist was dressed in formal ceremonial attire, dark robes trimmed with gold and silver embroidery reflecting the prestige of his newly founded Duchy, bequeathed to him by the king himself. Even so, he felt underdressed as his mother turned and beamed at him radiantly, the sun reflecting off her own light blue dress as she swept over to his side and pulled him into a deep hug. "Joe, you *stubborn* boy. You should've gone to Jotunheim a week ago. I'm married now, so get gone!"

"You think I'd miss this?" Joe softly chuckled through another muscle tremor. "I wouldn't have missed this for *anything.*"

Brenda hugged him fiercely then stepped back to look him in the eyes. "Thank you. Now, promise me you'll take care of yourself. I'm off on my honeymoon after this, and if you're here when I get back, I'm going to be absolutely *beside* myself with fury."

"I promise," Joe intoned mock-seriously, giving her hand a gentle squeeze. "Right after we're done here."

She laughed, dabbing her eyes lightly as Blas came up to stand next to her. "Good. That's exactly what I wanted to hear."

"So, stepdad…" Joe's light tone caused the man to look at him with suddenly suspicious eyes. "How long before I have a little brother or sister?"

Though he had been bracing himself, the newlywed husband still sputtered and looked at his wife with panicked eyes. Brenda only laughed and pulled him to her side, shooing Joe away as they started making their way off to the receiving line.

All around them, guests moved joyously through the plaza, enjoying a feast laid out along tables draped in colorful linens, loaded with delicacies from every corner of Midgard. Laughter echoed from every direction, interspersed with joyful greetings and reunions as old friends found one another.

Kirby waved enthusiastically from a table piled high with cakes and pastries, calling out loudly, "Joe! Make sure you're at the dance; I've figured out how to make the Ritual of Cloudstep work in an area—your mom is literally going to be dancing on a cloud. Well, kinda hovering, but same deal."

Big_Mo gave a hearty laugh as Taka finished telling him a joke, both of them already filling a plate from the buffet.

Hannah offered a shy wave, her eyes full of quiet gratitude as she conversed animatedly with Robert, who was trying unsuccessfully to keep from staining his new clothes.

Even Boris looked unusually relaxed, chatting animatedly with a small crowd gathered around him, thoroughly enjoying his role as the resident Scholar as he explained the exclusive reclassing benefit the sect had decided to keep as their personal tool for the time being.

"Hold on just a moment," Joe called both to Kirby as well as his mother, who was trying to slip away. He caught up to her after only a moment, reaching into his robes and retrieving an elegant scroll sealed with the crest of his Duchy. "Before you go... before *I* leave, I have a wedding present for you. Ahh... mostly for Mom, don't get too excited, Blas."

He handed the scroll to Brenda, who broke the wax seal with eager fingers. "What's this, now?"

"Exclusive trade route rights," Joe explained with a proud grin as she looked at him with a puzzled expression. "As of today, you're the *only* merchant authorized to make trade agreements for my Duchy. You'll have first pick of contracts, resources—everything. Feel free to set up trade routes, make deals, and assign taxes that will be deposited on behalf of the Duchy. Just, ah, play really nice with the Golden Greens Guild? I can't say they're working for me, exactly, but they are definitely helping me get something I desperately need."

Brenda gasped softly as he explained, her eyes growing misty. "Joe... this is incredible. The things this will do for my class...? My profession? I don't know what to say."

"Say you'll make sure Midgard is a place I want to visit as often as possible," Joe replied firmly. "Other than that, if this is something that makes you happy, then you deserve it."

The festivities continued, vibrant and merry, but Joe felt a mounting urgency as each passing moment increased his discomfort. Yet he stayed, committed to experiencing every precious moment of the celebration. Finally, the sun dipped below the horizon, and he knew it was time to say his good-byes.

"You're sure about Jotunheim?" Brenda questioned him as he went for a final hug.

Joe bobbed his head tiredly. "Grandmaster Snow's the best chance I've got. There's no one better at Mana Manipulation than she is... at least, no one else of her caliber who owes me a massive favor. I'm going to have her give me advice, then sit down in a dark room for however long it takes to make my mana work again."

"You're the First Elder of a Sect now. I'm pretty sure the novels just call what you're gonna do 'closed-door seclusion', or something of that nature." Brenda put on a brave smile and gently pushed him away. "What are you waiting for? Go fix yourself. We'll be here for you when you come back."

"It won't be too long. Besides," Joe embraced her tightly once more. "You're going to be so busy you won't even notice I'm gone. I'll come back stronger. I promise."

"I don't care about that, and you know it."

Joe acknowledged her point then started to walk away, only to be stopped by Mr. Johnson, who had an unsightly expression on his face.

"Mr. Joe," the bureaucrat managed to say somewhat pleasantly. "Since almost our entire... Sect is gathered for this event, I was wondering if you wouldn't mind making an announcement for me in your capacity as First Elder?"

He handed Joe a note, and the Ritualist almost fell over laughing as he read what it had to say. Wiping his eyes, he nodded at the sour-faced man. "It would be my pleasure!"

Casually jumping—using only his muscles and specifically *not* Omnivaulting, as he had made that mistake and fallen face-first to the ground twice this week already—to the top of a nearby building that hadn't lost any of its load-bearing walls, Joe took a deep breath and shouted into the night.

"Wanderers!" The area quickly went quiet as his call was repeated, and soon all eyes were on him. "A small announcement... the votes are in, and our Sect Territory has a new name!"

A cheer went up, and the slight tension that had built up melted away.

"I have the distinct pleasure of informing you that the official name is... 'The City of Towny Mctownface'!"

When the laughing and cheering finally died down, Joe decided to add a personal touch. "If you don't know me, I'm Joe the Ritualist, first Elder of the Wanderer's Sect. Let me tell you something. I know staying on Midgard has its benefits, but it's worth getting stronger. Get out there and learn what you can really do. Make mistakes! Get messy! Explore new worlds, then come back and tell everyone about it! Remember, Wanderers... not all who wander are lost-"

"-some of us are out there committing *war crimes*!" As he finished his impromptu, irreverent speech, the sect members listening on burst into laughter or added their own comments.

"Woo!"

"Now that's a mission I can get behind!"

"Abyssal *legend*, isn't he?"

"This is why we're the best!"

"This is why I joined this guild. Sect. Whatever. Bring it on!"

"Wanderers number one! Wanderers number one!"

Joe joined in the laughter as he swept a proud gaze over the area, then threw his hands in the air. "Let's get this party started for *real*! Someone pull out the *big* kegs, and let's get those bad boys untapped!"

ABOUT DAKOTA KROUT

Good. Clean. Fun.

Dakota Krout is a celebrated author known for infusing fantasy novels with fun, punny, and clean humor. With multiple best-selling series—including "Divine Dungeon", "Completionist Chronicles", "Cooking With Disaster", and "Full Murderhobo" —he brings joy and laughter to readers. Dakota's work, renowned for its wit and creativity, earned a place as one of Audible's top 5 fantasy picks in 2017, a top 5 bestseller rank featured on the New York Times, and was chosen by Audible as among "the top 100 fantasy books of all time" in 2024.

Dakota's journey in publishing has been filled with gratefulness, and a deep desire to continue bringing smiles and laughter to the readers. "*I hope you Read Every Book With A Smile!*"

Connect with Dakota:
MountaindalePress.com
Patreon.com/DakotaKrout
Facebook.com/DakotaKrout
Instagram.com/DakotaKrout
Twitter.com/DakotaKrout
discord.gg/MountaindalePress

ABOUT MOUNTAINDALE PRESS

Dakota and Danielle Krout, a husband and wife team, strive to create as well as publish excellent fantasy and science fiction novels. Self-publishing *The Divine Dungeon: Dungeon Born* in 2016 transformed their careers from Dakota's military and programming background and Danielle's Ph.D. in pharmacology to President and CEO, respectively, of a small press. Their goal is to share their success with other authors and provide captivating fiction to readers with the purpose of solidifying Mountaindale Press as the place 'Where Fantasy Transforms Reality.'

Connect with Mountaindale Press:
MountaindalePress.com
Facebook.com/MountaindalePress
Twitter.com/_Mountaindale
Instagram.com/MountaindalePress

MOUNTAINDALE PRESS TITLES
GameLit and LitRPG

The Completionist Chronicles,
Cooking with Disaster,
Damsels of Distress,
The Divine Dungeon, and
Full Murderhobo by Dakota Krout

Metier Apocalypse by Frank G. Albelo

Ether Collapse and
Ether Flows by Ryan DeBruyn

Unbound by Nicoli Gonnella

Lion's Lineage by Rohan Hublikar and Dakota Krout

Wolfman Warlock by James Hunter and Dakota Krout

Axe Druid,
Mephisto's Magic Online, and
High Table Hijinks by Christopher Johns

Tower of Jack by Sean Loomer

Dragon Core Chronicles by Lars Machmüller

Pixel Dust and
Necrotic Apocalypse by D. Petrie

Viceroy's Pride and
Tower of Somnus by Cale Plamann

Henchman by Carl Stubblefield

Incursion by Dennis Vanderkerken

Artorian's Archives by Dennis Vanderkerken and Dakota Krout

www.ingramcontent.com/pod-product-compliance
Lightning Source LLC
Chambersburg PA
CBHW020626020726
47494CB00001B/60